A Struggle
For Independence

A STRUGGLE FOR INDEPENDENCE
By p.m.terrell

Published by
Drake Valley Press
USA

This novel is a work of fiction. Any resemblance to actual persons, living or dead, is entirely coincidental except as noted under "A Note from the Author". The characters, names, plots and incidents are the product of the author's imagination. References to actual events, public figures, locales or businesses are included to give this work a sense of reality.

Cover photograph of Dusk, Killua Castle, County Westmeath, Ireland, copyright 2020, Willie Forde Photography of Ireland (https://www.facebook.com/williefordephotography/). Printed with permission.

ISBN 978-1-935970-48-4 (Trade Paperback)
ISBN 978-1-935970-47-7 (eBook)

Author's website: www.pmterrell.com

A STRUGGLE FOR INDEPENDENCE

By p.m.terrell

What reviewers have said about p.m.terrell's historical books:

"Terrell introduces a new level of excellence to the historical novel. Using the mastery of an artist, Terrell paints colorful word pictures and descriptive phrases that are so exquisitely well-chosen that the reader is magnetically drawn into the plot, taking on a role as an active participant in the intrigue of the story." – Richard R. Blake, *Midwest Book Review*

"Truly well written stories that grab your interest from page one, teaches you a lot of fascinating history and keeps you from realizing the passage of time as you read. Totally engrossing." – author Maggie Thom

"P M Terrell writes some amazing stories and her historical fiction makes me feel as if I can see the ruins, hear the cattle, smell the crisp air… P M Terrell has a marvelous ability to bring to life the characters and surroundings with vivid descriptions. I can see the stone fences and the patchwork quilt of the countryside. I felt like I was walking the meadows and the ruins." – Reviewer Sherry Fundin, *Fundinmental*

"I felt as if I had been to Ireland after I read this book *[April in the Back of Beyond]*. I got so engrossed I even went to my computer to read more about some of its history. Don't get me wrong, this is not a dry history book by any means. It's a story about its wars, its people and its beautiful scenery. It's one of those tales you just don't want to put down. The kind you keep looking at the clock thinking "just 15 more minutes" and pretty soon it's been a couple hours." – *Our Town Book Reviews*

Sometimes a woman comes to the realization
that she has built the perfect life
but with the wrong man.

1

February 1916

I stood at the window and watched the clouds kicked up by the horses' heels, feeling my freedom slipping away like grains of sand sliding through my fingers alongside each pound of the hoof toward me.

It had been a good run, this last one; for my husband, Stratford Berkshire Mather, a man with three last names impossible to shorten to anything close to endearment, had been gone for three full weeks. In that time, I had been a bird set free from its cage. The energy in the house had abruptly shifted; I could feel it in the relaxed shoulders of the household staff and their ability to meet my eyes instead of staring beyond me to some nonexistent point. I allowed the Irish wolfhounds inside to follow me about and curl at my feet as I read in the evenings, the warmth of the fire preferred over the bitter cold in their outdoor kennels. I wandered from room to room without the perception that someone was peering over my shoulder, spying on my activities, thinking me foolish if I while away the day sketching in the solarium or meandering along the meadow path.

The outline of the carriage came into view, and I pictured Stratford impatiently shouting to the driver that he was going entirely too slow, despite the precarious wobble of the top-heavy carriage. The cloud of dust should not even be there, as it was winter and the ground nearly frozen, a sign their hooves were digging deep into the Irish soil as they nearly galloped toward home. For the briefest of moments, I pictured the carriage overturning, the driver thrown safely aside, but my husband crushed, and then I shuddered not at the image but my heart's relief to it.

I heard the door open behind me, but I did not turn away from the window. Johanna had already brought and cleared my breakfast, made my bed, cleaned my room, and helped me dress. There would be no other reason for her to reappear, and if Stratford wasn't barreling up the drive, she no doubt would be in the stables keeping her beau Éamonn company. Then it occurred to me that she had most likely been there and seen the carriage before I happened to venture toward my bedroom window to spot it myself.

"Ma'am," she said softly.

"Yes," I answered, my voice sounding wistful, "I see him." Even her formal reference gave me pause; for the past three weeks, I had been Mistress Penny. Now I was Ma'am or m'lady, once again a woman with no name of her own.

I remained at the window even after I heard the door close gently behind me. The carriage disturbed the slow pace and serenity of the countryside, the tranquility of the sheep in the pastures like giant balls of cotton, the lazy roll of the clouds coming off the Atlantic, even the gay chirping of winter birds. As it drew ever closer, I pictured the staff assembling from the bottom step of the manor house and stretching into the marbled hallway like so many soldiers at attention, hoping their master would not single them out to berate them for some insignificant infraction.

Already the house felt smaller. I stood three levels above ground, and an attic level was beyond this one, a basement level below the others. I would have to traverse the long, winding corridor to reach the main stairs that curved their way downward in ever-widening grandeur. It was a journey best taken with measured intention so I would not be winded as I took my place at the end of the line of servants, angled to face the double front doors as the master entered. But already, the air had shifted and grown stale like a midsummer's heat lingering at face level. There would be no place I could go without his eyes upon me, without his criticism and ceaseless dissatisfied appraisal. I waited until the last possible moment before turning away and making my way to the bedroom door, feeling as though I was housed in the Tower of London and was now to make my way toward the chopping block.

"Aindriú is slowing him down, m'lady," Johanna whispered as we met at the top of the staircase. Aindriú was the Gaelic name for Stratford's manservant, who also preferred for some inexplicable reason to double as the butler. My husband favored his Anglo name, Andrew, and was so dependent upon him that he could not venture a trip without the man accompanying him.

I relayed my thanks as I descended the stairs. I knew Johanna would not follow me down but would rush to the opposite end of the corridor to use the servant's narrow stairwell, depositing her into the kitchen where she would take a meandering hallway toward the front of the house. Still, she was likely to beat me there as I slowed my step to one expected of the lady of the house.

The servants were lined up along the hallway as I knew they would be, nervously adjusting their caps as they awaited Stratford.

"Independence!" he roared as he entered the doorway, precisely at the moment I took my place. I knew it never escaped the servants that he was the only person to use my given birth name, and I wondered why I cared. I had always loved the name, it having been given me in honor of my grandmother and her name in favor of her mother and so on until it reached back to the fall of the Roman Empire, ushering in an age of British independence and later domination. Independence Christiana Pretoria Kingston, a mouthful in itself, was given to a premature girl when my father desired a son to carry on the distinguished family name, his disappointment intensifying when my mother's troublesome pregnancy resulted in an only child with no hope for another.

Nonetheless, my name had taken on a different meaning of late as an undercurrent of discontent had spread over Ireland, and my husband seemed to spit the name out much as he did when he spoke of Irish independence that he was convinced would never be and rightly so.

"Welcome home," I said, my voice clear as it rang through the monstrous, silent hall.

He tossed his hat to Andrew, who followed a few paces behind him as was proper. The manservant caught it in midair. Then as if it had been well-rehearsed for indeed it had over the years, Stratford turned about and spread his arms so his overcoat, dusty from the ride from Dublin, could be removed by the servant.

Another man stepped across the threshold behind the two, and I strained to catch a glimpse of his face. He was of medium height and wiry, his clothing, however dusty it might be, indicating an upper class. As he removed his hat and handed it to Andrew, his lips moved. I have never claimed to have had the gift of reading lips though many times I would have loved to have had the ability; however, it was clear from the servant's expression that the man had whispered his thanks. I liked him already.

"My wife," Stratford sniffed, waving a hand in my direction, "Independence Mather." Without looking me in the eye, he continued, "And our guest from London, architect Peter Bowers."

The man's eyes locked onto mine as he strode passed the servants. He had a high forehead and striking dark brows, a wide face, and a bushy mustache. As he drew close, I noticed between his smile and the gleam in his eyes that he was one who enjoyed a good joke or two. "Pleased to meet you, Lady Mather." He bowed slightly.

"You're Irish," I whispered, confused.

"You have a good ear. Yes, I hail from Kilkenny. I encountered your husband in London. It appears we share the same banker."

"I see."

Stratford's voice echoed right off the walls as he barked his orders—set an extra plate, prepare a room for our guest, there was dust on a table, and where were his slippers? The servants scattered to attend to all his needs at once. It was simply the way things were.

"Shall we have a cordial?" I asked, motioning to the drawing-room.

"We shall indeed," Peter answered, his smile a bit wider.

2

The shadows had grown long, the candles short, as the late hour approached. The servants had cleared the table except for our tea and an assortment of sweetbreads. Johanna stood just on the other side of the arched doorway, listening to the conversation so that when I indicated my nightly departure, she would be there to escort me and help me prepare for sleep. Though my body was tired, my mind felt more alert than it had in ages, and I was reluctant to bid my guest a good night.

I sat at one end of a table that seated fourteen; Stratford sat at the opposite end. These were our customary positions when he was home for supper. Should I want for something nearer his plate, a servant fetched it for me, striding up and down the table several times in the course of a meal. But tonight the atmosphere was different, cheerier somehow, as I listened to Peter's conversation with my husband. It consisted primarily of London and their mutual friend, the banker, along with specifications regarding the addition he wanted him to build.

Peter turned toward me, raising his voice slightly so I could hear, though I had heard everything they had spoken about thus far. "My apologies, Lady Mather. I am certain we have bored you with our ceaseless banter."

"Not at all," I replied. "I have enjoyed the conversation. I look forward to more of the same."

"Ah, if I could. I'm afraid I will be leaving at first light."

"Oh? Why the hurry?"

He shot a sideways glance at Stratford, who was busily devouring a hefty slice of fruit cake. "I have not seen my wife in over a week, and I am anxious to be back home for a day or two before beginning the work here."

"Of course," I said, taking a deep sip of my tea. "Have you children, Mister Bowers?"

"Peter, please. Yes, I have three. My oldest is Rory; ah, what a lad. He has only turned eighteen and has a bright future ahead of him. He will be attending Oxford in preparation for becoming a solicitor."

"You must be very proud of him."

"That I am. He has been my pride and joy since the moment he was born."

"And your others?"

"Girls, both of them. Bonnie lassies they are. Sosaidh is one year younger than Rory, and Mallaidh is fifteen."

"And your son—will he be apprenticing with you here then?" Stratford interjected. He spoke with his mouth full of food, oblivious as flecks sailed across the table, and equally inattentive to the conversation. I looked away as Peter answered.

"I'm afraid not," he answered patiently. "He prefers the legal profession over architectural design."

"You came with the highest of recommendations, Mister Bowers," Stratford said. "It is highly unusual for me to hire an Irishman for such an important task as this one, but our mutual friend tells me I can do no better."

"I will endeavor to live up to his recommendation and your expectations."

"And your workers—I will expect you to keep an eye on them at all times." He picked up a spoon and waggled it. "Any missing silver, and I'll have you to account for it."

"Stratford!" I breathed, the color rising to my cheeks.

The men continued as if they had not heard me. "I assure you," Peter said, his voice steady, "there will be nothing missing."

"You will need eyes in the back of your head."

"And I will have it. My brother Nicolas acts as my foreman on a project as large as this. You can expect the same level of commitment from him as you expect from me."

"Anything even slightly amiss, and I shall hold you both responsible." Stratford loudly tapped his china cup with the spoon. "Brandy in the drawing-room," he barked as the servants rapidly appeared. "And more cake."

I stood and was surprised to find Peter instantly stand as well as if in deference to me. Seeing his guest nearly at attention, Stratford pushed back his chair and stood as well, immediately grabbing a slice of pie with his hand and chomping on it as he made his way toward me. He stopped just shy of me and turned around. "Well?" he said to Peter. "Drawing room is this way."

As I looked from Stratford to Peter, I caught something in our guest's eye. It was not the first time I had seen such an expression. His eyes narrowed as if to protect his thoughts, but I knew they were roaming from my husband to myself. Stratford and I stood at eye level. Twenty years older than I, he had lost more hair than he had retained, and what remained behind was the color of his pale skin. His gray eyes bulged, and his bulbous nose was always red, the pores enlarged; the telltale signs of a man that imbibed too much. Now he had flecks of food on either side of his mouth, of which he was blissfully unaware. As Peter placed his napkin on the table, bowing slightly, I detected his eyes scanning our physiques as well; though Stratford had thin arms and legs, his belly protruded well over his belt. As for me, I'd heard myself referred to as curvaceous and sometimes Rubenesque but Stratford called me pudgy. I wondered which term was rolling around in Peter's mind at the moment.

I felt the heat rising in my cheeks as I said, "It is time for me to retire, I'm afraid. I wish you a safe journey to your family, Mister Bowers."

"Peter," he corrected.

Stratford continued past me toward the drawing-room, and Peter began to follow. He paused for a moment as he reached my side. "Thank you for a thoroughly enjoyable evening, Lady Mather."

"My pleasure," I answered as Johanna came to my side.

"M'lady," she said, curtsying briefly to us both.

"Good night, Mister Bowers."

"Good night, Lady Mather."

He waited for me to depart with Johanna before he strode after Stratford, who was already in the drawing-room.

"Tell me, Bowers," Stratford said as Peter entered the room, "did you happen to see the scum playing with their toy army in Dublin?"

I stopped abruptly to listen. There were only Johanna and me in the hallway. From the dining hall came the sounds of servants clearing the table as the clink of glasses resonated in the drawing-room. I strained to hear Peter's answer.

"I am not sure what you mean, Lord Mather."

"Their tiny toy army," Stratford persisted impatiently. "Surely you must have seen them marching on Dublin Castle. Perhaps twenty of them with brooms and sticks held as though they were rifles, marching in formation. Idiotic lot they are."

"I am certain Dublin Castle has nothing to fear, as they cannot overthrow the British with brooms and sticks."

Stratford cackled. "A man after my own thoughts." There was a moment of silence, and then he said more seriously, "I do expect you to hire only those not participating in such antics."

"You need not be concerned," Peter answered. "I will hire only the best, and you shall receive only the highest workmanship and service."

Stratford responded, but I could not decipher his answer as one of the servants exited from the drawing-room. Seeing me standing there, he opened his mouth but I held up my forefinger. Whatever words he had intended to speak were left on his lips as I turned my back on him and began to make my way to my bedchamber.

The clock struck two before I heard the low rumbling of men's voices in the corridor outside my door. I had not slept but had lain in bed watching the moonlight dance through the open window, the chill night air causing me to snuggle deep under the covers. The bed warmer at my feet—a stone left on the fireplace and then wrapped in several layers of linen—kept me comfortable. The fire smoldered now in dying embers in the fireplace across from me, and soon a chill would descend upon the room, overtaken by the night air. I could rise and close the window and draw the drapes, but I preferred it this way as if the open window might cure the claustrophobic veil that had descended upon me.

Two doors closed, the click of the latches resounding through the otherwise silent hall. I assumed the servants had placed Peter in the corner guest room at one end of the hall, while Stratford's bedchambers were at the opposite corner. My eyes moved to the door that separated our bedchambers, but I knew it would not open, and in fact, a few minutes later, I heard muffled snores resonating down the hall.

I rolled over, my back to the door, and closed my eyes as I prayed for sleep to overcome me.

3

I arrived in the dining hall the next morning to find it empty, the vast table cleared of everything except the customary doilies and silver vases. Today each sported several stems of coral bark intermingled with winter heliotrope. The drapes were open, providing an unencumbered view, the rolling hills still stubbornly green though patches of snow vainly attempted to overtake them. The aroma of fried meats and potatoes was unmistakable in the cavernous room.

"Ma'am."

I turned to find Johanna standing in the doorway. She was only a few years younger than I, her hair a soft brunette under her servant's cap, her eyes large and bright, a sprinkling of freckles spattered across her nose and cheeks.

"They tell me our guest, Mister Bowers, left before first light."

"And my husband?"

"Gone to Dublin, m'lady. We are expecting him back late this afternoon, as usual."

"I see."

"Léana thought you might wish to take your breakfast in your usual spot?"

By the time I had finished my breakfast at the kitchen table, I had devised a plan for the morn. It was odd, wasn't it, that I found myself far more comfortable eating at the table reserved for servants than in the formal dining hall befitting a lord and his lady. And yet there was something so reassuring about the stout woman already set about preparing the evening meal, rolling and kneading the dough at the opposite end of the table where I sat finishing my tea. The fireplace was somehow warmer in this room, cozier and friendlier than any of the ones in the living areas. I half-listened to Johanna as she chatted with Éamonn, giggling in response to his overtures. Stratford would believe them impertinent, as informal as they were in front of me now, but truthfully, I considered some of them more like family than my flesh and blood.

I rose, and Léana abruptly halted her work. "May I get you something else, m'lady?"

"No," I answered, aware that Johanna and Éamonn had quieted their conversation. "I plan to take a stroll." I picked up an untouched crumpet from my plate. "I will take this with me."

"Ah, let me get you some cheesecloth for that," Léana said, hurrying toward a basket.

"May I saddle your horse for you, Ma'am?" Éamonn asked.

"No, thank you." I allowed Léana to wrap several crumpets along with a few carrots. "I plan my usual walk."

"I'll gather your cloak for you," Johanna said, hurrying off before I could stop her.

"I'll be on my customary route, should you need to fetch me," I said. I did not meet the servants' eyes before I made my way through the kitchen toward the front hall. There would be only one reason they would need to come after me. They would leave me to myself until one spotted Stratford on the road coming toward Matherscourt, the estate that carried his name, and then they would rush to fetch me so I could be standing in my customary spot when he came through the door as if I had been sitting in the front hall all day idly awaiting his return.

I took the path from the main house toward the stables, a lane well-worn by frequent comings and goings. I caught a glimpse of Éamonn, who had left the kitchen by the back exit, already preparing to groom one of the stallions just outside the stable doors. The other horses were in the field, their bodies thick with their winter coats, their muzzles emitting bursts of condensation as they expelled the cold winter air. Just shy of the stables, I veered off on another path that took me alongside well-tended fences on one side and a deep and meandering pond on the other. Several from the herd having spotted me made their way toward me, and I rewarded their friendship with the bits of carrot from the kitchen. I stroked their muzzles and murmured to them before reluctantly moving on.

My stroll took me toward a copse of young trees, having been planted only in recent years to conceal several outbuildings. No matter how many times I ventured this way, I found myself rattling off their purposes in my mind like accounting for so many children: the smokehouse, a cookhouse once used before the manor house had an indoor kitchen, a dovecote, and dairy. There was another barn out here as well; unlike the stable that housed the horses, this much larger one once contained cattle that grazed the pastures during times past. It was vacant now, the pastures having been plowed and planted with food needed for The

Great War, primarily barley, wheat, and oats, which Stratford had determined to have lower overhead costs than cattle or sheep and presumably higher profits.

I stopped at a tiny structure, gazing at its miniature front porch as if greeting an old friend. And indeed, this one-room building was my friend in good times and bad. The air inside was bone-chilling, but there was a stack of kindling in the hearth. I quickly got to work starting a fire. As it began to ease into leisurely flames, the room appeared to come to life, my artwork stacked against the walls flickering in the light. It would not take long to warm it, as petite a structure as it was, and soon I was removing my over clothes, draping them over a prim wood chair.

Upon an easel was my latest charcoal sketch, a portrait of a man and a woman. The woman's face was my own, though, in my amateurish style, I doubt anyone would make the connection. The face turned upward so the neck was long and graceful; the hair removed from its braided confines to cascade past the shoulders and down the back. The man's face was not visible, for his attentions were turned to her nape, presumably his lips pressed against her skin. His hair was thick and dark, longer than the British hairstyle which tended to be short, even shaved along the sides; no, this was a bit unruly, the waves made even more apparent by the woman's fingers—my fingers—raked through the locks.

I settled in front of it, assessing its level of completeness before beginning to work on the detail of her cleavage, dangerously, deliciously close to the man's present attention.

4

When Peter returned, he did so with a caravan that stretched for nearly half a mile. Winter was still upon us, but the snow and ice had vanished, leaving in its stead a bitter cold that bit at the lips and tormented the eyes. A prudent man would no doubt have waited until spring was well underway before attempting a project that would break the soil, but not Stratford. His needs required instant gratification, and he had the money to make them happen.

The work would involve excavating stone from the near-frozen ground, and for that, Peter had brought a team of burly men in thin clothing, their sleeves rolled up above the elbows. He had traveled to Dublin before Matherscourt, so he also had cartloads filled with bought supplies, which they unloaded in the vacant barn across from my makeshift studio. My environment changed in a matter of hours, from my quiet refuge to a bustling, noisy workplace. But I was accustomed to changes beyond my control, so I swallowed my disappointment and told myself their presence would not interfere with my pastime.

I was on the veranda reading when I first spotted them, but they would have been impossible to miss wherever I'd happened to have been. The din of horses' hooves and wagon wheels was enough to shatter the tranquility of my little world. Stratford met them at the end of the drive on his favorite white stallion, a tall, handsome specimen of an animal.

Once the work was well underway unloading the carts, Stratford rode tall in the saddle back to the front of the house, where he was met by Éamonn, who had anticipated his master's needs and was ready to return the horse to the stables.

"Edmund!" Stratford barked, using the Anglo equivalent of the groom's name. Perhaps because he was unaware the servant had anticipated his needs or more likely because he wished to impress our returning guest, he bellowed orders in minute detail. Éamonn merely nodded with a polite "Aye, sir," as he led the horse away.

Two men had walked behind the horse from the direction of the old barn. I recognized Peter immediately; I had stood and was looking at him as he glanced up and spotted me on the veranda. He nodded his greeting and looked as if he might speak, but he did not. Perhaps he felt he was too far away, or perhaps that Stratford was too close. In any event, my husband began speaking to him, bellowing from several paces ahead, and he hurried his step to catch up with him.

My attention turned to the other gentleman. He continued his stride as if he was neither dragging his feet nor was in any great hurry. He was taller than Peter by several inches, and though he was not hefty by any means, he did not have the same wiry frame. He peered at me curiously as he walked past, smiling when we were almost even. I placed my bookmark in my book and made my way to the top of the steps.

Stratford and Peter were already there, crossing the wide expanse to the front door. Peter looked at me as if a greeting was there on his lip, but my husband was ushering him quickly through the door, instructions regarding his work coming fast and feverishly.

The second gentleman, being a few steps behind, stopped on the veranda. "You must be Lady Independence Mather," he said. His words were smooth, the pattern of a man of confidence.

"I am," I replied. "And you are—?"

"Nicolas Bowers." He bowed his head slightly. As he rose back up, I noticed his eyes on my hands; perhaps he might have taken my hand in greeting if I had offered it, but I continued to clutch my book. He smiled then, and I saw the resemblance between him and his brother; it was there in the crinkles around the eyes, the merriment that existed through the windows of his soul, and the ready smile that lit up his broad face.

"What will you be building, Mister Bowers?"

"Nicky, please. I must insist." The slightest of frowns gathered his brow. "Did your husband not tell you of his plans?"

I tilted my chin upward. "He did not."

He seemed to process this for the briefest of moments before he said, "It is an orangery."

"An orangery?" I repeated in puzzlement. "Do you mean a conservatory?"

His lips pursed, and he glanced toward the front doors, which had closed quietly behind Stratford and Peter. "I understand you already have a conservatory, Lady Mather."

"Penny. I must insist."

He smiled at my repeat of his words, and I heard a barely audible chuckle.

"And we have two," I added.

"Ah. So you do. I observed them as I was leading the workers to the barn; apparently, your husband feels the conservatories allow too much light through the glass roofs; he wishes for the orangery to have a slate roof and for there to be more substantial stone pillars and fewer windows."

"I see. And will he be growing oranges in the orangery?"

There was the smile again, and this time he laughed. "At this point, Lady Mather—Penny—I don't know."

It was my turn to chuckle. "Well, I suppose I shall find out when the orange trees arrive."

I sensed hesitation from him as he continued to study me in a slow and leisurely manner as his eyes wandered from the book I still grasped to my neck, where they hesitated only momentarily before tracing my jawline. When his eyes landed on mine, I was gazing right back at him, unblinking and unapologetic.

"I must—" he said regretfully, motioning toward the door.

"Of course, you must."

"It has been a pleasure meeting you."

"Will I see more of you, Nicky?" His name rolled off my tongue so easily that I surprised myself. I hastily added, "Your workers—will you be supervising them daily? Or will they be left to their own devices?"

"Oh no, Lord Mather made himself quite clear—only the best workers and supervision at every turn. I shall be here every day to ensure the job meets his expectations—and yours."

I turned as if to return to my chair at the far end of the veranda. "Then, I shall see you as work progresses."

I heard his steps, heavy and sure, and the unlatching of the door. It wasn't until it closed once more that I turned back around. I still felt his presence even after he was gone, and my heart was pounding in my chest. What a silly filly I am, I thought.

5

We settled into a routine as winter trudged on. Stratford left nearly every morning for his office in Dublin, tending to business matters of which I knew little about, only that he dabbled in real estate investments. I continued my walks through the meadow to my studio, where I spent long hours attempting to perfect my charcoal sketches.

As for the remodeling taking place at the rear of Matherscourt, the workers arrived shortly after dawn, gathering their implements from the barn before beginning a long workday broken only by a short break for lunch. They brought their lunches with them each day and sat under the trees that had stubbornly begun to bud even before the last of winter was yet round the corner. I remained a good distance away, though I sometimes watched through the window of my studio as Peter and Nicky instructed their team of workers. And ever so slowly, the orangery began to take shape.

It was an unusually warm day at the beginning of March, a time when the last of the cold winter winds customarily rolled in from the sea to sashay across the island. But on this day, I found myself removing my shawl and eventually rolling up my sleeves as I worked on my sketch. The fire was too dramatic, the flames dancing too high when I rose and opened the door and then the windows on either side of the cottage.

I stepped outside on the tiny stoop, a set of stones that had remained in place for decades, if not centuries. A stranger had arrived on a distinctly blond horse with a mane and tail as white as snow, and he and Nicky were making their way to the barn. Their backs were to me, and as I turned my attention toward the house, I realized I was out of sight of the workers.

I'd grown accustomed to events occurring without my knowledge; often Stratford found a new horse or carriage of his liking and once he purchased a motor car, though it remained virtually unused in the stable among the horses before being sold to another. He remodeled rooms and created additions, sold the cattle and sheep, and hired farmers to plow and work the fields, transforming my vista, all without speaking to me of his decisions.

I remained on the stoop for a few minutes and allowed the breezes to cool my skin. By that time, I was no longer in the mood to work on my latest creation, so I returned inside and closed the windows. I gathered up several cloths stained with charcoal—my preferred medium not for its characteristics but because it was plentiful without having to explain a purchase to my husband. I stuffed the cloths in a small basket and backed out of the cottage, pulling the door after me.

I had closed that door countless times, and never once had I stumbled, but as I stepped backward, my shoe caught, and I cried out as I grasped for something to stop my fall, but my fingers encountered only air. My back wrenched as I tumbled over the stones, and I felt myself descending toward the hard ground and rock below when strong arms halted my fall.

"Dancing backward now, are we?"

I instantly recognized the voice. Though we had spoken only once, I'd heard him calling out directions to the workers—and even if I hadn't, I would never have forgotten his deep, melodious timbre. My chest was heaving with my unexpected exertion, and I found his arms wrapped around my middle, so my back was against his chest. I swept my hair off my forehead and began to turn, noting as I did that the stranger on the blond horse was making his way past the house, spurring his stallion into a gallop as he neared the road.

"Are you quite alright then?"

As I turned completely around, Nicky dropped his hands from my waist but kept them positioned as if ready to help me once more should I need it. "I'm fine; thank you."

He peered down at the toes of my shoes, peeking out from under my dress. "Are you quite certain you haven't twisted an ankle? You were performing quite the waltz there."

I felt the blood rising into my cheeks, and my skin growing hot. "I imagine I appeared quite uncoordinated."

He smiled. "But that isn't what I asked you."

I felt quite certain I had indeed twisted it, but I told myself it was minor; certainly, nothing more than a soak in ice water would cure in minutes. "I'll be fine," I said. "Thank you for catching me."

"Oh, it was my pleasure it was," he answered.

I began to take the step onto the path, but the afflicted ankle was quite determined to attack me, wrenching further and causing me to reach out for his arm in alarm.

"Perhaps I'd better have a look at that," he said. It was not a question but a statement, and before I could stop him, he'd lifted me into his arms. I don't know how he opened the door with his arms so full, but he did it so fluidly that it was as if the door hadn't even existed. Before I knew it, I was seated in my customary chair, and he'd pulled my dress higher than my ankle to have a look.

I protested in vain as he pressed his fingers against the skin. When I cried out, he stopped immediately and peered upward at me.

"Ah, I fear it might begin to swell on you." He glanced around the cottage. "Would you happen to have something I might wrap it with?" Before I could answer, his eyes fell on the basket, and he grabbed one of the cloths. The charcoal immediately stained his hand, and he looked quite perplexed as he stared at it.

"I'm so sorry," I said, trying to rise. "I've fresh ones over—"

"Oh, no, you don't. You stay put. I'll get it."

"They're in that basket over there," I said weakly, pointing toward a table.

He stood, his eyes following the direction in which I was pointing. Then he became quite still as he gazed over the myriad of sketches stacked against nearly every available inch of wall.

"Please hurry," I said, trying to straighten. "Stratford will be home soon, and I must be at the house when he arrives."

He appeared not to have heard me. He stepped toward my latest creation—that of a horse in the meadow. "This is quite good."

"Did you not hear me?" I asked, becoming exasperated. "Stratford cannot know I am here."

He looked at me with a slight frown furrowing his brow. "Pardon?"

"He cannot know I was here. Please—help me get back to the house before he arrives!"

"He doesn't want you here?" He asked as if my words were not quite sinking in.

"He would burn all of these," I said, trying to rise to my feet.

"No," he said, leaning forward to the clean basket. "I'll wrap you up. We'll get you back to the house in no time." As he wrapped the cloth tight around my ankle, he kept his eyes riveted to the affected limb. "Why would he destroy these?"

"Oh, for heaven's sake," I said, trying again to stand.

He gently but firmly pushed me back into my chair. "I asked you why he would destroy these. You've quite the talent, you know."

"He—I—thank you." I glanced down at my ankle, the skin reddening above the cloth. "He cannot know I come here."

"I can carry you back to the house."

"No!" I nearly screamed, my voice sounding hysterical even to me. "Please," I begged, taking a deep swallow of air, "no one can see you carrying me."

He leaned back on his haunches. "You cannot walk far on this."

"Then—I—oh," I stammered. "Oh."

He gazed at my face for a long moment. "Does anyone else know you're here?"

My eyes widened as I stared into his eyes. Surely he wouldn't—he couldn't—no. He dared not. "The servants."

"All of them?"

"Most likely."

"Edmund?"

"Éamonn," I corrected. "Yes."

"Then I'll run to the stables. I'll have Éamonn get a horse to you straight away."

"Oh, please hurry."

He came to his feet and started toward the door. He was just about to close it behind him when he turned back round to face me. "You don't go together, you know."

I didn't need to ask of whom he referred. Most people only stared quizzically, as his brother had; it was a rare one that commented. My usual response was on my lips, having rehearsed it countless times over the past decade with a raised brow and chilly demeanor meant to cease any further discussion. Instead, I found myself saying, "I know."

He was as good as his word. He must have flown down the path, and he most certainly must have lit a fire under Éamonn as he was opening the door within a few short minutes. Nicky was nowhere to be seen as Éamonn carried me to my mare and lifted me upon her. "Can you ride bareback?"

"Yes," I answered, grasping her mane. I would have to.

He secured the cottage. "I didn't saddle her; Nicky said there was no time."

As he began to lead the mare toward the meadow, I said, "He was at the barn, gathering supplies when I—"

Éamonn glanced up at me. "You don't owe me an explanation, m'lady," he interjected. "Not at'al."

I swallowed. No, of course not. Then why did I feel the need to explain why Nicky and I were together? It wasn't as if—as if.

Éamonn stopped my mare at the kitchen door and carried me inside where Léana was busily preparing supper. At the sight of me, she dropped a kettle on the butcher block and rushed into action. By the time Johanna spotted Stratford on the road toward home, passing the workers as they left for the night, my ankle was blue from having soaked in a tub of ice water, but the swelling was gone. Léana re-bandaged my ankle, a bit too tight for my liking, but she said, "You can walk on it, ma'am, if you don't walk far."

As it turned out, Stratford paid no attention. I was there in the hall when he arrived, standing in my place at the end of the line, and when he made his way into the dining hall for a cordial as the servants set the table, he was unaware that I limped behind him, reaching for a wall or a piece of furniture at every turn to keep me from falling. I wondered if he would notice had I fallen, and I was nearly tempted to do, but I pushed the devil from my thoughts and carried on.

The scene was repeated at the end of supper, with him tossing his napkin onto his plate while he burped loudly and bellowed for the servants to bring his brandy to the east conservatory. He was out of the room before I'd risen to my feet. I only had to keep myself aloft until I passed the open doorway to the east corridor, but as it turned out, I needn't have bothered. All I saw was his back as he hurried to the conservatory, and I am quite sure he considered me about like the table upon which he'd eaten. He needed it there, but once finished, there was no thought of me at all.

Johanna was there on the other side of the doorway to help me up the stairs. When we reached my bedchamber, I discovered another tub of ice water, a high fire roaring, and my shawl ready to wrap about me. She never asked how I managed to wrench it, and I never offered an explanation. It was, as Éamonn had so succinctly stated, not necessary. Whether the groomsman had informed her of Nicky's quick emergence and instructions or whether either of them wondered how we'd managed to be together, I might never know.

Once I was in my bedclothes and situated in front of the fire in my overstuffed chair, my foot uncomfortably cold and my teeth chattering, she bid good night and quietly left. I sat for a time, simply staring into the flames. My chamomile tea grew cool before I reached for it. I snuggled deeper into the shawl as the heat from the flames began to melt the ice, and I nearly forgot my ankle. Truth be told, if no one was going to ask, and if no explanation was necessary, I rather preferred that I'd strained it doing something I might have enjoyed.

6

The fragrance left by the soft spring rain wafted into my studio, the mingling of grasses and flowers scenting the room like no bottled perfume could ever do. The door and both windows were open to nature as I worked, the fireplace cool, the charred wood remains now carefully arranged for my charcoal drawings. My studio had simultaneously become both my refuge and my prison, a place where my creativity had endless streams of outlets but also a single room in which the walls often appeared to grow ever closer. My company here came not in the form of flesh and blood visitors but from a one-dimensional canvass, the long hours alone turning my thoughts ever inward upon itself.

I turned around my canvas on the easel and painted the back of my latest creation with a thick mixture of resin, which I smoothed into thinner strokes. The resin worked from behind the sketch to adhere the strokes of charcoal to the fabric, preventing the picture from smudging. I hummed while I worked, pleased with the four drawings on four separate easels as well as those stacked against the wall. Each fabric was mounted with a wood frame, cut precisely, and nailed, so the fabric was properly stretched in all four directions. They would be ready for framing, and I offered a tiny prayer that wherever they ended up, the owners would enjoy them.

As if in answer to my thoughts, a carriage pulled in front of the cottage. I set down my brush and wiped my hands on my charcoal-stained apron.

Eliza Davies' dainty shoe appeared beneath her gown as it descended onto the carriage footstep, and once again, I found myself in awe of my friend and neighbor. Her hair was blond and fine, and today it was swept upward into an elaborate twist upon which a beautiful sky blue hat perched, a royal macaw feather accenting the side. Her gown was also sky blue, as were her shoes; her tiny waist accented by white lace which also appeared around her cleavage, setting off her hourglass figure.

"Penny," she called out, her voice gay.

I strolled onto the stoop, smiling. "Eliza," I breathed as she drew near, "You look ravishing—as always."

"Thank you, dear. How are you? It's been ages."

As we entered the cottage, her coachman tipped his cap in greeting to me before returning to his seat, where he would remain until his mistress prepared to depart.

"Yes, it's been too long," I said. "Tea?"

"Do you have any here?"

I chuckled. "Always." I retrieved a cup from the sideboard and filled it with water I'd boiled over a small fire first thing this morning. Unfortunately, the water had grown tepid, and a glance at the fireplace told me it would not heat in short order. "It's grown cold," I said regretfully.

Eliza did not appear to have heard me. "This is exquisite!"

I came to stand beside her and attempted to see the sketching through her eyes. There was a fox in the foreground, its face peering out from the canvass, the eyes wise and soulful. It was running so fast that its hind legs moved as one, the feet even with the front paws just before they were to kick back, the power in its thighs evident. In the background against a copse of trees were men on horses surrounded by hounds, all in hot pursuit.

"I know exactly who to sell this one to," she said as she removed one of her silk gloves.

"I have six for you today," I said. As she continued to admire the fox, I gathered the others and arranged them on the easels, holding the last in front of me. "What do you think?"

"Absolutely flawless. I'm simply stunned. This is your best work yet."

I allowed her a leisurely stroll around the studio as she admired the drawings I had for her. Besides the fox, there was one of the cliffs of Ireland as though viewed from the sea, two of horses, and two landscapes.

As she studied one of the landscapes, she said quietly, "I must get you proper watercolors."

"You don't like charcoal?"

"I love it. But Penny, think what we could do if these were in color!"

"I suppose," I said noncommittally.

"And this one!" She moved beyond the circle I had created for her works and was now standing in front of the couple I'd been working on for weeks.

"That one is not for sale."

"Of course, it isn't. It is quite obviously you."

I blushed. "Not really."

"Yes, really." She placed a manicured finger against her chin. "And the man… I passed him on the way to the cottage."

I laughed. "No, you didn't."

She whirled around. "Do I appear to be joking?" She smiled conspiratorially. "He is working on the new addition to your estate. Who is he?"

I looked past her to the sketch. "No. I began this before I'd even met him."

"A foreshadowing. Ah."

"It was not. It is simply a coincidence. Besides, it's only of the back of his head. How could you possibly identify him as anyone in particular?"

"My dear girl, a blind person could see it."

I frowned as I moved closer. "Then, I must get rid of it."

"Why?"

"It is clearly a self-portrait. I cannot allow myself seen with anyone other than my husband."

Eliza guffawed. "Sketch your husband, and it will be the only drawing you will be unable to sell. Besides, no one buying your works—" she waved her hand as if encompassing the artwork surrounding us "—knows you are the artist."

"What do you tell them?"

"I tell them the artist—male, of course—wishes to remain anonymous."

My eyes drifted to the signature at the right-hand corner of the canvass. The 'A' was elaborate, a swirl descending over the other, much smaller letters 'non.'

"Well," Eliza was saying, "I shall take all six, which shouldn't come as a surprise. I would take a hundred if you had them."

"I will in time."

"I'll have Brian load my carriage." She dipped into a tiny purse no larger than the palm of her hand. "Here are the proceeds from the last group."

I took the coins from her and slipped them into my apron pocket, my eyes never leaving hers. "Thank you."

"My pleasure." Her eyes drifted back to the couple. "Won't you please sell that one?"

"No. It's… for my eyes only."

"Ah." She seated herself in one of the chairs and arranged her skirts around her. "You never told me who he is."

"Nicky?" I blurted the name before I had a chance to compose myself, and now the name hung in the air. I could not take it back, no matter how much I wanted to.

"Nicky," she breathed. "Oh my, on an informal basis with him, aren't you?"

I sat in the chair opposite her and sighed. "No. I have no... dealings with him. Stratford has hired him and his brother to supervise the addition."

"Are they Irish?"

I nodded. "Kilkenny, I believe."

She frowned. "I know all of high society in those parts. Paltry few, I can tell you that. But I've never seen him before today."

"I don't know what their story is. Stratford said they were highly recommended by a London banker, a mutual friend."

"London?"

I nodded. "He was there conducting business, and he was introduced to Peter—Peter Bowers if you must know."

"And how is this Nicky related? Brothers, you say?"

"Yes."

"Married?"

"Peter, yes. Nicky—I don't know."

"Well, my darling, whether he's married or no, it doesn't matter. If I had him working on my estate, I would be laid bare before him in a heartbeat."

"Eliza!" I sucked in my breath.

"Don't look so prim and proper. We all do it."

"What?"

"You can't be serious." Her chin tilted downward as she peered up at me. "Surely, you can't be satisfied with Stratford."

I shrugged. Eliza and I had been friends for years, though she was nearly ten years older than I. When I first came to Matherscourt, it had been Eliza that introduced me to local society and helped to elevate Stratford's standing in the community. "You know I am not."

"He is still impotent?"

"I don't know if one recovers from that."

"No, I don't suppose they do." She studied her nails for a moment before continuing. "Dear Penny, if a woman was frigid, don't you think her husband would be on the steps of a brothel?"

"That's different."

"Is it? Times are changing, you know. The suffragettes are determined to elevate women to equal status, and I do believe they will succeed."

"Ha! I don't believe it, not in my lifetime."

"You don't believe it because you are here all day, every day. Who do you see when you are not required to be on the arm of your husband?"

"I'm not sure what this has to do with—"

"Nicky?"

I fell silent.

After a moment, she continued. "A woman has needs, you know. Or perhaps you don't know—if all you've ever had was a marriage to an impotent man?"

"You know our marriage was arranged."

"Of course I do. Stratford had some money, and your family had the name. But while you are sitting here by yourself—not that I don't appreciate your work, I most certainly do—Stratford has more than quadrupled his income because your name opened the right doors."

"Quadrupled, you say?"

"He's using your name, dear; your standing. Your family's standing. But what you could really use is for someone to use your body."

"I could never… cheat."

"It isn't cheating."

"Sex with another man, a man that is not my husband?"

"You are what—not yet thirty?"

I nodded. "Twenty-eight."

"And you've been married to Stratford since you were eighteen?"

I nodded again.

"Did you have someone you loved before being married off to him?"

I looked away, uncomfortable with the conversation.

"I didn't think so. So all you've ever known is a man that treats you like an elevated servant. And you are prepared to live the rest of your life like this? Sneaking off to a studio after he leaves, hiding your talents, pretending that all you do day after day is watch the windows for his return?"

I felt anger growing inside me—and something else, something I couldn't quite put my finger on. Maybe Eliza was right, and the queasiness I felt growing in my belly was a conviction that something had to change, and I was afraid of that change. For whatever my life had become, it was comfortable and predictable.

"You think Brian is simply my coachman?" Eliza was saying.

"What? No—surely, you're not suggesting—"

"I am not suggesting a thing, dear girl. I am telling you outright. The man is a stallion. If he didn't scratch my itch at least twice a week—"

I came to my feet. "How could you?"

"I am doing no wrong. All the society women do it. The marriage is for convenience. Our needs must be met elsewhere."

"But—do you love him?"

"Brian? Of course not. Are you daft?"

"Then, how could you?"

"I'll tell you how I could. The same as will happen today when we leave here: I will have him take me to a village some distance out, check into a room, and he will come up the back stairs and join me. And I will have my way with him for as long as I wish. Then he will leave, I will arrange myself, and I will meet him downstairs when he's brought the carriage around."

"But surely—people must talk—"

"There are places one goes. Same as the men. As long as you remain discreet, and you don't embarrass your husband with it, there's no harm done."

"No harm done?" I shook my head in disbelief. "I won't judge you, Eliza. What works for you is none of my business. But I know myself, and I could not do that if I weren't completely in love."

She rose and began putting on her glove, one dainty finger at a time as if she was savoring each movement. "Suit yourself, dear. But how is a married woman to fall in love with someone else?" It was her turn to shake her head. "Too messy. Too disruptive. Take it from me; a tryst is all you need." She cocked her head toward the house. "And I'd wager there's a man not far from here that would be very cooperative in that endeavor."

Before I could respond, she called Brian to load the carriage. I hadn't realized until then that I had never truly paid attention to him before. Today I felt my eyes wavering toward him, only to dart away if he glanced in my direction. He might have been my age; he was fit and strong, and from the way his biceps bulged at the fabric, I could imagine Eliza in his arms. I found myself blushing, and I turned away.

"Thank you, dear," Eliza called from the door. "I'll be back in a few weeks for more. Consider watercolors, won't you?"

I opened my mouth to respond, but by the time I had turned back around, she was gone, being helped into her carriage by her paramour. I waited until they had turned the carriage about and were heading for the road before I pulled the money from my apron pocket. As I began to count, I nearly lost my breath. It was six months' pay, at least! I made my way to the far end of the cottage and moved a trunk to the side. I pulled the rug back upon which the trunk had sat and lifted one of the floorboards. Below the floor was a metal box, and as I opened it, money spilled out of it. I was barely able to add the new coins to it and get it closed once more. As I returned it to its hiding place, arranged the rug, and slid the trunk back into place, I realized with more than a little pride that I was going to need a bigger box.

7

It was raining the next day, not the soft, steady rain for which Ireland is noted, but waves of thunderstorms and lightning that turned the drive from the house to the road into a river of fast-moving currents. The clouds were so low they appeared as if one could reach out and touch them. On the third floor, as I was at the moment, the mists morphed and danced outside my window as heavy drops raced along the glass.

I was in a study of sorts; my study, a room where guests never ventured. I hadn't the vast number of books found in the formal study downstairs, but this was a more comfortable room filled with overstuffed chairs and matching ottomans. But today, despite the chill that threatened against the tall windows, I was tucked into a window seat, my feet firmly planted, so my knees were upright. I was reading *Great Expectations* for the umpteenth time, pulled into a world in which misery and deprivation abounded, and yet somewhere inside a little boy was the seed that would grow into the man, a man that would overcome all.

My respite was interrupted by hurried steps along the corridor with brief stops and starts until Johanna arrived at my door. "m'lady," she said, holding one hand against her abdomen as she caught her breath. "I've been looking everywhere for you, I have."

I closed my book and dropped my feet to the floor. "What's happened?"

"Lord Mather is calling for you, ma'am."

Puzzled, I stood and placed the book behind me. "He is?"

"Aye, ma'am."

I arranged my shawl around my shoulders and slipped my feet into the shoes I'd abandoned in front of the window seat. "Where is he?"

"The orangery, ma'am."

"In this storm?"

"Aye, ma'am."

My mind was pummeled with half-thoughts as I hastened along the corridor to the front steps. I sped down two flights, past servants with ashen faces and pursed lips. What on earth could he want with me? I wondered. He was usually at work at this hour in the office he kept in Dublin, but a glance out the window reminded me why he was likely to be home. He was not, after all, one to brave such wicked weather.

I took the wrong turn on the main floor and followed a labyrinth of hallways that took me nowhere until I finally discovered the one to the orangery, reeled in by the sound of Stratford's voice calling my name. The wild thought occurred to me that he was like a huge, deep-throated baby pounding on their high chair, demanding immediate attention.

I discovered the orangery, stepping into it for the first time. Thankfully, the roof had been constructed the prior week, the rain bouncing off the new slate tiles. Most of the windows were in as well, the others covered in tar-soaked sheets to keep the rain from pounding inside. There was debris everywhere; sawdust and bits and pieces of scrap wood, tools scattered about and piles of material so high that I had to duck this way and that to find Stratford.

When my eyes fell upon him, he was standing next to a brick column with a book in his hand. He shook it at me as I neared him. "You are not permitted in this room!" he bellowed.

I stopped in my tracks. His face was bloated and red, his eyes bugging out, so he appeared rather like a praying mantis.

The book was held above his head as he continued to brandish it. "This room is off-limits to you!"

I took a step back and collected my breath. There were only a few feet between us, yet I had no doubt he could be heard through half the downstairs. "I have not been in here," I said, keeping my voice level. "This is my first time."

"Ha!" He shook the book more vehemently. "You expect me to believe that?" He thrust the book at me, nearly knocking me over with it. "Who else would read such rubbish?"

I turned the book over in my hands; it was *Anna Karenina* by Tolstoy.

"Do you take me for a fool?" he roared. "Are you truly expecting me to believe a servant would read such?"

"Of course not."

"This is my room! *Mine!*"

The sheet nearest us swayed, and Nicky stepped inside, carefully replacing it against an open doorway in an attempt to keep the rain out. He was drenched, his dark hair falling in waves about his face, his clothing flattened against his skin. "Am I interrupting, sir?" His voice was strong and confident, the voice of a man that might have been saying instead, "I am not interrupting."

"Where are the workers?" Stratford demanded.

"The storm has delayed them," Nicky answered evenly. "The bridge has been washed over, so it is dangerous to cross."

"Yes, well," Stratford replied, his voice losing its velocity, "That is no excuse for their laziness."

Nicky said nothing but looked at him, his face impassive. The chill in the air was palpable. Then his eyes fell upon the book I still held. "Ah," he said. "Lady Mather, you have found my book."

"Ha!" Stratford said. "And you expect me to believe you would read such?" he yelled, his face reddening more deeply. "There is no need for you to protect her, sir. She is my property." With that, he stormed toward the inner door. "I expect your workers to be here within the hour!"

He stomped down the hallway, his heavy boots echoing on the stone, his bellowing growing fainter as he put space between us.

I turned back to Nicky. "It is truly your book?"

"It is."

"*Anna Karenina*? It seems like an odd choice."

"Why? Because a female's name is on the cover?" He gently took the book and leafed through it. "In a way, it is a study of a world that is moving faster and faster. Unlike Czar Nicholas, his grandfather, Alexander II, was reforming and transforming Russia."

"Are you interested in Russia then?"

"I am interested in progress and forward movement. I study many cultures—the Americas, Russia, Germany… Britain."

"And what conclusions have you drawn?"

"Ah, what a question. And no doubt, you know the answer would be lengthy."

"Yes, I suppose you're right." I glanced toward the door. "And since I am forbidden to be in this room, I must go."

As I turned away, he caught my arm, stopping my progress. As I looked at him, he dropped his hand, but his eyes did not leave mine. "Does he always treat you thus?"

"I'm sure I don't know what you mean."

"Oh, but you do. You are a possession like the horses in the stables, not a life partner meant to share equally."

I meant to chuckle, but it came out forced, and he noticed it; I could tell from the slight smile he sought to suppress.

"Would you join me some time to discuss *Anna Karenina*?"

"I am sure you have more important things to do." My eyes rolled lazily over the tools and materials.

"There is nothing more important than an invigorating conversation with a beautiful lady."

I thought he was mocking me. His eyes and his smile appeared to be sincere, and my stomach tightened in emotional conflict. "That wouldn't be proper, Mister Bowers."

"Are we improper standing here together?"

"Yes. I'm afraid we are."

"Then why did your husband leave?"

I was at a loss for words, and he knew it. I made my way to the doorway. Without glancing back, I said, "Good day, Mister Bowers."

"Good day, Penny."

His voice hung in the air as I continued down the long, dreary corridor. The further I got from the orangery with its vast windows, the darker and more dismal the house became. By the time I reached the front part of the house, I didn't know whether the tears I suppressed were from anger or longing. The butler was rounding the corner and stopped when he spotted me.

"Mistress, is there anything you need?"

"Yes," I said abruptly. I turned and pointed down the corridor from which I'd come. "I want every bit of that dark wallpaper removed."

"Removed, m'lady?"

"Removed. The burgundy is much too dark for such an enclosed area."

He appeared puzzled. "What should it be replaced with, ma'am?"

"Ask Mister Bowers. Mister Nicolas Bowers."

"The architect, ma'am?"

I had no idea whether he was truly an architect, but I nodded. "Yes. I'm certain he can add the job to his list of duties." Before Aindriú could reply, I hurried to the front of the house where I took the stairs up to my study. I picked up the copy of *Great Expectations* I'd been reading, and then set it back down before making my way to the bookshelves. I knew I had a copy of *Anna Karenina* here somewhere, and if I was going to discuss it, I'd better have read it.

8

I suppose I'd grown curious now that I'd ventured inside the orangery. I'd grown accustomed to Stratford's constant additions. They were generally rooms that would rarely if ever be utilized, but they increased the breadth of the house, so when his business associates came to visit, it was theoretically more impressive. Rather than appear like a miniature version of the palace at Versailles, however, it had become more of a disorganized mosaic, an abstract in stone and mortar with hallways leading to nowhere, rooms opening into other rooms, rooflines that didn't match. And now, there was the orangery, and this room was to be off-limits to me.

The workers consistently arrived each morning, trudging past my breakfast room on their way to the barn, where they would gather their tools and whatever additional materials they'd need. Occasionally a wagon would be with them, and now that I'd seen the volume of tools and materials inside the orangery, my curiosity rose regarding additional supplies.

Each evening the men would leave, sometimes returning to the barn but often not. I inquired of Éamonn to discover if he knew where they went each night, as the distance between Matherscourt and Kilkenny was entirely too far to journey back and forth. He came back to me within a day or two, having learned they traveled to a boarding house in the slums of Dublin, where they could pay to sit on a hardwood bench to sleep, a piece of rope tied in front of them to prevent them from tipping over, or for more money, they could sleep in the same room but inside a designated roped area the size of a coffin in which they could at least lie down. Peter and Nicky, however, traveled to a private residence not far from the others. Éamonn could find out no more about it.

I'd started a low fire in my art studio and hung a kettle over it, and now I took a break from my drawings and poured myself a cup of tea. I stood back to critique my work, as always seeing the imperfections which would propel me forward in perfecting the piece. Eliza gave me a wide berth in the subjects I chose, but I'd learned that landscapes and animals sold fastest so I concentrated on those. Every now and again, I would return to the self-portrait, not wishing to declare it finished. Perhaps I was afraid that once I completed it, the souls of the two people portrayed would vanish, leaving me with a deeper hole than the one I customarily felt.

I heard the clang and jangle of a carriage and turned toward the open door. It was too soon for Eliza to return, but as I watched from the doorway, I discovered it was not Eliza at all. It was an open wagon with two men in the front seat. As they drove past me, I nodded my head slightly, but they appeared somewhat frightened by me. I glanced down to discover my apron was in serious need of a wash and wondered if I also had charcoal streaked across my face.

When I looked up once more, I caught sight of the back of the wagon before they turned around in front of the barn. At first glance, it appeared they had a coffin. I began to debate myself; it was too short in length to be a coffin. It was too wide to be a coffin. Why would they bring one to the barn?

I stepped onto the stoop, careful not to trip on those upturned stones that had caught me before, and sipped my tea as I watched. The men—boys, really, they looked no older than twenty—climbed down and seemed to be prepared to unload the box, but seeing me on the stoop, they stopped and appeared to be conversing.

The sound of another man's voice filled the air. I would have recognized it anywhere, though he was speaking Irish Gaelic. Nicky was walking past the meadows, and whatever he shouted, the men answered in the same tongue. I recognized the language, though it was banned; the servants often used it when conversing among themselves. I suppose it had been banned for precisely that reason; the English did not wish for their subjects to be speaking in a tongue they couldn't understand, as they might be planning an insurrection. Yet there it was, alive and well.

At the men's answer, Nicky turned away from the barn to look at me standing on the stoop. I raised my teacup in a slight greeting before sipping from it once more. He looked at the men, then back at me, and then quickened his pace toward the men. Before he'd quite reached them, he said something more in his native tongue. They nodded, glanced at me, and he abruptly turned around and made for my little cottage.

"And a good morning to you!" he called as he approached.

"Good morning."

It might have been purely a coincidence, but he blocked my line of sight to the barn. "Have you considered my invitation to discuss *Anna Karenina*?"

"I have, indeed, Nicky. In fact, I've been refreshing my knowledge of the story."

"Ah." He looked at my teacup. "You wouldn't happen to have another cup in there, would you now?"

"I do." The words were automatic, but I was rather surprised that he had invited himself. Still, I turned around and made my way to the fireplace, where I poured him a cup of tea and handed it over to him.

"How is your ankle?" He came to stand, so I was facing the back of the cottage with my back toward the open door.

I lifted my skirt just high enough for him to see my ankle. "The swelling only lasted a day or two. Léana and Johanna took excellent care of me."

"I've noticed you've been getting along nicely. No limp at'al."

"Have you now?"

"I've an invitation for you, Penny. If tomorrow is a sunny day, would you be interested in joining me for a chat about books?"

"Well, I don't—"

"Away from here. Away from prying eyes. You know how to ride, aye?"

"I do."

"In the back of your property, past the pastures and the crops, is a lone tree on a hill. Do you know it?"

"I believe I do."

"Would you meet me there tomorrow? Say around noon?"

The clang of the wagon began, but Nicky's eyes did not waver from mine. "Yes," I heard myself saying. "I will meet you at noon."

He downed the tea. "Don't be late. And bring your books."

I took his empty cup from him, and he made his way to the door, his boots heavy on the stone stoop. Without another word, he was gone. I sat in the chair for a long time, alternating between the open door with its view of the barn and my sketches. My tea had grown cold before I stood again, dumping the contents outside the door, and returned to my work.

The shadows were long when I snuffed out the fire and readied myself for the stroll back to the house. I closed the door behind me, listening for the telltale click that the latch had caught, and turned not toward the house but the barn.

I could hear men's voices carried on the wind and knew they would soon depart for the night. The clouds were low and fast-moving, the moon slithering in and out, creating ghostly silhouettes interspersed with muted light.

I was taking a chance; I knew I was. But as I squared my shoulders and quickened my step, I reminded myself that I was, after all, the lady of the house. I had every right to go anywhere I wished. Yet I could not shake the trepidation that was climbing up my spine as I tried to remain in the shadows while I crossed to the larger structure.

I did not take the main door, the one which had been used each time materials were delivered or removed. I went instead to the smaller door at the rear and slipped inside.

It took a long moment for my eyes to adjust to the gloom. Without the benefit of windows, I found myself stumbling over a variety of tools and materials, everything from hammers to nails to stones, wood, and brick. There seemed no order to it; a woman, I determined, would have had these things in neat rows, perhaps by the stage in which they might be used. Instead, I found it to be rather haphazard, wood piled in one place and then in another, all seemingly the same.

As shapes took form, I realized I was in the center of the structure with pens on either side, pens still filled with hay and which smelt of pig and cow, though Stratford had long ago sold the livestock, except for the sheep that kept the lawn tidy. A ladder on either side allowed one to climb upward to the loft, but I was not sufficiently curious to climb it. Though my ankle had healed, I did not wish to repeat a mishap, especially on an old rickety ladder.

I looked for the box that had been delivered only a few hours earlier but could not find it. The longer I searched in vain, the more determined I was to locate it and determine its contents that had been so secretive, but the minutes sailed past, and I was coming up empty-handed. I was not a fool—or so I told myself—but knew beyond any doubt that Nicky's task was to keep my eyes focused elsewhere while the supplies were unloaded.

Two could play at this game.

As the shadows lengthened, my intuition told me Stratford was on his way from Dublin, and I needed to be in my customary spot when he entered the great hall. I took one last glance about and then made my way to the rear door. I quietly slipped outside where the air had grown chillier, pulled the door to, and set off toward the meadow walk that would take me home.

I would have another opportunity, I told myself as I walked. And I planned to take full advantage of it.

9

The oak on the backside of Matherscourt was like no other. Purported to be more than 700 years old, it was a sapling when the Vikings invaded Dublin. It would have witnessed warring Irish clans and chieftains as the land switched hands over the centuries and finally would have watched the English conquer the island, relegating the native Irish to serfs. Its branches began at such a low level that I could easily sit on a branch as wide as a settee, simply by backing into it. The branches continued upward to rival a three-story house and were almost as wide. Beneath the branches lay a labyrinth of roots that at times rose above the earth like a drowning man's arms, only to recede a few inches later.

Nicky rested on a branch across from mine; we were like two people in a parlor except for the spring breeze, the sweet aroma of grass and flowers, and that earthy fragrance that would forever tie my heart to Ireland. Our conversation had ranged far and wide, from the underlying politics of *Anna Karenina* to the plight of the poor that Charles Dickens had hoped to bring to public light in so many of his works.

"The world is changing," Nicky was saying now. "The Great War—it will change the world forever."

"Surely, Britain will win," I said. "It is only a matter of time."

Nicky curiously peered at me for a long moment. "You sound so certain, you do," he said finally. "And I suppose you would, living the life you lead."

"I don't understand."

"The Germans are a formidable fighting force, and Britain is a small country in comparison."

"But they have their colonies."

"Like Ireland."

"Yes. Like Ireland."

"Over a million men have volunteered in Britain to fight in this war," Nicky said, his eyes wandering across the field as he spoke. "But it isn't enough. A place like this in France or Austria-Hungary or any number of places throughout Europe are right now serving as killing fields, some infantries wiped out as soon as they gather. It may become a war of attrition—and Britain does not have enough men."

"Are you saying Germany could win the war?" My stomach tightened, even as I spoke the words.

"I am saying it is a distinct possibility." Perhaps seeing my startled expression, he continued, "London is attempting to force Irish men into battle to fight for them, you know. That will bolster their ranks."

"Conscription?"

"Aye. They have not begun it yet, but there is talk of it. There is a lot of pressure on the Irish right now. Those that want to fight have already gotten into the fight. Those that remain…"

As his voice faded, I asked tentatively, "Why are you not at the front?"

"Ah." Again his eyes, a startling sea-green as they reflected the land around us, took on a far-away look. "And why should I fight on behalf of England, 'ey? They are invaders here, relegating the Irish to an underclass of serfs.

Why should we willingly fight to preserve their heavy hold on us?"

I sucked in my breath. "Surely you don't wish for Germany to win?"

"I wish to serve neither Kaiser nor King." He leaned forward, his expression earnest. "Ireland ruled itself for thousands of years with some of the greatest Celtic and Gaelic warriors history has ever witnessed. The last 700 our ancestors have been beaten down to believe we are slightly above those horses there." He gestured at his black stallion, and my gray mare lazily feeding in the pasture as we talked. "The British have an uncanny habit, have you noticed? Whether it is America or India or Ireland, those that oppose the British monarchy are subjugated in the world's eyes, portrayed as subhuman while the Brits assume the mantle of a master race."

"But surely you have not been treated thus—"

He chuckled wryly. "Oh, have I not? You live in your fine house, a mansion twenty times larger than any Irish home in my village, and you know not what lies beyond it."

"Are you insinuating that I am somehow wrong to live as I do?"

He hesitated. "No. You personally are not wrong. But the system is wrong—this system of governance that keeps those of one faith from owning land or voting, while it continues to give more to a chosen few. And the truth of the matter is that those chosen few would have nothing were it not for the rest of us."

"And would it be better, were we all to be speaking German?"

He laughed a hearty laugh. "No, I am not advocating that at'al. I wish to speak Gaelic, as my ancestors did."

"The British have outlawed that."

"Aye. But the language has not died. The Irish people may have been beaten down, but now, with this war, we are prepared to rise up again, to claim our rightful position on the world stage."

"Are you saying there are Irish willing to fight against Britain?"

He picked up a stick at his feet and drew in the dirt for a moment. "No," he said finally. "We haven't the means to form an army and turn a beautiful meadow such as this into a killing field. But things are changing, not only in Ireland but in the rest of the world. Monarchies are a dying breed. Democracies are the future now."

"And what would become of an estate like this under your democracy?"

He shrugged. "Does anything need to happen to it?"

"I don't know. Perhaps my husband is one of the 'chosen few' of which you speak. Surely under this new system, there would not be the same place for him in society?"

He leaned in so close to me that I felt as if I had entered a bubble in which only he and I existed. "What is the story between you and Stratford Mather?"

"Forthright, aren't you now?"

"I don't believe in beating around the bush, no. I ask a straight question, and I wish for a straight answer, I do."

The words that had always been on my lips during impertinent conversations such as this were uncharacteristically frozen there, eventually falling away like ice melting in the sun. "It was an arranged marriage," I said without flinching.

"Arranged. Your parents arranged it, you mean?"

I nodded.

"Why?"

I could not tear my eyes away from his. They seemed to mirror the green fields of Ireland, the black lashes beguiling, his earnest expression so honest, so caring, as if he spoke not from curiosity but through some strange concern for me. "Sometimes a family has a name," I began slowly, searching for words I had never spoken before. "A name that opens doors…"

"And yours?"

"The Kingston family—my family— is filled with dukes and duchesses, counts and nobles, going back centuries."

"So why do you need someone like Stratford Mather in your life?"

"Because," I swallowed, "sometimes a name is all one has. And one cannot eat a name, can they now?"

"And so you married a man you're clearly not suited for—" he waved his hand to encompass our surroundings "—for this?"

"For security. Yes." Had it been anyone else, I knew I would have left by now, shutting down the conversation with no hope for its future revival. But I didn't wish to end my time with Nicky regardless of where the conversation might lead. It was refreshing to have an intelligent conversation with someone; I could not cross that boundary with my servants, and certainly, Stratford was out of the question as he thought me a silly girl. I was pushing the boundaries here with Nicky, and uncharacteristically I felt myself throwing caution to the wind. "It is difficult to be a woman alone."

"Ah. A couple—or a family—ensures survival and always has, I suppose." He created spirals in the dirt at his feet while he contemplated this. "But even that is changing," he said abruptly, stopping to peer into my eyes once more.

I laughed. "I don't see how it could."

"Ah, but it is. In Britain, women are working in the factories now—even in Belfast, they are."

"But haven't they always?"

"The lower classes, aye, they've always worked; they've always had to, and the children, too. But industrialization is driving unprecedented changes. And with the men at war, even women in the upper classes are working in ways they might never have thought possible."

"But why? Is their money at stake?"

"Civilization is at stake, isn't it? What do you suppose would happen to all those dukes and counts and kings if Europe's map is redrawn? What do you think will happen to their estates, their banks, their holdings?"

I shook my head. "Surely, it won't come to that."

"It may not, after all." He stood and straightened his back.

"What would you be doing, Nicky, if you were not building this addition for Stratford?"

He smiled. "I would be building a cathedral."

"Would you now?" I rose as well and dusted my dress of tree bark.

"I would, indeed. I'm a master craftsman, or so I'm told. I've helped to build churches all over the island."

"And are you a religious man?"

He shook his head. "I am a spiritual man, aye. But not religious."

"What's the difference?"

"A man can speak to God in his own way and go where the Lord seems to lead him. That's spiritualism—being guided by the Spirit, even a Holy Spirit. Religion consists of man-made rules, brick, and mortar, cultural wars, the pressure to conform. So no, I am not religious."

I strolled to my horse. "And yet you build churches."

"For the coin in my pocket," he answered. He held his hands together, and I stepped one foot into them and pulled myself into the saddle.

"I have enjoyed our conversation," I said.

"Would you care to see the world of which I speak?"

I hesitated. "How could I possibly—?"

"Your husband will be leaving for London tomorrow; he'll be gone for three days."

"How do you know that? I don't even know—"

"Servants see and hear more than their masters know."

"I see." I gathered the reins.

"I must travel to the countryside tomorrow to gather more supplies. If you'd like to journey with me, I would be pleased with the company. It is only overnight; we shall return the following day. And I give you my word I will protect you and your virtue."

"That would be highly improper, Nicky."

"Yes, Penny. It would."

I looked into the distance toward my home, though it was well beyond visual range. "I must go now."

"If you wish to join me, I shall be at the barn in the morning, just after daybreak. I'll be driving a cart—for the supplies, you see."

"And who else will be accompanying you?"

"No one—other than yourself."

I clicked my heels gently, placing my mare into a soft walk. "Good day, Nicky."

I didn't know if he ever answered me. Between the clop of the horse's hooves on the hard ground and my own overwhelming thoughts, his voice was lost on the wind, but not as it turned out, in my heart.

10

Eliza lived in a frightening house; at least, I thought it frightening each and every time I journeyed up the long, desolate road, and this time was no different. It had been a castle in the time of the Vikings, small for a structure of that stature, to be sure, as it was once the home of a lesser Gaelic chieftain but imposing nonetheless. Its towers soared high, the blue-black stone melting into ominous clouds that always appeared to hover around it as if a curse had been placed upon it, even on the sunniest of days. And indeed, there were rumors of many curses as it had seen various battles and numerous enemies at its gates. The moat was still there as if waiting for another attack, the water bracken underneath two drawbridges consisting of one at the front and one at the rear, and the rear always seemed to be drawn up as if to keep its inhabitants from escaping. It was dusk, and the bats had just begun to appear, black and swarming against the skies.

The coachman drew up to the front and climbed down to open the carriage door. Stratford was the first to exit, ascending the steps to the front door while I relied on the coachman's extended hand to help me down the carriage step. Another coach was behind us, the gentleman having already alighted as well, and I watched for the briefest of moments as he assisted his lady from the carriage before I turned my attention to the steps before me. By the time I was escorted inside by the staff, Stratford had already found a drink and was joining a conversation across the room.

My name was called out to announce my arrival, and as Eliza and I made our way toward one another, the couple behind me was announced.

"So very happy you could make it," Eliza said as she kissed my cheek. A tray of cheeses and meats was offered in one direction while another tray of spirits was proffered in another. I accepted a glass of white wine to settle my nerves, as I had grown unaccustomed to such gatherings.

"Countess," Eliza said, glancing over my shoulder, "have you met Independence Mather?"

"I don't believe I have," the woman said as she joined us. She was taller than I and had an air of confidence about her, though her manner was a bit brusque as we were introduced. Her name was peculiar—Georgine Markievicz—and I wondered at the nationality of her husband. I explained her self-confidence away as partly due to her age; she might have been in her late forties, and it had been my experience that women of a certain age tended to be far less intimidated by life in general. I was strangely drawn to her, perhaps wishing her self-assurance would rub off on me. She was also wiry and lithe, her facial bone structure prominent, and her hair, though coifed, unruly as though it was unaccustomed to being arranged in a feminine manner. She was, I decided, completely my opposite.

A live band began to play, the harps singing as though they were selkies, and as the room continued to fill up, I found myself wandering from one small group to another, visiting with those I had known for years and introducing myself to the occasional newcomer. It was the latter that gained most of the attention from the group, as our lives tended to blend into one ordinary day after another while the new arrivals often brought fresh and unfiltered news of distant places.

The biggest news by far was the Great War. Colonel Rutland was in attendance, bringing information regarding West Africa, where Cameroon had finally fallen to the British and French forces, leaving but one German colony remaining. With the British converging on German East Africa with ten times the forces of the Germans, morale was high that victory—at least on the African continent—was within our grasp.

Europe, however, was a different matter, with the Germans renewing an onslaught on a tiny city along the banks of the Meuse River in northeastern France. I wasn't exactly clear on the strategic significance of such a site, but Verdun was on the lips of everyone before the evening was done, with the insinuation that what happened there would be of utmost importance.

We certainly hoped and prayed the tide was turning in Britain's favor after having suffered horribly in the Gallipoli campaign at the hands of the Turkish Ottoman Empire. The Brits and their allies had lost an estimated 250,000 men in the campaign, some of whom were Irish, and their retreat in January only a few weeks earlier still hovered over us like melancholy clouds. The Ottoman Empire was formidable, stretching from Southeast Europe well into Western Asia and North Africa with a ruthless Sultan at its head. With men from the front coming home on visits, they carried with them news of Turkey's atrocities, including the genocide of the Armenians, the Greeks, and Assyrians. There was no doubt if they won the war, they would seek to obliterate Western culture, including all forms of Christianity, perhaps perpetrating genocide on us as well.

Dublin and its outskirts, such as we lived, seemed a world removed from the suffering and horrors of war on the mainland, and I found myself once again grateful that there was a sea between Ireland and England and another between England and mainland Europe. Ireland was a stepchild of no import; wild and uninhabitable to the more refined neighbors to its east, save for Britain's heavy hand upon it. We were Britain's breadbasket and meat producer and nothing more.

Dinner was served promptly at 8:00 at a table so long that many indulged in conversations heard only by a few. As was the habit, men were separated from their wives, enabling each to visit among those we rarely if ever saw. But as the night wore on and one course after another was laid in front of us, and the picked-over plates removed, attentions began to shift toward the head of the table where Stratford was having a rather loud conversation with Eliza's husband, Lord Philip Davies.

"It is a crime," Stratford was bellowing drunkenly, "that each time I venture to my office, I must pass through the tenements. Cannot you drive the peasants out of the city?"

Philip chuckled. Physically, he appeared a stark opposite to Stratford. He was taller than most men and lean, his movements often quick and decisive. He had a full head of black hair and thick brows over perceptive blue eyes. "My dear Stratford, perhaps if landlords were not converting genteel housing to room rentals, they would not appear in abundance."

"They are too poor to afford anything more than weekly rents," Stratford announced. "And they are poor because they are lazy. They are drunkards, illiterate, and ill-mannered."

"Are they illiterate," Countess Markievicz spoke up from further down the table, "because they have not had the opportunity to receive an education?"

A unified gasp went through the room as all eyes turned first to the Countess and then to Philip and Stratford. It was highly unusual, if not downright scandalous, for a woman to interject herself into a man's conversation, most especially when it did not pertain to subjects more suited to a woman's place.

When neither man answered, Countess Markievicz continued, "I hear the mortality rate in the tenements is extremely high. Not far from your office, Lord Mather, are homes that were each built to accommodate one family. They have now been subdivided into as many as fourteen apartments, some a mere ten feet square. They have no running water. More than three hundred people share one outhouse. And the people have barely enough to eat—"

At this, Stratford snickered and interrupted with, "I assure you, Madam, the people have plenty to eat. I see their fat, round, disgusting stomachs every morn on my journey into my office."

"Their fat, round stomachs amidst their spindly legs and arms?" the Countess prodded.

"And their pimply faces," Stratford continued as though he hadn't heard her. "They eat chocolates apparently, and too much for their own good."

At that, many at the table laughed. I set my fork beside my pie, which no longer held its appeal for me.

"Perhaps another route into the city would suffice," Philip said genially. "We can certainly cordon off the tenements to prevent the inhabitants from being seen by those with fairer tastes. You should speak to City Hall about it, Strather, if it bothers you so."

I stirred my tea as I watched the Countess. Her expression belied an inner turmoil, her lips twitching as if to speak before being held in place like a vise by her upper teeth. Finally, she interrupted the conversation that had taken a turn toward other subjects.

"Have you noticed," she began, her voice projecting so that all other manners of conversation ceased around her, "the children of the tenements haven't adequate clothing? They do not own shoes. There are no coats for them, only blankets they wrap about themselves even as they wander the streets—blankets, I dare say, full of holes. The children, the women, and the men work long hours when they can find employment, day laborers all, often paid by the piece to sew clothes each of us is wearing right here, right now, or cook food they sell at stands while we 'pretty ladies' throw out more food each day than a family in the Dublin slums can consume—"

"Ladies and gentlemen," Eliza said, rising along with her husband, "shall we take our cordials in the parlors?"

Countess Markievicz continued, her words harder and sharper, something about Dublin having the worst tenements in all of Europe, even as the other guests were shepherded out of the dining hall and into adjoining rooms for their cordials. The men left her behind, retiring behind the closed doors of the study to smoke their cigars and drink their whiskey while the gentler folk made their way to an adjacent parlor and the gentle strings of the harp.

Only I remained behind, even after the Countess had been silenced, and the dining hall was empty save for the servants that were clearing the table. I rose on shaky legs, though I didn't know why I should feel so anxious inside, and made my way through double doors onto the veranda for the night air. Sometimes the frightening façade of a forbidding castle was preferable to the frightening façade of the inhabitants within.

11

I could sense that my decision to go would somehow irreversibly change the trajectory of my future. I had tossed and turned throughout the night, my resolve vacillating, so I had no clear intent, and what little sleep I had succumbed to was filled with nonsensical dreams. I was awake long before I heard Stratford's door quietly opening and closing, his boots upon the floor as he made his way past my bedchamber and down the stairs in the center of the corridor. I rose and watched from the window as he departed, the only difference between this and any other day the black luggage his butler carried. He'd never said a word to me about his trip and not so much as a farewell this morning. It was, I told myself, simply another sign that this was not truly a marriage but an impersonal business arrangement.

That no doubt weighed heavily upon me as I vacillated no longer and quickly went about packing a few things in an overnight bag. I left a note for Johanna that I would be returning the following day, possibly late afternoon, and to inform the staff they were not to worry. I then quietly made my way down the hall and stairs, following Stratford's path until I reached the ground floor. From there, I made an abrupt turn toward a side door, where I slipped out and found the path past the meadow and toward the old barn.

He was waiting for me. The carriage was turned about to head out, and he was closing the wide double doors on the barn when he spotted me. His face lit, and his smile was broad. "You came," he said as he narrowed the distance between us to take my bag.

"I did," was all I managed to say. I questioned my own intentions as I allowed him to assist me onto the open seat. He climbed in beside me, and as I adjusted my shawl to ward off the morning chill, he placed a threadbare plaid over my legs, adding another layer over my skirts. Then he clicked to the two horses, flicked the reins and we were off.

We traveled in an easterly direction before turning south at Donnybrook, and I found myself growing anxious as we approached it. Despite the fact the notorious Donnybrook Fair had ceased operation for more than fifty years, I had always associated the village with the reputation of the fair.

"It's where the term 'donnybrook' hails from, you know," Nicky said as if picking up on my trepidation. "The fair began in the early 13th century and was always a lively place from the tales passed down, but somewhere in the 19th century, things took a decided turn for the worse."

"Those are the stories I've heard."

"Ah. The stories of drunkenness and fights that often turned to riots."

"Yes."

As we entered the village proper, I searched for any place that might have served as the location for the annual fair, but truth be told, there were fields all about dotted with sheep and cattle, and it might have been anywhere—or everywhere—I looked.

One building, however, stood out. It towered above the rest of the village and appeared as large as all the other structures put together. Just as Eliza's house always frightened me, this did as well. It appeared to be several buildings perhaps built at different times, as they had varying roofs and heights, but they were cobbled together in a decidedly uncoordinated manner. There were few windows, some structures not having any, and they all appeared to face inward on themselves, perhaps to a center courtyard. What the walls did not conceal from the road, a formidable sign completed; for as we passed its gates, I was able to glimpse the small insignia and words: St. Mary Magdalene's Asylum.

"The laundries," Nicky said, flicking the rein to prompt the horses into speeding up their step.

"Laundries?" I raised my shawl further up my neck, though the chill was not from the winds but from my own unexplained trepidation.

"Surely, you have heard of such places?"

I shook my head and inched a bit closer to him.

"Don't worry, Penny. They won't come out and get you. I promise you that." He smiled, but perhaps seeing my doubtful expression, he placed a hand on mine. "It's said when a woman is pregnant out of wedlock, the sisters take her in."

"Oh." I began to relax. "Then, they help her give birth?"

"I suppose. All I know is many of the babes are never seen outside those walls, and many a young maiden has been close to middle age when she departs."

"Are you saying the women stay for decades?"

He nodded. "A bit like slavery, it is. Human bondage wrapped up in the name of Christ. I suppose that is why I've no love for religion. Spirituality, aye," he said, glancing my way, "but not organized religion. It is too easy for mankind to warp it."

As we passed it and the edge of the village was within sight, I said, "Have you ever known anyone that went in there?"

"One or two." He glanced at me again. "None that I put there, I can tell you that."

I felt myself blushing. "Tell me about where we're going," I said, wishing to change the subject.

"It will take us the better part of the day to reach our destination," he said. "Are you up for it?"

"I wouldn't have come along if I hadn't been," I chuckled.

"Good. We'll be meeting a few lads—and lassies—who will have our supplies."

"I see." I don't like surprises, especially when I am unaccustomed to venturing beyond my little world. Perhaps I should have confided in Johanna, so at least one person would have known of my whereabouts. But then, I debated myself, no one could be compelled to reveal my location should Stratford unexpectedly return home. My stomach tightened at this last revelation. "Are you quite certain my husband has gone to London?"

"Quite certain."

I nodded.

"I would not endanger you—or your relationship with your husband."

I peered at him. He appeared intent on guiding the horses onto another road, and I couldn't tell from his expression whether his statement was serious or sarcastic. "So, we're stopping where?"

"You've heard of Powerscourt?"

"The castle?"

"Aye."

"I—I didn't pack clothes for a castle visit."

He laughed so heartily that his head was thrown back. Deep dimples appeared, and when he glanced back at me, his eyes were filled with mirth. It quite disarmed me; I suppose I'd been accustomed to such constrained displays of emotion that I couldn't even remember the last time I'd seen such abandonment. "Then there's the two of us," he said. "No, darling, we won't be spending the night at the castle or visiting the residents there, though I have worked on the architecture—part of an enormous, never-ending team, I suppose. We'll stay in a nearby village within sight of it, and within sight of the most beautiful waterfall your eyes have ever beheld."

"Oh." With Nicky's contagious good humor, Donnybrook, and the asylum behind us and the Wicklow Mountains off in the distance, I felt myself relaxing. The sun had risen and finally burnt away the last of the morning mists, and I pulled my shawl away from my neck and arranged it more informally about me, and settled in for the ride ahead.

By the time we neared the tiny village of Enniskerry in the shadow of the medieval castle, my back was aching the same as if I'd spent the day hunched over my artwork, and my rear was decidedly unhappy. Unlike the carriage I was accustomed to with its upholstered plush seats, this was slightly more than a cart pulled by two horses, the boards growing thin and rough as the day progressed despite my layers of clothing. We stopped only once and opened a cheesecloth of meats and cheeses that Nicky had brought, for in my rush to get through the house, I neglected to think of food or water. Fortunately, he also had a bottle of ale, which we shared. I did, however, have some coins, but we saw little in the way of stores or pubs in which to use them.

He slowed the horses to a leisurely walk as we wound our way a short distance from Enniskerry, where a few cottages were sprinkled amongst the hills. Some had sustained fires, their thatched roofs caved, exposing the interior to the elements. As we approached, those tiny cottages in which life remained came to life as children in bare feet came running to greet us. They called Nicky by name, one or two jumping into the cart behind us before he shooed them off in a good-natured order.

He pulled up in front of the last cottage on the rutted lane as a man and woman made their way to us.

"Peter?" I breathed.

"Aye, and it is," Peter called out, though he certainly could not have heard me. "And my wife, Isibeal."

"Pleased to meet you." Isibeal curtseyed as I began to disembark. I'd no sooner than turned myself around to descend onto the carriage step than both Nicky and Peter were beside me, offering their hands. I accepted both of them and climbed down to the bare soil.

As three more people joined us, Peter continued, "This is my son, Rory and my girls, Sosaidh and Mallaidh—Susan and Molly in English."

"I prefer the Gaelic," I said, taking each of their offered hands in turn. It might have been my imagination, but I thought Peter raised a brow at my reply, to which Nicky only smiled.

The daughters were the spitting image of their mother, their slender faces sprinkled with freckles under thick copper hair and celestial blue eyes. Rory, however, looked like Peter might have when he was younger: tall and lithe with dark brows and hair, his forehead not as high as his father's. While the girls shyly murmured their greetings, Rory stepped up to take my hand. "It's a pleasure," he said, bending down to kiss it. Ah, another charmer.

"I am very proud of my son," Peter said, beaming. "He is leaving in a few weeks for Oxford."

"Are you?" I blurted, more than a little surprised.

"Aye, ma'am. I will be training to become a solicitor," Rory answered proudly. "It has been my life's dream to pursue law."

"Aye," Nicky said, "he's got himself a benefactor that will see him through the university and then he'll spend—what is it, Rory, six years as an apprentice, 'ey?"

"Eight, but it's called clerking. Once I've repaid my debt, I intend to return to Ireland and practice law here."

"That is very admirable. But," I continued, glancing at the cottages, "I thought you all lived in Kilkenny."

"Ah," Peter answered. "Our family is from Kilkenny. Isibeal's too. But there's more work up this way."

As I followed them toward the last cottage, Nicky explained, "Peter and Rory have been far and wide obtaining the needed supplies, you see."

"Only m' da," Rory said pointedly.

Peter stole a sideways glance at Nicky. "He does not want any part of it."

"Ah," Nicky said without returning the glance. Instead, he kept his eyes focused on the cottage ahead of us.

"I must keep m' hands clean, Uncle Nicky," Rory said.

"I understand," Nicky answered, his voice light. "But we'll discuss it later, 'ey? We've a guest."

As all eyes turned back to me, I said, "I suppose I'm a surprise to you all."

"Not at'al," Isibeal said. "We've always room for one more. Come. Sit. I'll make us some tea."

Her reply did nothing to answer my question, but if they were surprised to see me there, they did not let on. The luster of the sun was abruptly replaced by the gloom of the tiny cottage as we stepped inside. Rather than sit as I'd been sitting since dawn, I wandered about the kitchen—or what served as one—while we waited for the water to boil. I suppose the kitchen comprised half the cottage. There was no cook stove but only a fireplace, high and broad and deep, a style that might have been a thousand years old or merely a hundred. It was impossible to tell the age of the structure as it appeared to have remained unchanged through centuries, and yet here was a family settling into it as though it was home. The interior walls were the backside of the exterior, limestone I supposed with mud and horsehair holding the bricks together. A long table graced the center of the room and served for both preparation and eating, and I assumed for just about everything else. The chairs were mismatched, and I recognized more than one as a style the gypsies sold on their travels.

"The cottage was once just this one room," Isibeal was saying as she gathered some chipped cups from an open shelf. "It belonged to tenant farmers dating back, oh, three hundred years or more." She nodded toward an open doorway. "That room was added on about a hundred years ago." She chuckled. "They did not do a good job, I'm afraid, of leveling the floor first. If you go in, watch your step."

"May I?" I asked.

"Of course."

I wandered to the doorway. I could see now where the brick had been chiseled away to create the opening into the next room, and Isibeal was right indeed; there was a good two-inch drop into the adjoining room. I stepped tentatively inside, taking in the straw-filled beds on either side, one larger than the other.

"It's where we sleep," Molly said. She'd come to stand beside me, and while I was peering at the contents of the bedroom, she appeared to have been studying me. "My sister, mother, and I sleep in this bed here, and Da and my brother in that one."

"But only for tonight." It was a statement, but also a question as the journey and the destination made no sense to me.

"No," Molly said. "Every night."

"But—"

"Ah, and the tea is ready," Isibeal said, interrupting us. Molly quickly returned to the other room. I glanced about once more, taking in the small pile of clothing in one corner and the dingy bedding, before making my way to the kitchen.

"We'll have supper soon," Isibeal said as she poured the tea. "But this will warm your insides while we wait for the men."

"Where did they go?"

"Oh, they'll be swapping out the carriages," she said, her voice taking on a vague quality.

"So. We'll be staying here tonight, then?"

"Next door." Isibeal looked into my eyes as she sat. Her own were enormous in a narrow face, her skin aged beyond her years, yet her eyes were sharp.

"I noticed some of the cottages did not have roofs," I said, sipping my tea.

"Aye."

"Did the tenants not have the means to keep them roofed?"

Isibeal looked at me as though I had lost my mind, and Molly openly laughed before her face showed pain, and I suspected her mother had kicked her under the table. "They are eviction homes."

"What is that?"

"Are you quite sure you don't know?"

I shook my head.

"The tenants did not have the money to pay their rent, so the owner put them out and burned the roof so they could not inhabit the cottage."

"How late were they?"

"A day, perhaps."

"A day?"

"Rent is collected each week. If you don't have the money in hand, there's no sense in the owner allowing you to stay now is there?" Her voice was gentle, and despite her words, I sensed an empathy for those evicted.

"But," I said haltingly, "if he burns down the roof, then another tenant cannot rent it, either."

"Tenants with money are few and far between. If one appears with the coin in hand, the owner will give the tenants permission to replace the roof."

"They're paying rent, and they must replace the roof themselves?"

"Aye," she said, settling back with her tea. "It's the way of things."

I began to wonder why Nicky had asked me to accompany him, for surely, he would know that I would be left with more questions than answers. My naiveté felt as though it was slipping from my shoulders, and for the first time, it occurred to me that his invitation was not purely personal. There was something he wanted me to see or perhaps to experience and I wasn't sure whether I was up to it.

Supper consisted of stew and cornmeal. The stew was tasty, seasoned with more fat than I was accustomed to, but it lent the dish a hearty flavor coupled with a smoky taste from the peat bricks fueling the fire. The potatoes were on the downside, an age by which my servants would have been ordered to toss them, and now I wondered if they had eaten them instead. The carrots were even more senior with blackened sections that I noticed the others eating. The cornmeal, I surmised, was store-bought and made into patties over the fire, each person around the table receiving one.

"I noticed," I said tentatively during a lull in the conversation, "that some of the children looked very hearty. They must eat a lot of this delicious stew."

The room became silent, and when I glanced up, I noticed all eyes on me. "Their stomachs. They looked like they eat quite a bit."

"Their stomachs are distended," Nicky said quietly.

"Is that a medical condition?" I asked.

"I've been told," Isibeal said, "that it is due to a poor diet. We eat what we can, what God gives us, but sometimes it isn't enough. Many a child has succumbed to starvation while their stomachs appear rounded."

The conversation at Eliza's dinner party replayed in my mind. Ignorance, I thought. Bloody ignorance.

We had finished supper, and I was helping to clean the table when the door opened, ushering in a blast of chilly air that had descended after the final vestiges of sunset. I was surprised to discover a priest standing there; his eyes swept the room, taking in the numbers crammed into the tiny cottage before he closed the door and removed his cap.

Nicky was the first to greet him, and as they hugged, the resemblance was uncanny. "There's naught but a year between us," Nicky said as he gestured me over, "but growing up, we were always thought of as twins. Meet my older brother, Brendan. Bren, this is Penny Mather."

I had barely a chance to greet him before the others fell upon him with hugs and handshakes all around. The men eventually found themselves back around the table, discussing their travels and catching up on people whose names meant nothing to me, but I enjoyed the banter and talk between them. As the shadows grew long and the candles short, I wished the evening didn't have to end. I'd grown so accustomed to the silent meals with Stratford that I hadn't realized just how much I enjoyed others' company and the closeness of family.

12

I leaned against the fence post, or perhaps it was a carriage post as there was no fence at all, only an iron post that protruded from deep in the ground, perhaps having called that spot home for decades if not centuries. My eyes were drinking in the vista before me. The medieval castle loomed high atop a hill in the distance, the moon illuminating its turrets from directly over its tallest roofline. A half-moon drive stretched from the structure, winding its way along the hill on either side before joining into one lane halfway down. Acres of gardens were cradled between the two halves, the white flowers catching the moonlight and sending it back, creating an otherworldly effect.

It had been quiet when I came to stand in front of the cottages in the chilled night air. But as I grew accustomed to standing there, I determined it was anything but silent. Crickets chirped in a growing chorus while bullfrogs crooned in their baritones. Somewhere in the distance, a black-crowned night heron added to the orchestra, its voice raspy and soulful while the nightingale joined in with its flute-like voice.

The cottages had grown hushed, the children perhaps put to sleep and the adults settling in for the evening in front of cozy fires. Somewhere a pig grunted, and elsewhere a horse neighed as they, too, settled in for the night. It would be a short one for sure, as the days were growing longer with the promise of summer not far away. It was a time of plowing the fields and planting seeds, of shearing sheep and birthing calves, a time for renewal after a dark and cold winter.

"It's even more beautiful in the sunlight." The voice was soothing and calm and seemed perfectly suited for the other sounds of the night, like yet another instrument added to the nocturnal song. Nicky joined me while his eyes continued to leisurely scan the distant horizon.

"Why did you bring me here?" My voice was soft; perhaps I was afraid of breaking the tranquil spell cast over the countryside.

"I wanted you to see all of this." His voice remained low and reverent.

"Why?"

"It is beautiful, isn't it?"

"Yes, it is beautiful."

"What do you see when you drink in the countryside?"

I paused, closing my eyes against the night. "I see the way the moonlight dances off the flowers, the shadows of the copses, and the way the uppermost branches seem to reach for the moon." I opened my eyes. "I smell the fresh soil, recently overturned, and I hear the nocturnal birds venturing from their nests to soar through the night skies."

"And what do you see in that field come the morrow?"

I peered into the darkness to a flat area, one I could not view clearly in the gloom. "I see a mule pulling a plow, a young man—perhaps your nephew? He is behind the plow, guiding it through the soil, tilling it for the seedlings."

"And there, on the hillside?"

"Sheep not yet shorn, the lambs bleating for their mothers, the sun warm on their backs."

"That is why I brought you here," Nicky said, turning away from the vista and toward me. His face was partly in shadows, and I strove to see his eyes as he spoke. "Your artwork is beautiful, haunting in its detail. Yet I have the impression that you sketch from memory."

"I suppose I do."

"I wanted to give you more memories."

I didn't respond right away, his words hanging on the wind like something I should reach out and grasp as it dangled in front of me.

"The fire is warming the cottage where you'll stay for the night," he said when the silence had stretched out too long.

I glanced behind us. "That one?"

"Aye. The one adjacent to my brother's. It has but one room, and I've laid out the beds near the fireplace so you'll remain warm."

"Beds?" I asked, emphasizing the plural.

"Aye." He hesitated, his expression hardening, and his voice becoming flatter. "It is beautiful here certainly. But it can also be filled with danger, especially in the dark of night. I'll remain with you to protect you, but I assure you I'll stay my distance in the opposite bed."

"And what will you be protecting me from precisely?"

He didn't answer directly, but his eyes continued to roam the shadows forming in those valleys and crevices where the moon did not penetrate. "One never knows," he said finally.

"I assure you that I can protect myself."

"In your own home, I have no doubt. In the wilds… It's better to be safe. I promised you no harm would come to you, and I intend to keep that promise."

I nodded silently. Then, "Are you not married, Nicky?" He didn't reply, and I continued, nodding toward Peter's cottage, "Your brother does not seem much older than you, and he has a wife and a family. Surely a young lass has caught your eye—and you've caught hers."

"I am married," he said.

My insides felt as though they were plummeting inside me, the stew beginning to roil.

He placed a hand on my shoulder as if to steady me. "I am married to Ireland."

"To Ireland?"

"Aye. And she needs me now, more than ever."

Puzzled, I asked, "Ireland, the country?"

He smiled. "Ireland. The country." Before I could respond, he continued, his voice growing a bit weary, "We shall leave at dawn. We must arrive back at your estate while the sun still shines. I must unload the supplies while I can still see what I'm doing."

At the mention of returning, I felt a mixture of emotions that seemed to compete for dominance. I missed my bedchambers, and what I knew would be a more comfortable bed. I missed the ample suppers and sweet pastries. I missed my studio with my drawings and my routine. And yet I did not wish to return. I wanted to remain here for a time longer, to continue to soak up the wild country, to see how the sun glints off the dew and the way the waters reflected the light. I wanted more memories of which to sketch. Perhaps Eliza was right. I should turn to watercolors, where I could more adequately bring to life the beauty that was Ireland.

The flames danced and pirouetted like so many ballet members assembled on a stage, their movements mesmerizing, even hypnotic. The warmth, however, was wanting, with a single peat brick trying its hardest to do its job but failing like a tiny child not meant to go it alone. I felt sorry for it falling short of the success it strove so hard to achieve, and then I grew discouraged as the cold pervaded.

I lay on a bed of straw faintly scented with what must have been last year's lavender blooms, as it was too early in the current season for them to make their appearance. The straw packed under my weight until I felt the pricks from shoulder to knee, and as I turned from one position to another, I eventually felt the hard dirt floor upon which the bed was laid. The blankets meant to cushion and warm me were worn so thin, I could see the outline of my clothes underneath them, and despite wearing several layers, I could not get warm.

Nicky's breathing had been measured, but now I could no longer hear him, and I struggled to see him through the gloom. He lay facing me—that I was sure of—but the shadows prevented me from seeing the details my heart desired. We'd talked until he'd fallen asleep, seemingly unaffected by the cold, and now I longed to hear his voice again. Despite his height and his brawn, his voice was gentle and reassuring, so very different from Stratford's brusque and impatient tenor.

Shivering, I stood and gathered the blankets about me as best I could and made my way to Nicky's side. I dropped to my knees upon his straw, which was a great deal thinner than the bed I'd been given. I was surprised to find his eyes open and watching me.

"It will be warmer for both of us if…" my voice trailed off as I felt the heat rising in my cheeks.

He opened his blanket as if inviting me in. I crawled in beside him, my back to his front. Unlike myself, who was wearing every stitch of clothing I'd brought in an attempt to stave off the chill, he was wearing only a gray shirt and trousers. My cold stockinged feet found him, and he covered us with both our blankets and then wrapped his arm around me. I placed my hand upon his and snuggled more deeply against him.

"Are you warmer?" His breath tickled my hair as he whispered, his lips close to my ear.

"Yes," I said. "Much warmer." I knew he could feel the beating of my heart; it was thumping wildly in both my chest and my neck, and I felt as though I could not catch my breath.

He settled in behind me, and I tried to listen to the rhythmic breathing I'd heard when he first slipped into slumber, but it did not come. His arm grew heavy across me like a weighty coat determined to protect me from the chill. Then he shifted, his head moving down to my neck where his lips brushed against my skin.

I turned in his arms, and he came upon one elbow to peer into my face. The darkness enveloped us, and I found myself searching out his eyes with a longing to see into his soul. I placed a hand upon his face, running my fingers along his jawline, feeling the stubble that had formed there since his last shave. And then my fingers found his hair and intertwined around the thick locks.

"You don't have to do this," he said hoarsely. "I gave you my word."

"I know. But I did not give you mine." I pressed upward to find his lips, my own whispering across his, savoring the fullness and the sweetness before his lips parted, and he returned my kiss with a passionate one of his own. I became lost in his kisses, my body burning for his, the longing mounting within me. "You don't have to do this," I whispered when we pulled back for a brief moment. "Or do you want to?"

"Desperately," he answered as his hands followed the lines of my body as if memorizing the bend in my back, the flare of my hips.

"I love your curves," he whispered.

"I am a bit hefty," I answered, suddenly self-conscious.

"Oh, I beg to differ," he said, his voice becoming serious. "I love every curve. Your body might not be perfect, but it is certainly perfect for me."

I felt as though a thousand pounds had been lifted from my shoulders, and suddenly I felt like the most beautiful woman in the entire world. As if to drive home his point, he set about exploring each curve, and in the process, he set my body on fire. Mountains of clothing and blankets peeled away, and somehow, the peat grew warmer until the room was awash in our moans and our heat, our limbs intertwined, our skin glistening, and I knew with all the assuredness in my soul that I was precisely where I was meant to be.

13

The morning arrived too soon, the darkness that had surrounded us replaced by a lazy filter of promised sunshine, the fire snuffed out as the peat burned itself out. Nicky departed the cottage long before I had fully awakened, my curiosity discovering him beside a cart as he spoke to Peter, Brendan, and Rory. I let the curtain drop back into place and busied myself with becoming presentable so by the time the horses were ready, and he returned for me, I was waiting.

"Ah," he said when he spotted me, "you're up."

"I am. And I'm ready."

"Well, sit yourself down for a moment. I've brought you some breakfast."

"Oh?" I sat at the tiny table pushed against the far wall and opened the cheesecloth to discover a slice of ham and a block of cheese. As I began to nibble on the cheese, I heard the clip-clop of a horse's hooves outside the cottage.

"That would be Brendan," Nicky said, pulling up a chair beside me. "He's off to perform his duties."

"Oh, and I didn't have the chance to say good-bye." I began to rise, but he waved me back down.

"Go outside now, and all you'll see is the horse's arse. I hope there will be another opportunity for you to see him, 'ey?"

"I hope so."

"And Peter's family as well."

"I won't get to say good-bye to them either?"

"They left before dawn."

"Why?"

"Why to work, of course."

"All of them?"

"Peter and Rory are still about, but they'll be heading south shortly. The others must arrive at their jobs before the first light."

I took a bite of the ham. "What do they do?"

"They have good positions, all of them. Isibeal is an upstairs housemaid, and Sosaidh and Mallaidh are scullery maids."

"At the castle?"

He shook his head. "At a manor house. Very similar to your own," he added with a sideways glance.

"Nicky, there's something I don't understand. You said your family was from Kilkenny, but Mallaidh led me to believe they live here all the time…" My voice faded, the question barely at my lips.

"And you're wondering who is telling you the truth."

I did not nod or reply but simply gazed into his eyes. After a moment, he smiled, the grin causing the laugh lines around his eyes to appear.

"Our parents remained in Kilkenny and my sister, too. Peter's family moves about as work presents itself."

"And you?"

"Thanks to work at your estate, I have a room in Dublin."

"Just a room?"

He laughed. "Why would I need more, 'ey? I leave before the first light, and I arrive home well after dark. I've barely time to get a bite to eat before I am crawling into my bed."

"So this cottage—"

"—is not mine," he finished. "Only for one night. It belongs to Brendan. And now," he said, patting his knees, "if you're so inclined, we have a long drive ahead of us."

Things had changed between Nicky and me. During the past 24 hours, I'd gone from the employer's wife to something else entirely. I knew Nicky felt it too by the way he took my hand in his once we had left the watchful eyes of rural folk and were on the isolated road back to Matherscourt. His palm was rough, his fingers calloused, his grip on me both tight and gentle, and I loved it.

It was unseasonably warm, the changing of seasons happening fast and completely, but always with the knowledge, it could change yet again in a matter of minutes. I shook the shawl from my head and then from my shoulders, tilting my head upward to catch the sun's affectionate rays.

Nicky was talkative, much more so than he'd been the day before. He pointed out landmarks, spinning tales of knights and ghosts, love and betrayal, warring Gaelic clans, the invasion of Vikings and England's ongoing struggle to conquer the Irish.

"I've never seen mountains such as these," I said as we circumnavigated a mountain range.

"The Wicklow Mountains? Are you to say you've never seen them before?"

I shook my head.

"Your husband—he never took you to see them?"

I squeezed his hand. "He doesn't take me very many places."

"'Tis a shame, it is. The world is out there, Penny, to be thoroughly explored. Else how can you say you've lived?"

"How high do you suppose they are?"

"Oh, they're not even the highest. No, I suppose Lugnaquilla would be that, but she's a good distance southwest of us."

"You've seen it—this Lugna…"

"Lugnaquilla," he chuckled as I faltered. "Oh, aye, I have indeed. There is something about the mountains that beckon to a man, you know. The cool, crisp air, the icy mountain streams—best water you'll ever taste by far. The creatures there are different; majestic, I'd say. It's as if you're closer to the heavens in the mountains; why the clouds come down so close, they can wrap you up in their embrace."

"It sounds like you're very familiar with them."

"I am indeed. Once there was a time when, if I was missing, folks knew where to find me. I'd be at Kippure, where the Liffey Head Bog feeds the icy streams into the River Liffey. At least," he added, "if I was in these parts. I'd head for the Sally Gap to be sure. Now, if I was south of here—" He was interrupted by a wagon approaching us from the opposite direction. He narrowed his eyes and pulled our wagon off the pocked dirt road and onto the soft grass.

I pulled my hand from his as the rider approached. It appeared to be a lone woman dressed in layers upon layers of clothing as if she wore everything she owned. The carriage was nothing more than a cart of questionable wood that was splintered so badly in some places that no doubt anything placed there would fall straight through. A single mule was pulling the cart, its ears pricked as it approached us.

"And a good morning to you, Missus O'Rigley," Nicky called out as she called for the mule to stop alongside us.

She nodded, her sharp blue eyes traveling instantly to my hands in my lap. The message was clear; she had seen us holding hands as we'd approached. I felt the color rising in my cheeks as her eyes traveled upward to my face. Her eyes narrowed as though she was trying to place me, but I knew we'd never seen each other before and now, being caught with Nicky and feeling as if our night together was splayed out for her to see, I hoped I'd never see her again.

Her face was weathered; the creases deep, and her face tanned as if she'd spent a lifetime in the elements. Her lips were unnaturally sunken, and as she responded curtly to Nicky, I realized she was probably toothless.

"A bit far from home, aren't you there?" Nicky said pleasantly.

"No more than you, lad," she answered. She pointedly peered at me again as if expecting an introduction. Nicky didn't take the bait, and I bit my lower lip to keep myself silent.

"Aye, and you've a point there." He glanced toward the cart. "You've something to sell today?"

"Not selling," she corrected. "Trading."

"Ah." He reached into his pocket and pulled out a coin. "Take it, Missus O'Rigley. You never know when you might need it."

She scoffed and pulled away from his hand. "Now, what would I be doing with a coin in my pouch?" she asked. "What I can't get in trade, I don't need."

"Suit yourself," he said cordially as he returned the coin to his pocket.

"I always do," she said before calling to her mule. As the animal began walking again, Nicky bade his farewells, but if she answered, her voice was lost in the wind or within the mounds of clothing.

After a brief moment, Nicky called out to our horses, and we pulled back onto the dirt road to continue our journey. Only seconds seemed to pass before he returned his hand to mine, squeezing it gently. "You needn't worry," he said. "We've been off for supplies for your addition, should anyone need to know."

"And just how many estate wives travel with builders on their supply runs?" I asked.

He smiled but didn't answer.

"So, that would be none then?"

He gave me a sideways glance. "At least one." We both chuckled, and then he continued, "Now where were we before we were interrupted, 'eh?"

Was it only yesterday that I traveled down this same road in the opposite direction? So much had happened since then, and so much had changed inside me that it felt it had been a lifetime ago. The journey had seemed long and arduous the day before, my legs and backside smarting from the hours on the rough wooden seat. It was in such stark contrast to today's trip back. Today I wanted the hours to pass slowly so I could savor every moment with Nicky, and yet they sped past in a cruel twist. One moment he was holding my hand and speaking softly to me about all manner of things, and the next, we were approaching the outskirts of Donnybrook.

We had barely cleared the village and come round the bend in the road where we were to turn toward the north and Matherscourt when we spotted a roadblock up ahead. Two official-looking vehicles were parked on either side of the road while British soldiers stood in the center. As we approached from the south, a fine carriage advanced from the north, and as we drew closer, I sucked in my breath. It was, of all people, Lord Philip Davies, Eliza's husband. Instinctively, I pulled my hood over my hair in a panicked attempt to shield my face from his view.

Nicky slowed our approach, his eyes darting to either side of the road, but there were no available turns to avoid the checkpoint. Our eyes met; to turn around now would be too obvious. Nicky removed his hand from mine.

Philip's carriage reached the checkpoint first. His coachman was in the front seat, and as he stopped the horse alongside the soldiers, he said something to them that I could not hear. Two of the soldiers walked back to the shiny black carriage that sported the Davies family crest. A hand rested on the door sash, and for a brief moment, the soldiers chatted with the occupant. Then the hand was withdrawn, the soldiers each tipped their hats to the occupant, and the carriage continued in our direction.

I could sense Nicky's breathing had changed; it was more shallow now, and his body appeared tense, his lips pursed. As we pulled up to another set of soldiers, Nicky called out, "And a good day to you, sir."

One soldier appeared to be all of nineteen if that but puffed out his chest as though feeling rather important in his uniform. He did not answer but peered toward the cart's contents. "And where are you coming from?" he demanded.

I felt my spine grow taut, and I struggled to breathe.

"Kilkenny," Nicky answered. His voice remained pleasant, in stark contrast to the soldier.

An older soldier joined the younger one, and he too peered into the cart.

"Is there a problem?" Nicky asked.

Out of the corner of my eye, I watched the two soldiers. They took opposite sides and were walking slowly down the length of our cart. I knew the supplies we had retrieved had been loaded early this morning with several lengths of wood peeking out beyond the cart. Atop them was laid several cloths with more wood holding it down to protect against the elements; it was Ireland, after all, and a rainstorm was expected despite the current sunshine.

"We're inspecting all wagons today," the older soldier, who was standing near the center of the roadway, announced.

Philip's carriage was slowing as it approached, and now I could clearly see his dark hair through the open window above the door.

Nicky breathed, "I cannot allow them to inspect us."

Startled, I jerked my head in his direction. He was reaching underneath his open jacket, and I spotted the glint of metal.

I bounded to my feet, dropping the hood from my head. My eyes met the older soldier's as one brow shot up. My voice was clear and dominating. "I am Lady Mather. This man carries supplies to Matherscourt. There is no need to inspect."

I was acutely aware of Philip's fancy carriage stopping alongside us as the younger soldier puffed, "Ha! Lady, indeed."

The older soldier stated flatly, "We've orders to inspect all wagons, and there'll be no exceptions." He tossed a piece of wood that had been laid over the cloths onto the side and climbed into the cart. His hand was on the corner cloth when the carriage door opened abruptly, and Philip stepped out.

"My good man," Philip said in a booming, authoritative voice, "did you not hear Lady Mather?"

The older soldier stood, dropping the cloth. "I did, sir, but I don't believe—"

"Independence, my dear, please forgive these uncouth men. I give you my word I will speak to their superiors about this." Philip turned toward the soldiers. "And I give you my word that this is indeed Lady Mather and this gentleman is in her employ. Do not question them further."

"Yes, sir." The older soldier jumped down from the cart while the younger man's eyes swept from his fellow soldier to Philip and back.

The two soldiers that had been inspecting from the opposite direction joined us as Philip turned toward them. "Allow Lady Mather to pass," he said.

The men stood back, and Nicky nodded toward Philip. "Thank you, sir."

Philip did not respond, but as I seated myself once again and Nicky flicked the reins, we began moving slowly past the soldiers. I heard Philip's voice behind us, saying, "Now. What are your names?" I resisted the urge to gawk behind us, and when I swept my eyes toward Nicky, I noticed he was focused on the road ahead.

Once we were out of earshot and around a bend, he said quietly, "That was a brave thing you did back there, Penny."

I chuckled wryly. "Don't be ridiculous," I said jokingly. Then in a more serious tone, I added, "There was no need for anyone to inspect the wagon—or to question my identity."

There was a moment of silence before he stated, "You know Lord Davies."

"I do. His wife is my best friend."

He swallowed. "And will there be a problem now that he's seen us together?"

"No," I said with more confidence than I felt. "I have every right to personally select the materials for our new addition."

He nodded, but I didn't believe I'd convinced him. And truth be told, I hadn't convinced myself, either.

We paused at the junction where we would take our turn toward Matherscourt, but rather than directing the horses onto the road, Nicky turned them onto a smaller route that appeared no wider than a cattle path.

"I don't want to take you through the front gates of Matherscourt," Nicky said in response to my quizzical expression. "It would not appear… proper."

"I had wondered about that myself," I admitted. "When we left, the sun had not fully arisen, and no one knew I was leaving." I glanced upward at the sun. It seemed to be shining directly onto me as we approached, rather like the lamps used to light up a theatre stage.

"There is a rear entrance to Matherscourt. I imagine it was used when the livestock was guided toward the slaughterhouse in days past. We'll arrive at the barn from the south so you won't be seen returning to the estate with me."

I felt as though two people were arguing inside me. One wanted to thank him for his courtesy, while the other did not wish to hide. Dared I say I was falling in love with the man? But that was precisely what I'd expected when I accepted his offer. There would have been no burning desire to travel with anyone else to pick up supplies required for a room I was expressly forbidden to enter. No, I'd come because I wanted to be with Nicky. I wanted time to talk, to get to know him and where he was from... And last night had been beyond my wildest fantasies. I wanted to ride that drive straight through the front gates with him, but peering downward at the worker's cart, I knew it was not possible. I could not transport Nicky into Stratford's role as my husband and the owner of the estate and all his holdings, no matter how much I fantasied about precisely that.

We arrived at the rear gates much too soon. I sensed Nicky's reluctance as he stopped the horses. He sat for a moment simply gazing at the double gate, and then he turned toward me. In an instant, he had me in his arms, his lips on mine as passionate and as wanting as they had been during the night. His hands traveled along my back, pulling me into him, eventually traveling upward to my hair where his fingers caressed the curls that had fallen from my upswept bun. When our lips finally parted, he did not pull back but pressed his cheek, rough with a five o'clock shadow, against mine, squeezing me against him so profoundly that I lost my breath.

"I don't want to leave you," he whispered in my ear.

"I know," I heard myself answering, my voice breathy with wanting. "I know."

I don't know how long we remained there, but it wasn't nearly enough time for me to memorize every inch of him pressed against me. I gazed upward at the blue, cloudless skies and allowed the sun to spread its warmth over my face. I tried to memorize the gentle hills that surrounded us, the copses of trees here and there, the babbling of a brook. I inhaled the aroma of wildflowers and bluebells that carpeted the ground around us as if the angels had sowed the seeds themselves. And I inhaled Nicky's scent as if I could keep it with me forever; that unique blend of spring air and sunshine, woodlands and peat fire, of salty masculinity. I curled my fingers through his hair, feeling its fullness and softness, burying my nose into it, wishing it was yesterday, and our time was only beginning.

When he finally pulled away from me, he stared at my face, his eyes lingering on my hairline, my brows, my eyes, my lips, and cheeks, as though he, too, was seeking to memorize this moment. "This won't be the last of me," he whispered, his voice hoarse. "We'll find time together. We must."

I could only nod my head as I fought back the tears that pulled at the edge of my eyes. I did not want him to see me cry, and I did not wish to return to the house with swollen eyes and reddened cheeks.

When his arms and hands dropped away from me, I felt the void as if a part of me had been torn from my body. I watched as he dismounted and strode to the gates, unlatching them and pulling them wide. Without another word, he led the horses through, and when the cart was firmly inside, he returned to close and fasten the gate once more.

When he was once again in the seat beside me, I grasped his hand, holding it firmly until the old barn was within view. Concerned the workers might be there gathering supplies, I hesitantly withdrew, planting my hands in my lap where my fingers searched out one another in a futile effort to console myself. But no one was there as we pulled in front of the doors. Nicky lifted me down from the cart and held me briefly, kissing me atop my head. Then he grabbed my bag and handed it to me.

"Will you be alright to walk back to the house from here?" he asked.

I nodded.

"I wish I could walk you back myself, carry your bag for you."

"No," I said, my voice sounding more confident than I felt. "Someone could see us from the windows."

"Aye."

"Can I stay and watch you unload?"

He hesitated. "You'd better not. We're risking someone seeing us here." His eyes moved upward and past me, though I knew the great house could not be seen from this vantage point.

I nodded and turned to go.

"Penny?" His voice was soft.

I turned back around to face him.

"Sketch what you have seen. Remember the mountains, the waterfall, the cottages… Remember the beauty."

"I will," I said, a smile spreading across my face. "I will."

With that, I turned onto the path that would lead me past my little studio, through the meadow and to the rear of the house. I was home, and yet it did not feel like home anymore. I longed to be back in the cottage with Nicky in my arms.

14

I awakened at the first light of dawn. It took me a moment to adjust to my surroundings; I'd been dreaming of the cottage, the thin straw bedding, and the warmth of the fireplace and of Nicky's body next to mine. When I opened my eyes to the bed well off the floor and the layers of bedding, I found myself looking through the waning gloom for Nicky. As reality set in, I lay in bed, staring at each piece of furniture, realizing that any of them would be fancier than anything I'd seen in Peter's cottage. I wondered at the paradox of Peter's fancy suit, the recommendation from the banker in London, and Stratford's assumption that the Bowers family was of upper-crust stock.

And then there was Philip Davies to contend with. I felt a headache coming on, and I rose and made my way to the window to watch the sun rising on the distant horizon. Could Philip have come along at a worse time? Figure the odds of meeting him along the road so far from either of our estates.

I went to my writing table and wrote out a carefully worded note to Eliza. It was simply a request to call on her later that morning. I would give the note to Johanna and dispatch her right away to deliver it. Then I would dress and call for my carriage to take me to Davies Castle. I would tell her of meeting Philip along the road and ask her to intervene so word could not possibly get back to Stratford.

And how would I explain myself if it did? I folded the note and sealed it with candlewax, imprinting my seal upon it. Stratford would never believe me if I told him I was selecting wood for the addition; it was *his* addition after all, and he would be furious if I implied I was interjecting myself into his plans. That is if he believed me. What if he didn't? What if he suspected an affair?

I was not cut out for this. I'd always lived my life as others expected me to, remaining along the straight and narrow path, church every Sunday and all that. Leaving with Nicky was completely uncharacteristic of me, especially for an overnight stay. What was I thinking?

And yet I did not regret one moment of it.

Oh, how different life would be were he to awaken beside me here! If only he was the Lord here instead of Stratford… But then Nicky would not be a Lord, would he? And Matherscourt would not be Matherscourt…

My mind was jumbled, the thoughts continuing to arrive disjointed and fraught with worry until the minutes turned into an hour, and Johanna silently slid the door open. She was surprised to see me sitting by the window in my dressing gown, shivering against the morning chill.

"Are you well, m'lady?" she whispered as she entered and closed the door behind her.

"I am quite well, thank you."

Our eyes met, but I said no more. She had not asked—nor had any of the servants—where I had been, nor was it their place to inquire. I had called for a hot bath when I'd first arrived home, which had been arranged posthaste. Then I had eaten my fill in the dining hall, alone except for the servants attending me. I had then retired to my bedchamber and slept the night away, my body depleted of its strength, and my dreams filled with passion.

"A message came for you first thing this morn," Johanna said, passing the note to me. I recognized Eliza's handwriting immediately, and my heart skipped a beat. Philip had told her. He must have. As Johanna built up the fire, I cracked the seal on the note and read it.

Dearest Penny,

Should it be convenient for you, I wish to pay you a visit at our usual spot today as early as practical. No need to reply if this is acceptable, only if it is not.

Yours truly,
Eliza

I folded the note. "I wish to dress immediately," I said. "I'd like to take a stroll. Have the kitchen prepare a basket for me."

"Yes, ma'am." Having stoked the flames into resurrecting the fire, she slipped out the door. I knew she would be hurrying through the corridors to the kitchen to let them know of my breakfast plans. I hurried to the fire and dropped Eliza's note into the flames along with my own note. I watched as the paper was alighted, my ivory seal and Eliza's crimson one melting onto the peat.

Johanna returned quickly and helped me dress and style my hair. Then as the first warm rays began burning the dew off the grass, I made my way through the meadow with my basket.

It was mid-morning before Eliza arrived. I'd seen no one else that morning, not even the workers retrieving supplies from the old barn. I found myself looking for

Nicky's cart, disappointed that I didn't see it, relieved that my morning was not further complicated.

I spotted Eliza's fancy carriage from the window, wiped my hands of charcoal, and was standing in the door as she alighted with Brian's assistance. I felt an odd sort of kinship with them now. To an innocent observer, he was simply a coachman doing his duty, but as I watched, I saw how Eliza grasped his hand a bit too heartily and how his lingered on hers even after her feet were on the ground.

"Penny darling," Eliza said as she spotted me. She breezed up the steps to my little studio and kissed me on each cheek.

I invited her in and poured us each a cup of tea. I had barely touched the basket Léana had prepared for me this morning, and now I set out some of the sweets for us to nibble. While I prepared our little table, Eliza meandered around the room, pausing at this sketch or that. I watched her as I worked; those she lingered on longer than others were usually those that fetched the most money.

"What is this you've started?" she asked as she stopped in front of the sketch I'd begun only that morning.

"The Wicklow Mountains." I straightened, my hands folded in front of me.

"Ah. Is that where you were?"

I nodded.

She pulled her elaborate hat off with a flourish and set it in an empty chair, and then she sat in another. "Dear, why on earth did you travel that far?"

"Nicky—Nicolas Bowers, the gentleman overseeing the construction at Matherscourt—he asked me to accompany him as he picked up supplies."

As she sipped her tea, her eyes never left mine. She set her teacup in the saucer, which she held with gloved hands. "Yes. That is what Philip told me last night."

"Oh, Eliza. Please don't tell me he's going to say a word to Stratford."

"I don't believe he will," she answered thoughtfully, "only because he can't stand Stratford."

I sighed in relief. "What did you say when he told you?"

"I told him you had decided on your own project."

"What?"

"That's right." She carefully removed a glove before reaching for a tart. "Stratford Mather is not the only person that can renovate and remodel Matherscourt. His money comes from the connections he's made through your marriage. You have every right to do what you wish as well."

"But—"

"I told him you were building a gazebo."

"But, I'm not!"

"Well, now you must. Anyway, think about it. A gazebo was the least involved project I could have come up with. It could be built in a few days with very little in the way of supplies, especially compared to Stratford's orangery. Pick a place where you'd love to read or bide your time and have Nicky build it for you. Then you'll have covered yourself quite nicely."

"Oh, Eliza." I stared at my hands. I had touched neither my tea nor the sweets. "I'm not good at this."

"None of us are in the beginning."

My eyes swept past her to the sketch I'd made of myself in a man's arms. It seemed in retrospect like a premonition. "I've fallen in love with him."

She laughed. "Of course, you haven't."

"But I have!"

"You're feeling the euphoria of having been satisfied. Really, Penny."

"No. It's more than that."

"But it can't be."

"Why not?"

"Darling!" She paused with the half-eaten tart halfway to her mouth. "You have made a life for yourself here at Matherscourt. Your name and Stratford's money have cemented your position in high society. You're a *Lady*, for goodness' sake! Stratford is a Lord! You certainly cannot be falling in love with a peasant."

"Nicky is not a peasant."

"Philip said you two were atop a peasant's cart. It was not even a proper wagon. He was shocked to see you there."

The color rose in my cheeks. "It was a supply cart," I stammered feebly.

"What on earth were you thinking?"

"Well, didn't you tell me yourself that I needed someone else?"

"If I'd known how quickly you planned to act on it, I'd have given you pointers."

"Pointers!"

"For one thing, dear, select someone that can be seen with you without raising suspicion. Brian, for example, is my hired coachman. People expect to see him drive me into town or to various places. If I am coming out of a hotel and he is there to see me into my carriage, people would consider him simply doing his duty. They would not think we had been in the hotel together *in that way*."

"Surely you're not expecting me to have an affair with my coachman—Old Man—"

"No. I am not. I'd be surprised if he could even function in that way. But what I am saying, darling, is to hire your own coachman, someone who could serve two purposes."

"But Nicky already has a job. He is an architect like his brother, he builds churches and—"

"I'm not talking about Nicky. Find someone else."

"But I'm falling in love with Nicky!"

With a huff, Eliza stood. "You cannot be seen with him again, Penny. I've lied for you, and now you must have the man build you a gazebo. But do not sleep with him again."

"But I've told you—"

"You risk losing everything, Penny. If you're going to have someone scratch your itch—"

"It's not like that—"

"—then you must be discreet at all times." She began placing her glove back on her hand though I remained seated. "I will take those five sketches," she said, pointing. "I'll have Brian gather them."

I nodded silently.

"Your last fetched very good prices. You are improving." She opened her coin purse and pulled out a good bit of money. "Here you are. I'll be back in a few weeks to buy more."

As I rose, she called to Brian, who apparently had remained just outside the open door. I wondered how much he'd heard of our conversation, and when he entered my studio to gather the sketches, I found I could not look him in the eye. Eliza followed him as he exited, and I followed to the door.

"Remember what we've talked about," she said. "Build a gazebo." She pointed toward the meadow. "I believe that would be a beautiful spot for it."

I could only nod. I certainly would not have a gazebo built in the middle of my horse's pasture. Oh, this was a state for sure. I watched as Brian assisted her into the carriage, and with a tip of his hat to me, he climbed in front and flicked the reins. I remained where I was and watched the carriage bouncing along the narrow dirt road that would lead them past the meadow and around the estate until they were joined once more with the road. My sketches had been propped against the back of the carriage with a cloth covering them. As they jostled along, I saw in my mind's eye Brian and Eliza returning from one of their trysts, the bundle behind them, spotted by a member of polite society. She was right. They would think nothing out of place.

I had a great deal to think about now. My abrupt decision to accompany Nicky had placed me on a specific path. It was one I had chosen for myself; even if I had not admitted it as such to my conscience, my soul knew. It was also a path I had no desire to leave, though the upheaval in my life—even if it was only in my memories now—was enough to cause my stomach to churn.

I placed the money Eliza had given me with my previous earnings, tidied up from our tea, and gathered the basket. It was a warm day, and I laid my shawl over the basket instead of placing it about my shoulders. Then I closed the door securely behind me. On my way back to the great house, perhaps I could select the perfect spot for a gazebo.

15

I heard Nicky's voice before I reached the end of the corridor, followed by an unfamiliar one.

"I can get you as much Connemara marble as you need," the second man was saying.

"Aye, and I know that," Nicky answered. "But Lord Mather insists it is Italian marble."

"Does he understand there's a war going on?" the second voice rose in frustration. "I can't even get through to suppliers in Italy—"

"You'll just have to try harder." His voice rose as if speaking to someone further away. "Sean—the stained glass goes there, there and there—Sean, are you hearing me?"

I had stopped at the entrance to the orangery. It was nothing like I had imagined. I suppose I'd envisioned an indoor garden or orchard with as many orange trees that could reasonably be accommodated. What I found was more in line with a solarium but with fewer windows. The room contained elaborate crown molding and three sets of French doors leading onto a stone patio that joined another that led in turn to a garden. Nicky was pointing at a row of empty casings above the doors, but the man he spoke to was staring at me.

Sean might have been the same age as Nicky. He was shorter in stature, and his hair was a blend of brunette and auburn. His sleeves were rolled up above his elbows, revealing muscular forearms while suspenders held up baggy pants that appeared as though they'd seen better days. His eyes were fiercely green as he stared at me.

Nicky followed his line of sight. "Lady Mather," he said in surprise. He immediately began making his way toward me. "Is there something I can do for you, ma'am?"

"There is indeed," I spoke before he'd made it halfway across the room, my voice carrying so all could hear if they chose to listen. "I wish to have a gazebo added to your worklist."

He reached my side. "We'll be happy to oblige you, ma'am." His voice was louder than it needed to be. "Perhaps we could step away from all the din to discuss it." He gallantly spread his arm toward the corridor from which I'd just walked down and waited until I had strolled down it a few steps before I heard his footsteps behind me.

When I was confident there were no eavesdroppers, I hurriedly told him of Eliza's visit. "I know exactly where I'd like the gazebo built," I finished. "Next to the ancient oak at the rear of Matherscourt."

He rubbed his chin for a moment, his eyes focused on the floor between us. "You shall have your gazebo there if that is what you want," he said finally. "But for the benefit of covering your story, I suggest a second gazebo in the gardens closer to the orangery."

"Why there?" My brows furrowed. I never went into that garden at all. It was a maze of perfectly manicured hedges; easily lost inside while on the ground, it was completely visible from every window at the rear of the house—particularly from Stratford's bedchambers.

He smiled as though following my thoughts. "The old oak is so far removed from the house that if Lord or Lady Davies were to visit, it would be impractical for them to venture there. But I know the perfect spot right in the center of the formal gardens. It would be an easy stroll from the orangery, a room Lord Mather is certainly likely to show his friends."

"Ah."

"Would he approve?"

I felt my ire rising. "I do not require his permission."

"No. Of course, you don't." He grasped my elbow and led me further down the hall and around a bend. He glanced toward the opposite end, and I followed his gaze. It was empty; we were alone. He pressed my body against the wall, placing his palms on the wall on either side of me. "I miss you terribly."

I chuckled. "It was only yesterday we were together."

"It feels a lifetime ago." His lips brushed against mine, sending shivers through me.

It took only an instant for him to take me places I'd never been before meeting him. His fingers caressed my cheek and ran through my hair as his leg pressed against mine, his teeth nibbling on my lower lip… One moment I was standing in a corridor of Matherscourt, and the very next I was back in the cottage, slipping under the blankets, my skin against him, inhaling the scent of the man that drove me nearly insane with desire.

But it was more than that. I opened my eyes to find Nicky watching me, and as our eyes met, his crinkled just before he swept me into his arms and squeezed me so tightly, I lost my breath.

"I do miss you so," he whispered, his breath tickling my ear. "Meet me tonight. Tell me, you will."

"I will," I answered. "I can't."

He pulled slightly away from me to look into my face. The look of disappointment was devastating.

"Stratford—he should be home this evening."

"Ah." He held me again, his face pressed against my hair.

"We don't share a bed," I felt compelled to say. "Nor even a bedroom. It's just he expects me to be there—"

"I know." His voice was stronger. "Do what you must."

"Then, when?"

"Tomorrow. In your artist's studio."

"There isn't space—it isn't—"

"I'll find the space. I will be there for you tomorrow."

Before I could respond, the sound of footsteps echoed down the hall, and he abruptly pulled away.

"Yes, Mister Bowers," I said in a formal voice. "Two gazebos. One in the formal garden. I shall rely on your professional opinion as to the exact location. The second by the ancient oak where I may have more privacy for my contemplations." I began to walk away from him and toward the footsteps, which turned out to be Aindriú.

"Yes, Lady Mather. Perhaps I can show you some sketchings tomorrow?"

I paused to glare at him over my shoulder.

"Some measurements of the gazebos," he elaborated. "And a style befitting Matherscourt."

"Yes. Of course. Good day, Mister Bowers."

"Lady Mather."

I was eating in the kitchen when Aindriú once again appeared. As he stood in the doorway, his eyes were riveted on Léana, who was kneading dough for a pie.

"Lord Mather has returned," he announced.

The air changed in an instant. No sooner had Aindriú made the announcement than he was already rushing toward the front hall. I knew he already had Stratford's slippers and lounge coat ready should he want them, and it would be Aindriú whose face Stratford would first lay eyes upon as he entered the house.

Léana scurried into action as well. She would not be required to appear in the hall, but supper must be on the table within minutes of his arrival. If he wanted to eat immediately, it must not be too hot, and if he waited for a half-hour, it could not become cooled.

Johanna and Éamonn had been seated at the end of the long kitchen table, and Éamonn fairly flew off the chair as he charged out the door and around the house. He must be in the proper position to receive the horse and carriage from Stratford's coachman as the coachman opened the carriage door.

Johanna was required in the hallway procession just before me, though I never understood why; she was my servant, not Stratford's.

I had not changed my attire, though I was tired. I had waited as long as my stomach dared before entering the kitchen and settling into a hard chair. Léana had clucked over me like a mother, serving up a hearty bowl of stew and some fresh garlic soda bread. Now I left the bowl half-eaten as I hurried along the winding corridors toward the front hall.

I was standing in my customary position as Aindriú opened the double doors with a formal flourish. As he assisted Stratford out of his overcoat and top hat, I noticed my husband's face was ruddy, his eyes bulging. It would only take a moment for us all to understand why.

"Bloody idiots!" he bellowed. The entire line of servants tensed as if he was attacking them personally. "They tied up the streets all bloody afternoon, marching with broomsticks o'er their shoulders like little tin soldiers! What the bloody hell do they expect to do with a bunch of brooms? Sweep the English away?" He chuckled at this last, amused by his own wittiness. "I am starving! Starving!"

I stepped back as he barreled past without so much as a glance toward me. I waited until he had taken a few strides past me before I fell into line, walking silently behind him. The table was immaculately set and a feast laid out, though I had no idea how the woman managed it. I waited until Stratford was seated and then began to take my place at the opposite end, assisted in my chair by one of the staff.

Dinner was a lonely affair. Truth be told, I did not feel loneliness while sketching by myself. Neither did I feel it while I was walking alone through the meadow. I had not felt it when seated at the kitchen table, eating while filling my head with my own thoughts as Johanna and Éamonn whispered privately at the opposite end or Léana banged the wood every now and then while kneading the pie crust.

But I felt a painful sense of isolation as I sat at the opposite end of the table from Stratford. His newspaper was presented to him, and as he ate, his eyes feasted on the latest news. He did not tell me what he read, even when he grunted at this or groaned at that. Though it had been like this since we married, my heart ached this evening as it never had before. The silence became oppressive as I realized he had not asked about my week because he almost certainly did not care. I was a servant, seated at the position assigned to me, but as the servants, I was not to speak unless spoken to.

As I cut a piece of meat, I glanced at the opposite end of the table. I was not lonely for him. The thought of being in his arms as I had been in Nicky's filled me with revulsion. He was sloppy as he ate, emitting out his groans and grunts with a mouth filled with food that speckled the table around him. His arms were short, his fingers stubbly, and his belly was round and wide, his shirt buttons straining.

No, I must be honest with myself. I did not long for Stratford because Stratford simply was not Nicky.

I set my fork down and took a long drink of wine. Matherscourt should have been the perfect home. Set in the bewitching green hills of Ireland with elegantly manicured lawns and gardens, I thought serenely of the meadows with the horses glistening in the sun, of my studio where I loved perfecting my sketches, of the ancient oak where Nicky and I first spoke of Anna Karenina, Charles Dickens and a host of subjects that brought me alive.

In that instant, staring down the table at Lord Stratford Berkshire Mather, I realized that I had nearly created the perfect life for myself but with the wrong man. The only thing that would complete the perfection was if I could magically transport Stratford out of that chair and replace him with Nicky Bowers.

Yet I knew it was not possible. If Stratford died, I could perhaps inherit much of his estate as we had no children—and would never have children together as he could not… But I mustn't think of him dying. I silently asked God for forgiveness even as my fantasies took off, imagining how very different life here would be if only…

If only.

16

I slipped out of bed as the grandfather clock in the upstairs hall chimed the two o'clock hour. I had been awake since midnight, tossing and turning, slumber beyond my reach. I poked at the fire, but it would require a more concerted effort to coax it back to life and warmth, and I felt listless, unable to sleep yet too drowsy to fully awaken.

My dressing gown was woefully inept at keeping me warm, so I dragged the uppermost spread off my bed and wrapped it around me as I made my way to the window. I opened it slightly, though I don't know why as the chill of the night invaded my bedchamber. But with the hoot of an owl and another in response, I left the window open and settled into a chair where I could allow the serenity of nature to soothe my restless soul.

If I peered downward at a specific angle, I could see the dark outline of the hedges in the formal garden, and as my eyes adjusted to the gloom of the cloudy night, I began to pick out the pathways that existed within, all leading to the center. There was a pond there with an elaborate fountain where the water was continuously drawn upward to spray onto its surface, and I wondered how Nicky would manage to create a gazebo without removing it. For a fleeting moment, I considered Stratford's mood and the possibility he would become enraged at my little project, for he'd made it quite clear it was his estate that bore his name and while I was permitted to live within its luxuries, it was not mine to alter.

My eyes wandered to the opposite side, away from the formal garden. This side, I knew so much better. It had been a well-worn carriage path the servants took each morning to tend to the livestock, a path less traveled now that the fields had been turned to agricultural crops. This was the route I took each morning that led me past the meadows where the horses gathered at the fence to greet me. It also led beyond the meadow and through a copse of trees that hid my little artist's cottage, the old barn, and a scattering of other buildings that had been mostly boarded.

A flash of light caught my eye, and I leaned forward in my chair, my eyes instinctively narrowing. It appeared to have come from the rear of the estate, or as close to the rear as I could see from this vantage point. Before my little excursion, I would not have known of the rear entrance at all; I suppose I hadn't given any thought to how the livestock had been herded to slaughter or the crops were transported to market. But as I peered through the gloom, the light did not reappear, and I leaned back once more, content that it was only my imagination.

I listened to the bullfrogs and crickets that must have been gathered at various spots around the estate, their chorus welcome. I was settling in with my thoughts once more when I spotted it again. I stood this time and opened the window wide, so there was no barrier between myself and the light. Now I knew why it had disappeared; it was traveling along the back trail, and the trees were obscuring it from view as it entered the copses before exiting once more.

It was a yellow lamp, an oil lamp perhaps, and from the way it swayed when I could spot it, it was affixed to a carriage and not carried by someone on foot. It disappeared again, and my eyes searched a circumference around it until I was able to pick it up once more.

Who could possibly be wandering about the estate at this time of night? It certainly was not a servant; they would have come and gone through the main gates, regardless of the time. It was quite common for one to return as the clock struck midnight, their day off coming to a close as the new day was heralded in. I thought of the topmost floor where most of the servants stayed, and I wondered briefly if any were awake right now and watching the same strange light as I. In the next instant, I pictured them sound asleep as their work would begin in only two short hours.

As the light continued to meander, I considered alerting Stratford to the presence of a possible intruder, but immediately sanity came to my rescue, and I determined that was the worst course of action. I continued instead to simply observe.

A flash of lightning lit the sky, and for the briefest of moments, I thought I saw a wagon in between thickets and a grove of trees, but the flash was so temporary that I could not be certain what I saw and what my imagination might have invented. In any event, it was gone again in the next instant, and though I waited several minutes for it to appear, it seemed to have disappeared for good this time.

Perhaps it was the night air that eventually coaxed me back to my bed. When I settled in this time, I felt myself drifting off almost immediately. I remembered that I'd neglected to close the window and instructed myself to rise once more and close it, but as I floated away on distant dreams, the winds continued to howl until they slammed it shut for me, only for it to open again as the rains began to bucket.

I dreamt of the rain against the deep-set glass windows in the cottage as the pillows that lay against me became Nicky's arms holding me close in the night, the bed morphing from my comfortable padding to coarse straw and back again, the bullfrogs becoming ever more insistent as the rains came down.

17

I was in the studio when Nicky arrived. I spotted him in the same wagon we'd taken on our little excursion as it wound around the meadow. The door had been open since I'd arrived, the nighttime rains replaced with the scent of spring, the warmth of the sun and the birds chirping.

I stood in the doorway as he pulled up alongside my cottage. He wore a broad grin, and my heart immediately soared. As much as Stratford could change the air with his presence, Nicky could alter it in the opposite direction. Before disembarking, he grabbed a leather portfolio. His stride was long and eager as he came toward me, bounding up the stairs to envelop me in his arms. I heard the portfolio drop on the table behind me as his hands found my back and pressed me to him.

There was something about the way he kissed me that melted everything around me, so nothing existed but Nicky and me. I doubted I could ever get enough of him, yet when he finally pulled away, I set my palm upon his chest lest he return too soon.

"I've to get my breath back," I laughed.

"Ah, Penny, Penny." His eyes swept over my hair. "You're wearing your hair a bit different today, aren't you now?" Before I could respond, he continued, "It's that wee clip in your bun. A butterfly, is it?"

"Aren't you the observant one?" I teased.

"The color sets off your strands so beautifully."

"Do you always notice such things?"

"I notice beauty, aye. It's what I do. In fact," he said, turning toward the table to pick up the portfolio, "I've some rough sketches I'd like for you to consider."

"You're drawing now?"

"It's what I do." He opened the leather binding to reveal a penciled sketch of a gazebo.

"This is what you call rough?" I breathed. I leaned in to examine it. The gazebo consisted of eight sides, four of which were open to the north, south, east, and west. The flooring was to be made of Connemara marble to match the multiple shades of gray in the pebbled walkways that meandered through the formal garden. Four low sides were to be of the same marble as well as the columns that held up the roof. The roof itself was to be made of copper, and to top it off was a cupola finial that was a miniature version of the gazebo below it. "This is exquisite."

"Do you like it then?"

"Like it? I love it! How large is this?" I added in awe.

"Ah. I was out this morning measuring. I suggest twenty feet interior."

"That large?"

"I could go fifteen, but I would not make it smaller. You may wish to use it for entertaining someday."

"It's amazing."

"So, may I start it?"

"Yes. What do you need from me?"

"Only your verbal approval to move ahead."

"And the cost?"

"It will be added to our invoices."

"And the second one?"

"Ah. Happy you asked." He turned the page to a second gazebo very much like the first, but this one had only one open side with a gate that closed. "A bit more privacy on this one," he said with a sly smile. "And it's a bit cozier, I suggest twelve feet."

"I love it."

"I've a seamstress that can sew cushions for each of the benches in both gazebos."

"What a lovely idea."

"Perhaps you could meet with her—she would come to you, of course—to pick the material and patterns."

"Yes. Yes, of course."

"And that bit of drawing here? It was on the other one as well. They're flower boxes, all around each gazebo."

"Oh, how beautiful. I can completely imagine it."

"So, you're pleased?"

"More than pleased. I am thrilled."

"Good. Now down to the real business."

"Oh?" I asked as he swept me into his arms. "And what would that be?"

"I've a surprise for you." He kissed me briefly, leaving me wanting for more, before grasping my hand and leading me outside.

"Where are we going?"

"It's a surprise." Once I was down the steps, he returned to close the door before assisting me in the wagon. Without as many layers as I'd worn on our trip, the wood seat felt much rougher and uneven.

We meandered along the cattle trail leading toward the back gate but stopped between two groves of trees. There, he turned the horses toward the water. In the distance, I spotted the ancient oak; it might have been only a tree to be sure, but it would forever be joined in my mind with stimulating conversation, an opening of my consciousness to what could be.

"Where are you taking me?" I giggled nervously.

"Not to worry. We are remaining on Matherscourt grounds."

A couple of minutes later, he pulled the horses to a stop in front of an old stone cottage. It was such an interesting structure that I was dumbstruck when I saw it. It might have appeared like a simple cottage that was so prevalent throughout Ireland's tenant class, except it was elevated over the wide stream that wandered through the property. On either side of the bank, the stone swept downward in an arc, and from those arcs were wide stone steps. A short distance from the cottage was a smaller structure made from the same limestone blocks, the wide doors identifying it as a tiny barn or stable.

"What is this?" I asked, my voice barely above a whisper.

"It's a gatehouse. You've never seen it before?"

I shook my head. "Never."

"Ah, there's a lot you must learn about your properties then." He hopped down and reached back for me, lifting me from the carriage onto the ground beside him.

As we approached the structure, the sound of water rushing almost sounded like a waterfall. I stopped on the steps to watch the water rush under the gatehouse. Nicky was ahead of me, and he opened the door and beckoned me in.

"It's dusty, to be sure," he said as he moved around the single room and opened windows. Without the grimy glass in the way, the sunshine poured in bright fingers toward the stone floor. In the center of the room was an open fireplace filled with soot and ancient peat bricks that had been reduced to powder. Against one wall was a pallet of sorts, oddly out of place as though it had only recently been placed there. Atop it was a faded plaid blanket.

I became acutely aware of Nicky watching me.

"It's naught but hay, though you deserve down," he said quietly.

"You put that here?"

"I did."

"This morning?"

He appeared surprised but did not answer.

"Around two or three o'clock this morning?" I pressed.

"How did you know that?"

"I saw you."

"You—what?"

"Well, I didn't actually see you," I explained. "I saw the light from a carriage lamp."

"You did? From the house?"

"From my bedroom window."

"All the way out here?"

"Well, it was not that clear, and had you not had a lamp, I would not have seen you at all."

He stared at me in a queer way.

"Are you quite alright?" I asked.

It took him a moment to answer. When he did, he shook his head and laughed. "I thought I was surprising you, I did."

"But you did surprise me. I had no idea this place was here."

"Well, then, we must remember not to light a lamp while we are here," he said a bit conspiratorially, "lest it be seen from the house and raise suspicion."

"This is our little spot, then?"

"If you want it to be." He glanced upward. "She's solid, she is. She's a slate roof and no leaks. But I would not use the fireplace…"

"The smoke might be seen above the trees."

"Ah. My little rebel."

18

The light changed in the gatehouse as the sun made its way overhead. Buttery shadows emerged in the far corners, and the sound of rushing water underneath was threatening to lull me to sleep with its gentle lullaby.

I lay on my side, my leg thrown over Nicky's as he rested on his back. I ran my fingers across his chest, still moist with perspiration from our passions.

"Are you comfortable?" he asked. His voice was barely more than a hoarse whisper, and as I peered upward at his face, his eyes were only half-open.

"Very much so." I giggled. "I like this place."

"And you truly never knew it was here?"

I shook my head. "It makes me wonder what else is at Matherscourt that I've never seen."

"Oh, I'm hoping I've provided several new views for you," he chuckled.

"Ah!" I exclaimed with mock modesty. "I should be ashamed."

"For what?" he chided. "For being a woman? Hell of a woman, too, if I dare say it out loud."

"Stop."

"Have I told you how much I love your curves?"

"Several times," I tittered.

"And did I tell you I fell in love with you the first time I saw you?"

"No. And I don't believe you."

"Don't you, now? You were standing on the veranda. And when you stood and walked over to greet Peter and m'self, I could not believe my luck. I knew…"

"Knew what?" I prompted as his voice faded.

"I just knew."

"Knew what?" I repeated, laughing.

"I knew I had to see you again. I knew I was completely infatuated."

"You did not."

"Didn't I, 'ey? You felt it too. I know you did."

I stole a sideways glance. "I did," I admitted.

He rolled onto his side and then, half-reclining, rested his elbow on the makeshift bed as he looked at me. "You know, you're very much confined here," he stated.

"I do get out on occasion." I purposefully eyed his nude body.

"Hmm." He fell silent, and I watched his face for a moment. He appeared thoughtful yet distant somehow, his ready smile turning serious.

"What are you thinking?" I asked.

He looked into my eyes and then looked away as if he was struggling with something.

"Go on," I urged. "Tell me."

When our eyes met again, he was earnest. "Do you have a goal?"

"A goal?" I laughed.

"A mission. A purpose."

I considered his question for a moment. "I suppose I am living my purpose. I was married off to Stratford to secure my family's—"

"No," he interrupted. "Marriage to Stratford is not a goal, nor is it a mission. Your purpose in life must be accompanied by passion, a longing for what you do, who you are. Your passion does not lie with carrying the title of 'Lady Mather.' What about your sketches?"

"What about them?"

"They are your passion, aye? You see the world through the artist's eyes. You see the beauty in everyday things."

I shrugged.

"You know that you do." His voice became more urgent. "Did you know Lady Davies sells your sketches?"

"Yes. She pays me for them."

"But do you know how much she sells them for?"

"I don't really care. She pays me well."

"Ah."

"Do you?"

"Do I what?"

"Do you know how much she sells them for?"

"I do."

"How do you know?"

He lay on his back again. "She has set up an art gallery in Dublin."

"She has?"

"How did you think she sells them?"

"I suppose," I said, "I thought it was through her social connections."

He chuckled wryly. "Aye, I suppose she used her connections to get established. But she has made quite a name for her gallery; she is attracting the best artists in Europe, and you're among them."

"But—how do you know this?"

"I have been to her gallery."

"You have?"

"I have. It is across from the General Post Office."

"The GPO? In Dublin?"

"Aye. She has hired a gentleman that manages it for her; he is very knowledgeable in the arts. I noticed one of your sketches—framed now—in the window as I was going to the GPO. I went inside and inquired about it. He's quite a tale about how it was smuggled out of Europe as the war raged all around. Said the artist must remain anonymous or his life would be in danger."

I sat up. "Really?"

"I would not lie to you, Penny. Perhaps someday you can make the journey into Dublin and see for yourself. I've no idea what she's paid you for them—"

"She—"

"And it isn't my business to know. But you can see the prices on them for yourself, and determine for yourself whether she is taking advantage of you."

"I see."

"It is an easy trip, you know. Less than an hour from here. Stratford makes it every day."

"His office is across from St. Stephen's Green," I murmured.

"You could visit the gallery without going near Stratford's office," he said gently.

"And what of you?" I asked.

"Me?"

"You. What goals have you?"

"Ah." He sat up and took both my hands in his. His eyes carried a gleam as though a fire had been lit from within. "I shall have my place in history, dear Penny. I shall fight for Ireland."

"In the world war?" I felt my heart begin to sink.

He smiled indulgently. "You truly are secluded here, 'ey?"

"But I want to understand."

"Have you noticed the way your—shall we say, acquaintances—treat the Irish?"

"But, I am Irish."

He shook his head. "There are two worlds here in Ireland, darlin'. There are people like you whose ancestors arrived here from England centuries ago; they live on big estates and have money to burn, more food than they could ever spend, I dare say, and servants to attend to their every desire." He allowed this to sink in for a moment before continuing. "Then there are the people who lived in Ireland for thousands of years before the English turned it into a colony of the British crown. People like me."

"But your name—Bowers—is English, is it not?"

"It has been Anglicized, darling."

"Why? I mean, why not keep the name of your ancestors and be proud of it?"

He took a deep breath. "Because there are those of us that need to straddle the two worlds."

"The world of the estates and the upper class," I said slowly, "and the world of the tiny cottages and…" I remembered the meals prepared for me by Peter's wife, but I didn't know how to continue without offending Nicky, and that was the last thing I wanted to do.

"Aye. And if you consider the native Irish, how do your friends treat them? How does Stratford treat them?"

"I suppose like servants—"

"Precisely. For generations—too many to count—the Irish have been told they are nothing more than serfs. They are portrayed as unintelligent, uneducated, filthy and lazy, drunkards all. And each babe that is born is told they can never be more than what their fathers became or their fathers before them, which is to relegate them to serfdom for an entire lifetime—and their children, too. The cycle continues from one generation to the next." His voice had grown passionate, and yet he did not carry the anger of a man like Stratford, with his bellowing voice and red face. Instead, he leaned forward as if attempting to open my eyes to a reality I had never before had to confront, and his passion for the topic fueled my own.

I thought of Léana, who prepared all my meals; of Johanna, who helped me with everything from my bath to my hair; of Éamonn tending to the horses and stable, living in the loft; and Aindriú, Stratford's trusted butler who ruled over all the servants. His was perhaps the only position that often seemed to transcend the gap between the classes.

There were other servants as well, people of whom I would never know their names; tenant farmers and others that made Matherscourt what it was and yet would spend a lifetime as a nameless, faceless servant—at least to the upper classes. What were they to their families, their friends, their fellow servants?

"But there is a man," Nicky was saying, "Michael Collins. Have you heard of him?"

I shook my head. "Who is he?"

He smiled. "He is a savior, that's who he is."

"A religious man?"

"No, sweetheart," Nicky sighed wistfully. "He travels throughout Ireland, and he speaks to the Irish—the true Irish—and he is opening our eyes. People everywhere are discovering we no longer need to be serfs. We have become educated, many of us, despite restrictions that would have us remain illiterate. We have traveled abroad—some to London, others to Paris, still others to Berlin—even some that have gone as far as the United States of America, if you can believe it! And we have discovered there is quite a bit of support for the Irish to be free of England's heavy hand."

"What do you mean, be free? Do you plan to fight against England in the war?"

"No, not the Great War. We intend to demand our sovereignty right here at home." He grinned as if he was revealing a big secret.

"But—what exactly does it mean when you demand your sovereignty?"

He gently dropped my hands from his and rose, making his way to a window where he stared outside. I wrapped a plaid around me and rose to join him. We stood silently for a moment as he seemed to study the terrain beyond us while I studied him. Someday, I thought, I shall sketch him standing there in the window, pensively peering outside.

Finally, he said, "I know you are a gentle soul, Penny. I know you prefer to eat in the kitchen with the hired help. I know you treat Johanna more as a friend than a serf. I know you refer to each of your servants by their Gaelic names and not the Anglicized names Stratford insists they be called."

"I suppose you know all of this because servants talk."

He turned to me. "They talk, aye. They do. And they've had nothing but good to say about you."

"I see."

"You can trust Johanna; you can trust her with anything. Same with Éamonn. Léana… she is a good person, but tied to the old ways."

"An Ireland that is not sovereign."

He nodded. "Aye. And sovereign it must be."

"And Aindriú?"

"Do not trust him, Penny." His face took on a hardened expression. "Do not trust him with anything."

"But—"

He turned to me, taking my shoulders in his hands, silencing me with his intensity. His eyes were fixed on mine as he said, "We are rising, Penny. Soon we will be demanding equal rights, equal representation, even though we are Catholic and native Irish. And soon, we will pressure England to leave our country, returning it to the countrymen—and women—of Ireland."

"Rebellion." As soon as the word escaped my lips, I wished I could take it back. Surely he was not insinuating such. But his next words made no mistake of his intent.

"Aye, my Penny. Rebellion."

"War—"

"We do not anticipate a war—not like the rest of Europe is experiencing. Not battle lines of men with horses and rifles—"

"But certainly, you cannot demand your freedom with broomsticks!"

He laughed so loudly and so heartily that his head was thrown back. After a long moment of mirth, he said, "I can tell Stratford has been filling your head of toy soldiers with broomsticks, 'ey?"

"Yes," I said. "I suppose he has."

"Well, what he's seen is true enough. We have formed units based on the same rank and file system the British use—but thanks to Sean Mac Diarmada, it's been created in such a way that should one man be captured—or a hundred—they will not have the information—the intel—that could collapse the entire house of cards."

"And the broomsticks?"

"True enough." He laughed again. "Our men have been training with shovels and broomsticks and walking sticks, whatever they wish to put o'er their shoulder on any given day. And they've been training right under the noses of the British officers, marching right up to and past Dublin Castle."

"But surely you won't be able to—I mean, a rebellion—"

"—takes weapons. Aye, and we've been training on that as well. Do you know of Countess Markievicz?"

"Why, yes—I met her at a dinner recently. But surely, you're not going to tell me—"

"Aye, and I am! She is a crack shot, did you know that? I swear if she was on the front lines right now, the Great War would be o'er."

"But a woman!"

"We've women, Penny, women standing shoulder to shoulder with the men. We want it that way. The countess is high up the ladder, too, no mistaking it. She's using her estate to train men—and women—how to shoot for when the time comes."

"But you said there'd be no bloodshed." I shivered, realizing the sun had lowered, and gloom was beginning to settle into the room.

"Here, darlin', you're freezing. Get your clothes on. The day is getting late, and I've yet to get you back."

"But—"

"Come now." He walked me to the makeshift bed and gathered my clothes. "My skills are not as decent as Johanna's, but I can help you dress so you'll be acceptable enough." As if to prove his point, he gathered the items in the correct order and helped me dress while I made a mental note to figure out a way to wear less if I was to be involved in these trysts more often. Afterward, he made quick work of dressing himself, and then he ushered me through the door, closing it gently behind us.

As we made our way toward the wagon, I stopped and pulled him back to me. "Tell me there will be no bloodshed."

He wrapped his arms around me, one hand moving to the back of my head. He pulled me into him, so his cheek pressed against mine. "I cannot tell you there will be no bloodshed," he whispered against my ear. "Only that we do not desire it. But we shall be prepared for whatever comes our way."

He continued to hold me as though he was afraid that once he let me go, I would fill his ears with objections. Instead, as we pulled apart, I said, "And where do you see yourself in this new alignment of power?"

"It is my hope and prayer that I would be by your side." Before I could respond, he continued, "And I wish to show the world how the Irish build cathedrals—" he smiled wryly "—and estates."

"So you would continue doing what you do now?"

"Aye, and serving my country too, as she needs me."

He helped me into the wagon and then climbed up beside me. Like our journey had been, the return trip seemed half as long as the original, and all too soon we were pulling alongside the old barn. "I've kept you too long," he said with an eye on the darkening skies. As he assisted me to the ground, he said, "Will you be alright?"

"Of course," I said. "But Nicky—"

"Aye?"

"What can I do to help the rebellion?"

His eyes widened. Then he said, "Be there for me. Pray for my comrades, and for me that God will help our cause."

"You have that anyway. But I want to do more."

"I—" He shook his head. Then, "There is something you can do. Allow me a bit of time, and I'll let you know the details, 'ey?"

"Promise you're not leading me on?"

"Oh no, my Penny. I would never do that."

I nodded. "Alright, then. Whatever you need, I will come through for you."

"Of that," he said, "I have no doubt."

19

I spotted Nicky's wagon from my studio window as it rounded the north end of the great house before it was lost behind the trees and gardens. Almost at the same time, Eliza's carriage meandered around the south end, taking the path along the meadow. I held my breath, waiting for them to converge, but when Eliza reappeared at the near end of the meadow, Nicky's wagon was nowhere in sight.

She alighted from her carriage with her usual aplomb, the ostrich feathers in her hat fluttering in the breeze as Brian assisted her to the ground. I had come to perceive Brian with a different set of eyes; the way he held onto her hand a bit longer than necessary, how their eyes met and held, his appreciative expression as he assessed her gown—or more likely, her figure—under lowered lashes.

She climbed the steps and kissed me on either cheek before entering, sweeping off her right glove with a flourish. But after taking a couple of steps into the studio, her expression changed to one of near horror. "What have you done?" she breathed.

I followed her line of sight to the nearest canvas. I had sketched from memory the row of cottages where Nicky and I had stayed on our first night together. The cottages nearest the road were minus their roofs, charred marks on the limestone walls that still stood. An emaciated dog lay in the abandoned grass while two figures leaned against a railing, their faces upturned toward a spectacular sunset.

Before I had a chance to respond, she pointed to another. "And this!"

I followed her about the room, my silence and puzzlement growing as she pointed out one sketching after another with rising alarm—a stooped tenant farmer behind a plow and nearly skeletal mule; the stark walls of the Magdalene laundry; a family settled around a table with mismatched chairs and a bowl of stew ample for one man but meant for them all as the children eyed it hungrily.

"What have you done?" she breathed again, whirling to face me.

"You don't like them?"

"Penny!" she exclaimed as she pointed to the family around the table. "Look at this man's face, how thin it is, how sunken his eyes!"

"Yes. I know."

"The mule—it looks like it might drop dead at any moment!"

"It might."

"I can't—I don't know what to say—I'm speechless!"

I was at a loss for words as well, but before I could manage to reply, she dropped into the nearest chair, fanning her face as though she might swoon.

"They can't all be that bad," I managed to say.

"It's his influence, isn't it?"

"What are you talking about?"

"Oh, my God," she said, placing one hand to her forehead. "Penny, I can't possibly sell these."

"Why not?"

"*Why not?* They are disastrous!"

"They are the same style as I've always sketched."

"My dear, it isn't whether you portrayed them with the same stylistic technique. The subjects themselves are horrendous. No one wants to have a peasant farmer hanging in their parlor—or hungry faces staring back at them from their dining room wall. They want beauty! They want to see themselves stepping into the sketch. They want thoroughbreds in a meadow, a sunset over formal gardens, fat dogs sleeping peacefully on plush pads in front of a fireplace."

I sighed. "Don't you want to at least choose one and see what the reaction is from your patrons?"

"Absolutely not. I will not hang those in my gallery."

"Your gallery?" My voice turned icy, though I had not intended it to do so. I remained standing, my hands folded in front of me.

She stopped fanning herself. "Surely you don't believe I simply stacked your work against the wall in my front parlor? Of course, I have them on proper display."

"How much do you sell them for, Eliza?"

"I give you nearly all the money," she said, one brow raising. "After I pay the overhead of the gallery, I have nothing left."

"Nothing?"

"This is a hobby for me, nothing more." She stood. "I certainly needn't work to earn *money*." She spat out the word. "I shall return in a few weeks. If you do not have the types of sketches my patrons desire, I will not come back again." She popped out of her chair and made her way to the doorway. "Brian!" she called. "The package, please!"

She had stepped down to the ground as he carried a small rectangular package to her. She shoved it into my hands. "If I had known what I would find here today, I would not have bothered purchasing these watercolors for you. But here they are—brushes and all. Perhaps a new medium will return your sensibilities."

A loud bang sent us both jolting. I had not noticed Nicky's wagon beside the barn, and with the next boom, I watched him and one of his men setting long wood planks into the back of the wagon.

"Mister Bowers," Eliza called frostily, "it would seem to me, given your appointment, you would have brought sufficient men to load your cart so that you might supervise."

Nicky hesitated. He was standing atop the wagon, ready to receive the next piece of wood. "Lady Davies," he said, his voice filled with warmth, "how nice to see you. Yes, I could have ordered my men to retrieve supplies; that is true. But I never ask of anyone something I am not willing to do myself."

"Then perhaps you should learn to draw," she retorted. Grasping Brian's hand, she nearly lunged into the carriage. Her mood clearly darkened, Brian hastened to close the door before climbing into the front and setting off.

I remained at the door and watched the carriage until it was no longer in sight. I felt as though I had been dealt a blow to the stomach.

"Have a moment?"

I turned toward the barn as Nicky made his way across the road to me, his eyes still watching the spot where Eliza's carriage had disappeared into the meandering landscape.

"Of course," I answered, my eyes streaming past Nicky to his assistant.

"He's fine," Nicky said in a lower voice as he drew closer. "He won't say a word." My expression must have disclosed my reservations because he added, "If you'd rather, we can remain right here." He unrolled several papers, which I instantly recognized as the plans for the gazebos. "I know what you can do to help," he whispered.

I grasped one corner of the plans and kept my eyes downward. "Anything you need."

"This is quite difficult for me," he said. I glanced at him to find that he, too, was peering at the plans.

"Go on."

"We need money, Penny."

"Money?"

"Aye, and a lot of it. We need weapons and weapons cost money."

"How could you possibly buy weapons in Ireland?"

He glanced toward the barn. His assistant had disappeared inside, and he continued, "We have a lot of support for independence, darling. The Americans have already sold us some weapons, and the Germans have agreed to sell us more."

"The Germans!" I recoiled.

"Oh, now don't you go thinking we're going to side with the Germans in the Great War," he said, his face growing dark. "As I've told you before, we serve neither Kaiser nor Crown. But the Germans have weapons to sell us and their rifles shoot as well as another. But we need money to buy them."

I peered behind me. "I have money from my sketches."

"No. I won't take your money."

"Surely you aren't asking me to hold a fundraiser?"

He laughed. It was so instantaneous and so infectious that I very nearly laughed myself. "No, dear Penny," he said. "But Stratford has a great deal of money."

I inhaled sharply. "Steal from my husband?"

"No. It would not be stealing. You are his wife; the money is as much yours as it is his."

"Would a court see it that way?" I asked incredulously. "Or Stratford?"

"He never needs to know. You see," emboldened, he turned to look me in the eye. "I've a banker friend from London that can facilitate the transfer. Stratford has several accounts, some he's never even shown interest in."

"But I've never been to London. I've never traveled outside of Dublin, except with you."

"There would be no need to go there. He will come to Dublin; he does it all the time. He'll have all the paperwork completed, so all he'll need is your signature."

"How much would you require?"

"Not enough for you—or Stratford—to even notice it is gone."

"I—" I was caught short as his assistant made his way from the barn to the wagon, struggling under a heavy piece of wood.

"Here you are, Lady Mather," Nicky said, his voice loud enough to waft across the road. He pulled out the paper at the bottom and rolled it up, handing it to me. Then he made a half-bow and started back toward the barn, rolling up the remainder of the papers. "You'll be able to sit inside your gazebo within a week," he called over his shoulder.

I did not respond. Before he had reached the wagon, I had turned my back and entered my studio, closing the door behind me despite the stuffiness of the room. My hands were shaking, and it was some time before I realized I was holding the rolled-up paper. I stretched it open upon the table as my heart began to pound. In Nicky's writing was a Dublin address followed by a date and time. My mind reeled. It was tomorrow morning at ten o'clock; sufficient time for Stratford to have not only left for his office but to be firmly entrenched behind his desk. The address was only a few blocks from the General Post Office and not near Stratford's office at Saint Stephen's Green at all. It would be possible for me to travel there and back without my husband ever being the wiser.

But I hadn't given Nicky an answer. As I continued to stare at the paper, I realized he had already known I would oblige him even before he'd spoken to me.

20

Some nights are longer than others. This one was right up there with the night before my wedding to Stratford. On those rare occasions where I managed to drift off, I awakened thinking hours had passed when in fact, it had been only five or ten minutes at most. The rest of the time, I tossed and turned, throwing covers off me only to pull them back moments later, readjusting the pillows time and time again, and finally arising to pace the floor.

It did not help that a storm had blown in from the sea with lightning that illuminated the room in brief, violent flashes to be instantaneously followed by the rumbling growl of thunder.

I must have traveled to Dublin a dozen times in my mind; with the raging storm, I envisioned the roads muddy and treacherous, the waters rising dangerously below the bridges. What if Stratford decided against traveling into Dublin on such a day? Or what if he decided to wait until the roads were drier while I tried to cool my heels upstairs, waiting for him to depart? What if I came upon him on the road?

A host of situations presented themselves as I awakened in my mind a dozen times over to start the day. I was still awake, tired, and cranky and my brain as foggy as the swirling skies when I heard Stratford's door open and close, his heavy footsteps making their way down the corridor toward the stairs. When I could hear them no longer, I arose and tried my best to become presentable.

The storm cleared out as the sun rose, leaving behind only a heavy mist that made visibility difficult, for I could see no further than a few feet from my window. By the time Johanna poked her head inside, I was dressed and struggling with my hair.

"Allow me to do that for you, ma'am," Johanna exclaimed, rushing to my side. "Had I known you were to be up early, m'lady, I would have been here to assist you, I would."

"I could not sleep," I muttered as I watched her expert hands take hold of my long hair and braid it into an elaborate bun. "The storm, you know."

"Aye, it was a bad one, it was."

"I feel as if the walls are closing in on me," I said slowly.

I caught a glimpse of her surprised expression in the mirror before she quickly masked it and continued with my hair. "Would you care to go for a walk then, ma'am? Perhaps with a basket of food. Or would you like breakfast first?"

"Perhaps a wee basket," I answered. "And a ride. Have Éamonn ready my carriage."

There it was again, the look of surprise before the mask rolled in once more. I suppose it was to be expected. I was a creature of habit, after all. Stratford left for Dublin six days a week, and I rose in more leisurely a fashion, usually took breakfast in the kitchen, and then strolled past the meadow to my little studio cottage. I didn't even remember the last time I had asked for my carriage.

Johanna finished with my hair and eyed my clothing. "Is there anything else, ma'am, before I summon Éamonn then?"

"That is all."

"M'lady." She scurried to the door, slipping through and closing it silently behind her.

My heart was pounding. My mind was at war within itself; sluggish and bouncing, it moved swiftly between fog-induced drowsiness and over-stimulated thoughts and back again. My body followed suit, too sleep-deprived to move quickly, yet my insides felt as stirred up as a raging fire. The result was nauseating and dizzying.

By the time I had made my way to the front doors, Aindriú was standing expectantly beside them with a queer expression on his face. As I approached, he opened the door, so my gait was not altered, but as I passed, I thought I heard him sniff impertinently. Johanna stood outside on the top step under a broad umbrella. She accompanied me down the sweeping steps to my carriage with the umbrella expertly carried above my head, where Éamonn stood with the door opened.

"A basket is in your carriage, ma'am," Johanna said, "with both a breakfast and a luncheon, should you be several hours."

"Thank you, Johanna."

"Will you have need of my services?"

I stopped at the carriage door. "No, that will be all."

"M'lady." She handed off the umbrella to Éamonn before she curtsied and backed away, finally turning to make her way back up the steps.

"Have the workers arrived this morning?" I asked in what I hoped was a nonchalant tone.

"Some of the builders arrived this morn, ma'am, if those are the ones you're asking about?" Éamonn answered politely.

I nodded. *Some* of the builders did not tell me whether Nicky or Peter was at Matherscourt, but what had I truly expected Éamonn to say? It had been silly of me to even ask. I had hoped Nicky would be in Dublin today; his presence would provide me with confidence and ease my anxiety, but here I was, standing at the carriage. There was no turning back.

Once I was confident Johanna had returned to the house, I handed a note to Éamonn that contained the address. If he recognized either the address or the area, his expression did not reveal it. He merely said, "Yes, M'lady" before assisting me in the transport. The umbrella was folded and stood against the front wall across from my feet before he closed the door. A brief moment later, the carriage shifted with his weight as he settled into the coachman's seat, and we were off.

The General Post Office, or GPO, was only a few short blocks from the River Liffey, and as we passed, I gazed out my open window to watch the scores of people making their way in and out of the building. It was an impressive structure that towered over the surrounding block. Because taxes were assessed on the number of windows, many of the establishments had bricked them in to reduce the tax burden. It made the dozens of windows in the monstrous building all the more ostentatious and if that weren't enough, the half dozen columns in the Greek Revival style that heralded the entrance were both striking and intimidating. Traffic was slow here; a mixture of horse-drawn carriages and mechanical vehicles fought for dominance, and a cacophony of sounds surrounded me from horns rudely blowing to voices chattering to the sounds of construction nearby.

As we briefly stopped directly in front of the GPO, I tried to memorize its features so I might sketch it later. Perhaps, I thought, it could be my first watercolor experiment as the aged gray walls against the blue skies would be easier to master than a more colorful subject. The building was nearly a hundred years old and constructed in a manner more tuned to British tastes than Irish with the display of the Royal Arms as well as Mercury on one side and Fidelity on the other with Hibernia in the center.

The entire exterior was rumored to be of Portland stone, though it would have been easier to transport limestone from one of the Irish quarries. Instead, perhaps to line the pockets of those in Britain, the stone was delivered from England. I imagined how many loads might have been required, as the building loomed three stories tall in addition to a basement and must have had 18 windows on each floor just on this side alone.

The carriage jerked forward as we began to move once more, and a moment later, the GPO was behind me. As we traveled toward the River Liffey, the streets became even more clogged and noisy, so I was relieved when Éamonn turned the horses down a side street and a block or two later, turned once more into a quiet lane.

He pulled the horses to a stop in front of a row of brownstone townhomes. They might have appeared forlorn as most of the windows had been bricked over, had it not been for the brightly painted doors. A splash of red here and yellow there was enough to brighten the spirits, and as I waited for Éamonn to dismount and open my carriage door, I tried vainly to tamp down anxiety born of both excitement and trepidation.

"M'lady," Éamonn said, offering his hand to assist me in descending the two iron steps to the walk below. He nodded toward a bright blue door. "We have arrived, ma'am."

"Thank you, Éamonn," I said, attempting to keep my voice light as if I traveled to places such as these regularly. "Please remain near. I should not be here long."

I took a deep breath as I climbed the steps. I opened the door onto a tiny foyer where a young lady was typing, the clacking of the keys loud in the confined space. She stopped as I entered. "Lady Mather?" she asked politely.

Surprised, I answered, "Yes. I believe I have an appointment."

"Aye, and we've been expecting you, we have," she said with a broad smile. She came round her desk. "Follow me, please." She led me down a narrow hallway past several closed doors. The air was musty and stale, in dire need of open windows and fresh Irish air. It was eerily silent, my intuition telling me there was no one behind those closed doors and no other meetings taking place. In the absence of light, the corridor grew darker with every step I took.

I felt breath against the nape of my neck. Startled, I whirled about, but there was no one there, only the vacant hall which we had just walked down. When I turned back around, the young lady was standing at the end of the hall beside an older man.

He had a very high forehead, short dark hair, and bushy brows that matched a mustache that appeared more like a mop resting atop his upper lip. He wore a dark suit—trousers, vest, and jacket—even though the establishment was quite warm. He walked toward me with fast, long strides, both hands extended. "Lady Mather," he said genially, "I am honored to meet you." He grasped my hands in both of his. "Come, come. I've been waiting for you."

He waved his arm toward the end of the hall, so I stepped forward. I couldn't shake the feeling that he was assessing me from behind. We entered a small room that contained a desk and two chairs, one behind the desk and one in front of it. The desktop itself was empty except for a single sheet of paper. A minuscule fireplace inset in one wall made the room overly balmy, and I wondered how he could remain dressed in his vest and jacket, given the temperature.

"I understand we have mutual acquaintances," he was saying, pulling the chair out for me to sit. "And of course, Lord Mather and I go back many years. His investments, you see." He spoke with a cultured English accent that sounded a bit nasally and more than a bit bored.

"Yes, I—"

"Oh, and I have the paperwork already prepared." He rested against the side of the desk and turned the paper toward me. "I will only require your signature here. Quite painless." He moved around his desk to extract an inkwell and pen from a drawer.

I turned my attention to the paperwork. It was short and simple, stating that monies were to be transferred from one investment account to another. I stared at it for a long moment. There was a disembodied voice at my shoulder, urging me to stand and leave. Though my eyes were focused on the writing, in my mind's eye, I saw the sparsely furnished front office, the closed doors, and the meager banker's office. This was not a bank; that much was clear. It was interesting during times like these when the war within oneself rose between recognizing suspicious circumstances and remaining polite, and for some inexplicable reason, the need to remain polite was always triumphant. "And you handle my husband's affairs in Manchester," I said.

"London," he corrected.

"Yet, you do not have a bank in Dublin?" I smiled politely.

"Ah, but we do," he answered without hesitation. "But I thought it would be more—shall we say—discreet—to meet here."

"Ah. Discreet."

"You see, a mutual acquaintance has explained to me how you wish the funds diverted. Many share your convictions, Lady Mather, and many do not."

"And where do you stand on the matter?"

"Where I stand is of no consequence. As a loyal and trusted banker, I do not question my clients' motives. I simply facilitate them."

"And signing this paper will do that."

"It will, ma'am."

"And exactly what will it facilitate?"

For the first time, his eyes flickered as though he was unprepared. He cast his eyes down at the paper. "The funds will be moved from this account," he pointed, "to this one."

"And what will that do precisely?"

"It will facilitate the fulfillment of your motives, precisely."

"And who is our mutual acquaintance?"

"Ah." He laughed softly. "I understand, Lady Mather." He took a breath as I waited patiently. "I must remain prudent, as I am certain you can appreciate. All I am at liberty to divulge is I am also the banker for the Bowers family. I believe you are acquainted with at least two of the brothers—Peter and Nicolas—and they are currently building an expansion to the Matherscourt main house." He dipped the pen in the inkwell and offered it to me.

I accepted it but paused over the signature line. Nicky asked me to do this, I reminded myself. It was not through a third party, nor was it through a handwritten note. He asked me with his eyes looking into my own. I signed, *"M. Stratford Berkshire Mather"* and handed the pen back to him.

He smiled more broadly.

I rose. "I trust you will remain… discreet."

"Of course."

He walked me to the door and began to escort me down the hall when I stopped. "There is no need," I said. "I doubt I can become lost in this corridor. I can clearly see the foyer from here."

"Ah. Well then, Lady Mather, I only wish to say I appreciate your business, and if there is ever anything I can do for you, I will be most happy to oblige."

"Good day, sir." I continued by myself. I felt the hallway grow empty, and I turned around to verify that he had returned to his office. The young lady's back was to me as she continued clicking away, and I quietly opened one of the doors. There were stacks of boxes against one wall and a good inch of dust on the floor. It was exactly as I suspected. When I saw Nicky again, I was going to have a lot of questions.

It wasn't until I had bid the young lady farewell, exited down the steps, returned to my carriage, and we had started off for home that I realized I had never gotten the banker's name.

21

As the raindrops fell upon the gatehouse roof, they created a musical melody that was enough to lull me into blissful complacency. The outside world could not reach me here, and I could no longer remember what life had been like before Nicky.

He laid beside me now, his arm pulling me close. His eyes were closed, his breathing regular, the cool air from fresh rain wafting through the open windows to brush away perspiration that had formed on us both. Only his fingers lightly rubbing my shoulder told me he was not asleep but only resting, a brief respite before we made love all over again.

My existence had been permanently altered. I knew that now, and I also knew I was barreling toward a reckoning of which the details were hidden from me, and I could only have faith that this was where I needed to be… and who I was meant to be with.

I did not see Stratford in the mornings as he departed each day at the break of dawn. When he arrived home, I was no more than the candlesticks on the table, a tiny ray of light he would never acknowledge but expected to remain in a given place. One evening I simply did not stand in the hallway when he arrived home, having given Johanna the excuse that I was under the weather should he inquire. But when she reported back to me later, she said he did not ask for me, and from the reports of the others, he went about his dinner as he always did, as though I was seated at the far end of the table.

It was not a relationship; I understood that now. It was a business arrangement; it had always been a business arrangement and nothing more. I had been naïve to believe it might ever turn into something else. Nor did I want anything else with him, I realized. The mere thought of him touching me was enough to turn my stomach. I was thankful for his inability to consummate the marriage.

Nicky squeezed my shoulder and pulled me ever closer to him. My days were completely different from my evenings; I lived for the hours between dawn and sunset. I still took the path along the meadow each morning but an hour or so earlier than I had in the past, and it was not long before Nicky arrived to whisk me away. Sometimes we strolled along the water at the rear of the estate, far from prying eyes. Other times we picnicked beneath the ancient oak, discussing all manner of things. Sometimes we rode our horses to the far corners of Matherscourt. And always, always, we ended up at the old gatehouse. It had become our haven.

The gatehouse was diminutive, but I was serenely comfortable here. The rushing waters under the structure sounded like a constant lullaby, and on days like this with a steady rain tapping against the roof, I felt wrapped in its cocoon. The makeshift bed had been made plumper over time thanks to Nicky overstuffing it, and my contribution had been some bed linens from the house, enough to cushion the top so we could no longer feel pricks from the straw. Someday I planned to stuff it with eiderdown; I simply hadn't figured out the logistics of that as yet.

Meals, wine, and ale were all brought in a basket, and Léana never once gave me any indication that she was puzzled by my sudden voracious appetite, though she must suspect I was not eating it all by myself. Still, I had grown a bit plumper. I had even managed to move in some old chairs and a table with Nicky's help, and a few peat bricks kept the fire going.

Yes, we had set up our own little home here, and while I knew we could not expect to live out our lives in a gatehouse on Stratford's estate, I was content to let the days slip by.

"The money you transferred was enough to put us over the top," Nicky said, his voice barely over a mumble as he laid there, his eyes still closed.

"Now, that's romantic."

He chuckled, his eyes opening as he turned on his side and rested on his elbow. "Sorry, darling. My mind is filled with so much these days."

I brushed a lock of hair from his brow. "So tell me; what does 'over the top' mean?"

He smiled. "We bought the weapons, Penny."

"From the Germans?"

"We did. It's happening. Between the weapons we bought from the Americans and those that are coming from the Germans, we are nearing the day we declare our independence."

"And how will that happen?"

"There's so much more I want to tell you, darling. So much. But I can't..."

We were silent for a moment. Then I said, "But is that all it will take? You show your weapons, declare Ireland's independence, and the Brits just walk away, just like that?"

"They've been weakened by the Great War. They've been fighting for nearly two years now, and the Central Powers are a formidable enemy. Who knows who will win?"

"Surely, you don't want the Central Powers to win?"

He shrugged. "Britain has kept my people as mere slaves for centuries; they decimated us in war and through starvation—committed genocide in the north—then evicted us from our homes and removed any possibility that we could better ourselves. Could the Germans be any more brutal?" Before I could answer, he must have seen something in my expression because he continued in a softer tone, "As I've told you before, darling, we will serve neither Kaiser nor King. We simply want Ireland to be independent. And once that occurs, whoever wins the Great War will become trading partners, and we'll seek to live in peace alongside them."

"Even if it's the British?"

"Even if it's the British."

"When will this happen?"

"Easter Monday."

"Easter Monday," I repeated in a whisper.

"All across Ireland—from north to south and east to west—a declaration of independence will be read aloud, declaring our sovereignty."

"And will you be reading it?"

He chuckled. "No, dear Penny. I am nothing more than a foot soldier. There are so many men in high positions in our struggle for independence—James Connelly, Patrick Pearse, Tom Clarke, Joseph Plunkett, Sean Mac Diarmada—so many more—"

"But what does that mean, a 'foot soldier'? Will you be carrying a weapon?"

"I will not be in danger, Penny. I give you my word. Britain's men are at the front; they haven't the forces here nor the will to fight on their western front. They've lost all the lands they'd gained at St Eloi, Belgium, you know, in a German counter-offensive. Though they're going back and forth now, I hear casualties are high. And that's not even the half of it—the Brits are fighting in so many countries now, multiple continents, and they haven't as many men as they need."

"But surely with the Americans on our side—on *their* side—" I corrected myself.

He shook his head. "We will peacefully declare Ireland's sovereignty. We wish for no war with England, and as the declaration is read all across the island, people like myself will step in to keep the peace and maintain order. That is all. I doubt that I will even have an opportunity to fire my weapon."

"Easter Monday," I whispered.

"Ah, and I have already told you far more than I should have," Nicky said, pulling me under him as he kissed me. "There are many more important things on my mind now."

His touch was electric as it always was, and his passionate kisses were enough to force all other thoughts from my mind. I surrendered completely to the moment—the rain upon the roof, the gentle breeze that wafted through the windows to stroke our skin, the perfume of spring flowers, and a new season of grassland—and Nicky, always Nicky, completing my world.

22

I was humming when Eliza returned to my studio. Oblivious to anything but the watercolor painting I was focused on, I didn't realize she had arrived until she called my name from the doorway.

"Penny dear, those are absolutely beautiful!" she exclaimed as she waltzed inside to stare at a previous painting of a pasture alongside a meandering stream. "I knew to transition to watercolors was the right call. Oh my, oh my!"

"I'm glad you like them," I said, blushing. I set down my brush and stepped back to take a critical look at the painting on which I was currently working. It was another pastoral scene, this one with a series of lakes and streams as seen from a hill.

"We'll be able to get four or five times the income from these as we did from your charcoal," Eliza said as she came to stand beside me. "The greens and blues are absolutely gorgeous."

"I have several for you today. Not this one—it isn't quite finished yet; besides, it's wet. But those against the wall. If any don't look quite up to your standards, I'll understand. I've been experimenting."

As she studied the paintings I'd pointed out, I poured some tea.

"I'll take them all," she said finally. Removing one of her gloves, she joined me at the tiny table near the window. "Funniest thing happened," she said as she took her first sip.

"Oh?"

"That last batch I picked up from you. Brian accidentally took one of the sketchings I hadn't chosen."

"Which one?" I passed her a small plate of crumpets.

"An old lady." She laughed. "Wizened face, threadbare scarf."

"On a cart?"

She continued to laugh. "That's the one. With a worn-out mule pulling it."

"Just bring it back," I said. "I know you didn't like those themes."

"That's just the thing," she said, her eyes gleaming. "Somehow or other, it was displayed amongst far better-known artists, their work worth thousands."

"Oh, no," I said, the color rising in my face.

"Oh, yes. And someone came in and offered more for that sketch than anything else you've ever drawn."

"What?"

She reached into her purse and drew out a fistful of money.

I eyed it in disbelief. "Do you know who it was?"

She shook her head. "I wasn't there; my man sold it to him. His name is in the books, though. Austrian."

"Austrian? What's he doing in Ireland with a war going on?"

"Older gent, from what I gather, and obviously with a great deal of money. A man like him wouldn't be at the front, dear."

I looked down at my hands. They were sprinkled with various colors of paint. "Of course not," I said, folding my hands neatly in my lap to hide their condition.

"Not that I want you to do more of those," Eliza was saying. "On the contrary. I still want the more beautiful scenes like these," she waved her hand toward the watercolors. "Serenity. Tranquility. Beauty. That's what the public wants in times of war. Something they can get their minds lost in."

"Of course."

"So, you'll be at the party on Sunday?"

"Party?"

"Well, of course, dear. Didn't Stratford tell you?"

I shook my head. We rarely saw one another these days, and when we did, I was treated more like the wallpaper than a living, breathing human being. "It must have slipped his mind," I said.

"Men." She took a dainty bite of a crumpet. "Well, it's going to be lavish; you know me. The servants are hiding prizes in the formal garden for the children to find. Easter egg hunt, you know."

"Easter is Sunday?"

She giggled. "Not at all surprised you don't know. You've had your head in the clouds with Nicky, haven't you?" Before I could respond, she continued, "Anyway, come dressed to the hilt. Everybody who is anybody will be there. An entire afternoon of food and spirits, a dinner that will be the envy of Dublin, followed by music, dancing, and more spirits."

"I look forward to it," I lied. Truth be told, I preferred my little studio and paintings to a gathering of people, especially a formal one. I was already beginning to fret over my attire; it must always be a gown no one has seen before; otherwise, the rumors get started that one is in financial straits.

Eliza stood. "Wonderful. I'll see you there." She called Brian through the open door and pointed to the watercolors he was to load. He carried each one to the back of the carriage, where he secured it with a piece of material, handling it as gently as one would wrap a baby. "Don't be late," she was saying as she joined him. "It's going to be a grand time."

I watched Brian finish loading the paintings before escorting Eliza down the steps and then into the carriage, his hands going around her waist as he helped her to ascend the single iron step that dangled from the carriage door. He tipped his hat to me, and I nodded in return before he assumed his position in the coachman's seat.

I don't remember watching them leave, but I must have because sometime later, I was still standing in the doorway. My mind filled with the refrain that Sunday was Easter. That meant Monday was to be the day that Ireland would declare her independence.

23

I think when all is said and done, I prefer to sleep when the rains are upon me. There is something about curling up beneath layers of warm, cozy covers and listening to the raindrops against the glass or even the stronger pelting storms with their thunder and lightning that cause me to become lulled to contented sleep. But on nights like this, when the air is still and silent, time becomes stuck, and I feel suspended in wakefulness while sleep gathers just beyond my reach.

I rose, sliding my feet into my slippers and donning my robe to tread across the cold floor and poke the peat in the firebox. It was stubborn tonight; seeking the same slumber that evaded me, the remnants of earlier flames nothing more than a spark and a flicker. I finally gave up and began to make my way back to my bed, where warmth, if not sleep, awaited me. I paused at the window to note the frost forming in the lower corner, a late frost that could damage the flowers just beginning to bud to officially herald the spring and promise of summer. The skies were clear, the customary clouds nowhere in sight, the half-moon brilliant even though we were midway between full moons.

A flash caught my eye, and I turned my attention from the night sky to the ground below. I spotted it again, a glint and a glimmer, and it was gone as quickly as it had appeared. Forgetting the chill for the moment, I strained my eyes as I peered into the shadows, the moon unable to penetrate the copses of trees between the great house and the structures beyond the meadow.

I tried to pinpoint where the flashes were occurring and came to the conclusion they were at the old barn across from my little studio cottage. I thought vaguely of Stratford, asleep and snoring in his room down the hall, and knew I would not awaken him to the possibility of trespassers, nor would I rouse the servants from their beds. Completely and fully awake now, I felt my senses pricking at my mind, urging me to venture there myself.

I dressed quickly in dark clothing and carried my heavier shoes in my arms as I slipped outside my bedchamber and quietly closed the door behind me. The corridor was dark, and I groped at the walls as I made my way away from Stratford and down the stairs. The house was surreally quiet, objects that seemed ordinary or innocuous during the daytime, suddenly morphing into ghostly beings that loomed over the rooms to watch my departure from the house and into the chill of the night.

The windows of the great house became murky eyes that followed my progress around the east wing and into the shadows cast by the trees, rushing from trunk to trunk lest I be exposed to the intruder's eyes. I unlatched the gate to the meadow and slipped inside, not wishing to take the path for fear those at the barn would venture down it and discover me there. I remained to the glooms until I'd reached the other side, breathless and perspiring despite the cold. From there, I moved toward the back of the old cottages, remaining in the darkness, trying to avoid the light of the moon I had admired only a short time earlier.

When at last I came upon the barn, I watched as several men closed the large double doors and joined others in a cart—Nicky's, I thought, but just as quickly I realized his wagon was as common as Irish grass and this one could belong to anyone. When they began to move, they took care to remain as silent as possible. I waited until they were on the path toward the back gate and began to follow them, keeping to the trees well beyond the light. They moved slowly with one man at the horse's muzzle, perhaps to hold onto the metal in the bridle to keep it from clanging. My own breathing sounded loud and hoarse as I inhaled the stinging air, and with each footstep upon the soft leaves beneath the trees, I was certain they would hear me, and I would be discovered. That it was my property didn't seem to placate my fears, as these men that came under cover of night would not respect the owner any more than they respected the contents of the barn paid for with the owner's money.

When they reached the point where they should have continued toward the back gate, I was huffing. Unable to keep up, I had fallen some distance behind, and now, as they halted, I stopped as well and leaned against a tree to catch my breath. I was astounded a moment later when they turned the wagon toward the wide stream that wound through Matherscourt and straight for the old gatehouse.

An advantage of being on foot was while they followed the gutted path that meandered around the woods, I could pass through at nearly a straight line. They still arrived before I was able to, however, and I hunkered down amongst the trees to watch. They turned the wagon around so the bed faced the gatehouse door and all but one man went inside.

Without cloud cover, I could clearly see the man that remained. I inhaled sharply and then covered my mouth quickly lest he heard me, for it was Peter. He climbed down from the wagon on the opposite side from me and wandered toward the far end of the gatehouse. Before I had time to think it through, I sprinted out of the cover of the woods. I rushed to the nearest end of the gatehouse. I slipped out of my shoes before sliding along the bank until I was up to my hips in water. I stopped beneath a window and held onto the corner foundation to keep me steady.

"Double check," Nicky was saying. "Make sure you've accounted for all the ammunition as well."

"Aye," another man answered; I thought I recognized his voice as one of the builders. "We'll need every last one on hand, just in case they want to give us a bother."

Heavy footsteps resonated on the floor, followed by the sound of scuffling. I heard movement outside as if some of the men had left through the front door and were near the wagon, while another set made its way into the gatehouse.

"You've retrieved all the weapons from the barn?" Nicky asked.

"Every last one," Peter answered. "I checked it myself when they were done."

"Did you cover it up well?"

"The hiding place?"

"Aye. I do not want the Mathers to know anything about it."

I held my hand over my mouth and bit my lip. My breathing had become labored, my chest hurt, and the sound of my heaving too loud for my own ears.

"We covered it well," another man answered. "I even piled horse manure atop it. No Brit would bother shoveling horseshite."

The men laughed in unison.

"It's loaded."

There were sounds of the men leaving, and the wagon creaked as though they were climbing atop it.

"What about Penny?" It was Peter's voice, quieter now that the others were outside, and I strained to hear Nicky's reply.

"What about her?" he asked.

"Does she know?"

"No. And I want to keep it that way."

"She'll be looking for you."

"Aye. That she will."

"You'll leave without saying goodbye?"

"That's the plan."

"We're ready to head out," a man called from the door.

"Nicky?" Peter asked.

"Go on," he answered. "I'll be behind you. I've a horse tethered to the wood line."

"Aye. I spotted it. They're expecting us, Nick. Don't be late."

"I won't be. I want to cover up our tracks here. Won't take but a few."

"See you there then."

"See you there."

I eased toward the corner of the building and watched as Peter exited the gatehouse and climbed aboard the wagon with the others. "Don't use the lamp unless absolutely necessary," he said as they departed.

"We won't need it here," said the man I recognized as Sean. "Not like we did at the barn."

I waited until they had rounded the first bend, and they were out of sight, the horse's hooves and the creak of the wagon wheels fading into the night. Then I climbed out of the stream and made my way to the gatehouse door, my shoes still held in my trembling hands. Without drapes on the windows, the moon streamed in like branches of a tree, snaking along the walls and floor. Nicky was arranging our makeshift bed on the floor, returning the covers where they had last been. It was obvious from his attention to detail that the weapons and ammunition they had retrieved had been under the bed where we'd made love.

He was so focused on cleaning up that he didn't know I was there until he finally turned around and started toward the door. Then he stopped dead in his tracks, his eyes wide as the color drained from his face.

"Leaving without saying goodbye?" I asked. My voice sounded odd even to myself; it was cold and aloof with a slight tremble. I realized I was shaking as much from my discovery as the ice-cold stream in which I'd stood.

"It's not what you think," he said.

"And just what is it that I'm thinking?"

"You're wet," he said, his eyes taking in my clothes as they dripped onto the floor, the puddle growing around me.

I was freezing, my skin a series of goosebumps that shouted for me to rub warmth back into my limbs. Yet I remained still as stone simply looking at him. When he said nothing more, I said, "So this was all a setup, wasn't it?"

"Yes. No. It's not what you're thinking. I swear."

"Then start with the setup." I walked toward the center of the room, my gown heavy with water, so I felt as though I was still treading through the stream. I folded my arms in front of my torso in a vain attempt to stop my shaking. "The London banker, for example. You and Peter were looking for a wealthy man with property near Dublin and a place to hide your guns and ammunition for a planned rebellion."

"I told you about the rebellion, Penny. I didn't lie to you."

"You've been moving in large amounts of supplies," I continued. "Brick, wood, marble… and rifles. Bullets. All directly under our noses."

He took a step toward me, and I took a step back. "That much is true, Penny. I won't lie to you. We've worked our arses off building Stratford's orangery—"

"—and gazebo?"

"That was a pleasure," he said. "And aye, it's true we moved weapons closer to the city and the old barn—and aye, this gatehouse—were the perfect places to hide them. We knew no one would suspect Stratford Mather."

"Or his wife."

"That's right, Penny. No one would ever suspect you."

"And when you asked me to accompany you, we were moving weapons, weren't we?"

He remained silent.

"Ah. Your silence says it all. And I suppose I was asked because—well, if there was a road checkpoint, for example, Lady Mather could save the day, right? Only she couldn't, and it was Lord Davies' presence that kept us both from the Gael."

"No, Penny. It's true, we connected with Stratford to use this property. But I asked you to accompany me because—"

"I don't want to hear your lies. To think that I fell right into your trap, bedding you like a common whore."

"You're not a whore, Penny. And I—"

"And the night I spotted you moving in the darkness here at the gatehouse—you allowed me to believe you were readying a love nest for us, didn't you? Only you weren't. You'd found another place to hide your weapons. You only brought me here and made me think you cared for me to buy yourself time and assure my silence."

"No! You've got it all wrong. If only you'd allow me to explain—"

"And then there was the banker again; perhaps the same one that recommended your services to Stratford? And like a fool, I transferred large sums of money to someone who was using me."

"It isn't like that at all." His voice was louder now, and he took another step toward me. This time, I held my ground. "Yes, we were taking full advantage of Matherscourt—Stratford, not you. I've fallen in love with you, darling."

"In love?" I scoffed. "And when you're in love with someone, you leave without saying goodbye?"

"It's better this way."

I stared at him, completely speechless at his response. My heart felt as though it was made of delicate glass and was shattering into a thousand jagged pieces, and I struggled to catch my breath.

"Penny, I told you from the beginning that my highest priority is Ireland—a free and independent Ireland. And now I must go and do my duty."

"Men leave all the time for work or war, and I doubt they all walk away without saying their farewells—especially to the one they profess to love."

"I know, and you're right. But there's much you don't know, Penny. And I can't tell you about it, any of it. I must protect you."

"Protect me from what?"

He shook his head. Taking a deep breath, he said, "There is a possibility of war in Ireland."

"The Irish are already involved in the war—"

"No. Not the Great War. An Irish war. And when that happens, it won't be with carefully drawn battlefield lines and men firing across an open expanse. It won't be with tanks. It will be guerrilla warfare; it will be block-by-block in the cities, house-by-house. It will reach far beyond the cities, also house-by-house. I couldn't tell you about the weapons hidden at Matherscourt; if the Brits were to question you and Stratford, ignorance could save you both from hanging."

"You promised me you would not be hurt; that a declaration of independence would be all that would transpire, and then Ireland would be free."

"If I told you that, then it was my one and only lie to you, Penny. You must believe that."

I could not hold on much longer. I thought surely he could see my heart splintering into pieces that could never be put back together again; even if I tried, I felt forever damaged. It was all I could do to prevent myself from collapsing onto the floor in a wet and shivering heap. "Go," I said, my voice strong and louder than I had anticipated.

He stared at me, his brows furrowed, and face darkened. I saw in his eyes the mirror of my pain; tears that rose which he stubbornly tamped down and lips that trembled with words he could not say.

"Go," I said again. "Get out. Join your compatriots."

His mouth opened as if he was about to speak, his lips continuing to quiver as though silent words were escaping before he closed his mouth tightly, his teeth grasping his lower lip. He turned abruptly away from me and made his way to the door. He hesitated there, and I saw him out of my peripheral vision turn back, but I would not look him in the eye. "I love you, Penny," he said, his voice shaking. "Whatever happens, you must believe that I love you."

Before I could respond, he was gone.

24

There have been times in my life in which I experienced chronic headaches. I sat forlornly in one of the two chairs in the gatehouse, the other conspicuously empty. It occurred to me that my headaches were really tears that were never spent. I wanted to cry; I truly did. But I could not. The pressure built up as it had when my parents informed me they had consented to my marriage to a man I had never met, and again before the wedding and many times since. But now the pressure was nearly unbearable.

I had tasted love; whether Nicky had ever actually cared for me, I may never know, but I knew I had truly loved him with all my heart. And now the gatehouse that had been so filled with devotion and passion was empty, a shell without a soul. It was as though Nicky had taken the essence of the place with him when he walked out that door.

Time slipped by, and time stood still through each excruciating moment until I finally wrested myself from my thoughts and turned to the bed upon which we'd made love so many times. I pulled it into the center of the room and then focused my attention on the stones underneath.

At first, I was puzzled; I knew they had removed the weapons and ammunition from this very spot, but the floor appeared to have been in place for a century or more. I ran my fingertips around each stone but felt only the mortar that had frozen it in place all these years. It wasn't until I started to move the bed back into place that I spotted it: a thin line that would have gone unnoticed on a cloudy day. I traced it with my fingers until it ultimately formed a rectangle approximately two feet long and one foot wide. Try though I did, I was not able to raise it; whether there was a hidden switch somewhere or the piece was simply too heavy, I didn't know.

My soaked skirt grew increasingly heavier, so I replaced the bedding and left the cottage, taking one last look behind me. I immediately wished I hadn't as my stomach lurched. My heart reminded me in a blinding flash that it was shattered to its core. I forced myself to harden my mind against it, and I closed and latched the door. Then I made my way around the gatehouse and back into the stream, my shoes now discarded somewhere between the gatehouse and the water. It was freezing and if my teeth had not been chattering before, now they sounded like rocks being knocked together. I knew which window the bed had been under, and I made my way beneath it. I was waist-deep now, and when I bent low to run my hand under the gatehouse arch, the water poured over my chest. Gasping, I almost abandoned my little mission, but I pushed myself to search for a telltale sign. And there it was: an almost imperceptible bulge about a foot wide. I didn't know how deep it went but would have bet my life it was two feet. It was stone, which meant the hidden compartment had been constructed when the gatehouse was built.

As I hurried out of the stream, I pictured guards from centuries gone by using that space—for what, I could only imagine—and now, on the eve of a declaration of independence, it had been instrumental once more.

I raised my skirts and hastened back toward the barn and my studio. I'd spent far too much time following the wagon, speaking to Nicky, and sitting with a fogged brain. I had to get home and out of these clothes. By the time I reached the barn, clouds were beginning to form, and the wind had kicked up. I wanted nothing more than to tear off these wet clothes and find a place to sleep, but I knew I could do neither.

I was almost past the barn when I stopped and abruptly changed direction, entering the structure through the wide double doors. I kept them open for the moonlight to guide me, but at first, I saw only supplies that had not yet been used on Stratford's orangery or my gazebo. Then I remembered the comment about the manure and for the first time in my life—and hopefully, the last—I went in search of it.

I found it atop a bed of straw that filled one stall, and from the stench of it, the men must have picked up horse dung from half a dozen horses. Despite myself, I found the tiniest bit of humor as I dashed back through the barn and closed the doors tight. They were right; no British soldier would shovel that. And if the flooring had been made as well as the gatehouse, the hiding place would remain difficult to detect.

I reached the house before dawn, slipping through the kitchen door and making my way up the narrow servant's stairwell. The oil lights had not yet been lit, which told me none of the servants had ventured from their attic rooms as yet. I knew I was probably leaving a trail of water and debris, and they would no doubt follow it to my room, but they knew better than to question it. They would simply clean it up and let it go at that.

But when I reached my bedroom floor, I realized that Stratford would have to walk right past my door to reach the wider formal stairs. He might ignore me, but he certainly would not ignore a trail of water that could threaten to slip him up. I hesitated at the top of the servant's stairs and stripped completely naked, trying to wipe off any bits of grass or debris from my feet. I opened the first guest room door I came to and shoved the bundle inside and then sprinted down the hallway to my room. My heart was pounding, and my breath was rough, my eyes riveted on Stratford's door.

When I reached my bedchamber and was safely inside with the door closed behind me, I collapsed onto the floor. The events of the night—the trek through the woods, twice wading into the stream, and the trek back—had taken its toll, and the conversation with Nicky and revelations revealed were enough to finish me. After a long while, I cleaned up as best I could with the washbasin but made a mental note to have Johanna fetch a bath for me as soon as I awakened. I would also instruct her to clean or dispose of the wet clothing. She would be discreet. She would have to be.

I had once again dressed in my nightgown, the ends of my long hair wet and heavy from the stream, and I had just climbed into bed when dawn arrived. I had not yet closed my eyes when I heard Stratford's door open and his heavy boots making his way down the corridor to the wide central staircase.

When I finally knew I was completely alone, the tears began to pour. The loss felt overwhelming, the heartbreak as tangible as if someone had run me through. Each stab was sharp and deep enough to kill, and yet I felt forced to remain sadistically alive to experience each immense pain. I felt completely abandoned, utterly lovelorn, entirely broken. I had reached for the stars, and when they were within my touch, almost within my grasp, they shattered. And they shattered me.

25

Easter Sunday was unusually cool, discussions of an overabundance of rain on everyone's lips. There had been some flooding in parts of the island with some areas having received nearly two hundred inches of rain in the first four months of the year, more than they would normally have received in twelve months. I realized I hadn't noticed the deluge, though now that I looked back upon my memories, they were there all along; the lazy days of lying in the gatehouse listening to the rain on the roof, the nights I had awakened to thunder, the raindrops pelting the windows as I'd worked on my sketches and paintings.

I stood at the row of windows in the back of Davies Castle alongside other adults with cordials in one hand and hors d'oeuvres in another, remaining under the dry and comfortable roof while their children risked colds as they searched for Easter gifts. To Eliza's credit, they had erected tents throughout the gardens, and most of the trinkets were hidden there, but there was something rather unsettling at watching children in their slickers and wellies rushing around with their waterlogged baskets to find as many goodies as they could possibly carry. I rather felt a bit of sympathy for the servants scurrying about in the rain, assisting the littlest.

"What's with the long face?"

At the sound of Eliza's voice, I turned as she thrust a glass of champagne into my hands.

"Just the weather is all," I lied.

"Just think of how beautiful and green the lawn and gardens will be tomorrow. It's what I do."

"Too bad it couldn't have been today."

She followed my gaze through the window. "At the stroke of the bell, the servants have been instructed to herd the children indoors. While the adults are dining, the children will be dried and freshly clothed and fed separately. Then they'll all open their trinkets."

"It was so generous of you to do this."

"I enjoy it. Nothing better than a party, wouldn't you say?"

Another guest garnered her attention, and she excused herself as she moved further away from me. I spent the next few minutes mingling though my heart wasn't in it. I wanted to return home, curl up in bed and sleep for the next week, but I planted a broad smile on my face and pretended to listen to all the mindless gossip such an event always invites.

When the bell was struck, I was bored nearly out of my mind and grateful for a change—any change. While the children were ushered indoors through a separate wing by harried and soggy servants, Eliza struck her champagne glass with a spoon to announce lunch, though it was well past one o'clock.

As the others filed out of the solarium, I hung back. There was no need to hurry. The places would be set with each female flanked by males, the couples divided so each could converse with people they didn't usually see. After Eliza's announcement, I noticed men finding their partners to escort them into the formal dining hall, but Stratford was one of the first to leave, and of course, it never occurred to him to accompany me. By the time I entered the room, the others were settling in, I quickly found my place, and with the help of the two gentlemen to be my dining partners, I was seated.

By the time the main course had arrived, one could barely hear their seat partners due to all the conversations taking place at once. I counted eighteen seated opposite me, which meant there were thirty-eight in attendance, with Eliza at one end and Philip at the opposite. I was seated near the middle, so I was overhearing conversations from both ends of the table. My head had begun to hurt.

"Did you hear about the weapons headed for Ireland? Twenty thousand and no less!"

I stopped pushing around the food on my plate as my head jerked upward. It was the gentleman across from me, raising his voice to be heard by the seatmate to my left.

"The war is coming to these shores?" My seatmate, an elderly Baron Wilhause, asked with concern.

Earl Armstrong shook his head. "British intelligence intercepted information that some Irish peasants were siding with the Germans."

"What does that mean?" Baron Wilhause demanded indignantly. "Siding with the Germans? Going over to the enemy's side? That is treasonous, I say!"

A silence fell over the center of the table as others turned to listen in on the conversation.

"What is all this?" Countess Markievicz asked.

"Nothing to worry about, I can assure you," Earl Armstrong answered. "The Germans supplied weapons to the Irish to attack the English, it appears. But two days ago, arrests were made of key individuals involved in the plot."

"Do we know who these people were?" another asked.

"And what of the weapons?" Baron Wilhause asked. "Have they seized them?"

"I have it on good authority that the weapons are at the bottom of the Irish Sea," Earl Armstrong explained. "A man named Karl Spindler along with his crew scuttled the Aud—that's the ship's name—to prevent the British from taking the weapons."

"Only now the peasants don't have the weapons, either," the countess said pointedly.

"Perhaps," Stratford boomed near the end of the table, "they will use the broomsticks and mops they've been practicing with."

The table erupted in laughter except for Countess Markievicz and me. I sat stunned, my eyes roaming the expressions of the other guests. When they fell on Eliza, I noticed the blood had seemed to drain from her face, and her hand shook slightly as she raised the wineglass to her lips. Our eyes met briefly before she lowered her lashes.

"And where did this occur?" Earl Wilhause asked.

"Daunt's Rock."

"Daunt's Rock?" someone asked, puzzled.

"East of Carrigadda Bay," the Baron explained. "Not far from Cork Head and Roberts Head."

I looked down at my plate as though focused on the food, but my mind was soaring in every direction. I had heard of these places in passing conversations, and my mind sought to pinpoint them on an envisioned map of Ireland. They were well south of Dublin near the southern tip of the island in County Cork, I believed, too far south for Nicky to have been in the area—or so I thought. My mind began to war with itself, calculating over and over again how long it took for us to reach the cottages and how far it must be past that to reach County Cork. I thought Nicky had mentioned Michael Collins and Sean Mac Diarmada were from that county, but I dared not ask about them. The mere mention of names that should be beyond my knowledge could raise suspicion.

"And this Karl Spindler and his crew—they were captured?" someone was asking.

"They were. I believe the news reports have them en route to Britain to be held as prisoners of war."

"The Tower of London?" the countess asked, her voice so unnaturally high that it was piercing.

Earl Armstrong shook his head. "No, a regular prisoner of war camp. Although," he said almost as an afterthought, "Sir Roger Casement was arrested as well, and *he* is being sent to the Tower of London."

There was a collective gasp. Sir Casement had been born in Ireland, educated in England, and knighted by the Crown after serving for many years in the British Colonial Service. That he had been involved in a plot to bring German weapons to Ireland was almost beyond belief.

"He was on the Aud?"

"On a submarine."

"A German submarine!" other guests exclaimed in unison. "In the Irish Sea?"

"Whatever will happen to him?" the countess breathed.

"His fate will be worse than Spindler's, I presume. If convicted of treason, he could be executed."

Conversation dwindled after that as though half the guests were in a state of shock. Many of them knew Sir Casement—myself included—and this brought the situation very close to home. When Eliza announced coffee and dessert in the drawing-room, I discovered I hadn't eaten a bite of my food; I had only pushed it around my plate.

I wanted to be with Nicky and not in this room filled with people. I wanted to know how the loss of the weapons would affect the rebellion he'd been planning for months—if not years. And as we made our way into the opulent drawing room to be seated at more informal tables arranged around the room, I realized to my dismay that it had been Stratford's money that had helped to fund the German weapons. I knew little of the British Intelligence Services, but I knew enough to understand the matter would not end here. They would trace the weapons back to their sale and then follow the money, which would lead them to the traitors within Ireland.

And with rising panic, I realized I would be one of them.

26

There was a surreal quality to the sound of the harps. Amidst the ever-growing hum of voices from laughter to hushed gossip, the melody of the three harps in the corner of the ballroom found a way to twist and curve around the bodies, the drinks, and the food while maintaining an otherworldly purity. I longed to be alone except for the music wafting like the wind over my soul.

I felt alone. Utterly alone. Amid the crowd of revelers brought together by the excuse of Easter Sunday but truly together simply for the opportunity to party, I felt a solitary outcast, my thoughts determined to envision the Aud and its cargo of weapons, the crew scuttling the ship, preferring to sacrifice the weapons to the depths of the Irish Sea rather than hand them over to the British.

I could not turn my thoughts away from Nicky, either. He was on the ship's deck, a captain giving instructions. He was the crewman setting the charge. He was diving into the water before the explosion, forcibly rescued by the British Navy. And he was Sir Roger Casement morphing into Nicky's body, Nicky's face, coming ashore only to be arrested and sent under heavy guard to the Tower of London.

I knew he was none of those people from the logical fact that he hadn't the time or the circumstances to be there. Yet his face was everywhere.

Countess Markievicz made her apologies directly after dinner and hurriedly left, and I wished I had her courage to leave as well. Instead, I wound my way around clique after clique, feeling out of place among those people with whom I had nothing in common until I found myself at the far end of the ballroom at the edge of a discussion in which Stratford appeared to be at the center.

"I must watch the workmen constantly," he was saying, his voice booming. "They are lazy, every last one of them. Should I look away for a moment, they will have made their way from the orangery to the house and stolen everything they can get their hands on. They are not to be trusted."

I thought of the times in which I came upon the men in the orangery. Lean, the lot of them, due to hard physical labor and little food, and not at any time did I see them idle—if I didn't count, that is, the time Nicky spent with me and he certainly was not lazy in that respect, either. And while they might have used Matherscourt to hide their weapons, there had been plenty to steal in plain sight, and yet it all had been left for the rightful owners.

"You are quite correct," Baron Wilhause was saying. "I have never seen a more lazy civilization. They remain existing hand-to-mouth because if we did not force them to work, they would live their lives as drunkards in the nearest pub."

"I believe they work for the coin to get drunk," Stratford agreed. "Five minutes after they are paid, they are tipping the bottle."

As the circle grew around us, laughing in unison, I said, "Surely they are not all as lazy and intoxicated as you portray, for they built our homes and everything in them."

A collective gasp went through the crowd. In the silence that ensued, I realized the harps had stopped playing, their last song ended.

"You ignorant little schoolgirl," Stratford boomed, breaking the silence. "Leave the adults to discuss matters of importance of which you know nothing." He spat the last words out, the spittle flying around those nearest him.

I remained fixed in place, my fingers tightening around my wine glass. I felt the stares of those around us but tried though I did, I could not find the words in which to respond.

Stratford's eyes insolently roamed my body from the top of my head to my toes. As the silence grew uncomfortably oppressive, he said, "Why are you so fat? Why can't you look more like her?" He pointed in the direction of Baron Wilhause's granddaughter, who had come to whisper something in her grandfather's ear. She was a child of no more than fourteen with the delicate androgynous figure of one that had not yet bloomed into womanhood.

"It is no wonder I haven't a Mather heir," he told the others that had begun to laugh nervously alongside him. "For surely who would want to bed such a fleshy creature? Not to mention she is like a starfish in bed—fat in the middle and limbs splayed and lifeless!"

The crowd erupted into boisterous laughter. I felt as though I had been struck by a lightning bolt, the heat erupting in my skin, turning it a bright red and causing perspiration to bead. My eyes roamed one face after another, their laughter so loud and obnoxious that I could no longer hear them. I saw only their faces, their heads tilted back, their mouths open, and their bellies shaking with mirth at my expense. Women far larger than I examined my figure with critical eyes as though their own bodies were models of perfection—and Stratford, with a belly as large as a washtub, was still speaking as more peals of laughter commenced. Only Eliza and Philip, who had just joined the crowd, appeared shocked and revolted by my husband's words.

I turned on my heel to find the nearest door. I did not know where I was going; the corridors of which I was nearly as familiar as my own house seemed foreign now, the halls narrower, and the walls darker. I don't remember having discarded my wine glass, but by the time I burst through another door onto a terrace, my hands were empty and shaking. I came to stand beside the elaborate stone rail, holding onto it for dear life as my legs wobbled so violently that I feared to fall. Even the cold night air could not remove the heat I felt inside or calm the perspiration that magnified my embarrassment.

A sound escaped my lips that might have been mistaken for a sob, but no tears would venture from my eyes. Like they had when Nicky and I had argued at the gatehouse, they felt as though they were backing up inside my head, brick upon brick of unrequited sadness and longing.

"Are you alright then?" Eliza's voice was soft and sympathetic as she came to stand alongside me. She tried to hand me a glass of water, but I shook my head.

"We have never had sex," I managed to say, my eyes straight ahead as though I was looking at the distant trees, but in reality, I saw nothing but my own sorrow.

"I know," she said quietly.

"He has never seen me in bed, splayed or otherwise. He is impotent."

"He is also drunk."

"Are they all drunk, Eliza? All those that laughed at my expense?"

"They're fools."

"Then why suffer them? Why invite them into your home if they are so shallow?"

"You know why." She took a sip of the water I'd refused. "It is all part of the game, isn't it?"

I was silent for a moment, her words tripping over my consciousness before being carried off on the growing winds. Finally, I said, "Do you think I am fat?"

"Absolutely not."

"Nicky loved my curves."

"Past tense?"

I sighed heavily and turned to face her. "He is gone, Eliza. I don't know when—or if—I will see him again."

"The orangery is complete? Your gazebo too?"

"I don't know."

"I don't understand."

I caught myself from going too far. "He had business elsewhere."

"Ah." She eyed me curiously. "I hope he is not involved with the German weapons."

"Why? I mean—I don't know that he is, he never said anything to me about it, but—"

"Didn't you hear Philip this evening? The British are going to hunt down all those involved in the liaison with Germany and try them as traitors."

"He could not have been involved," I said lamely. "He has been at Matherscourt every day."

"You mean he has been with you every day," she said with a sly smile. "Forget Stratford's words. Nicky will be back after he's attended to his business. Find your happiness with him. I am certain he does not think you a starfish."

"No," I said, breaking into a shy smile. "No, he most definitely does not."

A spattering of raindrops began to alight on my skin.

"Come back inside," Eliza said, shivering. "It's so cold out here, and the dancing is about to begin."

"Thank you," I said, giving her a quick hug. "But I don't believe I will. Can you send for my carriage? I will have Éamonn drive me home and then return for Stratford."

"Are you quite sure?"

"Quite."

I made my way back inside, steering away from the festivities to retrieve my cloak. By the time I had ventured onto the front veranda, Éamonn was waiting for me. His face seemed downcast, and his eyes had a faraway look in them as he opened the carriage door and closed it behind me. It wasn't until we were halfway home that I realized that he, too, might have heard at Davies Castle that the weapons had been lost to the sea.

27

Easter Monday was a bank holiday, but it had not stopped Stratford from leaving at his customary time, even though he had not arrived home until the wee hours of the morning. I knew the precise time because I had not slept for more than a few minutes all night; I'd tossed and turned, paced the floor, watched out the window, and hoped this time for the telltale sign of the lantern bumping along the back road but which never came.

I'd dressed in finery and advised Johanna that I would have breakfast in the kitchen, after which I would require Éamonn's services. I could not bring myself to walk past the meadow to my studio, could not bear the thought of spending the day alone with my thoughts while constantly peering across the way at the old barn.

I heard the voices while I was still in the corridor, well before I reached the kitchen. Éamonn and Léana were having an argument. I slowed my step as I struggled to listen, eventually stopping just outside the doorway to press myself against the wall and out of sight.

"It is all for the best that it's done afore it started," Léana was saying forcefully. "Nothing good could've come of it, I tell you that for sure."

"How can you say that?" Éamonn demanded hotly. "We're fighting for our freedom!"

"What freedom is that, 'ey? Don't you have three hot meals a day set right before ya? I know y' do because I cook it and put it there!"

"But they dock our wages for it!"

"And you think as a man declaring your sudden freedom, you'll get your meals for free then? And what o' the roof o'er your head, a roof that doesn't leak and isn't made o' thatch! Or the clothes you wear, the uniform o' a coachman? You've had it good, young man, and haven't the sense to know it!" As her voice rose, her diction descended into a less formal language that was more slurred and rough than the one she used in my presence.

"All I'm sayin' is I want to be treated as a man. I want the right to vote and own land. I don't want my children to be born into serfdom without any chance of bettering themselves."

"Ha! What's been good enough for us is not good enough for your children?"

"No, Léana, it is not. I don't want my children treated as less than an Englishman."

"You'd best go to America then."

"With what? Last I checked the passage was not free. And why should I leave my mother country?"

"You've plenty o' time to save for it unless you're about to tell me your lass is pregnant."

"I am not!" Johanna's voice rose in panic.

"And a good thin' for sure," Léana snapped, "or you'd be carted off to the laundries to have the bastard there."

The argument descended into Gaelic, and I only recognized a word here or there as the three servants spoke over one another. Growing impatient, I stomped my feet along the stone and made a bit of a commotion as I entered the room. As I suspected it would, the conversation ceased immediately.

"Good day, m'lady," Léana said politely, though her face was flushed. "I've breakfast ready for you and your usual place set."

Éamonn had arisen from a spot at the far end, and now he quietly made his way to my side, where he pulled out the chair, politely waited for me to sit and then gently pushed me forward before returning to his seat across from Johanna. His face was beet red, as was Johanna's.

I spotted an open newspaper, and just as Léana made to remove it, I placed my hand upon it. "What is this?" I asked.

"Just some silliness, m'lady," she answered, peering angrily at the others.

"I see." I moved the paper closer to read it. *"No parades!"* the title read, followed by *"Irish Volunteer Marches Cancelled"* and *"A Sudden Order."* "There were to have been parades on Easter Sunday?" I asked.

I was met with an uncomfortable silence, and I began to read the short article. *"The Easter maneuvers of the Irish Volunteers, which were announced to begin today, and which were to have been taken part in by all the branches of the organization in city and country, were unexpectedly canceled last night."* The article contained a couple of additional short paragraphs and was signed by Eoin MacNeill, Chief of Staff, Irish Volunteers. "I see," I said as my plate was set in front of me. "These 'Irish Volunteers' were to have participated in a demonstration it seems?"

"Aye, ma'am," Éamonn answered as he stared straight ahead.

"And it says here it was called off at the last minute."

"The last-minute, aye," Éamonn said.

"I see. And this—demonstration—did it perhaps have anything to do with the weapons that did not arrive in Ireland?"

Léana made a strangled sound and turned away, shaking her head. Éamonn and Johanna simply looked at one another as though a family member had died.

"I see," I said again. I took a sip of my tea and continued, "I will be going into Dublin this morning."

"Dublin, ma'am?" Éamonn said.

"That is correct. There is an art gallery I wish to see. I am not quite sure where it is, but I understand it is within a block or two of the GPO."

"The GPO, ma'am?" his head jerked toward me.

"The General Post Office," I said though I was quite certain he knew the acronym. "Is there a problem with that?"

"No, m'lady," Léana said. "It is not a problem today."

I nodded and took a bite of sausage. "Then I shall be ready to leave once I have finished my breakfast."

As Éamonn left to ready the carriage, Léana began kneading soda bread for the night's supper. Johanna remained behind, her hands folded in her lap, and her food left untouched. The room grew so silent that I could hear my own lips smacking as I ate, a sound I detested because it reminded me of Stratford. But as the minutes ticked by, my heart grew lighter. I was going into Dublin today, a bustling, vibrant city I rarely visited, and I was going to see my art in a gallery.

The art gallery was so close to the GPO that I could see the imposing building with its enormous row of columns as I exited my carriage on Sackville Street and prepared to enter the gallery. I instructed Éamonn to remain at the carriage, as I assumed I would be inside no more than a few minutes. It had been the journey into the city that I had craved as much as anything, the simple act of breathing fresh air some distance from Matherscourt. Neither Nicky nor Peter had arrived to work on the orangery or the gazebo, and none of their men had either. I had to get out.

The gallery was hushed like a fine museum. Only one other couple was inside their whispered murmurings about each painting, the only sound. A gentleman came from behind a massive mahogany desk to inquire how he could help me.

"I should like to look about," I said as though I arrived at galleries such as his every day. "Is there anyone you particularly suggest?"

"It all depends upon your taste, Lady Mather. Dadaism is, of course, all the rage."

"No," I said. "I much prefer something more traditional."

"Ah."

"Tell me, what sells these days?"

"It all depends upon who is buying. The Swiss and the Americans prefer European avant-garde. Old families prefer fox hunting, landscapes, French Impressionism…"

"Monet?"

"Precisely. The more horrific the war, the more people crave serenity in their art, it seems."

"I should like to see those please, Mister—?"

"Declan McClearn, ma'am. Right this way."

I was led into the next room, and for the next few minutes, I became like the couple: my chin cupped within my hand, staring deep into each painting for the messages, inspiration, and emotion elicited there. Unlike the couple, I sought to understand the colors used, how they played upon the mood, as well as the style used and the focal point. I was very pleasantly surprised when I spotted my own paintings upon fancy easels flanked by famous artists, and I was comparing one of mine to a better-known work of art when Declan returned.

"Ah, you like that one?" he said.

"Who is the artist?"

"Anonymous. His paintings are smuggled out of war-torn Europe at great risk."

"Are they now?"

"Indeed. They are some of our more expensive works due to the high peril involved."

"They cannot simply ship them?"

Declan laughed, his chuckle sounding a bit condescending. "Not amid the Great War, ma'am."

"I see."

He cleared his throat. "The artist began with charcoal sketchings. I believe I have one or two still in the windows."

I followed him into the front room, where the couple was preparing to leave. They spoke briefly, indicating they would return later once they'd made up their minds, and then the gallery belonged only to Declan and myself.

As he began to remove one of the sketchings from the window display, my eyes looked past him to Sackville Street, where a growing number of people were marching down the center of the street toward the GPO.

"What is happening?" I asked.

"Oh, it is nothing," Declan replied. "The Irish Volunteers march down the street on a regular basis. They go to the GPO or Dublin Castle, demonstrate their marching ability, you know, and then they all go home."

"They march with broomsticks and mops," I murmured.

He chuckled. "That is correct. Broomsticks and mops. Now, if I could show you—"

"Then why are they carrying weapons today?" I asked.

He did a double-take and then, as if his eyes had deceived him, stepped outside for a closer view. I followed him, my eyes riveted to the tight formation and serious countenance of the marchers. Women marched alongside men, and ages ranged from teens to the elderly. Many of the men were dressed in suits and ties, and many of the women were in their finest clothing with feathered hats. Others wore a uniform of sorts complete with sashes. Most carried rifles over their shoulders, and all seemed to be smiling as if they were on display in a momentous parade.

A crowd began to gather, following alongside the marchers, and I forgot about the art gallery as I was swept into the flow. I heard Éamonn calling my name, and when I turned to look back, I found him trying to reach me through the throngs, and in the corner of my eye, I saw Declan closing and locking the gallery as he, too, joined the gathering.

"Lady Mather," Éamonn said breathlessly as he came alongside me, "it is not safe here for you. I must take you home."

"Come," I said, grabbing his hand. "Let us see what they're about."

I was proud of the Irish, I realized, as we were swept along. I was proud of their smiles, their determination, the passions burning in their souls to be free and independent people. I spotted several countesses from Eliza's parties marching in their midst, and as I realized this transcended social classes and monetary status, I wondered if Countess Markievicz was there as well. The movement rose above the divide that had existed between men and women, relegating women to a lower status; for here, they walked shoulder to shoulder as equals.

I tried to find Nicky in the marchers, but I could not. I knew he was there; he had to be there. I wondered which of those rifles and pistols had been hidden at Matherscourt. It was as if blinders were swept away from my eyes and I saw things not as two lovers finding one another atop a hidden cache of weapons, but of two souls caught up in something far greater than themselves. It was far larger than anything we could possibly have imagined in our lifetime, and I knew, I simply knew, I was part of history for here, right here in this very spot, Ireland as a free and independent nation would be born once more.

The marchers stopped at the GPO, and the crowd gathered around as one man began to take center stage. With a flourish, he unfurled a piece of paper he held in his hands, dabbing once at an imaginary tear—or perhaps, not so imaginary, after all—before his voice rang out clear and strong.

"Patrick Pearse," Éamonn whispered in my ear. "He's a poet."

"Irishmen and Irishwomen," Patrick began, "In the name of God and of the dead generations from which she receives her old tradition of nationhood, Ireland, through us, summons her children to her flag and strikes for her freedom."

As he spoke, an arm of the marchers broke through the doors into the GPO and shouts could be heard inside. Only a moment later, workers and customers began rushing out as the enormous structure was cleared. The British flag was taken down and another erected in its stead; a flag containing three bars, one each of orange, white and green. Another man appeared to be ordering the marchers with great authority. He was older than Pearse; handsome, his face kindly, he spoke politely and calmly, but I could not make out his words. With each group he spoke to, they rushed this way and that, following his orders.

"Who is he?" I asked Éamonn.

He searched the crowd for the man I pointed toward. "Ah. James Connolly. He's the founder of the Irish Socialist Republican Party."

"The founder, you say?"

Patrick Pearse was finishing his proclamation.

It occurred to me that when a rebel force rose up to change the leadership of a country, one might anticipate the current ruling party to push back; yet I did not see any British authorities at all. "Where are the British soldiers?" I asked.

A man standing next to me overheard my question and said, "County Meath. The races, you know."

"They've left the city?"

He shrugged. "Public holiday."

I began to feel a surreal emotion surging over me. Perhaps when the soldiers returned, the rebellion would have taken place, and the strategic buildings—of which the

GPO was one—would already be in the hands of the new government. There would be nothing left to do but for the British to return to their own island.

The proclamation read, the volunteer Irish soldiers began spreading out as a ripple went through the crowds. They were seizing not only the GPO but the entire city.

"I must find Nicky," I said frantically.

"Nicky?" Éamonn repeated, his brow furrowed.

"Are you part of this rebellion?" I asked, pulling him close so only he could hear.

He hesitated.

"Tell me now if you are."

He stepped back to look into my eyes. His were wide, intelligent, courageous. I watched as pride seeped in, and his backbone turned ramrod straight. "I am."

"Then go. Do your duty."

He took a step away from me before turning abruptly back. "But my duty is to you. I must get you home safely."

"Don't be silly," I laughed. "Go now. Join them. If you bother to take me home and come back, the rebellion will be over!"

He looked as though he wanted to say something, but after an awkward moment, he said simply, "Thank you, ma'am."

The last I saw of him, he was winding his way through the throngs of people and straight for James Connolly.

28

My initial euphoria morphed into despondency within a few short hours. I knew from countless conversations with Nicky that once the rebellion had begun, the leaders anticipated Irishmen and Irishwomen to rise up with them, increasing their numbers by the hour. But as I walked the streets of Dublin center, the city that I knew was no more.

In front of the GPO, a mob of angry women pelted the windows with stones, swearing at the rebels to give up the building. These were women whose husbands were on the front lines of the Great War, fighting alongside the Brits against the Triple Alliance. The soldiers' checks were mailed home, and with the post office closed, mothers were in a near state of riot, unable to feed their children or pay their rents until they received those checks.

Large numbers of the city's poorest inhabitants were already rioting. The art gallery, along with every shop within blocks, had been looted, their windows were broken, doors shoved in. Europe's most infamous slums were right here in Dublin, and every family down on its luck appeared to be taking advantage of the situation to steal everything from food to clothing to furniture—and even things they did not need. I saw young women dressed in rags wearing two and three fine feathered hats, one atop the other, pilfered from millinery shops, and I spotted barefoot women wearing fine furs. I witnessed men carting off furniture and even a piano. I watched as art was carried into the muddy streets and toted off, and try though I might I could not imagine the insanity of three generations existing in a one-room apartment with artwork on the walls worth thousands of pounds. The groceries had been looted as well, the shelves bare, the floors littered with spilled contents of opened boxes. Those shop owners that remained had either been forced to step aside, or they were brutally pummeled right before my eyes.

I watched as a rebel soldier here or civilian there tried to reason with the looters, urging them to join the rebellion and not destroy that for which they were fighting, but their appeals fell upon deaf ears.

I learned through murmurings during my wandering that the GPO was just one of several places around the city that had been seized in much the same manner. Saint Stephens Green, the square with beautiful gardens that Stratford's office overlooked, was under rebel control. So were Jacobs Biscuit Factory, Four Courts, South Dublin Union, and Bolands Mill. Nicky could be at any one of those places or rushing from one to another as I saw many doing.

My carriage was overturned and stripped alongside the road where Éamonn had left it as we'd followed the marchers to the GPO, and the horse was gone. I inquired at the GPO for Éamonn but was told he'd been given orders and was elsewhere—where the rebel soldiers did not know or would not say. My world was turned upside down amidst chaos, and I felt as though I was searching for my rightful place.

Amid the maelstrom, I realized a silence was falling upon the rioters like a heavy cloak as all eyes turned to the end of the street. I pivoted in the same direction to discover

British soldiers lined up on horses, the animals nearly shoulder to shoulder, so they stretched across the entire breadth of Sackville Street.

This street might have been one of the widest streets in all of Dublin. It was a major thoroughfare filled with people crossing from one side to the other, dodging horse-drawn carriages and automobiles. There was an eerie standoff of sorts as the soldiers simply sat there, a horse impatiently pawing at the ground or flicking a tail, against a ragtag group of civilians from the soldiers' wives to the looters to businessmen in suits and women such as myself, while the rebels remained inside the fortifications of the GPO.

Then a man in the front line center raised one arm high. When it was lowered, the cavalry charge began.

In an instant, everyone scrambled to get out of their way; women rushing for the safety of the building walls, men lifting children as they raced for cover. An elderly man could not move quickly enough and was struck down by one of the first horses and trampled by the rest. Merchandise was dropped in the street to be pummeled by the horses' hooves. And amidst the charge, the soldiers began to fire.

The silence had been replaced with men shouting, women screaming, and children crying. I realized I was also screaming, my voice filling my ears but drowned out by the chaos. These were civilians, my frantic mind raged. Yet they were being mowed down as though they were German soldiers on the front lines of a defined battlefield.

The images were seared into my mind—an elderly woman shot in the back as she ran for cover, a child maimed by a horse as her mother tried vainly to pull her to safety, a boy not quite a teenager shot multiple times.

Then I felt strong arms grab me from behind and yank me into a narrow alley. I screamed and fought, but my cries were lost in the pandemonium, my kicking feet and pummeling hands no match for the man I could not see.

"Lady Mather! Lady Mather!"

The words sunk into my mind, and yet I could not stop screaming. It wasn't until he placed a hand over my mouth to silence me that I began to recognize the voice.

"Lady Mather, it's me—Sean," he was saying.

I was heaving, and my heartbeat was pounding so fiercely I thought I would faint. But as he slowly let go of me, I forced myself to turn around to look at him. I remembered him as one of the workers in the orangery, a carpenter, I thought. Nicky had been giving him instructions when I'd come to talk with him.

"What the devil are you doing in Dublin?" he was asking. "It isn't safe here for the likes o' you!"

"I—the marches were called off!"

He cursed Eoin MacNeill under his breath before ending, "You must get out of Dublin. It isn't safe here for you."

"I see that!"

"Then what the devil are you still doin' here?"

I caught my breath, forcing it to slow to a reasonable rhythm. "My carriage has been destroyed; my horse is gone. My coachman has joined the uprising."

"Then find another horse or carriage. Steal one if you have to." He pointed toward the end of the alley. "Make your way through there and quickly. The soldiers will be spreading out, mark my words. Stay to the south and get o'er the bridges as fast as you can."

"Where is Nicky?"

"Nick—no. You cannot join him."

"I didn't ask you if I could. I asked where he is."

He took a step back and peered at me. "I don't know."

"You do—"

"We were all at Liberty Hall. I was given my orders before his unit was given theirs."

"You weren't together—?"

"—But Peter was sent to Dublin Castle."

"The castle!"

"It is not safe for you anywhere in the city, do you hear me? The countryside will be swarming with Brits and Irish as well. Your only hope is to get home quickly and remain there."

My mind was racing, his words barely registering.

"I cannot help you," he was saying lamely. "I've a mission to run." He slipped a piece of paper halfway out his pocket. "I must get this to James Connolly."

I nodded.

"That way," he said, pointing again toward the end of the alley. "And hurry!"

He gave me a shove, and I began to run, yanking up my dress to prevent tripping. Somewhere along the way, I lost my hat, and my hair began to come undone, but I no longer cared. At the end of the alley, I dodged this way and that as I raced down one alley after another, skirting looters, lines of drying clothes, muddy holes, and garbage.

Somehow I made it to the River Liffey, running along the waterfront until I found a bridge that was not manned and zipped across, afraid at any moment that the British would mow me down. If there was one lesson to be learned on Sackville Street, it was the fact that women, children, and civilians were fair game, and the Great War had come to Ireland.

Once across the bridge, heaving along the main thoroughfare, I passed the Christ Church Cathedral where people were being ushered in to escape the carnage, before winding my way around it and through this street and that until I was a block from Dublin Castle.

29

Dublin Castle was an odd structure, a mishmash of architectural designs that appeared to be squashed together as if strong winds had conjoined several structures of uniquely different styles until they stood wall to wall. Originally built in the 12th century as a medieval fortress with tall curtain walls and four distinct corner towers, a massive fire in 1684 destroyed much of it. As it was rebuilt over the following two hundred years, each addition was styled after the fashion of the day. Though the original castle was built upon a settlement once occupied by the Vikings, the structure had become a symbol of English oppression.

It was impossible to live in Ireland without hearing tales of the poor gathered outside the gates each evening as the wealthy English aristocrats supped. When they'd had their fill, they opened the gates to the poor and watched from the balconies as the leftover food was tossed onto the ground, where the peasants would fight over each morsel like a pack of dogs. I didn't recall hearing when this practice had stopped, but the wounds were still there and handed down from one generation to the next, for in Ireland events that had occurred hundreds of years before were recited as though they had happened only yesterday.

As I made my way around the buildings to the main gate, my eyes repeatedly drifted upward to peer at the windows, expecting to see rebels with guns drawn guarding the structure against attack, but I spotted only concerned faces appearing to look further into the distance of downtown Dublin.

Above the gate stood Lady Liberty, a statue that represented well England's opinion of Ireland. While Lady Liberty stood at many structures around the world, Dublin Castle was the only one in which she faced inward. It had given rise to a popular saying amongst the Irish: The Statue of Justice, mark well her station, her face to the castle, and her arse to the nation.

It wasn't the only anomaly regarding the statue. Lady Justice was usually depicted with a blindfold, symbolizing that justice was equal amongst all, but in this case, her eyes were open. And in what seemed particularly poignant on this day was the fact that Lady Justice was most frequently depicted with the sword pointed downward, the tip against the ground, but at Dublin Castle, the sword was raised as if ready to do battle. If that weren't enough, she was staring at the sword and smiling.

To my surprise, there were several British soldiers at the gate and standing along its nearly ten-foot-tall wrought iron fence overlooking the inner courtyard. There was tension in the air so thick it nearly cut off my breath. Peering around the wrought iron as I slowed my walk, I noted some soldiers coming and going and a very large pool of fresh blood near the front gate.

I began to tremble underneath my clothing, and I hoped it wouldn't be visible. I locked eyes with a guard at the gate, whose eyes narrowed as he watched me suspiciously. I wanted to run, but I had drawn so near, I knew if I turned away now, it would raise more distrust. I had never been much of a runner; I'd had no need, so I knew I might get only two or three steps out before they had me.

But in the role of Lady Mather, having been stranded in the city amid chaos, I had every right to inquire as to the current circumstances. I steeled my back, my eyes still locked on his, and when I came close enough for him to hear me, I opened my mouth to speak.

At that moment, a carriage pulled alongside me, and a clipped British accent called out, "Lady Mather! Whatever are you doing in Dublin?"

I did not recognize the voice, and when I turned to see Peter Bowers opening the door of his carriage, I was astounded. I felt the guard's presence directly beside me, and I answered in as haughty a voice as I could muster, "I have been stranded, sir. My carriage has been destroyed, and my horse stolen by ruffians."

He opened the door wider and stepped out. "I shall take you somewhere safe." He gestured toward the carriage.

As I began to ascend into the carriage, the guard stepped closer to Peter, who was dressed in a suit with a vest and a top hat. Only his shoes betrayed his true standing, and I hoped the guard did not look down.

"Sir, you'll need to get off the streets as quickly as possible. It is not safe for you here."

"Thank you," Peter answered. "I intend to do just that. Tell me, where do you suggest I go?"

"Outside the city center. We're closing off this area, and martial law is being declared."

"Martial law? Have you the men for that?"

"Soldiers are coming from England, sir."

"Very good. And when shall they arrive?" Peter peered around him in disgust. "If they take too long, the city—"

"We don't yet know, sir. Sir, there was fighting here earlier between Dublin Castle and City Hall; we've regained City Hall and arrested the rebels there, but it is not safe here."

"Very well." He was climbing into the carriage to sit beside me. He tipped his hat to the guard, who was stepping back in place even before Peter knocked on the carriage roof for the coachman to resume.

As we took off, both of us began talking at once.

"I am so relieved to see you—"

"Whatever are you doing in Dublin? It isn't safe here!"

"Your accent—"

"Listen," Peter said, his voice returning to the lyrical Irish brogue I knew. "You must get out of the city as quickly as possible. It's chaos here—"

"—I know—"

"—and people are dying."

"I know."

"You are sitting on a cache of weapons," he said with a wry smile.

I sucked in my breath, my hands going to the cushioned seat upon which I sat.

"I am running weapons from one location to another."

"But what happened at Dublin Castle? I expected you to be there—inside, I mean. In charge of it."

Peter sighed deeply and shook his head, his voice low. "I'd been sent to get more weapons. A group approached the castle and was stopped by the guard at the gate—he was unarmed; the name was James O'Brien. He was killed, Penny; possibly the first man shot in the rebellion."

"Oh." I leaned back in my seat.

"The group was then fired upon from the windows of the castle, and they fled. That means," he turned to me in earnest, "we were unable to cut the communications lines from Dublin Castle to the outside world."

"Which means they could contact London," I finished.

"Precisely. You heard the guard; they've already notified them of the uprising. British soldiers will be landing in Dublin."

"What will you do?"

"We will fight. It is all we can do."

"What of the men that tried to capture the castle?"

"Arrested; all of them. Sean Connolly was the leader; he's the one that shot O'Brien. When they couldn't take Dublin Castle, they took City Hall instead. Hell of a fight. Connolly was shot dead by a British sniper."

We turned down an alley and then another. As the carriage came to a stop, I asked, "Where is Nicky?"

Peter's face was grave. "Don't try to reach him, Penny. He can't be distracted from his mission."

"I had no intention of interrupting his duties. I merely asked where he was—for prayer's sake."

"Saint Stephen's Green. Now, I don't intend to be rude, but I shall need you to move so we can transfer these weapons."

As we stepped from the carriage, several men rushed from a nearby factory to unload them. I eyed the buildings at each end, where the street names were painted on the corners of the structures.

"I'll get you a horse," Peter was saying. "It will be easier for you to maneuver through the streets. Head south, and don't stop until you're well outside the city."

He disappeared inside a livery, and perhaps he intended me to follow him, but the moment he was gone, I was off like a shot, my skirt gathered high, so I could run through the alley and into the next one. I had no idea how long he might have been inside the livery and whether he saddled a horse, but I had no need for one. I knew enough of the city from my childhood to know I was mere blocks from Saint Stephen's Green.

30

Saint Stephen's Green was a 22-acre park in the city center. Before my betrothal to Stratford, I had spent many days there wandering the lush green lawns and Georgian gardens and feeding the ducks at the ponds there. My family once lived a few blocks from the site. After my marriage, they sold their property and moved to North Dublin, far from the city center. In the home where I was raised, my grandparents often spoke of the changes in the city and how the site where Stephen's Green now stood was once a combination of grazing land for sheep and marshland suitable only for ducks. In 1664, the park was established with a curtain wall around it, and land overlooking it was sold at premium prices.

The walls had long since been replaced by iron fencing, and the buildings that surrounded it ranged in age, including the offices of Stratford Mather & Associates. I was told when his name was first mentioned to me by my parents that he had been watching me each afternoon as I strolled the park, oblivious that he was peering through his window at me.

Eventually, he inquired as to my identity and then sought out my parents to ask for my hand despite never having met me. I was vehemently opposed to a marriage of convenience, but I was informed in none too gentle a fashion that I had no say in the matter. I strongly suspected he investigated my family name in-depth, and he made no bones about describing his wealth to my parents, who, as it turned out, had a name but no money thanks to some questionable investments my father had made. I was soon to discover that Stratford's wealth had been greatly exaggerated, and he had profited from my family's name and connections, yet selling their daughter was a means by which my parents could go on living their comfortable lives.

It might have been true that my family could not have gained financially on our own, and neither could Stratford. However, the morning after the wedding ceremony, I informed my parents that I would have nothing else to do with them. I had been sold as a whore so they could live nicely, and I could not, would not, forgive them. It was the last time we had spoken, and that had been over a decade ago. Of course, I had no idea Stratford was impotent and as disgusting as I thought he was, God in His mercy gave me that blessing.

I was pulled out of my thoughts and halted in my tracks when I was still some ways from the Green; motor vehicles, carriages, furniture, and other debris were piled at the entrances of each cross-street, barring access to the Green itself.

"What is your business here?" a gruff man shouted as I drew near. He aimed a rifle at me, his eyes narrowed, and his aim sure.

"I am Lady Mather, and I—"

"I represent the Irish Citizen Army," he spat, "and I don't care who you are. I asked you to state your business."

"I'm a friend of the rebellion—"

"Then state the code."

"The code?"

"Ha! Just as I figured." He waved his rifle toward the distant corner. "Off with you. You'll come no further."

I was no match for him and his weapon, but there was more than one way to get where I needed to be. I backed away, and when I was a few paces distant from the man, I turned down a cross-street. Twilight was beckoning, and soon shadows would descend upon the city, and with it came exhaustion that settled over me despite my best efforts to thwart it. I found it implausible that I could have wandered the streets for so many hours.

I eventually sat on a stoop away from the commotion on the main streets and watched as people rushed this way and that, taking no notice of me there in the shadows of the side street. I replayed the afternoon's events in my mind, of Éamonn offering to take me home just as the rebellion was starting and of Peter's fortuitous appearance at Dublin Castle. Perhaps I should have taken the horse he offered, but what was done was done, and I could not turn back the clock to decide differently.

I remained on the stoop as the shadows lengthened, listening to gunfire erupting around me; shots to the north, then one or two to the west, a gun fired here, a rifle there. Every now and again, there were shouts, mostly men with baritones, their voices authoritative.

With the disappearance of the sun came the biting cold, and I knew I could not remain outside all night. I had to find a safe place where I could lay my head. I rose, my muscles aching with the exertion of the afternoon, and I began to trudge along the street. I expected to see lights in the windows, but they were darkened, doors locked, and no one answered my knocks even though I sometimes heard voices within.

Eventually, I found myself in a narrow alley where the shouting was more distinct, along with sounds that I could not identify. The alley was filled with debris—chairs, desks, phones ripped from the walls, papers flying everywhere as the ever-present Irish winds picked them up to deposit them elsewhere. The entire city center appeared much the same, and now I wished for the fur coat I had spotted earlier. Perhaps that thief was smarter than I'd thought.

As the gloom settled upon me, I realized that I was at the back entrance to my husband's office. Like the storefronts, it had been burglarized, the windows broken, and the door bashed in. I stepped over rubble piled just inside the doorway and felt my way along the hall to the front office. The front door had also been busted down, and between the back alleyway and the front street, I was certain that the office contents had been strewn about several city blocks.

On a wall parallel to the doorway, I discovered a giant mosaic of photographs joined together to comprise several city blocks comprised of townhomes. The whole was mounted in a simple frame under glass, and what drew my attention to it was the fact that someone had written on the glass with a heavy black marker. Each townhome was outlined, and within the outline was a list of last names ranging from a dozen to more than eighteen. Names had been erased over time, leaving behind a blackened smudge, and another name written over the first. The lengthening shadows made it difficult to study further, so I turned back around to face the room.

I could see the Green from the doorway, I realized with a start. Cautiously, I made my way close to the door where I watched men making their rounds on the outside of the rail fencing, their rifles at their shoulders. Recalling the man that had halted my progress, I stepped back into the darkness of the inner room lest I be sent on my way again. Then remembering the staircase that led to Stratford's personal office where he had observed me from the window so many years ago, I raced back down the hallway and up the stairs.

Men were digging trenches just inside the railing. I felt like a bird in the trees as I peered down upon the Green, all 22 acres of it. Men dug feverishly as though they were at the front lines of the Great War, anticipating a battle come the morn.

Due to the distance from the Green to Stratford's office as well as the lengthening shadows, I could not identify whether any one of those men was Nicky, and I had enough wits about me to understand that I could not safely approach them in the darkness of night. I would wait out the night here in the relative warmth of my husband's office—there was no fire, and I would not start one, lest I give away my position, but I was out of the elements at least. And come the morning, I would try again to reach Nicky. I would not, as I promised Peter, attempt to dissuade him, but rather, I would come to be at his side to help in the fight for freedom.

I pulled up a chair just out of the line of sight from the window, lest I be seen, yet I could continue to watch the trenches being dug and men continuing to fortify the barricades. Yet I was there in the offices where they were apparently taking no notice, and just as I lost my battle to remain awake and slipped into an exhausted but fitful slumber, I realized their strategy made them sitting ducks.

31

I awakened to the sound of voices. Still groggy, it took me a moment to register where I was; I had fallen asleep in a chair beside the window sometime during a long and unsettling night with shouts and occasional gunfire penetrating the darkness. My back was aching horribly from the unnatural position I'd managed to get myself into, and I stood on wobbly legs in an attempt to stretch out my crooked spine. It took another moment for me to realize the voices were not outside as I'd originally assumed but were downstairs in Stratford's office.

My first notion was Stratford himself, returning to the city to resume his work, unaware his office had been burgled. That was followed quickly by a supposition that Nicky had somehow found me.

But as I made my way down the hall to the stairs, both were dashed by British voices, their accents distinct from all classes of Irish. I was at the top of the stairs when I was spotted. The soldier already had his weapon out and pointed it upward while shouting, "Halt, where you are! Hands up! Hands up, I say!"

My first impulse was to run, and I knew I would have a decent head start as he had to climb the stairs. But that was dashed immediately by the realization that I had nowhere to go. I held my hands high and responded, "I am unarmed. I am—"

"How many are with you?" he demanded.

His question took a moment to sink in.

"How many?" he yelled as more soldiers joined him.

"Just me," I answered.

They reached the top of the stairs, and the soldier closest to me whirled me around and threw me against the wall as he began to rifle through my clothing.

The wind was knocked out of me, and it took me a moment to find my voice. "I am Lady Mather—"

"I don't give a flying rat's ass who you are."

"Put her in that room there," another voice said. The younger soldier stepped to the side, and I laid eyes on a slightly older man. I did not understand British ranks, but from the way the others obeyed, I knew he was most likely the man in charge. "Fan out. Check all rooms."

"I am Lord Mather's wife," I said to him as I was unceremoniously shoved into the first office. "These are his offices."

He followed me into the room and gestured toward a chair in the corner by the door. "Sit." As I complied, he made his way to the window, where he peered onto the street below and into Saint Stephen's Green. He had a pair of binoculars and took a moment to further survey the surrounding area. Then he half-turned to me. "Yesterday, a Lord's wife meant something. Today it means nothing."

"But you are trespassing! This is my husband's office!"

"And where is your husband?" His eyes narrowed.

"All's clear, Major," a soldier reported, sticking his head into the room.

"Cover all windows facing the park. Get ready for my signal." He turned back to me. "I asked where your husband is."

This time I forced myself to look at his nameplate. "Major Clarke, I do not know where my husband is."

"Is he there?" he nodded toward the Green.

"He is not. We are loyal British subjects."

He eyed the office. "What does your husband do?"

"Financial transactions. Investments."

He turned back to the window. "Like weapons?"

"Like land."

Two soldiers returned to the room. Now that I had caught my breath and my initial surprise had abated, I leaned forward in the chair to observe and began to formulate my plan, even though I had no idea whether I would be permitted to leave. The two soldiers facing the major were markedly different. One was a young man, possibly no older than twenty. His eyes were as wide as saucers, his hand appearing permanently attached to his weapon. The other was perhaps in his thirties, but his countenance caused him to appear much older. His skin was weathered and his eyes were nearly soulless, the eyes of a man that is looking beyond what is in front of him. Unlike the other, his weapon rested against his back shoulder by its strap. I realized immediately these were the reinforcements expected from Britain. The older soldier had most likely seen plenty of combat in the Great War, while the younger had possibly never seen fighting before now.

Major Clarke had resumed his observation through the window. "Sergeant," he said, beckoning the more seasoned of the two to his side. He handed him the binoculars. "You see that building over there? That would be the Shelbourne Hotel. British troops are amassing there now. When the firing begins, you'll see friendly fire—alert the troops to that. We will all be firing down upon the square."

"Yes, sir." The sergeant started to hand the binoculars back to the major.

"There's more," Major Clarke said. "The United Services Club there." He pointed as the sergeant dutifully peered through the binoculars. "Those are British troops there as well."

"Yes, sir." He turned to the other soldier. "Private, alert all troops along this side of Saint Stephen's Green that firing will begin precisely at seven o'clock—just as daylight is beginning. Instruct them to open all windows and assume positions. They will hear my voice when firing is to commence. Alert them to the location of our other forces."

As the private quickly left on his mission, the two remaining men spoke in lower tones, their attention on the park below. My mind began to race. I had been to the Shelbourne Hotel many times. It had originally been three separate townhouses overlooking the square, but in 1824 a wealthy Irishman from Tipperary acquired all three and converted them into a hotel. He'd named it after William Petty, the 2nd Earl of Shelbourne, an Irish born British loyalist who had served as the Prime Minister in the waning years of America's Revolutionary War, eventually securing peace with the new nation.

The building itself was five stories high in addition to an attic and roof, all of which could easily be used to fire down upon the unsuspecting rebels below. Made of brick and concrete, the rebels' handguns and rifles would be no match for the British fire; the British soldiers need only point their scopes downward and have men in their sights, while the rebels would have to return fire by aiming specifically at the windows or roof. I was obviously no soldier, but I would much rather fire down than up.

Like the Shelbourne Hotel, the United Services Club was made of brick and concrete and was only slightly shorter, boasting four stories with five at its center. Unlike the hotel, however, its roof was flat, which made it ideal for shooters to lie prone, nearly invisible as they shot the men below.

My stomach began to twist inside me. I had studied history in school—as did most of the Irish in my class—and I remembered well the stories of Gaelic Irish kings fighting the Vikings, the Normans, and the British. They always sought higher ground. Castles were built to fire down upon invaders; curtain walls were built in place of trenches for the same reason.

And now I realized the tactical blunder these Irishmen had made, and Nicky was among them. I pictured the actors, the poets, the school teachers that Nicky had spoken of; these were their leaders. Was there a true soldier among them? I didn't think so. The more educated might have been accountants, lawyers, architects—but would any of them understand the need to take the higher ground? For surely, my racing mind argued, those buildings were emptied the day before as they were digging their trenches below.

"Countess Markievicz," Major Clarke was saying, "our spies tell us she is dressed in a uniform of sorts, but she wears a unique hat—large, with tall feathers. If you spot her, let me know. We're to take her out. Their leader is Michael Mallin. Unfortunately, I'm told his description is similar to half the men under his command."

I heard running in the hallway behind me, and a moment later, soldiers assumed their positions at the windows. To my horror, they were not bearing rifles, as the Sergeant and Private had; they were bearing machine guns.

I felt all the blood drain from my body, leaving my skin covered in cold perspiration. I could no longer feel my heart beating or my breath escaping me, leaving me to wonder if I was succumbing to shock.

The shadows in the room began to lift much more quickly than I prayed they would, for, with every minute that passed, we drew closer to the sunrise. The mists were still heavy, and the sun barely a sliver when Major Clarke, having apparently been waiting for a signal from the hotel through his binoculars, gave the sergeant the command. The sergeant leaned only slightly out of the window and shouted the command in a booming voice that reverberated through the room. As the command was picked up and shouted along the line, the world erupted in gunfire.

I witnessed the scene unfolding before me in slow motion as if time had somehow been warped so the images could penetrate my being in a scene I knew would haunt me the rest of my life. The soldiers below had clearly been caught off guard. I heard men scream in the distance as if they'd been hit and with every shriek, I knew it was Nicky, and I prayed it was not.

Then my body came to life, and my feet found their footing. With the men concentrated on the battle and my presence seemingly forgotten for the moment, I ran. I raced down the empty hall past rooms filled with men firing, their backs to me as they faced the square. I rushed down the staircase and into the alley behind the building, only to find it filled with army vehicles and occasional soldiers guarding them as the fighting commenced.

I slowed my step and straightened my spine, and I walked straight past them, never meeting their eyes. I forced my face into stone, my eyes as soulless as the sergeant's I'd left behind, my head high and my hands clutching my shawl against the morning chill.

It was only when I had managed to get several blocks away, moving from alley to alley, that I stopped and dry-heaved against debris piled up in the street—bicycles, furniture, and household items. As men began rushing from the surrounding homes, pulling on their suspenders as the fighting registered and mothers shouted for their children to get down and remain in place, that I began to run.

32

The entire city was burning. The landmarks I had known since I was only a child had been bombed into rubble, the roofs collapsed and bricks crumbled into tall heaps. Wood structures, primarily habitats of those less fortunate, had been set afire, whether on purpose or the result of an accident as fire reigned down. It appeared as though the Great War had arrived with a vengeance on Irish shores, brought here by a small group of Irish dreamers intent on shaking loose Britain's hold.

But the British had two years of seasoned fighting behind them, of charging into battle against the German's formidable fighting force, of bloodshed, maiming, and killing. In comparison, the small band of Irish—perhaps numbering in the hundreds, certainly not the thousands—had only handguns and rifles.

As I wandered the streets of Dublin, I discovered they were spread around the city center, and the streets leading in and out had been blocked by British troops that were descending on the island in the thousands. It was a noose, and I was caught in it, and it was closing ever more tightly as the British took more ground and made additional arrests.

The Irish people that James Connolly, Patrick Pearse, and Michael Mallin, among others, counted upon to join their rebellion did not rise up. They met the British troops with cheers, bringing them food and water. And as the rebels were captured, they spat upon them and jeered at them as they were brought to Kilmainham Gaol. Women fared worse, called whores and harlots, their hair was pulled, and they were pummeled by other women before British soldiers were forced to step in to protect them.

And still the small band of Irish patriots fought on.

I could not reach Saint Stephen's Green. Machine guns and cannon fire had pelted it beyond recognition. The streets were filled with rumors, some outrageous and others possible when I heard the rebels that could still walk had retreated to the Royal College of Surgeons of Ireland.

I knew the building but had never ventured inside. It was two stories of brick at the corner of York Street, a formidable building in normal times, but these were not normal times. I had but two options in my thoughts: to believe Nicky was still on the Green or believe him to be in the RCSI.

If he was on the Green, it meant he was wounded or dead. I could not think the latter; I simply could not. And if I pictured him wounded on the field, bleeding out, I became frantic with the knowledge that I must go to him and help him despite any risks to my own safety. As I made my way around the Green, I found I could get no closer than two blocks away, and even from that distance, I heard wounded men calling out for help. I wanted to go to them, to patch their wounds with my unseasoned hands, to bring medical care to them the best I could, but my efforts were thwarted at every turn.

Eventually, the cries stopped. As the gloom of dusk set in, I did not know if those men whose voices I heard had succumbed to death, or their cries had grown softer with weakened bodies, or they had been carried from the field.

If they'd been removed, it was the British that had taken them; for, when the Irish retreated to the RCSI, the British had gained the ground left behind.

The air was filled with black smoke, the acrid odor of gunpowder and fires melding together and carried on the heavy winds. I had not eaten since the day before, and I fought an ever-growing weakness as I made my way through the streets and alleys. The racing I had done earlier had slowed to walking and now to a weakened amble, my feet blistered, my head aching and my clothing permeated with the stench of battle.

I sat down heavily on steps in front of a rowhouse that stood darkened and desolate. I no longer knew where I was; as I peered around me in the growing shadows, I supposed I had reached the slums of which Stratford had complained.

I had only been on the stoop for a few minutes when the door cracked open behind me. "What in God's name are you doing sitting out there?" a woman's voice whispered hoarsely. "Did you not know there is a curfew?"

I stood on shaky legs and grabbed hold of the railing to steady me.

"Get in here with you," the woman said, opening the door slightly wider.

I followed her inside, and she shut the door behind me. It took my eyes a moment to adjust to the darkness. No candles were lit, no oil lamps burning. As I adjusted, I spotted her moving down the hall away from me, and I lamely followed.

The doors were open along the hallway, revealing a state of squalor I had never before experienced. I knew these rooms must have been parlors, dining rooms, children's nurseries, and other living areas, but each room had been converted into an apartment of sorts, and some had makeshift walls sectioning one room into two. My mind struggled to grasp that each space was meant to house a family, and one after the other, I saw a mother, a father, and several children staring back at me.

When I entered the back room, I was astonished to find another family huddled around a tiny table laden with material, and I quickly realized every member of the family was put to work hand-sewing clothing. I had heard this occurred in Dublin; I had heard they were paid by the piece, no matter how long it took them to sew, and I had heard their payments were meager, barely enough on which to live. Now their eyes grew wide and questioning as I entered. There was but one candle burning in the middle of the table, too weak to provide light beyond their frightened faces.

"Have a sit," the woman said.

A boy of perhaps fourteen jumped up to offer his chair, and I gratefully sat down. As I joined them, I counted seven faces ranging in age from the mother, who might have been close to thirty, and six children from a girl of perhaps sixteen down to an infant she bounced on her lap while she sewed.

"My name's Nora," the mother said. She poured me a glass of water from a dented tin pitcher and plopped it in front of me.

I drank it as though I had been in a desert, my first liquid since the day before. "I'm Penny," I answered as I finished.

"What on earth are you doing wandering around such?"

"I was caught in the city when the fighting began."

"So you're not from Dublin, 'ey?"

"Just outside of Dublin."

She leaned back in a chair across from me. "Well, you won't be returning home this night. If the British had found you on my stoop instead of myself, you'd be on your way to gaol this minute, you would indeed."

One of the younger children sniffled, causing my attention to skirt from one to the other.

"My husband's at the front," Nora said, "if you're wondering where their father is."

"I wasn't, but I appreciate his service."

She sniffed. "At least someone does. Two years he's been gone now. All over Europe, he's been, risking his life day after day. Then a group of misfits and ne'er-do-wells take over Dublin, deny me my weekly check, and how am I to feed all these children without it?"

"I wish I could help you," I said. I fumbled for the tiny coin purse in my skirt pocket.

"Nonsense," she said, brushing my efforts away.

"Then thank you for the water," I said, rising. "It's the first I've had since yesterday morning."

"And just where do you think you're going?"

"I—I have to try to get home."

"Not tonight, you don't. Did you not hear me that the moment you walk out the door, you could be arrested?"

"But—"

"You'll stay here. There was an eviction here yesterday, so a room is vacant unless another has moved in. The landlord's manager will be back in the morning for sure but you might not be detected if you leave bright and early. Otherwise, you'd have to pay for your night or be jailed as a squatter."

The eldest boy stood. "I'll go check on it, Ma."

"That's a good boy, Jamie."

As he left the room, I protested, "But I couldn't possibly—"

"Yes, you could, and you are." She cocked her head. "Do you hear that?"

I hesitated as I listened. "I don't hear anything."

She cackled. "The silence is our neighbors listening to *us*." She rose. "It's best we be quiet now. With darkness setting in, we all need to sleep, and perhaps with the morning sunrise, all of this will be over." She picked up the smallest child from her daughter. "I wish I could offer you something to eat, but I have nothing. As I said, the check—"

"I understand. I only wish I could do something for you."

"It's what neighbors do, 'ey?" She arranged her blouse. "At least this wee one will eat, won't you now?" She nodded to her eldest as she began to breastfeed. "Show her the way, Afric."

"Thank you," I answered. "I will not forget your kindness." As Afric led me into the hallway, I was struck by the darkness. "The candle—"

"Everyone wants it dark," Afric said. "Best the British think we've fled than to call attention to ourselves by a light."

Her skirt swayed in the darkness, the lighter pattern assisting me in the most primitive manner so I could find my way behind her. Up a narrow set of stairs, we went, stairs that creaked and groaned under our weight as if they were ready to collapse. The railing consisted of a hodge-podge of wood that was so rickety that I thought it best not to rely upon it at all. At the top of the stairs, Afric turned toward the last doorway. "That's the room there."

I held onto the wall to make my way to the rear bedroom. Along the way, I passed several bedrooms that might have been an adequate size once upon a time, but now each had been divided into two apartments. With the gloom setting in, I could barely make out the silhouettes of each family, and I felt more than saw them watching me as I made my way to the back room.

Jamie met me at the door. "I cracked the curtains a bit," he said, "so you could see your way to the bed. Be sure to stay away from the window, though, other than to close them."

"Am I safe here?" I whispered.

His eyes grew wide as though he'd been taken aback by my inquiry. "Safer in here than out there."

"Thank you," I said, but he was already starting down the hall.

There was no door. Instead, I found myself facing a wall right down the middle of the open doorway. On one side was a family, so I squeezed through to the other side. The slight bit of light that managed to make its way inside shed a finger across a thin pad on the floor before making its way up the wall to the window, which was shared by both sides. I made my way there first, gently pulling the thin curtain aside enough for me to survey my surroundings. I was peering into a courtyard that was crisscrossed with laundry lines where a sheet and a few items of clothing still hung as though forgotten. At each corner, the square opened into a street only narrow enough to be an alleyway. All the windows remained dark, though as I continued to stand there, I heard a murmur of voices next door. Nora hadn't been joking; the walls were as thin as paper. There was absolutely no privacy at all.

Eventually, I made my way to the pad, keeping the curtains open so I could see my way. With all my clothes on—even my shoes—I lay across the thin mattress, feeling the wood floor beneath my bones.

I was roused from slumber by the sound of voices and heavy pounding. I jumped up from the bed and quickly made my way into the hall, where all the families were gathering. A woman was screaming in the rowhouse to our right, and children began to wail. A young man's voice rose above the others, but his words were lost amid other voices, older men's voices, issuing orders.

From across the courtyard, other voices began in the same manner. Women screamed, children cried, men issued orders.

Then more pounding began, and this time, it was at our ears. It began simultaneously on the floor below and as though in concert, the walls of both floors began to crumple as men on the other side hacked their way through with axes and sledgehammers.

"What are you doing?" a young woman screamed as the children began to cry.

I reached for one of the smallest—a girl perhaps no more than two years of age—and lifted her into my arms. As she began to wail, I bounced her on my hip as I stroked her hair and tried vainly to calm her as I leaned over the balustrade to watch the people below.

"How many men have you here?" One of the soldiers demanded as they stepped through the wall from one rowhouse to the other.

"Have you no manners?" I heard Nora bellowing below. "You can't be bothered to go back down the stairs and out the door to knock on mine?"

The soldier closest to her slapped her across the face. I gasped as she fell backward, the wall behind her preventing her from falling to the floor. "I won't ask you again!" he roared.

"There are no men here," I said, my voice sounding firmer and more confident than I felt. Several of the soldiers below stared up at me. "Her husband is at the front lines fighting for Britain."

"No men, 'ey?" Another soldier hollered. I leaned further over the railing to find him holding Jamie by the scruff of his neck as though he was a kitten.

"He's only a boy," I insisted.

Nora rushed toward him, but she was caught by one of the soldiers. As the men fanned out, they inspected every room and every hiding place, turning over furniture and scattering items, the discordant sound of glass breaking coming from every room. When they were finished some minutes later, they had hauled Jamie and all the men they'd found to a heavily guarded wagon parked in the street. The soldiers left behind began to hack their way into the house to our left.

When the melee was done, I realized there were perhaps three dozen people roused from their sleep on the floor I was on. Each of us could stand in the center of the floor, upper and lower, and peer into every rowhouse up and down the block. The chaos continued all night long, the chorus of children howling and women screeching never-ending as men of all ages—from boys barely teenagers to old men barely walking—were locked up in the wagons.

To the women's demands for answers, they were told only that the men were being taken to gaol, guilty of whatever charges were being placed against them. This was war, and they insisted all men were combatants. In response to the women insisting otherwise—including Nora, who could not make them believe they were British loyalists and her husband was fighting at the front—they were told only to shut their traps, or they would join the men.

Mothers, all of them, were forced to choose between joining their sons, husbands, and fathers in gaol or remaining with the other children. As the soldiers moved further from us, I began to assist the others in righting the furniture and straightening their belongings. Long after we all settled down to sleep once more—this time, looking squarely into the neighbors' apartments—the blocks began to fill with the moans and cries of the women.

I lay in bed with two children, one on either side, my arms wrapped around them. I tried to tell them fairytales to distract them from the unfolding events. Long after they were silent and sleeping, I continued those fairytales to distract myself.

33

I was frantic to find Nicky. I could not imagine, even if someone opened my chest and drove a knife through my heart, that it could ache any more than it did now. I had seen two dawns since the rebellion had begun, each more frightening than the one before. As waves of soldiers continued to arrive on Dublin's shores, I knew there would be no peaceful solution, no passive ending.

I had arisen before the break of dawn, extricating myself from the children I had comforted through the night, tiptoeing down the stairs and out the door, trying not to relive the horror of witnessing Jamie and so many young boys being taken away. I knew the images were seared into my brain, and they would not be forgotten, and I knew once this was over, I would paint them. Perhaps it was just my way of processing what had happened, and perhaps it could help someone else. I soon forgot my plan as I placed distance between myself and the slums as I tried once more to find the Royal College of Surgeons.

Surely the powers that be, those mysterious powers that drove our lives in directions we could never have foreseen, would not have been so cruel as to place Nicky in my path, allow me to fall so hopelessly in love with him, only to wrench him from me in a wicked blink of an eye.

I replayed our last conversation a thousand times as I poked and prodded the circle around the center of the city, those ever-tightening nooses that were wound about the rebel strongholds. I chastised myself thousands of times over; I had been thinking only of myself, only of our love, and I had not seen that larger picture that now slapped me in the face with every turn.

He had told me once that he was wed to Ireland. Nicky had a purpose far broader than the love of a woman. I knew now that he loved Ireland so much he was willing to risk his life to set her free. I would not, could not, allow myself to believe he had already paid the ultimate price, for it was the hope he was still alive that propelled me along, forcing the strength to return to my legs and breath to my lungs even as I struggled with lack of food and water, my skin streaked with the smut of burnt embers and spent gunpowder.

The fog of war hung low over Dublin, mixing with the Irish mists to create unique soot that descended upon everything and everyone. I could not breathe, resorting to ripping a piece from my skirt hem to hold against my nose and mouth. My eyes burned so that everything became like a dark watercolor painting, edges blurred, and objects running one from the other like multicolored paint dripping down the canvas.

I asked everyone I passed if they had word from Saint Stephen's Green. Some swore at me, threatening to turn me in if I had sympathies for the rebels. Others simply shook their heads and moved on. Occasionally, someone would stop and inquire of whom I sought, but the name meant nothing.

Yet it never occurred to me that I should seek a way out of the city and home to Matherscourt. Life with Stratford had been a shallow business arrangement and nothing more, and now that I had loved and lost, I could not give up my search until I found Nicky. Perhaps, I told myself with declining faith, I had not lost him. Perhaps he was somewhere fighting still, the odds so stacked against him yet bravely battling on.

I did not know what I would do once I found him. I understood enough that he would not leave with me, nor should I ask him to; rather, I should stand and fight by his side. It had not been my cause, but his, and yet I could not ask him to do it without me. I would find some way to ease the stress of his calling. I had to.

I rounded a corner and bumped headlong into three men that nearly knocked me down in their haste. When I caught my breath, I asked, "Do you come from the Green?"

"Who is asking?" asked one with narrowed eyes.

"Do you know Nicky—Nicolas Bowers? He was there fighting."

They each shook their heads. One took several steps forward, beckoning for the others to make haste and follow.

"He was fighting on the Green?" another asked me.

I looked into his eyes. They were a brilliant blue, set off further by the streaks of grime that turned his face nearly the color of coal. "Yes," I answered. "He supplied many of the weapons."

"Is that the architect?" the third man asked. His hair might have been carrot red, but now it, too, was streaked with grime.

"Yes," I answered excitedly. "The architect. Nicolas and Peter Bowers—the brothers built cathedrals—"

"He was shot," the man with blue eyes said flatly.

"Where is he?"

He shook his head.

"Is he at the College of Surgeons?"

The man several paces ahead urged them to hurry, his impatience obvious.

The red-haired man shook his head. "They got him out, I think—along with several others."

"Where were they taking him?"

"Lady," the impatient man said, stepping back so I could hear him clearly. "He's most probably dead, and if we don't hurry, we'll be dead, too."

"Shot in the shoulder," the blue-eyed man said. "And the thigh."

I recoiled. "Twice?"

"I'm leaving without the likes of you," the impatient man said, his voice growing husky. The red-haired man began sprinting with him, the two disappearing into a dusky alleyway.

"Wait," I begged, grabbing onto the blue-eyed man as he began to follow them. "Where are they taking the wounded?"

"Out of the city is all I know—if they can. If they stay, they'll be arrested, wounded or no."

"Which direction?"

"What the hell does it matter?"

"Please! Which direction?"

"South."

With that, the man was gone, joining his comrades around the corner, disappearing into the heavy, grimy mists that descended like rain.

I was a horse thief now. There was no sense in trying to sugarcoat it; if I was caught, the punishment would be severe, and my life as I'd known it would never be the same.

But then, I knew my life had changed forever. It changed when I met Nicky.

I'd spent the afternoon trying to get out of the city center, finally finding an alleyway that was sparsely guarded at its end, and when the soldiers made their stroll to the next alley, I seized the chance to rush across it and down another. I heard shouting behind me, but whether they were yelling at me to halt or to someone else, I will never know. I never slowed but zigzagged like a rabbit down one serpentine alley after another until I was far from the city center.

On the outskirts of the city, I stumbled past a stable—God's intervention, I choose to believe—and it took me another hour biding my time until the stable boy had left at sunset. Then I simply waltzed in as though I belonged there, choose a horse, saddled it, and I was off. By the time darkness had set in, I was well south of Dublin.

I chose to believe I was simply borrowing the mare. Somehow when this was all over, I would return her if I could ever find that stable again. Perhaps I would place an advertisement in the Dublin paper—if it managed to survive the insurrection.

With the sun's last vestiges, I found myself at a crossroads. I could turn to the right, and within minutes, I could be at Matherscourt. I could tell Stratford that I had been caught in the city, made my way to his office—in search of him, presumably—and that his office had been ransacked and then commandeered by the British. And yes, it had taken me two more days to get home.

I could have Johanna pour me a piping hot bath in front of the fireplace, and I could soak the grime, soot and gunpowder stench off my skin. I could feel my satiny smooth gown against me, eat a hearty dinner and drink my fill of water and wine, and sleep like there was no tomorrow.

Instead, I spurred the horse onward toward Kippure in search of where the Liffey Head Bog fed icy streams into the River Liffey.

As heavy darkness descended, the silence grew oppressive, each cottage I passed darkened as if empty. I pictured the people inside as Nora and her family had been hiding in plain sight, hoping the soldiers would simply pass them by.

But there were no soldiers as I made my way through Donnybrook. The single road I found myself on was hushed; the only sound that of a distant owl hooting in the darkness. As I continued outside the village, I slowed the horse to a walk. I knew I could not expect it to make the full journey without a rest, and I was contemplating where to stop when the sound of vehicles made the decision for me.

I swiftly guided the horse into a wooded area nearly obscured by long shadows and lack of moonlight, leading her past the initial row of trees where we would be less likely to be spotted. I watched as three vehicles made their way along the road like a convoy. The outline was high, and though I had seldom seen British Lorries, I deduced them as such.

The counterattack against the rebels had reached beyond the city.

34

It was my shivering that awakened me.

I had buried myself in the underbrush, perhaps a quarter of a mile into the woods, tying the horse to a nearby tree. I hadn't believed I could sleep; my mind was filled with the memories of everything I had witnessed and fears of that which I had not yet seen.

Then I heard rapid hooves pounding the ground, and I sprang upward, not bothering to brush the debris off me. I saw the horseman as I made my way to the edge of the woods; alone, he rushed forward as if his life depended upon it. My eyes swiftly roamed the road behind him, but I could see no one in pursuit.

I dashed forward into the roadway as he neared, throwing my hands up to stop him. The horse reared dangerously near my head, and the man swore breathlessly as he quieted the stallion.

"What the devil? Are you daft?" he demanded.

"Please," I begged, coming alongside him, "what word have you?"

He hesitated. Then, "Three people were executed yesterday in Dublin."

"Who were they?"

"Two journalists covering the rebellion and one Irishman; killed by the British."

"Why?"

"The military called them traitors." He made a sound as if to chuckle, but it was obviously forced. "The journalists were British sympathizers," he said incredulously.

"But—"

"There was no trial. They were executed by firing squad."

"Is that what the country has come to? Executing people without trial?"

"Aye, and a lot more than that. You'd best get off the roads and go home before you're caught, accused, and shot."

"But—" He made to spur his horse forward, and I blurted, "Do you know Nicky Bowers?"

His eyes widened before he forced himself to look away from me. "No. I do not."

"But you do," I said, grasping the reins to prevent him from leaving. "I saw it in your face there."

"'Tis your own imagination, it is. Now away with you. I've work to do."

The jingling of a carriage reached both our ears, and he froze, his hands tightening on the reins despite my grasp of them further down. Then he relaxed, but his face was stern as he ordered me to release my grip or be dragged by the horse.

I managed to peer around the horse's head to see an old wagon moving toward us, a figure stooped in front as a tired mule moved along. As they neared, I called out, "She knows me!"

The man looked from the old woman to me and back again.

"You saw me here with Nicky Bowers," I called out, rushing in between the two travelers. "I'm trying to find him."

The old woman's wizened face peered into mine for only a second before looking at the horseman.

"You're Missus O'Rigley," I blurted. "Please, I have to find Nicky!"

"Do you know her?" the horseman said.

She nodded and spoke to him in Gaelic.

He turned to me. "Are you here to help him?"

"I am. I heard he'd been shot, and they were trying to get him out of the city."

"You heard right."

"Do you know where he is?"

He shook his head. "He was bleeding out. You'd best go home." With that, he spurred his horse onward, and the rein slipped quickly out of my hand.

I watched him rushing forward as he had when I first spotted him. He had news, I thought; news beyond the executions. I knew it with all my heart.

"Do you know Sally Gap?" the old woman asked.

I stared at her for a moment as her words sank in. "Is he there?"

She nodded so slightly that I wasn't sure if I'd seen it. "His condition is grave. 'Tis a miracle, it is, that they got him that far."

"But he's alive?"

"As of last evening, but I don't know if he survived the night…"

"But he was alive last night," I said excitedly. "How do I get to Sally Gap?"

35

The road to Sally Gap was undoubtedly at the highest elevation I had ever experienced. The terrain here was wild and sparsely inhabited, and the road not much more than a cattle trail, the skies so close I felt as though I could reach up and touch it. As Missus O'Rigley guided her mule along the precipitous mountain edge, I followed on my horse, hoping the animal was sure-footed for surely a tumble would kill us both. We passed through the clouds—for certainly, that was what they were—mists that swirled around us in such heavy folds that they turned white, and I could no longer see the horse's hooves beneath us or the rickety cart in front of us.

I would never have been able to find this location alone. There were no signs, and the cottages we passed here or there appeared vacant. No dogs were running about, no sheep or cattle on the thick green grass—nothing to show me residents had ever lived here. Occasionally the clouds would clear, and I would look out upon a vista so heavenly it took my breath away. The lakes were pristine, reflecting the skies in all their glory, the shades of green mesmerizing.

Had I been there with Nicky, I no doubt would have wanted to stop and simply gaze until the images were imprinted forever on my mind. I would have yearned to go below to those stunning lakes even if all I did was sit on the banks and allow my soul to experience them.

But today I felt as if each minute was an hour, and with every hour that slipped through my fingers, I wondered if Nicky's life was slipping too. I tried—oh, how I tried!—to convince myself that God would not have placed him in my life only to take him away. I said I was sorry a thousand times in my mind for our last meeting, and if I could be granted only two wishes, I longed to take back all the words I'd said, all the horrible things I'd thought, not realizing that of course there were things bigger than the two of us and he had never meant to use me. The second wish, of course, was we would arrive wherever Nicky had fled to find him walking around with nothing more than a flesh wound that was rapidly healing, a tiny scar the only memento of his part in the insurrection.

Missus O'Rigley did not speak, and I doubt I would have heard her if she had, for the cart jiggled and bounced along the rocky ledge as if it was ready to fall apart at any moment. This was not her emergency, and escorting me into the back of beyond was never meant to be her undertaking, and yet she continued hour after hour until I witnessed the dusk beginning to wipe out the last remnants of the sun.

As the last vestiges of light disappeared, we began a slow and tedious descent along a serpentine trail. Without the warmth of the sun, the cold that set in chilled my skin and reached all the way to my bones. The winds kicked up as though the moon had blown its giant breath into the clouds, at times catching my horse off guard. At those times, he righted himself but hesitated to move onward, spooked by the apparitions that danced in cloud's clothing and the occasional howl of a distant wolf or coyote.

Finally, we found ourselves in the tiniest of villages, if it could even be called such. There were perhaps ten cottages splayed out in a glen, the mountains on either side sheltering it from view. As we made our way past them, a grizzled man or suspicious woman would part their curtains or appear briefly at their doors to watch us go past before the curtain was dropped or the door closed, leaving us to our silent journey.

I longed to get down off this horse; my legs and back ached, and I was so hungry and thirsty I was concerned I would faint. But the horse continued with one step after another until we had passed the cottages and appeared to be heading downward yet again.

Then abruptly, Missus O'Rigley stopped her cart. She took her time settling the reins and climbing out of her cart. I slipped off the horse and waited for her, amazed that she was barely over four feet tall.

"Come," she said after tying the mule and horse to nearby trees. She took off down a trail thick with vines and underbrush that seemed to stand sentry before us and fell back into position as we passed. The trees blackened out any moonlight that might have been, leaving us in complete darkness. I hurried on her heels, afraid she would disappear only feet in front of me, and in the heavy woods, I would be unable to find her or my way back out.

Then the trees parted, and I found myself in a clearing. The tiniest cottage of limestone sat before us. It appeared uninhabited, and my first thought was Missus O'Rigley meant for us to spend the night; despite my exhaustion, I wanted to argue that we continue until I found Nicky. Then the door opened a crack and then wider as we drew near. In the shadows was a tall man. I nearly ran into his arms, but something stopped me; this man was leaner than Nicky. He stepped onto the stoop, his dark hair and the lengthening shadows of dusk shrouding his face.

"Rory!" I called out.

He raced toward me, gathering me into his arms. "Shh," he cautioned. "We ne'er know who may be about." He stepped back from me. "But oh, am I so happy to see you."

"Nicky—is he—?"

"Inside."

I dashed the rest of the way and through the door, but then stopped short. It was a tiny cottage comprised of a single room. Along one side was a fireplace that dwarfed that wall, but only a low fire was smoldering perhaps barely enough to warm the small structure. A strange wood chair sat beside the fire; the back stretched from two or three feet above the seat all the way to the floor, and the seat consisted of four pieces of wood, three which fanned out and one across the front. I'd expected to see Nicky sitting upon it, but I spotted no one.

There was a stirring on the other side, and out of the shadows, Peter's wife Isibeal stepped forward.

"Isibeal," I breathed.

"Oh, Penny, Penny," she said, wiping tears from her eyes.

"Where is he?"

She waved toward the floor in the corner. I surged forward, dropping to my knees on the hard stone floor. It took a moment for my eyes to adjust, and still, I could not see him. "A candle," I said, barely looking behind me.

A moment later, Isibeal moved forward with some of the kindling in an old metal dish. "There are no candles here," she said, her voice weary.

I accepted the dish from her and held it close to Nicky's face. He laid still, his face ashen, his eyes sunken. I could not bring myself to ask; I simply could not. Handing the light back to Isibeal, I placed my head on his chest but could not hear his heart. I held one wrist and then the other.

"Is he—can he be—?" I stammered.

"He is barely alive, but alive nonetheless," she answered. She lowered herself to the floor to sit beside me. "He comes to every now and again," her voice caught, "and when he does, he calls your name."

"I am here, Nicky," I said. His facial expression did not change. "It's me, Penny. I am here."

"The physician says he can hear us," she said, dabbing at fresh tears.

"So, he's been seen by a physician?"

"Aye, and he has. He would be dead now if it weren't for Old Doctor O'Toole."

I held one of Nicky's hands in both of mine. Despite the chill in the air, his skin was scorching.

Isibeal reached into a bucket of water for a torn piece of material and wrung it out. "The water is cold," she said, handing it to me. "I've been trying to keep his temperature down, but…"

I placed the material across his forehead and wiped off the perspiration before bringing it down the side of his face. It was some time before I realized that I was crying. My tears were pouring down my own face and intermingling with the perspiration on his. My heart ached so strongly, so sharply, that I could not imagine I could live through the pain. All the years in which I could not cry seemed to culminate in this one moment, and now I could not stop. My breath grew shallow, each intake searing my throat like no fire ever could. My chest became constricted as though I was held in a blacksmith's tongs. With no regard to the temperature inside the little cottage, my flesh was chilled and heated and chilled yet again until I felt I could no longer go on.

I didn't know when Isibeal left me or when Rory followed. I only knew that I cried until I could cry no more, and through it all, I never stopped pressing the cold fabric to Nicky's temple or his chest or his arms. I had no words, but I knew, somehow I knew, that he heard them in the pine of my heart, the desire of my soul, the yearning of my flesh. He knew I loved him, and he knew I needed him.

When Isibeal returned, it was with a cautious opening of the door. As she joined me, I said simply, "I heard he'd been shot."

"Twice, I'm afraid."

I wiped my burning eyes once more. "Where?"

She pulled back the thin blanket that covered him. "His shoulder there. Shot clean through." She lowered the blanket. "And in the thigh. The bullet was still in him, it was. Doctor O'Toole dug it out and stitched him up."

"Why isn't he awakening?" I whispered hoarsely.

"He lost a lot of blood before they reached us. Truth is he nearly bled out, so he did. So he's weak, and he's a fever."

There was movement behind us, and I turned to Rory.

"Missus O'Rigley is staying the night in the Flattery cottage," he said. His voice, like his mother's, was weary. "And I moved your horse into an old stable and gave him hay and water."

"Thank you. Was it you that brought Nicky here?"

He shook his head. "I tried to stop him—and I tried to stop my da, too." His voice took on a trace of bitterness. "I told them to wait; that guns and fighting was not the answer. I wanted to—" his voice broke "—to go to university and get my law degree and fight for our independence in the courts, not like this."

"Were you in Dublin?" Isibeal asked.

I nodded. "I've been searching for Nicky."

"Did you happen to see—I mean, of course, you wouldn't—"

"Peter? I did. I did, indeed." My face brightened. "He was well when I saw him. In fact, he was riding in a fine carriage right under the noses of the British, and they didn't suspect a thing. He's got quite the British accent when he wishes, he does."

Isibeal laughed, her voice soft. "He enjoys poking fun at the Londoners when he returns from his trips."

"Well, the imitation came in quite handy." I squeezed her hand. "He'll be alright."

Behind us, Rory made a choking sound.

"The volunteers are trying to keep us informed," Isibeal said. "Have you heard the latest?"

I told her of the man on horseback and how Missus O'Rigley arrived in time to take me to Nicky. "The man said the journalists were actually British sympathizers, but they were shot by the British anyway, and I don't know anything about the Irishman, I'm afraid."

She nodded. "It's a sad time for sure. I'm surprised you didn't pass another volunteer on the road, but I suppose he would have hidden had he seen you first."

"Are you saying someone has been here with news?"

She nodded. "Only a few hours ago. I suppose this is the end of the fourth day, is it not? I have lost track…"

"Yes," I said. "It is."

"He said Dublin looks like the war-torn cities of France or Belgium."

I nodded. "It did when I left it."

"He said the backbone of the insurrection has been broken," she went on. "He doubted there were more than two locations where the volunteers still held."

"Did he say what they were?"

"The GPO and fighting was thick. The other was a factory, I believe."

I looked at Nicky, who had not moved one whit. "And Saint Stephen's Green?"

"Taken."

"What of the men there?"

"The British are rounding up all the men—women, too. He said Countess Markievicz was arrested, along with Michael Mallin."

"Any word of what will happen to them?"

Isibeal shook her head sadly.

"Can you rest, Isibeal? I am here now, and I won't be leaving Nicky's side. You look like you could use some sleep."

She nodded and stood, holding the old stone wall for support.

"Have you any food? Not for myself, but for Nicky…"

"Only a bit of bone broth."

"Can you spare a bit?"

"Of course we can, Penny. I'll bring it straight away." She turned to go but then turned back to face me. "I'm glad you're here, Penny. I am so glad you are here."

36

Missus O'Rigley left before dawn, the only evidence she was ever here a small pile of potatoes left at the door. They were mealy, mushy, and pitted, and I could not keep myself from the memories of potatoes far better than these that were routinely thrown out at Matherscourt. Now this meager bit could mean the difference between hunger and satiation and for Nicky, life or death, so I set about making thin potato soup.

Nicky had moved some during the night, but his fever had not broken. I'd slept fitfully, lying on the floor beside his bed, awakening at every perceived sound. His breathing was shallow and faint, his skin pasty and gray. As Isibeal and I changed his bandages, I was appalled at the condition of his leg, and though I didn't dare share my distress with her, I became concerned that he would have to lose it to save his life.

The doctor had not returned, and as Rory set off to find him, Isibeal and I dressed in layers to begin a trek to a stream where we would fill several buckets with water. Before we left, we made a low fire in the fireplace as she explained that fires were only advisable when the mists were thick else the British might see the smoke. It was a surreal observation, one that brought home yet again that our world had changed.

"Where are the girls?" I asked as we labored across uneven terrain on our way to the stream.

"At the cottage where we last saw you," she answered. "They work in the old castle there, you know."

"They are still employed?"

She nodded. "They are as far as I know."

"Didn't you work there as well?"

"I did." She sighed heavily. "I was fetched the day that Nicky was brought here. There is a network of spies, you may as well know. They carry word from one to the other; sometimes, I think they know of dozens of men and their fates, and on their travels, they must find one person or another to pass along the word… I thought they had come with word of Peter."

I wanted to squeeze her hand reassuringly, but we were too far apart, each focused on navigating the rocky landscape.

Before I could respond, she continued, "Instead, they told me of Nicky. I sent the girls to the old castle with word that I'd been called away to tend a sick family member. Rory was there, and he insisted on coming with me."

"How did they know to bring him here?"

We reached the stream, and she set down the two water buckets she'd carried and wiped her forehead. "I suppose the volunteers scattered the men across the countryside. They carried with them word of Dublin, and it clearly was not safe for any volunteer to remain inside the city."

We filled the buckets to the brim, knowing some of it would be sloshed out before we'd made it back to the cottage. I began to fret before we'd arrived back, fearing Nicky would pass while I was away, remembering how they'd said he'd called my name in his delirium. But though we were gone close to an hour judging by the sun, he was still just as we'd left him. I placed one of the buckets beside his bed, dipped a cloth inside, and began again the process of bathing his skin to keep the fever down.

The hours passed into days. Rory grew increasingly impatient, his anger and frustration mounting as time passed. The volunteers that had provided such necessary information during that first critical week of the Easter Rising had disappeared, and we were left to wonder what the world had become outside our tenuous haven. Isibeal grew more silent and withdrawn, and I knew she was worried about Peter, for we did not know whether he was yet alive or had perished in the fighting or perhaps was somewhere as Nicky was, being tended hour by hour in a feeble effort to keep him alive. At least, I consoled myself, I was with Nicky; Peter might have been taken to complete strangers.

It was in the wee hours of the morning that the door opened. I felt it rather than heard it; I felt the chill of the night air swirling inside to rob us of the meager heat the fireplace had offered so many hours before. We could not begin it again until the mists began to obscure our location, and Rory and Isibeal had bedded down in front of it while I had crawled into bed beside Nicky and wrapped my arm around his cold body. I thought my body would take the chill off him, but instead, he robbed me of my warmth until my teeth were chattering, yet I could not drag myself away from him.

Rory was the first to rise. In the windowless cottage, I saw only the sliver of light that made it past the man in the doorway to find the boy standing there with fists balled and ready to fight, but in an instant, he had dropped his stance and cried out, "Da!"

Isibeal leaped up and into Peter's arms, the three of them huddled together in a tight embrace until Peter said, "Best close the door now, or we'll all catch our death of cold."

As the door was closed, I heard footsteps coming close to me. "Penny, are you there?"

"I am, Peter. Welcome home." My voice caught in my throat, and I found myself unable to continue.

"And Nicky?"

"He hasn't regained consciousness."

"I'd heard…" His voice faded.

"Sit," Isibeal said. "You must be famished."

"I brought you some food," Peter said. "It isn't much, but a bit of cheese and lamb…"

I slipped out from under the blanket and tucked Nicky in the best I could before joining them. "Have you word?" I asked.

He rifled through a carpetbag and handed me a paper. "'Tis the *Irish Independent*," he said.

There was not sufficient light in which to read it, so I slipped outside with the newspaper leaving Peter alone with Isibeal and Rory. They did not need me there anyway, I thought; best they have their privacy.

I made my way to the old barn, a stone building not much different than the cottage, save for the larger doorway and the hay strewn across the floor. There were two horses there now, the one I had stolen and another, which I assumed to be Peter's. I stood in the doorway under the light of the moon, shivering as I read the latest news.

37

I cried out, the sound of my voice lost in the Irish wind, the pain buckling my legs, and bringing me to my knees.

The Easter Rising had been a complete failure.

When the last of the rebels—now called Republicans because they wanted an independent Irish Republic—surrendered at the GPO, the military tribunals had begun. The British considered the rebellion an act of war and not a civilian disturbance. The distinction meant there would be no public trials, no appointed defenders, and no delay. One after another, the Republicans were declared guilty and sentenced to execution.

I turned back to the newspaper's date. Could it truly be May? Had it been weeks since I'd left Dublin, weeks now that I had remained by Nicky's side as he drifted further into unconsciousness? But there it was, staring at me, followed by the leaders' names and dates of execution:

Thom Clarke executed May 3;
Thomas MacDonagh executed May 3;
Patrick Pearse executed May 3;

Joseph Plunkett executed May 4;

Michael O'Hanrahan executed May 4;

William Pearse executed May 4;

John MacBride executed May 5;

Ed Daly executed May 8;

Con Colbert executed May 8;

Sean Heuston executed May 8;

Eamonn Ceantt executed May 8;

Michael Mallin, the commander Nicky had served under, executed May 8;

Thom Kent executed May 9;

Sean MacDiarmada executed May 12;

And the last of the leaders, James Connelly, executed on May 12. He had been injured at the GPO, his leg so badly mangled that he had been unable to stand. The British had strapped him to a chair in the courtyard at Kilmainham Gaol and executed him by firing squad.

Countess Markievicz had also been sentenced to death, but it was commuted to life in prison, the British having determined that it was not worth the bullets to shoot a woman.

Roger Casement, who had failed in delivering the German weapons to the Irish Republicans, was also sentenced to death, but the sentence had not yet been carried out. Unlike the others, he had been transported to England and was at Pentonville Gaol in London awaiting execution.

There was no count regarding the number of men and women in prison. Hundreds had participated, and the newspaper told a detailed account of them being paraded through the streets on their way to gaol as citizens that supposedly had not participated in the uprising taunted them, spit on them and called them horrific names. A few of the commanders had been stripped naked and forced to walk through the streets, humiliated in public while suffering from the bitter cold. Seared into my memories was my time in Dublin, the looters, the innocents, the rebels… I thought my soul would be wrenched in two.

There were more stories along with warnings for anyone that had participated and had not yet been caught: the soldiers were coming for them. They were fanning out across the island, moving from house to house, county to county, searching out rebels that would presumably also be sentenced to death. That meant Nicky and Peter were wanted men; it meant their lives could never be the same. It meant they would not be finishing the orangery at Matherscourt or the cathedrals they were so proud to design; their vocations would be crushed by the stigmas on their heads. They were not safe anywhere in Ireland and to leave Ireland meant to run a watery gauntlet of British sailors that controlled the seas around the island.

I clutched the doorframe and hauled myself back to my feet. The doctor had never returned to attend to Nicky, and Rory's efforts at finding him had come to naught. Now I wondered which side the doctor was on. Would he turn in Nicky's location to the authorities? Were we no longer safe here? Or was he considered a conspirator, having attended to those injured Republicans? Was he rotting in gaol even now, perhaps tortured to disclose the locations of those he had treated?

A storm had blown in, mirroring my own tumultuous thoughts, the squall shrieking as it wound its way around the stable like a banshee in search of souls. The sound had grown to a fever pitch, and I had not heard Rory calling my name until he was upon me. His lips moved, but I could not decipher his words in the gale until he placed his lips next to my ear and yelled, "Hurry!"

It took another moment for me to come out of my stupor, and I dashed into the rain. I turned back only briefly to find him struggling to close the stable doors, and then the water came down like sheets of a waterfall, blocking him from view.

I was soaked to the bone when I reached the cottage. With the rain effectively obscuring the view from the mountains, Peter was busy stoking the paltry fire into something that might warm the single room. But it was Nicky's voice that nearly brought me to my knees again.

He was calling my name, his voice feeble and faint. As I drew near, I found Isibeal trying to still his arms as he thrashed.

"I am here," I said, grasping both of his hands in mine. "Nicky, it's Penny. It's me. I am here."

He was fevered, his face blotched red and perspiring, and I gratefully accepted the cloth Isibeal offered, placing it upon his forehead. "You're safe here," I managed to say through tears that had begun once more. How could they come again in such a torrent when I thought I had been completely cried out? Yet they were there, and as he drifted back into unconsciousness, I laid my head upon his chest and cried until the thin blanket was soaked in my tears and his sweat.

38

I hugged Rory for so long, he had to extricate himself from me. I was truly reluctant to see him go. I had come to know him well over the past weeks, and I couldn't shake the feeling that I would never see him again. I knew I had to admit to myself that there was nothing to keep him at the tiny cottage, and there was a great deal waiting for him once he left us.

"Enjoy your time at Oxford," I said, trying vainly to hold back the tears from forming. "Come back a solicitor."

"That is my plan, dear Penny," he said warmly.

Peter finished saddling a horse. A single satchel contained all the possessions the three had arrived with, and though their belongings were meager, the tiny cottage felt empty without them.

"We're so anxious to get back," Isibeal said as she hugged me farewell. "We've not been able to get word to Sosaidh and Mallaidh, and we yearn to see them—most especially me."

"All of us do," Peter said, placing a hand on her shoulder.

"And once we've returned, I can obtain the necessary papers to attend Oxford," Rory added. "My benefactor told me a few months back that he would assist me in retaining a job through the summer, which will provide great insight into the workings of the law."

"Well, and you may be using those teachings to assist those of us that have had occasion to be on the wrong side of it." We all turned toward the door to find Nicky leaning against the frame, a broad smile stretching across his thin face. He held a walking stick in one hand, which he had fashioned himself after Isibeal and I had ventured out one day in search of suitable sticks. He was getting stronger—regaining consciousness was a great start—but it had been the lack of food that finally propelled Peter to suggest that the three leave. We had debated quite earnestly, but there were so many advantages to their heading home.

"Ah, do not get the boy started yet again," Peter said, shaking his head.

That, I decided, was something I would not miss. Rory had debated the rebellion nearly every night; he had been opposed to it from the beginning, and now that the results had been so catastrophic, it drove his point home. He was convinced more than ever that the only way to effect change was through legal means. He had lofty aspirations; once he had become a solicitor and had made a name for himself, he would run for public office, perhaps one day even ending up in Parliament.

Nicky made his way to the group as his sister-in-law climbed upon the horse. There was but one horse to share between them and a long journey ahead.

"You'll be fine here for as long as you want to stay," Peter said. "I'll stop on my way out of Sally Gap and make inquiries as to provisions for you."

"I thank you," Nicky said, giving his brother a hug. "But only if you truly trust the person."

"Of course."

"Find out what happened to the doctor if you don't mind?" I asked tentatively. Nicky had made a remarkable recovery, but his wounds—especially his thigh—had not healed as I thought it should.

"I will, indeed." Peter nodded, and Rory began to lead the horse along the narrow path through the woods. As they passed through the underbrush, the fauna closed behind them as though they had never been there. A moment later, Peter was following them.

We stood for a moment, our eyes glued on the copse into which they had vanished. Then Nicky stepped behind me and wrapped his arms around me. An eagle soared above us in a widening arc, its dark brown wings stretched wide.

"Ah, to be an eagle right now," I sighed, my stomach aching for a decent meal.

"I would rather be a man," he said, dipping his head to kiss the nape of my neck, "with an empty cottage for a change."

There was no better place to be than within Nicky's arms. When we were apart, even for a moment, memories of the past or worries of the future consumed my mind, but when we were together, there was only the present moment. I sought to savor those times, committing them to memory because as beautiful and idyllic as our world was becoming, I knew it was only an illusion that could be shattered when the outside world eventually found us.

We spent our nights wrapped in one another's arms, sharing our heat as temperatures dropped, the promise of summer just around the corner, and yet still out of reach, a reminder that the hottest summer day and the coldest of winter might only vary by twenty degrees in Ireland. Nicky spent his days learning how to overcome his thigh wound as we fished in the crystal clear waters, picked wild strawberries and raspberries, and even discovered an apple tree.

The bullet had pierced a thigh muscle, and we conjectured that when the doctor was trying to dig it out, he had cut rather vigorously through the muscle. It was a long and slow process for it to mend well enough to walk without a walking stick, and bending was clearly painful. We had nothing for the pain and with the world around us falling apart, neither wanted to venture far from our cottage hidden deep in the woods in search of a remedy.

Yet time and again, my mind wandered to Matherscourt as if it was trying to call me back. I relived the moment when I stopped at the crossroads, knowing I could turn toward Matherscourt and easily explain away my days-long absence. I did not regret my choice to find Nicky; in fact, I knew had I chosen the safer path, I would forever have regretted not coming after him. But as the days turned to weeks and the weeks to a month and then two, I wondered if Stratford cared what had happened to me, or if he had resumed his daily journeys into the city as he had always done.

I worried about Éamonn and wondered if he had been captured and was imprisoned, or whether the executions that had begun with the leaders was now making its way down through the rank and file. I worried about Johanna, knowing she was in love with him. And I missed Léana, especially when we awakened famished as we always did, and I remembered the plentiful bounty at Matherscourt and her delicious cooking.

It was a beautiful day. The sun's warmth stretched through to my bones, allowing me to shed some of the layers that had covered me nearly constantly since my Dublin departure. The stream gurgled as the ice-cold water found its way from higher lofts to the valley below. The fish were spawning as huge numbers were migrating, ensuring we would have enough meat in our diets for the foreseeable future. The plentiful fruits and vegetables that grew wild here were tough to find and tougher to forage, but we'd settled on a few prime spots that would serve us well.

I was stooped over a fallen silver birch so decomposed that I could easily peel the bark off it. Perhaps there was a time in which I would dry out the bark and use it for kindling, but this particular tree would serve a greater purpose. The long, thin strips I extracted would be used for unique sketchings.

I had already amassed quite a bit of the soot from the fireplace, storing it in the corner of the deep fireplace itself. I would use that medium to draw on the silver flesh of the birch that which I had seen in Dublin. The memories of the rowhouses with holes large enough for the soldiers to walk from one to the other were seared into my mind. So were the soldiers firing down on Saint Stephen's Green as the men lay in their trenches like sitting ducks, the household items piled up at the ends of streets to block the soldiers' way, the dead lying in the streets.

I'd read in the newspaper Peter had brought so long ago why it was that James Connolly surrendered the GPO. He'd been injured himself days earlier but had been determined to fight on to the last man when he looked out the window and spotted a citizen trying to retrieve his own vehicle. He was an elderly man, and Connolly could hear him shouting out to the British soldiers that he only wanted his vehicle so he could leave the city center. After a few minutes of terse words between the old man and the British, he'd set off for his vehicle and was shot dead in the street. At that moment, Connolly realized the soldiers would not kill only those involved in the insurrection but any and all Irish, and to stop the vitriol and senseless killing, he'd made the decision to surrender.

I had not been there to witness the scene with Connolly, but my imagination drew Sackville Street, the debris littered as far as the eye could see, the GPO pitted from bullets as

Connolly watched from the window while the old man tried to reach his vehicle. I would take each of those elements and transfer them to my makeshift canvas, preserving for all time the imagined memory of that day.

"Ah!" Nicky said excitedly, turning a small table upright. "And it's finished it is. Not my best work, but my best by far with neither hammer nor nails!"

I piled the rest of the birch strips into the cloth I'd laid out upon the ground and joined Nicky to admire his work. He'd found a tree that had been cut down, the trunk presumably carried off for fuel. With only his hands and rudimentary tools that he'd fashioned from tree branches, he'd dug up the root ball and cleaned the dirt off the bottom until he'd fashioned a rather interesting pedestal that culminated in the nearly flat top.

"It's large enough for the two of us to put our food, aye?" he asked, his hands on his hips.

"Definitely. And it will feel so good to have a table again."

"It will 'ey, and I'll give you that."

"I wish I'd known…" I started.

"Known what?" he asked when I didn't continue.

"Oh, nothing really. It's just—well, if I'd known I would end up here, I could have loaded my carriage with things from Matherscourt and set out for the cottage here. I could have made our stay much more enjoyable."

"But that is what Life is all about, isn't it now? We never know from one moment to the next where our paths will lead or what we will encounter. It's part of the adventure. And I beg to differ with you," he said, grabbing me and holding me close. "It has been a totally enjoyable time."

A flash of light caught our attention, and instinctively, he pulled me behind him.

"What is it?" I asked nervously.

"Stay to the shadows," he said. "The trees will shield us here." We waited for a protracted moment before he pointed. "There. On the ridge. It must be binoculars."

"The British?" I breathed as my heart skipped a beat and then two. "Do you think they spotted us?"

"No. We've stayed in the shadows, and any sound we've made could not be heard from that far."

"How far are they?"

"Were they to travel down to the valley here, it would take them the better part of a day—and that's if they knew the way."

"What do we do?"

"We'll go home in a wide arc around the eastern edge. That will place us further away and on higher ground so we can keep a watch on them."

"What of the fish?"

"We'll grab them as we cross the creek."

"But what if the soldiers have spotted them?"

He turned to peer at me, a lop-sided grin on his face. "And what if they have? They'd be expecting a fishing pole or two now wouldn't they? Not some rocks piled in the stream to catch the fish as they swam. Grab your birch wood, and I'll maneuver this table onto my back."

I did as I was told as I kept a wary eye on the distant ridge. Had it not been for the sun glinting off the binoculars, we would most likely never have known they were there. I began to fear our time in our rustic paradise was coming to an abrupt end.

Our trek around the eastern edge was long and arduous. Unable to lug the table upon his back and remain steady on his feet, we each took hold of opposite sides and carried it together. In his other hand, Nicky relied on the walking stick he'd fashioned to keep him upright while I carried the birch and the fish we'd caught in our makeshift rock dam, all piled together within a pitifully thin cloth.

We spotted the group of soldiers several times during our journey back home, and each time they were further from the cottage. By the time dusk had arrived and we were tripping on extended roots and uneven terrain, Nicky had declared they were not heading into the valley.

But as we continued walking, we grew silent, each with our own thoughts. Mine was filled with a fear that they would return while we slept, kicking in our door and rousing us from one another's arms.

39

When a knock came at our cottage door, it was not the soldiers that I had feared, but Sean, the carpenter that had worked with Peter and Nicky at Matherscourt and who I'd seen again during the Rising. He was thinner than I'd remembered him, and his clothing was dusty and threadbare, but the smile was still there along with a weary twinkle in his blue eyes. He was clearly happy to see Nicky and pleased that we were together, but he brought news that would bring us both to our knees.

It was after dinner that he finally told us why he had come; a dinner of fish breaded in crushed nuts and cooked over the open fire that rested between grilled wild turnips and fresh strawberries. It had become a favorite meal for us, for it was hearty and filled with a wild taste I had never known before, but I noticed Sean had barely touched his meal.

I was proud of Nicky for making the table and chair; we'd started with one chair, and he'd made another that I suppose was never meant to match it. We'd spent many an hour sitting in front of the fire on cool nights, for even in late spring and early summer, the nights could become chilly once the sun had gone down. I never wished for a third for two was plenty enough, and how were we to know we'd be found in the bowels of Sally's Gap?

We had no windows in the tiny cottage, but I had the door open wide as we carried on our conversation.

"I'd be telling you true, you could not find your way about Dublin today," Sean was saying. "It has changed it has and not for the better."

Nicky nodded. "I've been biding my time here, waiting for things to calm before I resurfaced."

"You may be waiting a good long while."

"That bad, even out of the city?"

"I suppose it is even worse when you get out of Dublin if such a thing could happen."

We sipped on ale made from old apples, and now Sean grimaced. I wondered if it was the tartness of the ale, but with his next words, I nearly dropped my cup upon the floor.

"I need for you both to listen," Sean said, setting his own cup on the table and pushing back. "I do not have the emotional fortitude to tell you this but once."

"What has happened?" Nicky said. I had been standing by the fire, and now he grabbed me and pulled me close to him so I was nearly sitting on his knees.

"I knew you were here," Sean began. "Peter told me when he and Isibeal first returned. I had been staying at the cottages near Powerscourt." He shook his head sadly. "I suppose I should say I checked in on the cottages instead. Sosaidh and Mallaidh stayed in one, and I tried to be there for them in the absence of their parents."

"That was kind of you," I said.

"But you didn't stay there, you say?" Nicky asked.

He shook his head. "After the rebellion was put down and Dublin calmed a bit under martial law, the soldiers began fanning out into the country looking for others that either participated in or had been sympathetic to the cause of a free Ireland."

"Ah," Nicky said. "Well, you can stay here as long as you wish."

Sean sighed heavily. "We have known one another since we were wee ones. You and Peter," his voice broke, "have always been like brothers to me you have."

We remained silent. Sean's mouth moved as though he was about to say more, but then he appeared to be chewing on the inside of his lip. Somewhere in the distance, a coyote howled and another answered.

"The soldiers, they come through on an irregular basis, you see," he finally continued. "To keep us off guard, you know. And well, one night, Peter and Rory were with the women at the cottage."

"Have they been arrested?" Nicky stood. "We could have been after them hours ago."

Sean let out a noise that I could only describe as a sob wrenched from his insides. It took me off guard, and Nicky and I stared at him. My mouth had gone dry, and I reached for the table with one hand and Nicky with the other, hoping either could steady me.

He shook his head. "Nick, the soldiers have been terrorizing the Irish ever since the uprising. They've been looking for men, and the age hasn't mattered." Another anguished cry escaped his lips.

"What are you saying?" Nicky asked.

"They interrogated the family for some time—"

"Were you there?"

He shook his head. "Sosaidh found me. She knew where I laid my head."

"The girls—did they—?"

"No, praise the Lord. They did not. But—"

As another sob and then another escaped his lips, Nicky said, "For God's sake, Sean, spit it out. We can take whatever you tell us, but not knowing is twisting my insides."

"You can't take it, Nick," Sean bawled. "I have tried, but I can't."

"What is it?" I asked, coming around the table to take Sean's hands in my own.

His voice was broken. "They executed Peter and Rory in front of their women."

"Executed!" Nicky bellowed. "On what grounds?"

"On the grounds that they were men, they were Irish, and they were there."

"What the bloody hell! Did you get names, can you identify them? We'll find a solicitor—"

"No, Nicky." He peered up at him with anguished eyes. "The Ireland you knew—we all knew—it's gone. There is no law. Some soldiers do whatever the hell they feel like doing."

"But they deserved a trial—an opportunity to prove themselves innocent—"

"Aye, and I agree that's what they both deserved. But it isn't what they got. What they got was a firing squad in the middle of a pasture."

Nicky placed both hands on the table. It teetered, so it seemed like he and it were about to topple. "Did they have evidence of Peter's involvement?"

"None from what the girls told me."

"But," I interjected, "Rory was never involved. He was against the uprising. He—he was going to Oxford to become a solicitor—"

"He was the eldest son, and that's what they are after."

"The eldest son?" Nicky said, his face growing crimson as his voice rose. "They are killing the eldest son like the Egyptians did in the Bible?"

Sean nodded sadly. "And the age did not matter. Missus O'Rigley's grandson was but nine years old, and Old Man Neeson's son but twelve—"

"Killed?"

"Killed. Murdered in front of the mothers."

"What could children do?"

"They were guilty of being Irish." Sean dried his eyes. "So you see, Nicky, my friend, and brother, right here is the safest place for you to be. They haven't made it anywhere close to Sally's Gap though I suspect with time, they will."

I sank into the chair as Nicky continued to hold himself upright with the help of the table. "And how are my brother's wife and the girls?" he asked after a long moment.

"What you can expect. Their employer keeps them on so they are not in danger of starvation, and they have the roof over their heads. But emotionally…"

I needed air. I rose abruptly and stepped to the open door where the chill was still hours away. With the promise of summer had come longer days, but now as I stared at the crystal blue skies and the thick green vegetation, I wished for darkness to fall. Perhaps I yearned for the cloak of night to wrap itself around me; perhaps I ached for tomorrow's morn to erase all that Sean had told us. Just like Sean, I had not been present when the murders had occurred, but I knew in my mind's eye that I would never forget the images his words invoked.

"But," Sean said, his voice becoming a bit stronger behind me, "if there is a silver lining, the killings have meaning to them, Nicky."

"What are you saying?"

"The world is learning of Britain's form of 'justice.' Every day at dawn, the leaders of the Easter Rising were executed at Kilmainham Gaol. They did not receive a trial, Nicky; none of them did. They received nothing more than a military kangaroo court, and the entire world knows it."

"But what good does it do us even if the world knows? Our leaders and our men—"

"And now with the additional killings of men and their eldest sons—without even the military trial mind you, but simple murder by men not fit to judge—it is reaching the rest of the world. And the rest of the world is responding."

I turned back to them. "In what way?"

"Do you know of Éamon de Valera?"

"He was one of the leaders sentenced to death," Nicky said.

Sean shook his head. "He's in America now."

"He wasn't arrested?"

"He was, but he isn't Irish."

"What?" I asked.

"He was born in America, which makes him an American citizen. The Brits stopped short of executing him because the United States put pressure on them to let him go."

"But," I said, "His mother was Irish—"

"And his father was Basque. He holds citizenship, I suppose, in all three regions. But the important one is America."

"So he's in the States now," Nicky said. "I fail to see how he can help us now."

"Oh, but he can. The Great War won't go on forever, Nicky. And when it's ended, they'll come a time when the victors sit down at the table and decide the fate of nations. And de Valera is determined for Ireland to be free."

"Are you saying the rebellion isn't over?" Nicky and I said at the same time.

"Far from it."

"But the Irish didn't rise up like the leaders intended," I said weakly.

"No. Not during the Easter Rising. But as the soldiers invaded homes throughout Dublin and now throughout the rest of the island, seizing men and boys and executing them for no reason at all, the tide has turned. The Irish are rising up now, and we need you, Nicky."

"Are you saying the Irish are fighting?" Nicky breathed. "What land do they hold?"

"None at the moment. But this is a fight like no other, brother. No one is occupying a building and firing out the windows while the soldiers shell it into oblivion."

"Then, how—?"

"It is a guerrilla war. We're forming small bands of men that are separated from other bands, so if one is captured, he knows little of what the entire body is doing. We are getting arms from America, smuggled into Ireland every week that passes. Ammunition, too. And we're waging war on the soldiers—sneak attacks, quick kills, and then we disappear."

There were a million reasons why I should have objected to what I knew Sean was asking of us. The British were a formidable force; they had been for centuries. The Irish had been flattened by them many a time and even now did not have the rights of a British citizen on their own native Irish soil.

"Where are you getting the money for the weapons?" Nicky asked.

Sean smiled. "There are more Irish Americans than there are Irish, my friend."

"Americans?"

"You heard me right."

Nicky rubbed his beard.

"Do you need time to think it through?" Sean asked. "I know it's a great deal to absorb."

"No," Nicky said. His voice was strong. "Count me in."

"Are you sure now?" Sean glanced at me.

"Without a doubt. I am committed to a free and independent Ireland."

I made my way to the stream as the men's voices grew faint behind me. It was a beautiful day. Ireland's weather can be fickle, providing all four seasons in one day, but today had been summer through and through. To be sure, the summer temperature was perhaps 20 degrees different from the winter's, but it was warm all the same. The birds were out in all their glory, finding mates and laying eggs, the tiny chirps of those just born mingling with the songs of the adults.

There was an aroma in the air, a unique combination of blooms and grasses, fresh air and distant waters, salt, and wood. It seemed to pass through my body until I was part of it, part of this idyllic countryside, the rolling mountains and steep cliffs of Ireland.

I sat on an overturned log a short distance from the stream, a log upon which Nicky and I had spent many an hour while we waited for the fish to be corralled into the rocky chambers we'd set to snare them. Our time had been filled with conversation and intimate moments, times that had been etched into my soul that could never leave me.

And in the beauty that joined my soul with Ireland, I cried. All the tears that had welled up inside me, all the cries that had not been spent the night that I found Nicky, found their way from the depths of my heart to spill onto my clothing and form puddles on the ground.

I cried because the world I lived in had been changed forever. I had been born into a genteel family, Irish, to be sure but British in its loyalty, and I had every expectation of living a privileged existence until the day I passed from this world. I was schooled in history, governments, and sciences, the anticipation of an orderly country with set norms and the comforts of routine, even though I sometimes disagreed. Yet there was something reassuring on the most basic of levels that each morning found scores of people going about their business as they had the day before and as they would again on the morrow.

There was a calm in routine, the monotony of a personal day, as well as the predictable mechanics of a government, slowly turning, the infighting nothing more than civil disagreements from parties that both loved Ireland but had varying ways of showing it. There was reassurance in the establishments that opened at certain times and specific days and closed just as predictably. That the butcher was out of particular meat or the seamstress was slow in her latest alterations was the most unpredictability I had ever had cause to experience.

Oh, there was Stratford. Yes, I thought there was that. Yet even under those circumstances, there was a lineage behind me that had walked the same road as I; centuries of women that married not for the sake of love but for the protection and security a man could provide for her. Even that was part of a routine in which I was compelled to play my part.

I cried for Ireland because, in a few days' time, our world had been changed, and all routine and predictability had flown away on the Irish winds, dissipating over the Irish Sea and leaving us in abject turmoil.

I cried for Isibeal and her girls. There could not be much difference in age between Isibeal and myself; surely, she had expectations as well and at their core a belief in a marriage that would last into old age. The interaction between Peter and his wife was a world apart from Stratford and me; perhaps in their world, they did marry for love. Perhaps as they gazed at their infant son, they predicted all the wonderful things he would someday accomplish; perhaps they moved from one Irish county to another to open doors for his future. They had been on the cusp of witnessing their hard work and sacrifices, allowing Rory to attend Oxford and return home as a solicitor, most likely the first in their family's long lineage.

And in an instant, all the days that had stretched into weeks and months and years were erased. They had simply been erased. All the longing for a future better than the current one had been dashed in a few minutes, a hasty condemnation, and a hastier execution. All the things Isibeal might have said to Peter and Rory but hadn't because it was never the right time had been forever lost on the winds.

In its place was a heart heavier than a stone that literally felt broken in two. Like a cart divided down the middle, it was impossible to understand how the two parts could be put back together to enable forward movement—or any movement at all. The journey appeared halted in its tracks.

And yet I knew Isibeal and her girls were not the only ones that were crying on this day. They were not the only women lifting their faces to heaven to ask how a just and loving God could have allowed these senseless murders. They could have arrested them, my mind cried out, and tried them for their perceived crimes. And in the end, perhaps Peter would have been found guilty of treason and sentenced, while Rory would have been released because he had played no part in the uprising.

I thought of Jamie, the young man—truly, he had been just a boy—in the Dublin tenements, taken like so many others from a mother's arms, a wife's embrace, a child crying for their father. Where would it end if not the total annihilation of the Irish people? Was that truly what Britain wanted?

It was as Nicky had said; it was Biblical. Like the Egyptians, they sought to butcher not only the father but the sons as well—and then would it continue for every son born? Without men, it would not take long for the Irish to be eliminated. And then Britain would own all of Ireland, lock, stock, and barrel.

But that is not possible, my practical mind argued. Surely the rest of the world would not stand idly by and allow the British to practice genocide on an entire country's men.

I tried to dry my eyes, but new tears formed, determined to find their way out of a body wracked in pain. I had been content in another life, wandering the lane past the horses in the meadow, settling in with my biscuits and tea as I sketched and practiced watercolor landscapes. I had made my peace with a man that had never loved me, a man that had never truly wanted me apart from the name that would open doors for him.

But the contentment had shattered in an instant, though not in the vile way the Bowers family had experienced. Mine had led to greater love, not the lack of it, to a brighter future, not the carnage left. I had been led into the arms of the only man I had truly loved with all my being, a man improbable for me considering our diverse backgrounds and culture. Yet I had known every time my mind had wandered to Nicky that he was my future; he was my everything.

I cried because I felt that future slipping out of my fingers as rapidly as water might flow over them. I sobbed because now that I had found love, it would leave me to join the fight for Ireland's soul. I wept because my heart had grown larger and fuller, and Nicky could not leave without wrenching a part of it from me.

40

Sean left at sunset. His departure at that hour was yet another indication that our world had changed; people had always traveled during daylight hours and never in the cold, dark night if they could help it, for the ground was uneven, and often a misstep could mean the difference in whether a man could continue to provide for his family. But then, the world had changed beyond Ireland, hadn't it now? Men were coming home maimed from the war, and now the war had come to our own shores, a possibility most Irish had never entertained.

It hadn't been long after Sean's parting that Nicky had pulled me into our bed. He had hesitated over me as if he wanted to memorize the way my hair had fallen across the pillow, unraveled from its customary braid to cascade from one side of the bed toward the other. His eyes had traced the outline of my cheeks and jawline, had moved to my throat and back up again to lock onto my eyes.

I wanted to pull him toward me, to feel him against every inch of me, but I, too, paused. I, too, wanted to memorize this moment, to sear it into my soul so I could relive it again and again because I knew these memories would be all I would carry with me until we were joined yet again. I touched his hair, thick and a bit unruly, traced my finger down his jaw to feel the soft beard he'd grown since the Easter Rising, my eyes wandering to his arms as his palms were set on either side of me. Such strong arms, I thought, and once upon a time, I had envisioned those arms taking care of me in any situation. Yet now I fought to push Saint Stephen's Green out of my mind, to dispel those thoughts of men lying in wait in deeply dug trenches only to be fired upon from the windows of my husband's office, the bullets streaming down like so many raindrops.

His finger touched my bottom lip, and only then did I realize it had been trembling. "I promise you," he said, his voice husky, "I will return to you, Penny. I promise you that."

I could only nod, the words refusing to form as if I was at war within myself. I wanted him to remain with me; hadn't these past weeks been unspoiled? Like two people in a cocoon, the world had been closed out of our lives. Yet his words so long ago came tumbling back at me: "I have a wife. She is Ireland."

He bent low, his lips grazing mine, and as his eyes closed, I discovered the tiniest tear attempting to escape. I held him close, my arms wrapping around him as tightly as I could muster while I felt his tightening around me. We became one as the moonlight found its way through the open door; our souls and our bodies so intertwined that I no longer knew where he ended and I began.

"You cannot stay here, you know," Nicky said as dawn was breaking.

We'd made love throughout the night as many times as we could possibly attain as if both of us knew it could be a long time before we were together once more—if ever.

"Why can't I?" I asked sleepily. "We have been safe here; there is no one about that could bother me."

"Aye, we've been safe enough. But you heard what Sean said, and we've seen the soldiers along the ridge ourselves."

"But they didn't come down into the valley."

"But they will sure enough. Once they've realized the men they seek are no longer in their customary places, they will know we have gone into hiding. And they will eventually come here, mark my words."

"So what if they do? You won't be here," I said, squeezing myself against his side as he laid flat, his arm encircling me.

"And that's the point of it, isn't it now? You would be a woman alone with no one to protect you. You don't even have a weapon to protect yourself—nor should you, for a man won't venture here alone. They will come with a score of men, expecting to find rebels, prepared to find them, and they could take their hostilities out on you."

"They wouldn't," I breathed.

"You are not Lady Mather here. You are Penny, the partner, the lover of a known rebel."

"But they wouldn't know of our relationship."

"Then how would you, a noblewoman, explain the fact that you are living in a one-room hut, wearing the same clothes every day for weeks now?"

"I would explain that I'd been caught in Dublin—"

"How long ago was that now?" He turned to face me. "And just how would you explain that you reached the fork in the road and took not the one to Matherscourt but one that would lead you into the back of beyond?"

I fell silent. I could not explain it; only he and I would ever understand my need to find him in those awful moments. I could never have returned to Matherscourt as if nothing had ever happened and expect life to remain as humorless and pointless as it once had been.

"You must return to Matherscourt." Nicky's voice was blunt.

"What?"

He turned onto his side so he could see my face more clearly. "It is the only place where you can be safe."

"What are you talking about? I can't go back there—!"

He placed a finger upon my lips as if to silence me. "You must, Penny. You will be sheltered there from callous soldiers. Stratford is well-known as a British loyalist, and you'll be back in a circle of friends that are well connected with the highest in the British government."

"But—but—I can't!" I managed to blurt as I fought back the tears of frustration.

"You must. I cannot go if I don't know you are safe. I cannot focus on the things I must do if I am worried about your welfare—where you are, how you are surviving."

"Then come away with me. We can go into hiding together; if this place is not safe, there must be another—"

He smiled sadly. "I can't, darling. As much as I want to, I can't."

"Then Europe—America—"

"How would we get there with no money?" Before I could respond, he said, "Besides, Ireland is a part of us both, isn't it now? It would not take long before we would long for her green hills, the way the salty air sweeps its way across the isle, the sound of surf and gulls, the sheep and the cattle dotted across the slopes and valleys, the stone fences like a patchwork quilt upon the landscape..."

I kissed him then; I kissed him to stop him from talking, to slow the passage of time, to push my tears, my anguish and my broken heart so deep inside me that I would not, could not, find it again until after we were parted.

Yet I still could not imagine returning to Matherscourt; it was akin to a man appearing on the steps of the gaol and asking to be let in.

41

We waited two days before we left. Once the decision had been made, there was a surprising bit of work to be done. Not knowing if or where we could eat along the road, we smoked fish in green leaves and gathered berries. Being a woman, I refused to leave the tiny cottage unkempt, so there was a great bit of airing out, cleaning the fireplace, sweeping the floors with branches of Scots pine, and replacing the straw in the makeshift mattress.

But truth be told, we waited two days because neither of us wanted to go, though I could sense Nicky's growing impatience to get on the road and back with his compatriots, wherever that might be. Apparently, while I was outside crying my eyes out a few days prior, Sean was inside telling Nicky that he was to accompany me to the old gatehouse at Matherscourt, where he would find a bicycle and additional instructions written in a boyhood code only the two knew. He had also warned Nicky to keep us off the roads, travel only at night, and get rid of the horse as quickly as practical. The only thing worse than discovering a rebel, he said, was discovering the rebel was a horse thief with his stolen property beneath his arse.

I closed the door and latched it so the wind and rain would not find its way inside. The sun was setting on the distant horizon, and a heavy cloud cover had rolled in, good omens so Nicky thought. I wasn't so certain.

The landscape was unfamiliar under the cloak of darkness. I had grown accustomed to the area around our tiny cottage, but as we saddled up the horse and Nicky mounted in front of me, it already appeared empty and foreign. I could not resist peering back at the cottage, only momentarily visible through the trees and then gone as if it had never truly existed at all. I wanted to rush back, the single, windowless room beckoning to me as no home ever had. I buried my face against Nicky's back and squeezed back the tears that threatened to flow. There would be another time, I told myself, another place. All the sadness, the longing, the heartbreak I would deal with once I was alone.

Alone. I held on tighter to Nicky. He murmured something that I didn't quite decipher, but I was in no mood to talk as the horse wound its way up steep, narrow trails that were shrouded in shadows. Pebbles loosened beneath his hooves, and I listened as they clattered down cliff walls.

I asked God time and again, what I had done to deserve such a fate. I had never wanted to marry Stratford; the marriage had been arranged without my input and I, the dutiful daughter, had done what was expected of me to preserve my family's place in society. And yet God had placed Nicky into my life. Against all the odds, married for a decade, a hermit at Matherscourt, and yet there he was. We both knew; we had to know that we were meant for one another, and if it meant living the rest of my life in that one-room cottage, I would be happy there. I could not be happy returning to Stratford.

And I could not be happy allowing Nicky to walk out of my life.

I understood—at least I tried to, I did—why he must join his compatriots. I thought of all the women around the world forced to see their men depart for faraway places to fight in battles of which we women could not imagine. I considered all the women that received those visits they dreaded, those words that would change their lives forever: their men were not coming home. Throughout history, other men had returned that were changed forever; the scars of atrocities etched permanently into their psyches. Others were visibly maimed, their contributions to the world ended at tender ages.

And with the Easter Rising, the Great War had come to Ireland's shores. Britain would pour as many resources as possible into eliminating the threat. For all the signs declaring that the Irish served no man, neither Kaiser nor King, the fact remained that weapons had been purchased from Germany, and the Germans had been willing to fight alongside the Irish. The enemy of my enemy is my friend. Yet now, having aligned with Germany, their fate could be ours, even if it had been only a minority of Irishmen involved in the rebellion.

I forced the thoughts far from my mind; there would be time enough to process it all, I told myself, once Nicky was gone.

The horse moved slowly, and for that, I was grateful. Nicky winced more than once, a reminder that his thigh had not healed despite weeks of recuperation. Perhaps now that we were leaving the remote valley near Sally's Gap, he would find a doctor that could place him on the road to real recovery. His leg was still blue and black, the black inching wider, and he'd come to rely more and more on his walking stick. God would not allow him to die, I told myself. He could not be that cruel. And even if he lost the leg, we would make do somehow.

Sounds traveled as though we existed within an echo chamber, especially once we cleared the valley floor and found ourselves along a plateau. Owls screeched in the darkness, and it was impossible to tell whether it was one or many, their voices circling us as though we were the prey. An unexpected mechanical noise such as brakes squealing was enough to freeze us in our tracks as Nicky, and I searched our surroundings with narrowed eyes. Our horse's tilt of the head or prick of the ears was enough to halt us yet again, knowing the very moment we were discovered could be our last.

It was impossible not to think of Peter and Rory, my heart breaking all over again for the women they left behind and for such promising lives left unfulfilled. It was impossible as well for hatred of the British not to well up inside me. A mere six months ago, I would not have believed I would become a traitor to Britain. Tonight, I could not imagine remaining loyal to her.

As the night wore on, the cold and damp set in. The mists rose around us as though the clouds had descended to our level, twisting and dancing, advancing and encroaching until the mists themselves became a wild animal we could not tame. My hair and clothes grew dank and heavy, and I shivered involuntarily as I sought yet again to lengthen my dress sleeves to their fullest extent. I pressed against Nicky as much for his warmth as his essence as we road in silence, too fearful our voices, however low might travel across the fields and miles.

The sun had not yet risen when we cleared the mountains. Had I not had Nicky to cling to, I might have fallen from the horse in fitful slumber, my eyes weighty, and I knew whenever we bedded down once more, I would dream I was still upon the horse's broad back, and he was still plodding forward one heavy hoof at a time.

Roads were more plentiful here. Some were gravel, constructed by famine victims some decades prior, each excruciating mile back-breaking work by those paid with only a meager meal. Others were dirt roads turned into mud and slop and back again. We avoided both.

"Trust me," Nicky had whispered as we entered a copse of trees, meandering among the shadows in a circuitous route. "I know where we are going."

I could only squeeze him tight in silent acceptance. I had no choice but to trust him.

We paused at the edge of woods as Nicky surveyed our surroundings, quietly calculating the next field to be crossed when we could not venture upon the field at all. Then he would flick the reigns, and the horse would turn, and we would ride low yet again, dodging the low-slung branches of greedy trees that reached through the murky darkness to grab at our clothing and hair.

A sliver of color emerged along the distant horizon, the glint of light seeking its way through the thinning clouds, and Nicky urged the horse onward despite the long night. I had begun to worry about the animal walking hour upon hour without rest when we came to a set of fields divided by stone fences.

Nicky stopped the horse and remained still for longer than usual as we both peered ahead of us. A brownstone house appeared in the distance, thin trails of smoke wafting from dual chimneys, eventually spiraling into the mists until it was impossible to determine where the smoke ended and the mists began. A series of outbuildings in varying stages of neglect surrounded the house without apparent design.

Nicky turned in the saddle and peered in each direction, eventually climbing down and offering his hand to me. My thighs ached as I slipped off the horse, my legs screaming against once again coming back together. My back throbbed as well, my spine having been unnaturally bent as I'd tried vainly to stave off the cold and damp. I was bone-tired.

"Remain close to me," Nicky whispered. "Allow the horse to shield us."

I nodded though I didn't understand. When he began to walk the horse toward the house, I fell in behind him, ducking low as he did so our heads were not visible from the other side. The dawn was our enemy, and my pulse quickened as we drew closer to the house.

Curtains shifted inside so carefully that I thought it my imagination. But a few seconds later, the door opened, and a man stepped outside. He did not speak but beckoned silently toward a barn. Nicky steered the horse along the well-worn path from the house to the barn. The group of us converged upon the doors at the same time.

We slipped inside as silently as possible. The man did not speak until he had closed the doors behind us.

"The horse stays here," he said finally. "You two will sleep in the calf shed." As Nicky removed the saddle, the farmer laid out fresh hay. "Haven't seen the two o' you before now. Have you any notes you want to be passed along?"

"Notes?" Nicky asked.

The farmer stopped long enough to appraise us before returning to the hay. "I suspect not." He signaled for us to follow him yet again. We squeezed through the door and trudged along a slender path to another building. Slipping inside, we heard the soft sounds of calves that could not have been more than a few weeks old while a pungent smell wafted upward to greet us.

The farmer stopped beneath a ladder. "Up there," he said. "Soldiers were through here yesterday; if they stay on schedule, they'll be back tomorrow."

"When we're ready to leave—?" Nicky began.

"You're to leave your horse in the stable. Take the mottled white horse; she'll get you where you need to go."

Nicky patted his pockets. "I owe you—?"

The farmer waved him away. "You owe me Ireland's freedom, that's what you owe me." He nodded toward the loft. "You'll find stew up there. It's cold, but it's all I've got for you."

"That's plenty," I said. The farmer did not look at me as I spoke.

"Thank you," Nicky said.

"If you come back through here again, you can leave a note with me. Name and village on the outside of it; it won't be opened."

Nicky nodded, but the farmer did not wait for his response. He was already through the door, closing it softly behind him.

42

We arrived at the back gate of Matherscourt before dawn the following day, having slept the daylight hours in the loft and traveling another long night under cover of darkness.

I had managed somehow to maintain the appearance of outward calm though my insides were roiling like an Irish storm. I knew better than express my insecurities, for they were mine alone to overcome. I reminded myself repeatedly that throughout history, there were men who left home for war or for purposes far less dramatic, and no doubt there was at least one woman behind the majority of them. Some women would cry, visibly meltdown, or issue ultimatums, but I was convinced all that did was create additional turmoil that served neither of them. If the man acquiesced, he would resent his inability to follow his destiny or show a side to the world that could be construed as cowardice, and the woman would resent him if he followed through with his plans.

No, I decided, it was better that I kept my anxieties to myself. There would be time enough once Nicky was gone for me to have the inevitable emotional collapse.

Still, it required all my fortitude to prevent myself from running away from Matherscourt. We stopped at the gate, and Nicky dismounted. As he helped me to my feet, he said, "We should walk to the gatehouse from here. Can you make it?"

I nodded, afraid to utter a word lest my voice was to divulge my inner turmoil.

He unsaddled the horse. We had little other than that, and he arranged it over his shoulder as he slapped the horse's rear, causing her to run back in the direction from whence we'd come. "She'll find her way home," he said, though I sensed a bit of doubt in his voice.

"I know we can't risk being found with her," I said. "It could expose the farmer's role…" My voice, already hushed, faded completely.

We walked in silence as the sun rose on the distant horizon. Birds began to stir, announcing a new day with their songs, and for a time, I could almost forget the Easter Rising and return again in my mind to those carefree days we had spent together. The mists and the clouds cleared as the sun came up, revealing a beautiful blue sky. I finally pulled my shawl away from my neck and shoulders and allowed the warmth of the sun to find me.

We had not yet laid eyes on the gatehouse when Nicky spoke again. "Penny, I'm staying with you for another day or so."

I glanced at him. I had thought he would see me safely here and depart immediately.

"I need to tend to my thigh," he said. "It's taken a bit of a beating these last two days. I need to be rested when I rejoin the others."

"I understand. I'll do whatever is needed for you."

"For us," he said. "There is no *you* and no *me* anymore, Penny. There is only *us*. Please remember that when I am gone."

"Gone temporarily," I stressed.

"Gone temporarily," he said. "I promise you."

The brook babbled a few yards away, the spray a reminder that crystal clear water was cascading over the rocks beneath the gatehouse. I sat in a tiny clearing while the branches of nearby shade trees attempted to stretch their branches over my head to join one another. The sunlight that found its way between them shed gentle rays over a set of birch bark purposefully laid out at my feet. I sat on a tree stump, busily working on yet another piece of birch, my pen a twig no larger than my finger that I expertly dipped into soot from a long-ago fire.

"That's amazing," Nicky said.

I hadn't heard him approach behind me, so engrossed was I in my art. I paused, glancing over the birch in front of me. There were a dozen pieces laid inches apart from one another. On each piece was a charcoal etching that, laid side by side, formed an intricate picture like pieces of a puzzle that appeared nonsensical by themselves yet together created a sweeping vista.

As Nicky knelt to study them, my eyes swept over the forefront: a vast mansion not unlike Matherscourt, the details conveying something akin to a palace with manicured lawns, rows of windows stretched over four stories, turrets and gables. But allow the eye to wander and just beyond the bastion of wealth are cottages with thatched roofs caved in, a skeletal dog sleeping between them, women in rags tending the potato fields in bare feet.

"Is it too depressing?" I asked.

"It is too realistic." He sighed. "It tells a story, it does; the more one stares at the individual components, the more the story unfurls much like turning the pages of a book."

I tried to see the pieces as he did. I thought them rather crude, as they were sketched onto pieces of birch and not a smooth canvas. "I will do better once I have my supplies again."

"No," he said. "This is perfect." He sighed and then peered into the distance. "A creative person sees the world differently from others."

I chuckled. "I have always been different; I never seemed to fit, as though I was from a distant planet and simply dropped here amongst humans."

"Ah," he said, looking back at me and smiling, "a creative person is not meant to be like everyone else. See that tree over there?"

I followed his nod to an ancient oak. Unlike the woods we sat in, the tree was set apart on a knoll.

"The average person sees a tree. Perhaps their mind registers the green grass underneath or a blue sky above. But the artist sees in their mind's eye the veins in each leaf and how the leaves are brought perfectly together in branches and how they, in turn, relate to the trunk. They see the way the light strikes the individual leaves and how it plays into a mosaic, Nature's piece of art."

I was silent as I surveyed the oak.

"The poet," Nicky went on, "seeks to place what he sees into words worthy of its beauty, a melody that conveys its essence." He smiled. "And a novelist sees characters beneath the tree; scenes unfolding. A battle, perhaps, or a budding romance. The tree becomes the setting around which the action unfurls. In the writer's mind, the tree morphs from spring blossoms to summer maturity to autumn splendor and winter's hibernation."

"And the musician," I added, my voice soft, "seeks to recreate the tree's unique energy, hopeful as spring, the diversity of summer storms or lazy afternoons. Autumn is the tune of mellowness and winter, sadness, and loss, yet hope arrives again in the spring."

"Aye," Nicky said, standing to peer at the tree and then back at me. "You see, a creative person should never experience the world as others do. It is in their imagination that we see beyond mere eyes to the stories that lie within. And that," he added, "is precisely what you have done with your art."

"Do you think—?" I hesitated.

"Go on," he urged.

"Do you think you might be able to pass these along to someone? I don't know how they would use them precisely..."

"They tell a tale," he said. "A tale of one place yet two very different realities. They live side by side, but each has unique experiences unto themselves... much like Ireland."

"Yes. That is what I sought to convey. It is the purpose of the revolution, is it not?"

"To level the field, aye." He pointed to the women portrayed in the potato fields. "They could still choose to tend their fields if that is where their heart leads them. But they should not be forced to labor there to make another wealthy beyond means. Yes, I will take them with me—if they can be packed so the sketches are not damaged?"

"I'll make sure of it. And then, if you find yourself in a position to pass them along..."

"I will do precisely that." He sighed. "I wish I could remain with you forever," he said at last. "I wish I did not feel this pull to rejoin the rebellion. And yet, what kind of a man would I be if I hid amongst the forest in my lady's arms while my countrymen risked their lives to make mine free?"

He stood only inches from me, and as I looked upward into his face, I fought back the tears once more. I seemed to be intent on making up for all those years in which tears would not come. It felt as if my heart had been ripped open and was yet to heal.

He reached out to take my hand, pulling me upward to him. "Do not be sad, Penny," he said. "I must leave tonight, and I want to remember you as content and brave. You will return to your art, and I shall return to you as quickly as humanly possible."

I opened my mouth to speak, but he did not wait to hear my words. His mouth was upon mine, hungry as a starving animal, determined to have his fill. As his arms wrapped around my body, mine encircled his. I wanted him so close that our bodies melded into one, our energy transformed so that when he must leave, a part of me was carried with him.

"I am told that Michael Collins himself rides a bicycle about Dublin every day," Nicky said. He was leaning on his elbow, his body glistening in perspiration even though the breezes had found us under the canopy of trees.

"With the British about? No. I don't believe you."

"Sean told me himself. You see, the Brits have a preconceived idea of what Collins looks like—rough, dirty clothes, a sod of a man." His voice became animated, his eyes dancing. "He wears a suit, you see, and a fine overcoat—and a hat like the Dubliners wear. He rides his bicycle right under their noses, says good day to them, he does, and they never know the man on the wanted posters just rode by."

"Will you do that with yours?" I eyed the bicycle leaning against the gatehouse.

He chuckled. "I doubt it, love. I'm too junior for all that, you know."

"What will you do?"

He became thoughtful, almost melancholy, and I almost wished I hadn't asked. Yet there was something within my soul that needed to know, if for no other reason than to picture him doing his part to free Ireland. Those images, I knew, would be all I had to maintain some sanity until we were together again.

"Sean said that the Irish Volunteer Army is well organized," he said pensively. "Yet they travel in small groups. They make their strikes like a coiled snake and then retreat quickly into the countryside. It is far more difficult for the Brits to fight a guerrilla war."

"Why is that?"

"They are accustomed to battle lines. Their men trained at the front lines with a defined enemy across from them. They take a hill, a village, a place of strategic importance. But here in Ireland, they have owned it all for centuries—nearly 700 years—so there is nothing for them to take. The men carry on as they always have, not changing up their routines, and then when they are least expected, they lash out, do their damage and disappear."

"But," I said, "If they do not alter their routines, what will you do? Surely you could not return to Matherscourt to finish the orangery."

"Forgive me, my darling, for I will not finish either the orangery or your gazebos. Not now."

"I don't care about that; only that you are near."

He nodded. "I will not know where they will send me or what duties I will be given until I report. Sean left a note with the bicycle."

"Yes. I saw it. One word—'selkies'."

"Aye."

"It was code, was it not?"

"It was. Of course, you know what a selkie is, yeah?"

I laughed. "Of course I do. They are mythical creatures that can transform from human form to seals and back again."

"Mythical, 'ey? So you don't believe in them?"

I almost answered but caught sight of his lop-sided grin.

"Sean and I have known one another our entire lives—we're only a few months apart in age, you know. And there was a place where we went as wee ones, waiting for the seals to be transformed under the full moon..."

"Will you tell me where that was?"

"Best you don't know, love." He leaned over me and kissed me. "In any event, it is only where I shall meet him. From there, I'll be given a new destination and a mission."

"How will I know—I mean—?"

"How will you know if I am alright?" he asked, his voice low. "Write me letters, Penny. Keep them with you at all times. And I shall write to you. One day you shall be paid a visit, and they shall hand you a note… and you should hand them your notes to me."

"Oh, Nicky," I breathed.

"You shall be with me," he said gently. "You shall remain right here." He touched his heart. "Regardless of my travels or my assignments, whether I venture far or near, I will carry you with me. And someday, you shall look up, and it will not be a messenger but me standing before you."

He kissed me again, his passion resurfacing, his embrace insistent. The fire between us grew as the shadows descended into the late afternoon, and with every moment that passed, I longed to get it back, to stave off nightfall and his inevitable departure.

43

I remained at the gatehouse for two days after Nicky left. Perhaps I hoped he would return for me. Or maybe I was simply delaying the unavoidable reunion with Stratford.

Shortly after his departure, I discovered a note he had written to me on the back of Sean's single-word directive. Unable to read it in the darkness, I'd waited impatiently for the dawn, as it was too dangerous for me to light a fire as the smoke would surely be detected by those at Matherscourt.

He had written a poem to me, and the Lord only knew where he had found the pencil. I kept the poem against my breast, close to my heart, the words etched into my memory.

Sun-streaked hair of fawn and flaxen
Beckon me with every turn
Soft and sensual, my lady, my lady,
How you make me yearn.

Eyes stormy as the Irish Sea,

They reach into my soul
Soft and sensual, my lady, my lady,
It is you that makes me whole.

The poem continued until he had run out of room on the tiny notepaper. If there was one thing that touched a woman's soul and caused it to soar with the eagles, it was the knowledge that a man utterly and completely adored her. I had pondered when it was that he had watched me without my knowledge, perhaps memorizing every last piece to carry with him in his heart. I'd spoken to him so many times in my thoughts since he had left, reliving every moment we'd ever had together, craving his return.

Fate was capricious, was she not, to allow a great love into my life only to whisk him away yet again?

I forced my thoughts back to my present situation. I had been largely silent as Nicky had declared Matherscourt to be the best place for me, but I knew better.

I was changed, irrevocably altered. I could feel it as strongly as a bolt of lightning coursing through my body. I was no longer the mousy Independence that had raced to the front foyer to greet a husband indifferent to my existence, standing meekly in line with the rest of the servants. I would never again attend an event in which a hard-hearted man sneered and criticized me in front of others to make himself feel taller, unfeeling of my humiliation. I would not, could not, suffer through another silent dinner with a callous clod of a man that had needed my name more than I had ever needed his money, regardless of my parents' opinion.

In fact, I thought as I strolled toward the barn and studio, the events of the past year had so entirely transformed me that I felt the courage welling up inside to turn my back on my own parents if they could not honor my wishes. I knew—oh yes, I knew—it had been societal norms that had compelled them to arrange their daughter's marriage to a man they had to have known would never have suited me. Yet despite that knowledge, I felt the bitter taste of anger rising inside me as I considered their acceptance of their only child existing for an entire lifetime with Stratford, never knowing love or even respect.

My parents could not have known he was impotent, and the mere thought that money was more important to them than their daughter's circumstances was repulsive as I shuddered while thinking what might have been my fate.

I was so engrossed in my thoughts that it was sometime before the odor of burnt wood reached my nostrils and registered in my mind. I halted and looked up and into the distance.

I had traveled most of the way from the gatehouse to the clearing where the barn, my art studio, and other outbuildings had been. But now, as I looked upon it, I hardly recognized it. My feet moved of their own accord, slowly, tentatively, as I sought to adjust to these foreign surroundings.

The buildings had been constructed largely of stone, which had kept them standing for a century or two. As I came first to the barn, I tried to remember its construction as I stared at its charred ruins. The stones were yet standing—at least most of them, the others buckled with the weight of a collapsed roof largely made of wood rafters. The door, too, was gone, transformed into a heap of embers and kindling. I peered into the barn through the opening. It no longer existed in shadows, the sun now able to shine its full intensity upon every square inch of it. The stables that had lined the sides were gone, the wood crumbled and burnt. The supplies so carefully transported in wagons by Peter and Nicky's workers were also destroyed, save for the stones meant for the orangery floor.

I tried to remember the last time I stood here. My eyes sought out the heap of hay under horse manure but found only ashes.

Somewhere in the distance, I heard a horse leaving Matherscourt, the hooves thundering with the urgency of its rider. It forced my attention away from the barn and toward the house.

The big house stood as it always had, intimidating and foreboding, a hodgepodge of architectural elements with no master plan, rooms upon rooms that were never used but simply built to impress. But as I stood there attempting to wrap my mind around the altered terrain, I realized that I had never been able to view the house from this clearing before. The woods that had sheltered me from watchful eyes had been decimated, only stubby trunks of charred wood remaining here and there.

I could, for the first time, witness a rider leaving the house along the circuitous drive that led to the main gates. My horse stood in the meadow as it always had. Now she caught sight of me and galloped toward the fence that appeared to be recently rebuilt. I caught sight of three people leaving the house, their destination clearly where I now stood.

I forced a deep breath from my lungs. I had been sighted. The horseman no doubt had been sent to fetch the husband I never wanted to see again, and the people coming toward me—

I narrowed my eyes. These were not servants. They were soldiers.

I stepped across the clearing and waited for them outside my tiny studio. The contents had been burned to the ground; all my paintings, canvass, and art supplies were gone. As my eyes settled on the interior, it was obvious that my studio was a total loss. I fought back the tears that threatened to sting at the corners of my eyes. I could rebuild, I told myself. I've lost everything, my soul responded inside me.

"Lady Mather?" one of the soldiers called out as they approached.

I turned away from the studio and squared my shoulders.

"Are you Lady Mather?"

One man strode before the others, his eyes fixed on me. He was short and stout like a teakettle, his hair the color of a sunrise, his skin leathered. He narrowed his eyes, but I could still see him assessing me from top to bottom and back again. No doubt I looked a fright; I was wearing the same clothes I'd left Matherscourt in on that distant day, an innocent in search of an art studio in Dublin. Sure, I'd washed them countless times since but I still felt like a vagabond.

A man on a horse rode swiftly from the direction of the newer stables closer to the house, coming to a halt near the man and quickly dismounting. The four men approached me with wary eyes.

"You are to come with us," the man in front stated.

"I will not."

Two of the men separated as though they intended to encircle me.

"That was not a request," the orange-haired man continued. "It was an order."

"Lady Mather," the horseman said, "I have brought a horse for you."

I pulled my shawl tighter to me. "I shall walk," I said before taking my first step toward my prison.

The house had changed. I tried to place my finger on it as I was led through the front door and up the wide main staircase. Aindriú was not at his customary place beside the door, the first time I noted his absence in all the years I had lived here. Johanna was also nowhere in sight. No maids were clearing the house of imaginary dust or polishing items that did not require it. And yet there were noises, not the hushed tones of servants cognizant of their employers but a distinct jangle from boot spurs and the baritone voices of men upstairs, a place that had been off-limits to all but female servants, excepting Stratford and me, of course.

As I made my way up the stairs between the orange-haired man in front of me and two others behind me, the heavy cloak of oppression bore down on me so deeply that I considered bolting, perhaps throwing myself out an upstairs window. Yet that momentary insanity was quickly replaced with the logic that I was unlikely to die but simply maim myself so not only would I be imprisoned here, but I would also be physically prevented from leaving even if the opportunity arose.

As we reached the top step and the orange-haired man stepped aside, I expected to see Stratford in all his fury and myself with only a lame excuse as to my disappearance these past weeks. Instead, I found myself meeting the eyes of Lord Philip Davies.

"That will be all, thank you," Philip said.

Reluctantly, the men turned about and started back down the stairs. Philip waved me into the center room. It was an odd room, to be sure, one of those architectural designs that made absolutely no sense whatsoever. The wide double doors faced the grand staircase and had always been left open to reveal a lounge complete with settees, ornamental tables, and European art. Yet the room was circular so it extended across the hall as an open bridge that peered down onto the main foyer below. This meant that it was open on both sides as it crossed the hallway. It was impossible not to pass through it when taking the center staircase, leaving it a room that was not actually a room.

"I have sent for tea," Philip said, "and for your handmaiden."

I could only stare at him as my mind tried to wrap itself around his presence and the absence of my husband.

"Come," he said, beckoning me to a set of chairs by the fire. "Sit. We have much to discuss."

A servant entered the room and set a tray of tea and biscuits onto the table between us. She quietly poured the tea into the cups and set several biscuits on each plate with the use of silver tongs. The tongs I recognized; the woman, I did not.

"That will be all, thank you," Philip said.

As the woman left us alone, he settled into one of the chairs.

I found myself perched on the edge of the chair. Though my stomach cried out for the food and drink, my nerves prevented me from following through. "Where is my husband?" I asked.

Philip placed two sugar cubes into his teacup and stirred. "The real question," he said, "is where you have been these past weeks."

I straightened my back. "It is not necessary for me to answer to *you,*" I said pointedly.

"Ah. But it is." He set the spoon down and sipped his tea. "I have been appointed by the king to assist in putting down the rebellion. You might have noticed that Matherscourt has been—shall we say—appropriated for that purpose."

"You have seized my home in the name of the crown?"

"That is such a strong word, Penny. I prefer to say it is temporarily a headquarters… But before we discuss that, it is critically important while we find ourselves alone that your presence these past weeks be fully accounted for."

"Are you asking on behalf of the crown, then?"

"I am." He pointed toward the tray. "You should eat, Penny. You've clearly lost weight while you have been… detained."

"Detained," I repeated.

"I will tell you where you have been," he said, leaning forward so quickly that I found myself drawing back. "You will listen, for I shall only tell you one time and one time only. Do you understand?"

I nodded.

"Your coachman brought you to Dublin on April the 24th. You were there selecting artwork for the new addition to Matherscourt."

My mouth grew dry, and I clutched the arms with whitening knuckles.

"You were caught, as untold others were, as the rebels seized buildings around Dublin. We discovered your carriage not far from the General Post Office, though it is unclear whether the rebels destroyed it or the soldiers did as they responded. Whatever the case, though the carriage was a complete loss, the horse was not. Miraculously, he found his way home within days of the uprising."

I swallowed. "That is a relief."

"I thought you would want to know. Eliza tells me how much you love your animals."

"Yes." I dropped my hands into my lap, each one holding the other to prevent myself from nervously fidgeting.

"Unfortunately, in the maelstrom, your coachman left you stranded," he continued. His teacup was poised halfway to his mouth, but he was staring at me over its rim. "And as you searched for him to take you home, you were knocked unconscious."

I met his eyes now, unblinking as well.

"It is unclear, as it was with your carriage, whether your injury was due to rebel activity or responding soldiers... though we strongly suspect rebel traitors." I started to speak, but he held up his hand to silence me. "You could not know, as they came from behind. Unconscious as you were, you are indeed fortunate that your life was saved when others stepped in to remove you from the area."

The sound of the downstairs door seemed like an intruder between us. He glanced once at the double doors and then back at me, fixing me once again with his stare. "Unable to tell others of your identity, they could only nurse you back to health as best they could. Amnesia is a terrible thing, you see. But as your memory began to return and you were able to travel, of course, you made your way home as best you could. You had no idea that several weeks had passed as you lay unconscious."

Footsteps sounded on the staircase, and we both turned to see Johanna standing in the doorway.

"And my coachman?" I asked, tilting my chin upward.

"Kilmainham Gaol," he answered. "Sentenced to death for his treason." Seeing my face no doubt pale, he added, "But world pressure has commuted that."

"To what?"

"Life imprisonment." A tense moment passed between us, and then he said, "I assume you wish to remain at Matherscourt now that you are home."

"I do not." The words surprised me as much as him; though I had carefully considered my future ever since Sean's visit, I had not intended it to be presented so abruptly.

"Ah. Then perhaps you will allow your maidservant to gather your things and spend some time as my guest at Davies Castle." I began to protest, but he held up his hand to silence me again. "I insist." In a louder voice, he said, "Please gather your mistress' belongings."

Johanna looked at him and then at me. "Aye, sir," she answered.

When we were alone again, I asked, "Where is Stratford?"

"Your husband?" he asked, his lip slightly curling. "I am afraid it will be impossible for you to visit him."

"And why is that?" I asked stiffly.

"He is in London. If you wish to write a note, I will ensure it reaches him."

"London," I repeated.

"London. He has been imprisoned at Reading Gaol."

44

I stood at a bedroom window at Davies Castle as Johanna unpacked my belongings behind me. The blue skies had given way to dark clouds, ominous clouds that seemed forever to linger over the castle as if the gods knew of dark secrets buried here.

"How long have you been here?" I ask without turning.

"Ever since the soldiers first inspected Matherscourt," she says. Her voice is low, almost halting.

"And do you know why the soldiers intentionally burned so much of the woods and buildings?"

"Oh no, m'lady, it was not the soldiers. No, not at all."

I turned then to peer at her. She held one of my gowns in her hands, half-folded. It was a gorgeous gown, shimmering gold with gossamer lace and pearl buttons, and it felt as though it belonged not to me but a stranger. "Then who did?"

"Well, ma'am, 'tis a long story, it is…"

I swiftly moved to the table where two chairs waited by the fire. "Sit," I directed. "And tell me everything."

"Everything?" she said, placing the gown upon the bed and joining me.

"Everything. Start at the beginning."

"The beginning… I suppose I should begin on the day you and Éamonn left for Dublin. Master Mather was home early that day with tales of rebels taking over the city, including the area around his office. It was not considered safe to stay."

"That was true enough," I said, remembering my own ordeal. "And did he ask of my whereabouts?"

Johanna avoided my eyes.

"The truth, Johanna."

"I am afraid he did not."

A long moment passed. Then I sighed heavily. "Go on. What of the fire?" I needn't have been surprised.

"Well, ma'am, after some days had passed, the Brits they began sweeping the countryside, looking for rebels, you see."

"And they looked at Matherscourt? Why?"

She swallowed. "They said they had a tip that weapons had been stashed there."

"A tip?" I felt the warmth rush from my face, leaving me clammy and cold.

Johanna held my gaze. "Master Mather did not know where all the buildings were located, ma'am. They searched the house, and they searched the stables, but…"

"But he was not aware of the old barn?"

"Aware, aye. But not the precise location."

"How curious."

"Aye, well, ma'am, I was asked if I knew so I led the soldiers past the meadow and into the clearing there… and Master Mather followed as well in his carriage."

"I see. And did they find anything?"

"Their spy said the weapons had been hidden in the barn, so they searched it, loft and all. Turned over much of the supplies for the orangery that had been stored there…"

I grasped my hands in my lap, thankful the table was between us so she could not see them trembling.

"So, did they find anything?" I asked again.

"No, ma'am. They did not."

I frowned. "But they burned the barn anyway? That seems rather unprincipled."

"They did not burn it, ma'am. Master Mather did."

"What?"

"While the soldiers were searching the barn, he began asking questions of me regarding the other buildings. I could not keep him from entering your art studio, ma'am—" She hesitated, her eyes filling with tears.

"No. I am quite sure you could not."

"He flew into a rage. Began destroying your paintings, m'lady." She dabbed at her eyes.

"So Stratford set the fire."

She began to cry then. I rose and quickly strode the length of the chambers to find a handkerchief. She had been using her apron hem to wipe away the tears that flowed so readily down her cheeks and gratefully accepted my offer of the handkerchief. I simply placed a hand on her knee and squeezed it as I sat, a rather sad display of empathy, I suppose, but I was aware that I was crossing the line between a lady and her servant. As I kept my hand there, patting her reassuringly, I realized I no longer cared.

Finally, she began again. "That night," she said haltingly. "After the soldiers had gone, I was asleep in my room when something awakened me. He had gone back to the barn, ma'am, and to your studio, and he'd set the whole lot of it on fire."

I pictured Johanna in an attic bedroom, her window providing perhaps the most advantageous view possible from the house. In my mind, it became a portrait; the flames red and orange, shooting into the night sky as a single face behind imperfect glass, framed in the tiny window, watched it burn.

"I could see it all quite clearly," she continued, her words flowing faster as if she needed to recite it all. "The flames, you see, they lit up the night sky like it was midday. And not a raindrop in view when it was the very time it was needed most. He was a madman, Lady Mather; I know he is your husband, and I shouldn't say such, but…"

"So he burned the buildings to the ground," I finished for her.

She nodded. "It was out of control so quickly; we all thought the flames would reach the house, but thank the Good Lord above that they did not." She crossed herself. "Then the soldiers returned, m'lady, right then, right in the middle of the night."

"Why did they return?"

"Some of the servants were outside, you know. Not helping to put it out, it was quite clear the Master did not wish it extinguished. But watching and listening. And—"

"And what?"

"They thought he was trying to destroy evidence. He'd come back to the house by the time they arrived, but there wasn't one among us that wanted to protect him, begging your pardon, ma'am."

"So that's why they arrested him," I breathed.

"Oh no, m'lady. No."

"Then, why?"

"I cannot say." She averted her eyes once more, staring into the fireplace.

"You cannot say, or you will not?"

"It is not my place to say more, m'lady. I cannot."

I leaned back in my chair. Oh, and sure I wanted to prod her as my curiosity was quite raised by this point, but as she continued crying, I realized I could not push her. It simply felt inhumane. "Do Lord and Lady Davies know the reason?" I asked instead.

She nodded while still avoiding my eyes.

"And how did Lord Davies come to work at my house?"

"He saved it, m'lady. Master Mather wanted to burn it all down. Lord Davies saved us—the servants—as well, ma'am. The soldiers, they were convinced…"

"Did they hurt you?"

She shook her head. "No."

"Do they know of your relationship with Éamonn?"

She shook her head again.

"Does Lord or Lady Davies know of it?"

She hesitated slightly and then nodded.

I rose from the table and returned to the window. I heard her sniffling a bit and then some scuffling as if she'd arisen and returned to her duties. After a moment, I said, "You should know, Johanna, in the strictest of confidence that I do not intend to remain here. I wish only a decent bath, fresh clothes, and some sustenance."

"Aye, ma'am. Lady Eliza is due home tomorrow—she's off visiting a friend, I believe I heard—and I was told to inform you that you could eat in the dining hall or in your room. I've already arranged bathwater to be brought up."

"What of Lord Davies?"

"He arrives home late each night, ma'am."

"I see."

"I'd best see what's keeping that bathwater."

I heard the door open and close behind me, and only then did I turn about to survey the room. It was monstrously large with a separate bedding area at one end, a dressing room nearby, and the table and chairs by the fire. A settee was also arranged by one long, narrow window.

But I missed the tiny cottage at Sally's Gap. I would have given my heart and my soul to turn back time. I didn't care that it had no oil lamps where this single room had a dozen. It didn't bother me that we had to keep a watchful eye on the mists and clouds to start and snuff out our fire, lest we were discovered. I never minded that my bath was taken in the startlingly cold spring or that I had no soap.

I was happy and content there and in the gatehouse. Money and frills meant nothing to me, but the love of a good man meant everything.

I wondered where Nicky was at this moment. I tried to believe he would remain out of danger; otherwise, I would simply go crazy. I remembered my promise to write to him, and on a whim, I scoured the room for stationery. I found some in a drawer and carried it to the table, where I began my first long letter. I would keep it on my person and would await the inevitable visit by a volunteer courier who would carry a note from him. I only wished it did not take long to arrive.

45

A week passed, and then two and I was no closer to leaving Davies Castle than when I'd first arrived. I'd been back to Matherscourt to wander the rooms and inquire of each of the servants but I could not bring myself to remain there. I felt as though I had not been the woman that had lived there, only a stranger peering into the rooms of the wealthy and still pining for the simple cottage in the woods.

I knew from Philip that Éamonn was imprisoned in Dublin, and because I was not a direct relative, I was unable to visit him. He also advised me not to render support of any kind, lest I be considered a co-conspirator, which would place me and those around me in danger. Johanna had been beside herself with grief over his sentence of life imprisonment, and Philip promised he would discretely look into his situation and provide her with updates through me.

Most of the other servants had disappeared, presumably to join the rebellion, or had been arrested out of hand during any one of the routine soldier visits. All of that had stopped, however, when Philip made the house a headquarters of sort, indicating that the owners—Stratford and myself—wanted to support Britain in this wartime effort, despite Stratford's imprisonment.

Only Léana remained. I thought for certain she would be judgmental about the servants' involvement in the Easter Rising, so I was taken aback when I visited her in the kitchen and found her fully in support of the rebellion.

"'Tis not right," she said in a huff as she kneaded soda bread. "We've laws in this country, have we not? Laws that required those arrested be tried and an appeals process to boot. Instead, they're brought up on charges that wouldn't stick in a court of law, especially not our Éamonn."

I sat at the kitchen table where I had eaten so many of my breakfasts. At the end of the table was a stack of newspapers, and I began absent-mindedly perusing them as she went on.

"And then to shoot them as they did! The leaders, I'm talking about, not poor Éamonn," she said with a lift of her brow. "Every morning at dawn, another was executed. Murdered, if you ask me. It's not right. It's not what an advanced civilization is supposed to do."

She'd kept all the newspapers from *The Irish Times* detailing the Easter Rising, the executions, and its aftermath. Roger Casement was the only one left whose sentence had not been commuted, and he was scheduled for execution in London sometime this summer. My stomach began to turn somersaults inside me.

I turned over one of the papers to view below the fold and stopped as I felt the blood drain from my face. My heart racing, I opened the paper fully to look at the date at the top. "London," I breathed.

"What'ya say there, ma'am?"

"Nothing," I said, my throat so dry that the word came out in a hoarse voice that didn't sound like me at all.

"Ah, the London *Times*," Léana said, glancing at the paper. "Lord Davies prefers it over the Irish papers, I believe." She peered more closely at me. "Is there something amiss, m'lady?"

I took a swallow of tea before I answered. "No," I answered carefully. "Just this picture here, it took me by surprise."

I heard her voice as she answered, but she sounded distant, her words lost somewhere in the short distance between us. I was focused on the picture that took up a good portion of the front page and the article below it. Of course, I recognized the sketch immediately—it was Missus O'Rigley, sitting in her dilapidated cart, her face drawn and wizened as shoe leather, her clothing threadbare and ragged. The mule that pulled it was nearly skeletal, the saddest animal I think I'd ever laid eyes upon. I vaguely remembered sketching it and seemed to recall Eliza taking it by mistake, but how it traveled from her shop to the front of the *Times* was beyond me. I felt completely surreal as I stared at it before forcing myself to read the story underneath.

Contrary to what I would have expected from an English newspaper since the Easter Rising, I found indignation regarding the condition of Irish peasants. The story went on to say the woman in the picture—that thankfully remained unnamed—was trading mealy potatoes for other necessities and had no home to call her own but slept in her cart wherever she happened to find herself. I tried to remember what little I knew of Missus O'Rigley and wondered whether a journalist had found her or was simply filling in the story with his imagination. Regardless, the sketch and the article had obviously made an impact with the editors for there it was on the front page, just below the fold.

"Had it not been for Lord Davies," Léana was saying, "all the servants in this house—including myself, mind you—might have been carted off to the gaol, they were that determined when they made their rounds."

I forced myself to set the paper aside and gather my wits. "So Lord Davies was here immediately then?" I asked.

The teakettle whistled, and she paused to freshen my cup and place some crumpets on a plate. "He was. Uncanny it was, how he seemed to know what they would do and where they would go."

I sipped my tea for a moment. "Do you know what happened with Lord Mather?"

She peered at me, a startled expression on her face. "What do you mean by that?"

"Did you know he's been sent to prison?"

She began kneading the bread as the color rose in her cheeks. She avoided my eyes, much as everyone else had when I'd brought up my husband's name.

"Well?" I prompted.

"I'd heard as much."

"Do you know why?"

"Do you?"

"I asked if you did."

"And I asked the same of you. Begging your pardon, ma'am."

I chewed on a crumpet. It tasted too sweet to me now, and I found myself thinking of the berries I'd picked not long ago and a world away. "So, you do know."

"It's a crime against God hisself," she said, shaking her head.

"What is?"

She slapped the bread into a pan. "Master Davies will be looking for me. I beg your pardon, ma'am, but I've work to do."

She had never spoken to me in that tone before, and I felt the heat rising into my cheeks. The world had certainly changed in my absence. "No, I don't believe anyone would fault you for feeding the mistress of the house," I said. "So, you shall remain here until you are dismissed."

Her eyes widened. She opened her mouth to speak and then closed it again before making her way back to her spot. She looked at the bread in the pan for a moment as though it held a lot of interest for her. Then she began pulling out vegetables, washing, and chopping them. "Have you enough there to eat?" she asked after several silent minutes. "Or would you like more tea or biscuits?"

"I am fine at the moment." I left the crumpet half-eaten. "What of Aindriú?"

She made a noise as though she was exasperated and flung down the knife she was using. I jumped, stunned by the noise of the blade hitting the table so close to me. "Lady Mather," she said, her chin rigid, "If you have any questions regarding Lord Mather or the butler, I strongly suggest you take it up with Lord Davies. It is not my place to discuss it, and Lord help me, I never will."

With that, she stomped from the kitchen, leaving me alone with my thoughts. It hadn't been as though I hadn't asked Philip—or Eliza, for that matter. And though Eliza had been my dearest friend, neither of them wished to discuss it. They both had the same response to me, as though they'd rehearsed it: I would know soon enough, and for now, I must regain my weight and my strength and focus on my future.

I folded the London paper and tucked it under my arm. I had work to do.

I had considered my future many times over since my return, and I thought of it yet again as I strolled from the house to pet my horses in the meadow. I was cognizant of eyes upon me; perhaps it was only my imagination, but it seemed the walls had ears, and the windows were full of spies these days. I could imagine no future here, but my role was beginning to become apparent to me. In fact, I'd felt rather like a ship foundering at sea, but amid the storm, a lighthouse had appeared on the horizon, and the beacon was growing brighter by the minute.

I fed carrots to the horses and leaned against the railing for some time. There were matters to be considered, of course. I could not continue living on Eliza's goodwill indefinitely. Philip had indicated that I could return to Matherscourt, but I knew it was not where I belonged; I would be throwing in the towel somehow and returning to a former life I hadn't wanted then and most emphatically did not care for now. With Stratford tucked away in a London prison, I would not have to endure the negative cloak of energy that always seemed to precede and follow him, but something still hung in the air here.

With the woods burnt, I could see the orangery from where I stood—or what would have been the orangery, had it been completed. Apparently, none of the workers had appeared for work the day of the Easter Rising, and none had returned after. I had no idea how many were imprisoned or—like Nicky and Sean—how many were on the run, waging guerrilla warfare against the British.

I turned toward the clearing. I had not ventured there since that first day I'd arrived back home. Home, I thought. No, it most definitely was not that for me anymore, if it ever had been. Perhaps I could move into the gatehouse. The thought appealed to me. I could select furnishings from the house, hire workers to transport them, and set up a rather comfortable existence for myself.

No, the other half of my brain argued. Nicky could return at any moment, even if just for one night. As far as I knew, no one was aware of the gatehouse, as isolated as it was. I could not risk exposing it and possibly exposing Nicky in the process. Best that it be kept as secret as it had always been.

I strolled toward my old art studio, despite my reservations about seeing it again. Imagine, I thought, all the times Nicky and I had been in the throes of passion at the gatehouse, never knowing Philip Davies and British military were stationed in my house a short distance away! I would have been terrified, had I known—terrified for us, but more so for Nicky. He was a wanted man now, from what I knew.

I missed Peter as well, and my heart broke again for him and his son. The violence and the vengeance were too close to Nicky to ignore.

The studio was as I'd last seen it, except more rain had fallen upon it, creating deeper mounds of soot and mud. The roof was completely caved in. I stood just outside the window and remembered all the times I'd been inside and watched for Nicky to come down that meandering path toward me. Those were simpler times; had I known it at the time, I would have savored each moment more fully.

I stifled a gasp as my thoughts turned to the sketches and paintings Eliza had procured from me. I came around the front of the tiny cottage and stepped through the doorway, my slick shoes no match for the wet slime. I passed by mounds of canvass burnt almost so that they were unrecognizable. I discovered my paint set only because the rainbow colors had streaked across the stones, muted now due to the ever-present rainfall and mists so they appeared like a reflection of a sad rainbow.

It was difficult trying to figure out exactly where my hiding place had been, but eventually, I found the rug, burnt and charred, and it took me quite some time to dig it out. The metal case in which I'd hid the money would surely be ruined under all this, and it was too much to ask that the coins and especially the paper would have survived. Yet I was compelled to search for it.

I had not noticed anyone approaching the tiny cottage until I laid hands upon it. Trembling, I opened the case, the clasp warped from the fire. I gasped as I looked at the contents; it was all there. Every bit of it was there.

"Found what you were looking for?"

The voice alarmed me, and I almost dropped the case as I turned to look at Philip standing in the doorway. "I did," I said.

"May I see it?"

He made his way over the debris much as I had done, and I handed him the case. He rifled through it for a moment before handing it back. "Eliza told me she had been purchasing your artwork."

"Yes," I said, swallowing.

"It is good that you have it," he said. "Stratford's assets have been frozen until his trial."

"I see."

He offered his hand. "Allow me to assist you."

I took his hand and allowed him to lead me back to the door. He relinquished his hold on me once I had set foot on the firm ground outside the cottage.

"You should paint again," he said, eyeing me.

"Where would I sell them?"

"Eliza would buy almost anything you paint," he said, a small smile beginning to form.

"So the art gallery—it was not—?"

"Destroyed? Completely. And the curator disappeared; probably returned to England. Who would wish to remain in Dublin if they didn't have to? Still, there could be others. And it might be therapeutic for you."

"I agree." I held the box in my hands and considered the weight of it. "I have the means to purchase the supplies I'd need."

He eyed the box. "I would say so."

We began to stroll back toward the meadow and the house beyond. "Philip, what are the charges against Stratford?"

He sighed but did not answer.

"I have a right to know, Philip. I am his wife."

He stopped and turned toward me, placing his hands upon mine as I held my little money box. "You do have a right," he said. "But might I refer you to Eliza? She can explain it far better than I—"

"I doubt that. And I have already asked her; could you think I would not? She simply looks away, as everyone has whenever his name has been brought up."

"I've no doubt." He placed his hands behind his back and continued to walk.

"Or I could travel to London myself," I said.

"No," he said. "Best you remain here. I will advise Eliza to tell you of his circumstances."

"Thank you." I found the words odd, even as I'd spoken them. I knew had it been Nicky arrested, I would have moved hell itself to discover the charges and arrange for adequate legal representation. Pangs of guilt threatened to assail me.

Philip simply nodded, his mouth set and eyes dark. Several soldiers were riding up the road toward Matherscourt. Unlike the horse-drawn carriages I'd become so accustomed to, they rode in trucks that puttered and spit, the tires grating on the gravel, breaking the serenity of the countryside. It might have been my reason not to purchase the things, but Stratford had other reasons—the cost and the maintenance. He had a stable boy that was adequately trained but to purchase a vehicle meant to employ a mechanic, I think he called it. And apparently, that was very expensive.

The crown apparently had quite a bit of money, I thought as I witnessed the small caravan. Philip offered his apologies and hurried toward them, eager for any bit of news that he no doubt would keep from me.

But now, I had his permission to speak to Eliza—and apparently, she knew everything.

46

The lighting was perfect as it streamed through the open window. I was upstairs at Davies Castle, not in my chambers, but in one of the many reading rooms, my easel, and canvass adjusted to catch the thin streams of muted light that managed to find their way through the ever-present clouds that hovered over the castle like malevolent spirits. I was simply following the light with my paintbrush, casting a pale yellow glow over the nearly-finished painting.

On the left side of the canvass was a simple white cottage, the door ajar, and smoke swirling from the single chimney. It was set in the foreground of a copse of woods that wound their way behind a clearing before reemerging on the other side in the foreground. Following the light through the window as I was, created an effect as though the sunlight was streaming through the forest canopy.

"Ah. There you are."

I looked up to find Eliza in the doorway. She swept in, her long skirt sashaying about her ankles.

"Am I interrupting you?" she asked as she came to stand alongside me.

"Not at all," I said, setting down my brush. I stood back to survey my work.

"It is simply stunning," she said. "Perhaps your best work yet." She stepped forward, peering closely at it. "This technique you're using—what is it called?"

I followed her finger as she pointed toward the chimney and then toward two of the trees in the right foreground. "Do you like it?"

"It is magnificent. But I have never seen that technique used before. You must tell me about it."

I chuckled. "It's something I invented, actually. I wasn't quite sure how it would turn out." I pointed toward a larger tree in the foreground. "I began to collect tree bark from my strolls around Davies Castle, and I wondered how it would appear if I used them atop a few of the trees I'd painted."

"They appear to pop right out of the canvass," she mused. "But how do you get it to stay there?"

"Paint," I said. "And tree resin."

"Tree resin?"

"It acts as a type of glue. Mixed with the paint, it becomes stronger, I suppose."

"And you thought of this yourself?"

"Idle minds," I laughed.

"It's brilliant." She peered more closely at the house. "And the chimney?"

"Bark as well, just laid sideways and painted as though they were stones."

"Positively brilliant."

"Now that you're here," I said, "do you mind if I ask you a question?"

Eliza strolled around the room, admiring more of the paintings I'd begun. With the money I had recovered from my art studio, I had purchased several easels, watercolor paints, and palettes. The painting had helped me immensely to while away my time as the days stretched onward with still no word from Nicky. She stopped near the fire. With her back to me, she said, "I've been expecting more than one."

"Philip told me you knew why Stratford has been imprisoned." The words tumbled out bluntly and not at all what I had rehearsed.

"Do you want the short answer or the details?"

"If you stood in my shoes, which would you want?"

She turned to face me, her dainty hands folded in front of her. "Sodomy."

"What?" I felt the room tilting precariously, and I fumbled to find a handhold on a nearby chair.

"You'd better sit," she said, but I had already begun to make my way around the overstuffed lounge chair to sink into its deep cushion.

"But," I managed to say, "That's impossible. Stratford is impotent."

"Apparently not." She moved closer to me but did not sit.

"What? How?" I struggled to form the questions that were roiling through my mind.

"A lot happened while you were away."

"Apparently."

She smiled weakly before quickly growing somber. "Rumors flew regarding the insurrection. As more troops landed in Ireland and they gained control of the city, they began to fan out into the countryside."

"Yes. I'd heard."

"There were—*are*—spies everywhere. And apparently, someone tipped off the authorities that weapons had been stashed at Matherscourt."

"Yes. Philip told me as much."

"Then he might have told you of the fire Stratford started?"

"He didn't, but Johanna did. But I don't understand the connection—"

"It raised additional suspicion—perhaps that he was trying to cover up evidence that had not been found during the first raid." She paced toward the window and peered out as if she could see Matherscourt, though it was several miles in the distance.

"Ah."

"And Philip knew they would destroy Matherscourt looking for it. He stepped in—as many loyal British subjects were doing—and offered to seize your estate on behalf of the crown." She turned back to face me.

The questions began forming in my mind, tumbling one over the other. "Philip had been in the Armed Forces, hadn't he?" I asked in a low voice.

"He had, yes. Years ago, which is how he obtained his title."

I nodded.

"He could not go to Matherscourt alone; he took a small unit with him. It included, unfortunately, Lord Alderidge, who outranked him." She returned to the chair across from me and held onto its back with pale, genteel hands. She peered at me curiously. "When they arrived, they did not knock—they simply burst into the house."

A pregnant pause ensued. In my mind's eye, I envisioned the great estate, so formidable and commanding, being brought to its knees in the wake of the rebellion. Finally, I said, "And?"

"And they found Stratford and your butler—Andrew, I believe?"

"Aindriú." I swallowed.

"—engaged in his chamber."

I felt the color drain from my face, and my lips grew cold, my hands clammy.

"Would you like more details?" she asked.

"No." My voice came out far more forcefully than I had intended.

She took a deep breath. "Had it been Philip in charge," she went on, "he might have been able to—shall we say, conceal the incident. But Lord Alderidge was there and immediately had them both arrested."

"I see."

Eliza came around to the front of the chair and sat on its edge, reaching her hands out to mine. Gathering my cold hands in hers, she said, "You needn't remain married to him, you know." My silence might have given her the courage to say more as she continued, "Everyone knew it was a marriage of convenience. You two were never suited to one another."

I nodded.

"Now that the charges are public, no one could fault you for leaving him. After all, you had been fighting to regain consciousness somewhere in Dublin. He should have left no leaf unturned in the search for you. Instead, he was… inappropriately and illegally engaged elsewhere."

"What will become of him?"

She shrugged her shoulders. "Do you care?"

"I suppose I do, in a way."

"He has not yet been sentenced. You might be too young to recall the trials of Oscar Wilde."

"I was in my teens," I said. "And I remember the salaciousness of it all."

"Then you know he was imprisoned at Reading Gaol—the very same place Stratford is right now—for the very same charge."

"He received two years' sentence at hard labor, did he not?"

She nodded. "It broke him."

"I devoured his books once upon a time… *The Picture of Dorian Gray* was always my favorite. And I read *The Ballad of Reading Gaol…*"

"As I've said," Eliza said, fixing me with a compassionate gaze, "No one would fault you if you left Stratford."

I nodded.

"It says a great deal that you did not wish to remain at Matherscourt."

"I imagine it does to outsiders. But it isn't enough to know when it is time to leave. One must have a destination in mind."

"And you haven't discovered one?"

"I am close to it… There is simply so much uncertainty in these times."

"Oh." Eliza abruptly pulled her hands from mine and removed a piece of paper from her pocket. "I'd forgotten why I came up here in the first place."

As she handed me the paper, I recognized Nicky's handwriting immediately as he'd neatly written my name on the outside. My head jerked upward.

"Have you one for him?" she asked, cocking her head. "It is never read by anyone save the recipient—unless it is intercepted, of course."

"And was this note—" I swallowed "—intercepted?"

She smiled. "No. It was not."

I fumbled inside my breast pocket to retrieve my note. It felt strange now that it was gone; I had carried it with me day after day, pulling it out only to add to it.

Eliza was on her feet now as I handed her the slip of paper. "It will make its way to him," she said as she strolled toward the doorway. "It might take a few days or even a few weeks—but it will reach him. I give you my word."

"Eliza," I said as she began to leave. I rose from my chair as she turned to face me. "Are you—could you be—?"

Her smile grew wider. "Let's just say you were not the only woman involved with a servant on the side of Irish freedom."

Brian's face raced through my mind. Consumed by my own thoughts and worries, I hadn't realized until that moment that I had not seen him since returning to Davies Castle. "He is not imprisoned, I hope?"

She shook her head. "No. Staying one step ahead of it."

"Good. Let's hope that becomes several steps… And Philip?"

"He does not know of Brian, of course."

"Of course."

She turned back to the doorway, but I called out to her again before she passed over the threshold. "Eliza, Philip served in India, did he not?"

She turned slowly. "He did."

"With Roger Casement," I added.

A small bittersweet smile crossed her face. She nodded, and then she was gone.

47

I could hear Nicky's voice in my head as I read his letter. I could feel his warmth surrounding me and could sense his presence as strongly as if he had just entered the room. Though they might have been mere words on paper, it felt as though he was reaching across the miles to caress my soul.

I had retreated to my bedroom, where I could read his note in private and without interruption. It had begun only hours after he'd left the gatehouse with the words, *"I miss you more strongly with every mile that distances us. I want you to know I fell in love with you the first time I laid eyes upon you. I know that sounds ridiculous, doesn't it? And yet it is true. You are the woman I thought I would never have the good fortune to find."*

The sentences below those were written on different dates, as if he'd kept the note in his pocket and added to it as the days had turned to weeks.

"I have arrived at my new job, an apprentice with much to learn." I hesitated, allowing the words to sink in. Of course, I told myself, he could not tell me where he was in the

event he was detained and the note discovered. But with these words, I knew he had found his rightful place in the rising rebellion. I wondered what he meant by becoming an apprentice and what he was to learn.

"It is a soft day," he wrote on another day. *"And I remember all the soft days we laid in one another's arms. Do you miss me as I miss you?"*

A soft day. I looked upward through the window, remembering all the times in which the rain was only slightly more than a mist. Had he written those lines on one of those days where I'd stood at the window staring into the distance, wondering where he was?

"At my new assignment now," he wrote. *"Taking advantage of those places I am most familiar with."* Sally's Gap, perhaps? How I wish I was there now!

I continued reading, and when I was finished, I began again, looking for clues. Nicky had joined the rebellion, was trained, and was assigned to a unit. They were, perhaps, placing men where they best knew the terrain and the people and would know who they could count on and who might betray them.

I read the letters twice and then three times before I settled in a chair where my eyes could wander over the gently rolling hills and valleys, dotted with sheep and patches of vegetables.

I could not remain at Davies Castle; that much was evident. Eliza and Philip had been most accommodating, but my life stretched before me, and I was wasting time.

I heard the roar of a vehicle before I saw it winding around the hills toward Davies Castle. I glanced at the clock on the mantle. Philip was home early.

And I would be meeting him as he stepped out of his car.

"Penny," Philip exclaimed when he saw me.

"I must speak with you," I said, bypassing the usual formalities.

"Of course," he said. He nodded at the driver in the open car. "That will be all." Turning back to me, he said, "Perhaps after dinner, we can chat. I haven't been around for that much lately."

"Yes," I answered. "I would enjoy that as well. But I wish to inform you—I would like to go to Dublin tomorrow."

"Dublin?" A frown began to cross his face. "Whatever for? It has changed, you know, Penny, there are soldiers everywhere—"

"I could care less about the soldiers. Stratford's office had been ransacked during the rebellion. I would like to get it in order."

"I see." He cupped his chin in his hand as he eyed me thoughtfully. "You know his assets have been frozen."

"I do. And I suppose the court has appointed someone to oversee *our* holdings?"

His eyes widened briefly as I stressed the word. "That is correct."

"And who would that be, precisely?"

"Lord Alderidge."

"The same Lord Alderidge that discovered my husband… indisposed?"

"Yes. Look, Penny—"

"Then I should like to see him tomorrow as well." I folded my hands in front of me and steeled my spine.

After a moment, he smiled. "I shall be delighted to accompany you into Dublin tomorrow. We shall visit Stratford's office, and I will send word to Lord Alderidge that we wish to call on him as well."

"Very well." I returned his smile. I felt a mixture of relief that I would not need to argue my position with him and a bit of trepidation regarding what hurdles I may still be required to navigate. It was humiliating, to say the least, to look people in the eye knowing they knew of Stratford's situation, but I had already formed a plan to deal with it—and my future.

48

The next day dawned a beautiful summer morning without a cloud in sight. Philip and I met briefly for breakfast; Eliza generally slept until noon. Then we were off with a soldier driving the vehicle while Philip and I rode in the back.

Dublin had changed yet again. In the space of a few months, it had gone from the Dublin of my childhood—a city that had rarely changed over the decades—to a war zone. Now it was an occupied city with soldiers stationed everywhere I looked. They patrolled the streets with their rifles at the ready, staffed checkpoints and cast a long shadow over the city.

The GPO was open again, yet as we passed, I could not ignore the telltale signs of the shooting that had occurred there. Though the windows had been replaced, there were pockets in the brick where bullets had sought to seek entry, a grim reminder of what had transpired there.

The art gallery was still closed, the windows and door boarded up, and a somber pall was cast over everyone. Though I witnessed a few soldiers cackling or laughing at jokes I could not hear, most of the population went about their business with long, drawn faces. I suppose since we were in a military vehicle, our progress was steady, but I could not resist comparing it to those dark days in which navigating a block took hours.

We parked directly in front of Stratford's office. Saint Stephen's Green was mostly hidden from street view, though some of the hedges that had lined parts of it were still pitifully chewed up from the fighting that had occurred there. I was surprised to find the offices along this stretch to be repaired with new windows and doors as if nothing had ever happened.

As we alighted from the vehicle and made our way to the door, I found myself searching for bullet holes in the brick and was somewhat surprised I didn't see any. It was a stark reminder of the ambush the Irish had encountered as dawn had illuminated the green; it appeared as though the fire had gone in one direction only.

I steeled my back as Philip opened the door and escorted me inside.

There were two men in the front room; both of them I recognized from having been introduced years before, but now I could not remember their names. One was short and stout with a pockmarked face and bulbous nose, while the other was young and slender.

"Mister Addington," Philip said to the older of the two. "You remember Lady Mather." He spoke the words as if the man would certainly not have remembered me.

Mister Addington nodded in my direction. "Ma'am," he said curtly. Though I held out my hand, he did not take it.

"And this is—?" Philip said as he stepped toward the younger.

"Bradford Beckwith," Mister Addington said. "My apprentice."

After shaking Philip's hand, the young man stepped toward me, took my hand, and kissed it so gently that I barely felt his presence through my glove. "M'lady," he said.

"Lady Mather wished to pay a call to the office here," Philip said as his eyes roamed the walls.

"Did she now?" Mister Addington said, his contempt barely concealed.

I walked to the wall I remembered from my last visit there, where I remembered studying the montage of photographs joined together to depict several city blocks comprised of townhomes. The medley was mounted beneath a single frame under glass. Despite what had occurred here, each of the townhomes was still outlined and contained a list of names, as though the soldiers had had no interest in the markings. I was surprised the glass had not been broken.

"And what is this?" I asked.

"Nothing," Mister Addington responded. "Only your husband's properties."

"And if my husband had asked you to explain it, would you have answered that they were 'nothing'?" I asked icily.

He did not respond, and I stared at it for a long moment, attempting to memorize the layout of the homes as well as the names within them.

"Are there others?" I asked.

He shrugged.

I looked at Philip.

"Lady Mather asked you a question, sir," Philip said. "I suggest you answer."

The color rose in Addington's face until his burgundy nose appeared to grow even larger. He waved his hand at the other walls and a smattering of photographs on a nearby desk. I took my time wandering the room. Some of the photographs appeared to be of townhomes fit for the upper crust of society, gauging from the exteriors. Others were under glass as the largest one was and contained names written with heavy black markers.

"And are these properties rented to all these people?" I asked.

He did not answer, and I looked again at Philip.

"Answer the Lady," Philip said.

"They are," he said curtly.

My memory was thankfully very good, as was my math skills. I counted perhaps a hundred townhomes. "All of these are in Dublin?" I asked.

Addington shrugged. "I would have to check."

"Would you like for him to check?" Philip asked me.

I shook my head. "Not at the moment, no." I made my way to the stairwell. I peered up the stairs, remembering how I had stood at the top, staring down at the soldiers that had occupied it before dawn on that fateful day.

"There is nothing upstairs," Addington said.

I continued staring upward. "Nothing?" I asked.

"Nothing."

"Then why have a second floor?"

"There is a second and a third," he answered, not attempting to conceal his distaste. "But they are all used for storage."

"All?" I asked.

"All," he replied.

"I see." I turned back to Philip. "I believe Lord Alderidge is expecting us."

"He is indeed," Philip said. He offered his arm to me and escorted me back to the front door.

As I started to step over the threshold, I turned back. Addington was rustling papers on the desk, clearly agitated. The young man—Bradford Beckwith—smiled at me. "Good day," I said.

The young man answered. Addington did not.

As Philip and I approached the vehicle, he said, "I wouldn't take Addington's attitude personally. You're a woman, you know."

"Yes, I seem to remember that."

He smiled. "It's highly unusual for a woman to be involved in her husband's business."

"I suppose," I answered as I climbed into the vehicle, "it is highly unusual for a woman's husband to be incarcerated for sodomy as well."

Lord Alderidge's home was situated in a Dublin neighborhood far removed from the city center. Here the homes were arranged on lots that appeared to be ten acres apiece, many with wrought iron fences or stone walls separating them from the winding road. Lord Alderidge's home was a formal Georgian estate built of limestone. The double doors were in the center with three windows on either side, all of which sported identical draperies. Above the door rested another window and then three windows on either side to match those beneath. There were no shutters, and the house seemed quite barren of personality.

The boxwood was square and formal, the pungent scent reaching my nose even before we had exited the vehicle. The hedges gave way to English Ivy that roamed up the side of the house, framing some of the windows.

Philip pounded the large brass knocker once, and as we waited for the door to open, I noticed the cornice above the doorway with the date the home was built: 1780.

Both doors were swung open wide to reveal a butler in a stiff black and white uniform. "Lord Davies," he said politely. "Lord Alderidge has been expecting you." As I crossed the threshold, the butler bowed slightly. "Lady Mather."

The foyer consisted of a large square with an inlaid marble floor. In the center was an oriental rug upon which a small round table perched. A vase filled with fragrant flowers overpowered the table, the fauna so plentiful that even the vase was nearly obscured.

"May I take your hat, sir?"

I kept my bonnet on as Philip relinquished his tall hat to the butler.

"You may wait in here," he said, beckoning to the first room on the left. "I will announce your arrival."

We made our way into the room. One wall was covered completely with cabinets, the shelves overwhelmed by the number of books, which easily numbered into the hundreds. Two large windows overpowered the opposite wall, a narrow table between them containing a lamp and a few pieces of bric-a-brac.

Philip motioned toward a settee that faced the fireplace. Though it was a warm summer day, a small fire was going, which made the room a bit stifling. As I sat in the middle of the settee, Philip took one of the two leather high-backed chairs beside the fireplace.

A moment later, Lord Alderidge arrived, followed by a servant in a black uniform with a starched white apron. She carried a large tray, which she set on the table in between the settee and chairs and efficiently poured three cups of tea while Philip and I rose to greet our host.

"Sit, sit," Lord Alderidge said as he made himself comfortable in the chair opposite Philip. Though he was of medium height, he was portly, his middle straining at the buttons of his vest. As he sat, his pants rose so I could view his ankles thick with gout. His gray hair was thinning, but what hair remained poured over his collar as if the length was intended to make up for the lack of volume. He rather reminded me of paintings I had seen of Benjamin Franklin.

We chatted for a few moments about the weather and our ride into Dublin before the conversation turned to Stratford.

"Lady Mather wished to visit her husband's office before our meeting with you," Philip explained. "We were rather surprised to find it operating as usual."

Both sets of eyes turned toward me, and I found myself in the disadvantageous position of being seated on a lower, softer settee while the men occupied the higher, more formal leather chairs, so I stood and made my way to one of the larger windows closer to the fireplace. As both men made to rise with me, I waved them back into their seats.

"That is correct," I said. My voice carried across the room, but I did not lower it. "Perhaps you can explain to me what Misters Addington and Beckwith were doing in my husband's office."

"Of course," Lord Alderidge said genially. "Mister Addington has been in your husband's employ for more than a decade. He manages the properties."

"And Mister Beckwith?"

"He collects the rents."

"And how often are the rents due?"

"Weekly."

The servant handed me a cup of tea on a dainty china saucer. I thanked her and took a sip before turning my attention back to the men. "I will not waste your time, Lord Alderidge, which I am certain is quite valuable, so I shall come straight to the point: I wish to run my husband's business."

Both men appeared shocked.

"And what do you know of running a business, Lady Mather?" Lord Alderidge asked after he managed to recover.

"Quite a bit," I answered. "I know, for example, that when the wealthier residents left the city center, Stratford purchased their properties en masse. I know that he then converted them to tenements—"

"I would not call them tenements," Lord Alderidge chuckled.

"*Tenements,*" I pressed, "housing as many as eighteen families under one roof. I also know that many of those tenements were partially destroyed during the rebellion."

"Is that true?" Lord Alderidge asked Philip.

Philip accepted a plate of sweetmeats before answering. "If Lady Mather says it, then it is true."

Thank you, I said silently, hoping Philip could sense my appreciation. "And," I continued, "with my husband incarcerated, I am certain you understand the benefits of continuing to operate his business—*our* business—so the properties do not fall into further disrepair."

"That is precisely why Addington and his apprentice were brought in," he answered.

I set my cup and saucer upon the mantle and turned to face the two men fully. "That is precisely why I am here." Before either could respond, I continued, "I wish to occupy the office. I want full disclosure to anything I may ask of Addington or Beckwith with the firm understanding that they report to me now. I want access to the accounts held jointly in my name and my husband's. And I want the power to do anything in his absence that he might have done had he not been… otherwise detained."

There was a stunned silence. I remained standing, my hands gathered in front of me. I squared my shoulders.

"We have no reason to doubt your husband's loyalty to Britain," Lord Alderidge said after a long moment. "I assume the same can be said of you."

"Of course."

"This is highly irregular," he went on.

"I assume you do not have the time to monitor our business," I said. "I am certain you are kept rather busy with your own."

He chuckled. "That I am."

"I am prepared to allow Matherscourt to remain a regional headquarters," I continued. "Lord Davies can remain there with British soldiers for as long as necessary. I wish to remain in Dublin, where I can better monitor our business, prevent any losses, and optimize profits."

"I believe the law allows for that, sir," Philip said.

"Yes. Yes, it does," he said. He rose, setting his tea and sweetmeats on the mantle beside mine. "I am sure you understand that I will need to oversee things," he said, his blue eyes fixed on mine.

"In what way?"

"Simply to ensure there are no losses," he said, throwing my own words back at me. "And to ensure profits are optimized."

"Certainly."

"Only," Philip said, rising as well, "because Lord Alderidge has been appointed as guardian since your husband's incarceration."

"And why you, Lord Alderidge, and not myself?" I asked.

They stared at me for a long moment.

"Because I wear a skirt?" I offered. "Perhaps once you understand I can run the business as efficiently as my husband, you will petition the court to transfer guardianship to the woman that rightfully owns it."

"I knew your father," Lord Alderidge said, his eyes narrowing a bit, "I grew up with him, in fact. And I know your family to be upstanding and honorable. It is a pity that he and your mother relocated to London after the rebellion. Though," he added, "I suppose it is perfectly understandable."

"You may be insinuating," I said, raising one brow, "that my father is better qualified to run a business built by Stratford and myself. I can assure you, sir, that he is not."

He nodded. "I shall visit the books each week."

"Of course."

"Then, she has your permission?" Philip asked.

"She does."

"To run it as I see fit," I clarified. "To reduce losses and optimize profits."

"To run it as you see fit," Lord Alderidge answered.

"Then I appreciate your hospitality, sir," I said, glancing at Philip. "But I must take my leave. I have much work to do."

49

Bradford smiled and greeted me warmly as I entered the offices a second time, and Mister Addington's roll of the eyes was not lost on me, either. I marched straight to the desk in which Addington sat. "I'd like a list of all properties owned and managed by this firm."

"I am busy at the moment," he answered curtly.

I placed both palms on the top of the desk and leaned forward. "I'd like a list of all properties *now*."

Addington slid his eyes past me to Philip, who was standing to my left. While Addington's face was red with growing ire, Philip's was one of amusement. "I work for Lord Stratford Mather," Addington said, "and I did not hear orders from him."

"No," Philip said, "you heard orders from the other owner of this firm, and I suggest you comply."

"Lord Alderidge—"

"Lord Alderidge has given Lady Mather full control of this establishment." Addington opened his mouth, but Philip cut him off. "Full control," he repeated.

Addington swore under his breath, but at that moment, I felt a light tap at my shoulder. Turning, I found Bradford standing beside me, a list in his hands.

"Here you are, ma'am," he said. "All properties are in this ledger here, along with the renters and amounts due."

"Thank you," I answered, accepting the ledger. "Bradford, is it?"

"Or Brad, ma'am. At your service."

"And you are whose apprentice exactly?"

"I was hired by Lord Mather."

"I see. And how long have you been employed here?" I heard Addington huffing behind his desk, but I ignored him.

"Three years, ma'am."

"Three years. And has that been sufficient time for you to learn what is required here?"

Addington's huffing became louder.

"I think so, ma'am."

"I see." I turned back to Addington, whose face was the color of a beet, his cheeks puffed up like a peacock. "That is all," I said.

He mumbled something under his breath that I could not quite decipher and took to his pen and paper, stabbing the latter with the pen as he wrote.

"I said," I repeated, "that is all."

He looked at me and then at Philip, who was appearing quite entertained.

I folded my hands in front of me. "Your services are no longer required, Mister Addington."

His eyes widened, and to prove his skin could grow redder still, it did.

"Do you have a key, Mister Addington?"

He fumbled at his pocket.

I held out my hand. "Then, I shall require it."

"This is preposterous!" he bellowed, his thick fingers fumbling so at his pocket that the key dropped to the floor.

As Brad stepped forward and picked it up, I said, "What is preposterous is your behavior, Mister Addington. Kindly get your hat and leave these premises. You are not to return."

"I—Lord Mather—"

"You are fired, Mister Addington."

He stared at Philip.

"Lady Mather has *full control,*" Philip said after an awkward silence. "Now and tomorrow and every day after that."

With a curse, Addington stomped across the floor and grabbed his hat from the peg near the door. He turned as if to say something, and from the expression on his face, I knew it would be cruel.

"There is nothing you can say," Philip said, cutting him off, "that will improve your circumstances."

Addington grabbed the door handle and propelled himself through, slamming the door behind him.

After a few seconds, Brad said, "Your key, ma'am."

I accepted it from him. "And do you have one as well?"

"No, ma'am."

"Then you shall have one by the end of the day. You shall be my assistant manager, Mister Beckwith."

A broad smile inched across his face.

"I shall take my leave if I am no longer required," Philip said. "Shall I send transportation for you later?"

"There are a horse and carriage in the back," Brad said, "and I will be honored to escort you wherever you need to go."

"Thank you," I said. I turned back to Philip. "Perhaps, because of the roadblocks, you wouldn't mind sending your man to fetch me—say, around six o'clock?"

He smiled. "I shall do precisely that, Lady Mather." He made his way to the door. He turned back to gaze at me, and then his eyes shifted to Brad. "I know you will have a very productive day."

I watched as he departed, closing the door quietly behind him. Then I turned to Brad and pointed toward the large set of photographs on the opposite wall. "Do you know where those rentals are located?"

"I do, ma'am," he said. "I collect the rents each week."

"Ah. Then please ready the horse and carriage. I should like to pay them a visit."

"This is the place," I said, directing Brad to stop. In contrast to the empty streets I'd encountered during the rising, they were now filled with children playing in the streets. A game of baseball was taking place with sticks for bats and pine cones for balls. Having no real idea of how this game imported from America was played, they appeared to be making up the rules as they went. I was able to peer between the blocks across the street where laundry was swaying in the Irish breeze, while a few women gathered around a pot placed upon a fire. I saw no men at all of any age.

I looked over the ledger I held. "I'm looking for Nora."

"Nora Murphy?"

"You know her?"

"I collect rent payments from her each week."

"Ah," I said. "I suppose you do."

"M'lady, you may as well know, and I suppose you could fire me right this instant—"

"What is it, Brad?"

His face turned red with embarrassment. "I was supposed to put all these tenants out last week, but I just couldn't do it."

"Who ordered you to do that? Mister Addington, I presume?"

"It's the way things are done, ma'am. Rents are due weekly, and if they don't have it, they are put out immediately."

"And why didn't they have it?"

His face was drawn and sad. "It's been this way since the rising, ma'am. Some of the women, well, their husbands are at the front, and some of the checks were missing on account of the GPO—"

"I see."

"—and work has been hard to come by. You see, many of the renters work by the piece, and some of the employers won't venture into these parts since the rising..."

I had climbed down from the carriage as Brad hurried to my side. He had the look of dread about him as if he was trying to steel himself to put out entire buildings of renters. He scurried after me as I approached the door to the second from the end, reaching around me to open the door for me.

As I walked in, I was assaulted by memories. Giant holes remained in the walls where the soldiers had busted through, and I found myself peering into the adjacent rowhouse where a bevy of tiny faces peered back at me. One was coughing, and from the sound of it, it was coming from deep within the chest. She looked pale and skelctal, and even on this fine summer day, she was wrapped in layers of threadbare blankets.

A hush fell over the inhabitants, and I could feel eyes upon me, stretching all the way down the row as mothers were notified of a stranger in their midst. I wondered if any of them recognized me from that fateful night. I certainly recognized them.

Brad had gone on ahead of me. I followed the sound of his voice to the back room.

"But you're a day early, you are!" It was Nora's voice exclaiming in alarm. "Rents are not due until the morrow, Mister Beckwith."

"Aye, and I know it, Nora, but you did not pay for last week, and neither did the others..."

"Oh, please don't put us out. You can see we're hard at work, sir, and I'm to be paid on the morrow. My husband's check, it never arrived, and it's put us back, it has—"

I stepped to the doorway and peered around Brad. Though my line of sight was mostly blocked, I saw her throng of children's fingers busily sewing pieces together at the table where she'd so graciously taken me. An infant bounced on someone's knee—her eldest, I presumed.

"I'm sorry, Nora," Brad was saying. "The owner is with me today, you see—"

I cleared my throat, and Brad stepped to the side, allowing me entry. "I apologize, Lady Mather. This is—"

"Nora!" I exclaimed, crossing the room to hug the startled woman. When I pulled back, her face was filled with confusion. "Do you remember me?"

Her eyes quickly moved over my clothing and my face, but she said nothing.

"I did not know I owned this property when I was here last," I continued.

"Oh!" she cried out. "Oh, I am so embarrassed!"

"You've no need to be embarrassed. You should be proud of taking in a stranger and for giving me a roof and warmth during a dark and frightening night." I felt something at my hand and I looked down to find one of Nora's daughters peering up at me.

"I remember you," she said. "You held me."

"Yes," I said. "I held you, sweetie." I blinked back tears as I ran my hand through her pale yellow hair. "And Jamie? Is he—?"

"Here, ma'am." Jamie stepped forward from the corner shadows.

"Did they detain you?"

"Aye, ma'am. At Kilmainham. But I did no wrong, ma'am—"

"Of course, you didn't. How long did they keep you?"

"Six weeks, ma'am, more or less."

"He was released due to his age," Nora offered.

"I see." I didn't know how well-informed the woman truly was or how much she chose not to reveal, but I knew of the pressure mounting against England after the leaders were executed so swiftly. I knew that word had traveled regarding the scores of men and boys sent to gaol, including the long imprisonment they faced without the benefit of a trial. It was that pressure, particularly from America, that had forced England to release the youngest and commute the sentences of many a man—and woman—caught up in the maelstrom.

"I apologize, ma'am, my manners," Nora said. "May I offer you—" she peered around the tiny room.

"No, thank you," I said. "In fact, I was wondering if I might borrow you and Jamie for a while. It won't take long."

"Borrow us, ma'am?"

"For only a short while."

A look of panic swept over her face, and I realized that many a tenant was not only put out when the rents were not paid but could also be imprisoned for non-payment. "I may have a job for you both," I added hastily.

"A job, ma'am?" Her eyes swept over the sewing that continued despite our presence.

"I see you're all very busy with work," I added. "I suppose this sustains you?"

"We never know how much work we'll be offered," Jamie said. "It comes in by the day."

My eyes swept over the children at the table, many of whom appeared to be the same age as those playing outdoors. They were all pale, their hair disheveled, their cheekbones prominent, and their fingers mere bone. It crossed my mind that each of them could be older than they first appeared, as I had no doubt they were all undernourished. Then my eyes wandered to the corner from where Jamie had stepped. A flatiron rested upright on a short table, the steam still rising from it while a nearby chair on one side held a stack of wrinkled clothing and one on the other side held neatly stacked and folded clothing.

"And is your deadline this evening?" I asked.

"Tomorrow at dawn," Nora answered. "But we were hurrying on account of…" Her eyes cut over to Brad, who had remained quiet during our exchange.

"Then I promise not to keep you for longer than an hour."

Nora wiped her hands on her apron before removing it. She nodded to her son.

As we made our way out of the rowhouse, I was aware of many more eyes on me than when I first entered. Word had traveled quickly that the owner had arrived, I suppose, along with the man that collected their rents. Brad assisted first me, and then Nora into the carriage and Jamie settled on the seat beside Brad.

I opened the ledger to a separate page and held it forward for Brad to view. "I wish to go here," I answered.

"Are you sure, ma'am?" Brad answered, his brows knitting.

"It is only a few blocks from here, is it not?"

"Aye, ma'am, but..."

"But what?"

"It hasn't yet been renovated, ma'am."

"You mean divided."

"Aye, ma'am."

"Yes. Well, that is precisely why we are going there."

50

The vacant rowhouses were at the edge of the tenements, a square block almost identical to the others but in far better condition. Though the exterior clearly needed upkeep, the interior might have been vacated only the day before by a family firmly ensconced in high society. With Brad's monstrous ring of keys, we were able to enter easily, and we spent a bit of time strolling through the main floor.

Nora was a slight woman, so thin she appeared as though a strong wind could pick her up and set her back down anywhere on the isle. Her hair was the color of straw, parted down the middle and gathered at the nape of her neck in a tidy bun. Her eyes were clear and bright, as blue as the sunniest day and so large they seemed to take over her face entirely. Her smile was hesitant, I suspect due to rotting teeth apparent when she spoke.

When we reached the back room, I turned to the others. "Nora," I said, "I need someone I can trust to clean up these houses. If you're interested, you're hired."

"Aye, ma'am, I am indeed," she said without hesitation, "But my sewing—"

"The job would not end there; far from it," I interrupted with a gentle hand to stop her. "You can see from this floor alone that it has not been renovated as apartments. I suppose you know people who are hard workers and can divide them?"

"I know many in construction, ma'am, many indeed."

"Then you would oversee their division. The people you hire will reflect upon you. Hire well, and you'll be paid well. Hire poorly, and I'm afraid your job will be short-lived." I stopped for effect and to meet her large eyes. After a moment, I continued, "Jamie can run your errands for you; find the men you'll list, for starters. If the men are truly qualified, they will be able to provide an inventory of materials with the correct quantities. The inventory is to go to my Assistant Manager, Mister Beckwith."

Nora's eyes met Brad's before returning to me.

"Mister Beckwith will arrive at a budget for renovation, and you're to remain within that budget. He will also determine a time table which you must meet." By this point, I was strolling down the center hall. I stopped at the banister. It was richly engraved and highly polished. "You are to maintain as much of the original workmanship as possible; this banister, for example, the crown molding and baseboards, the trim around the fireplaces and windows."

I peered upstairs. "Three more things, Nora. There are to be no more than three apartments per floor, and preferably two."

"Lady Mather—" Brad began.

I held up my hand to silence him but continued looking at Nora. "And you are to select one floor to be your own, in either this house or any of the adjoining ones."

"An entire floor, ma'am?"

"An entire floor."

"Could it be the top floor, ma'am? On a corner unit?"

I smiled. "It can be any place you'd like." I glanced away as I saw tears forming in her eyes, lest I begin bawling along with her.

"And the third thing, ma'am?" Brad asked.

"The people you hire to renovate will live in these units. They will be assigned once they are completed to my satisfaction. When this square is complete, you'll begin renovating your former home and the square around it, so it matches these."

"But, ma'am," Nora exclaimed as though she had just thought of it, "the rents—they would be so much higher-"

"Your rent and your workers' rents will be included as part of your compensation. You'll be paid weekly for all hours worked, so you'll have to maintain proper records, Nora. No fudging or everyone's positions will be in jeopardy."

"Of course not, ma'am, I would never—"

I cut her off to provide the rate of pay for Nora, her son, and the initial workers.

"But, ma'am," Nora said, "That's more than twice our pay now!" Then she clamped her hand over her mouth as if to take back her words.

"Then, you will have to do an excellent job to maintain that rate," I answered. "Your children can still sew if that's what you—and they—wish to do." My voice softened. "But I do hope you will send them to school and also allow them to play. Children grow up all too quickly."

"When shall we start, ma'am?" Jamie asked.

"Today or tomorrow, depending on your commitment to the sewing." I began to walk back through the house toward the front door. I felt more than saw Brad falling in line behind me. When I reached the door, I hesitated and turned back to peer into Jamie's smiling face. "One more thing, Jamie," I said, "I shall need two strong men at my office tomorrow. Mister Beckwith shall give you the address. I would like some furniture moved."

"Aye, ma'am," he said, nearly laughing in his joy. "Aye, ma'am, and you shall have them!"

Brad and I were almost to the carriage when we heard Jamie's whoop and holler ring out, followed by Nora's high-pitched laughter.

"Do you think they'll be alright to get back home?" I asked as I settled in.

"Oh, aye, ma'am, and they will," Brad answered, clucking to the horse. "'Tis only a few blocks, and the way they're feeling, they'll run it for sure."

"Keep a close eye on things, Brad. I want this done right."

"I will, ma'am," he answered, smiling. "I will… May I ask you something, ma'am?" he added thoughtfully.

"Of course."

"How do you know precisely what to do—with the subdividing and rents and so forth?"

I chuckled. "I paint," I answered after a moment. "I merely look at the houses as a painting and decide what should be done and how. It is your job to watch the money—incoming and outgoing."

"I'll do a grand job for you, ma'am."

"I know you will, Brad. Of that, I have no doubt."

The men were waiting on the stoop when I arrived the next morning. They rose as Philip's driver pulled in front of the offices, each holding their hats in their hands. I found Brad already at work inside, but my instructions would change his morning.

Three hours later, the offices on the second floor had been completely changed about to make room for all the furniture from the main floor, for the exception of a desk and chair for myself that would remain on the ground floor. Brad selected the office he preferred with my urging, settling on one at the top of the stairs overlooking Saint Stephen's Green. He was quite beside himself with the view and the accommodations.

Two overstuffed chairs meanwhile made it down the stairs to sit in front of my desk in the front room—but they would not remain there.

I found a good amount of paint, brushes, and supplies in the storeroom to the rear of the front entrance, separated from the front room by the hallway. My instructions were clear, and by mid-afternoon, the men had combined all the supplies into one room further down the hall and closer to the alley door and had finished a fresh coat of white paint in the backroom that would become my office. With the paint still drying, they moved in the ornate desk from the front room, my leather chair, and the two overstuffed chairs on the other side of the desk.

Then they set about painting the front room.

The shadows were long when Philip's driver returned to fetch me back to Davies Castle. Brad had been busy all day between the workers at the office and Jamie with his lists and had left only a short while earlier to perform a daily inspection of the properties under renovation before heading home himself. I'd languished along each wall, watching the waning sun scatter muted beams of light throughout the front room. This was the perfect room for an art studio.

51

The past week had passed by in one quick blur. I had managed to set up an art gallery on the main floor that was set to rival the one Eliza had owned near the GPO. I had no art as of yet, but the walls had been painted, screens set up to create both a flow for foot traffic as well as additional space for mounting paintings, and the walls had been painted a serene eggshell blue. The front picture window had been cleaned to the point where it very nearly appeared invisible, allowing a beautiful view of Saint Stephen's Green, which bustled with energy so that it was difficult to remember what had transpired there.

My office in the rear of the main floor had also been meticulously arranged; though the office did not have a window, my desk had been placed so I could see across to the front. It allowed me to keep one eye on the door as well as observe the myriad activity on the street outside.

Upstairs had also been transformed into a set of offices. Brad's was at the top of the stairs, and Nora's office was across from his, though she was rarely there. I could find her from dawn to dusk at the rowhouses; she seemed to be everywhere at once, directing the carpenters in subdividing the property, the painters in brightening everything up and even landscapers clearing the underbrush that had grown so quickly. She'd wasted no time in selecting the top floor, corner unit with a beautiful view that peered away from the tenements and toward the city center. Her furniture had been moved the first morning. Though it had not yet been divided from the rest of the house, she and her family were settling in.

Now Brad and I stood at the end of the second story hallway as he fumbled through a separate set of keys he'd found in Stratford's desk, having exhausted all his tries from the large ring of keys that constantly jangled from his belt. "Ah," he said now. "This is it."

The door opened outward into the hall, revealing a dark and narrow staircase. At the top of the stairs was another door leading onto the top floor.

He handed me the key. "Would you like me to accompany you, ma'am?" he asked meekly.

I hesitated. "I'll call down when I reach the top. I assume it's the same key, wouldn't you think?"

"Aye, ma'am. I'll wait here then."

The staircase smelled musty, and the dark wallpaper peeled away as if to expose the age and condition of the structure. As I made my way up the uneven stairs, I assumed I'd find myself in a stale and mildewed attic, and I would be right back down almost as quickly as I'd gone up. But when I reached the door, the key unlocked it as gently as if the lock had been recently oiled, and as I opened it, I was flooded with light.

I called down to Brad to let him know I was fine by myself, and as he departed from the doorway below, I turned my attention to what confronted me. Rather than the dreary attic I expected, I found myself in an opulent apartment consisting of a sitting room, a bedroom, a bath, and even a small kitchen.

I crossed to the front windows overlooking Saint Stephen's Green and pulled back the heavy draperies to allow more light to stream inside. I found to my surprise that the initial light that had greeted me upon opening the door was due to several glass panes set into the slate roof above, allowing in the Irish sunshine. It was the perfect place to paint, I thought excitedly, but it would require a complete renovation.

The walls in the sitting room and bedroom were covered in dark burgundy wallpaper, the crisscrossed pattern in gold. The settee and chairs in the sitting area were of engraved mahogany, the upholstery in burgundy. The tables were of black marble, the gold veins matching the color in the wallpaper.

As I made my way into the bedroom, the scent of Stratford's cologne hung heavy in the air. The bed was tall, the posters of elegantly engraved mahogany. The cover was of deep burgundy velvet with animal skins scattered at the foot and on a side chair. A bearskin lay in front of the fireplace, now cold and neglected. A soaring wardrobe reached nearly to the ceiling, which was so unusually high that I came to the conclusion that he'd had the original ceiling removed to reveal the attic rafters, now painted in black. Inside the wardrobe were several sets of clothing from loungewear to formal suits.

I made my way to the bath, where I peered in at a gold claw-foot soaking tub and a matching gold sink. It must have cost a fortune to plumb the third floor. A window opened onto the back alley, which, to my surprise, revealed a beautiful view of the city as I stood higher than most of the surrounding buildings.

I dragged myself away, crossing from the marble bath floor onto dark hardwood and oriental rugs as I crossed to the kitchen. It was simple but functional, a tiny table for two tucked beneath another window. As I wandered toward the window, I realized it was actually a door, and I quickly slid the table and chairs out of the way. I opened the French doors and found myself on a narrow wrought-iron balcony, too small for any furniture but enough to allow in fresh air during morning breakfast or a wine-capped dinner.

"Amazing, isn't it?"

The voice startled me, and I turned to find Eliza peeking into the kitchen.

"I had no idea this was here," I said, returning to the kitchen to close up the doors.

"What will you do with it?" Before I could answer, she added, "I love what you've done with the first two floors. You've utterly transformed them."

"Yes," I said, smiling. I met my friend at the doorway to the kitchen, hugging her though it had only been a few brief hours since I'd left Davies Castle shortly after dawn. "Care for some tea?" I eyed a teapot. "I'm certain he has some..."

"I'd love it."

As I busied myself with boiling water and discovering china cups with matching saucers, a crystal container filled with sugar cubes and gold teaspoons, I watched out of the corner of my eye as Eliza made her way around the walls, studying the artwork.

A few minutes later, I set a tray onto a table and handed her a cup of tea. "We've no cream," I said apologetically.

"No bother," she answered. She sipped it genteelly before settling in on the overstuffed settee. "So, what will you do with it all?"

I studied the room. "I plan to gut it," I said finally. I smiled slyly. "Do you think Stratford would mind?"

She eyed me thoughtfully. "Philip believes he will be in Reading Gaol for two, possibly three, years. It will be months before he goes to trial and judging from other sentences for the same crime, I don't see how he can return to face society here..."

"Am I foolish for empathizing with his situation?"

"Foolish? No. It's who you are, Penny. But will you stay with him?" She touched her dress a bit self-consciously, and my attention turned to the ruffles around her cleavage.

"You don't have—?" I leaned forward.

"I do." She smiled and dipped her hand past the ruffles to retrieve a note.

As she handed it to me, I noted my name in Nicky's handwriting. My heart leaped and then plummeted as I realized it was a single, small note and not the long pages he had written before. I opened it gingerly. *Our regular spot midway between the summer and autumn solstice. Love, N.*

"You love him," Eliza said.

I glanced up to find her gazing at me, her eyes a bit teary. "I do," I answered. "I suppose I always have."

She nodded and took another sip of her tea.

"You were never having an affair with Brian, were you?" I asked gently, folding the note and slipping it into my pocket.

She cocked her head. "What gave me away?"

"It didn't fit with yours and Philip's relationship, Eliza. The more I've come to know Philip, the more respect I have for him. I'm relieved, to be honest, that you haven't been cheating on him."

"He is most definitely a good man."

"Then why concoct an affair? It seems to be there could have been other subterfuges."

She shrugged. "It's funny, isn't it? It is perfectly acceptable for a woman of wealth to carry on an affair; scratch the itch, you know, even while her husband is doing the same elsewhere. But to agree with a peasant's politics… Oh, that is quite surely a mortal sin."

"It's a strange world we live in." After I moment, I asked softly, "And how is Brian?"

She looked away from me but not before I caught the panic in her eyes.

"Eliza?"

She set her cup on the table and stood, making her way to the nearest window to peer at Saint Stephen's Green. "He was with the 2nd Battalion of the Dublin Brigade of Irish Volunteers." She smiled weakly. "Quite a mouthful, isn't it?"

"Did he see fighting?"

"I've heard bits and pieces. They were sent to Jacob's Biscuit Factory, midway between Saint Patrick's Cathedral and the Green here."

"In the tenements?"

She nodded. "The Irish attacked them, not the British."

"What?"

Her voice grew softer. "Many of the factory's workers lived in the tenements. While the rebels held the factory, they couldn't work, and of course, if one does not work…"

"They don't have money for food or rent."

"Precisely."

There was a moment of silence before I said, "But did the British attack them?"

"Only sporadically. The leader, Thomas MacDonagh, eventually surrendered them as it became obvious their cause was lost."

"Thomas MacDonagh," I repeated. I tried to remember that day that seemed so long ago now when I stood in the doorway of the stable and read the newspaper listing the executions. "Was he…?" My voice faltered.

"He was a brother-in-law to Joseph Plunkett, did you know that? They married sisters, Muriel and Grace. He studied to become a priest before abandoning it to become a teacher. He was never a soldier; not really. His passion was poetry." She turned toward me as the sunlight caught the tears rolling down her cheeks. "MacDonagh was executed on May 3rd by firing squad, the same day as Patrick Pearse and Tom Clarke and the day before Joseph Plunkett was executed."

"Oh, Eliza."

"Two others were executed from the 2nd Battalion."

"Not Brian?" I breathed.

"Michael O'Hanrahan; he was Vice-Commandant. He argued against taking the factory; he said it placed the tenements in jeopardy if the British were to attack, as they were hemmed in by the tenements on all sides. He was concerned for the women and children and other non-combatants."

I thought of Nora and Jamie and the scores of families packed into the tenements before quickly pushing the memories away of the soldiers axing their way through from one house to the next. "And the other?" I whispered.

"John MacBride. He wasn't even part of the planned rebellion; he'd been living in Paris with his wife, a Frenchwoman, before returning to Dublin. He only joined the fight after the rebels began taking control of the city."

"God rest their souls," I said. I waited what I hoped to be an appropriately silent moment to grieve their passing before adding, "So Brian was not executed?"

She shook her head. "Arrested, though. And I'm afraid his trail has gone cold from there."

"But can't Philip find out what's become of him?"

"He's tried. General John Maxwell ordered 3,400 arrested. One hundred and eighty-three people were tried without a jury or defense. I believe they were all found guilty." She chuckled, but it was obviously forced. "Not surprising, is it?"

"But they stopped the executions."

"They haven't released all the prisoners," she said. "And somewhere, Brian is imprisoned."

"He'll be released," I said, but my voice did not carry much conviction. "The pressure is mounting against the British, from America to Europe and beyond."

We were interrupted by the sound of Brad's voice in the stairwell. "Ma'am?" he called.

I arose and made my way to the top of the stairs.

"Sorry to interrupt, ma'am, but Lord Alderidge is here to see you."

"I must be going," Eliza said, drying her eyes quickly. "See you tonight at Davies Castle?" Her eyes swept the apartment. "Or will you be staying here?"

"I shall see you tonight," I said, squeezing her hand. I followed her down two flights of stairs, reluctantly saying my farewell before welcoming Lord Alderidge.

"So you see, Lady Mather, I was just as surprised as you," Lord Alderidge said as he blew his nose rather loudly into his handkerchief.

"But it simply cannot be true," I insisted.

"I thought the same, but I've come from a meeting with his banker, and I am afraid it is." He rifled through his pocket to retrieve a calling card. "Ah. There it is." He glanced at it briefly before handing it to me.

I did not look at it. "It cannot be true," I said again. "He is mistaken."

"Well, it appears, Lady Mather, when one routinely spends more than one earns, this type of thing occurs."

My mind moved sharply to the orangery, still half-finished as it stood the day before the Easter Rising. I pictured the odd assortment of additions with rooms we never used, rooms built only to impress.

"It appears the only thing that can be done," he was saying, "is to liquidate everything except Matherscourt."

"What are you saying?" I breathed.

"You must protect your estate," he urged. "By ridding yourself—" he waved his hand in the direction of the office "—of all of this, you can afford to remain at Matherscourt with a roof over your head. That is," he added, "if you live frugally enough."

"Get rid of all of what, precisely?" I asked, my back straightening.

"Why, this business, of course. The poor investments your husband made—the tenements, other landholdings. It isn't as if he is here to manage them, and he won't be for quite some time from the sound of things."

"How long do I have?"

"I can hold off the banker for a month; two, at the most. If you visit him yourself, you might be able to buy yourself more time. He is generally in London, but he led me to believe he will be in Dublin for a few more days. I would not dawdle if I were you."

"London?" My voice was barely over a whisper. I opened my palm to reveal the calling card. "Simeon Reginald Watkins," I read.

"Do you know the Dublin main bank?" Lord Alderidge said. "It is only a short walk from here."

"I do," I said. "It's on the other side of the Green."

"That it is." He rose and replaced his tall black hat. "I shall take my leave. It isn't every day I must inform one that they are destitute, and I regret having to do it today…"

The rest of his words were lost on me as only the single word *destitute* hung in the air like a black storm cloud. I don't remember walking him to the door, but I must have as sometime later I found myself still holding onto the door handle. Then I shook myself out of my stupor. Brad might not have overheard our conversation, as he had remained on the second floor while I had descended to the ground floor to usher Lord Alderidge into my office. I called upstairs to him to let him know I would be taking a short stroll. I tossed a shawl about my shoulders, grabbed my small bag, and set off, the bell still chiming in my ears as the door opened against it.

52

I saw a wave of recognition wash over Simeon Watkins' face as I strode through the massive double doors. He had been standing near the bank of tellers, and when he spotted me heading in his direction, he turned his back to me. Though he made a few steps in the opposite direction, he wasn't fast enough to avoid me.

"Mister Watkins," I said, my voice ringing out in the hushed, hallow confines of the bank.

He turned to face me, his eyes imploring me.

"Lord Alderidge gave me your name," I said, loud enough for the closest tellers to hear me. "I am Lady Mather, and if you have a moment, I should wish to speak with you about the affairs of my estate."

"Of course, Lady Mather," he said, gently taking the hand I extended to him. "Right this way, please."

He led me to a side office and beckoned me to sit in the chair across from an imposing desk. Taking the tall leather chair behind the desk, he said in a low voice, "Thank you very much, Lady Mather, for not mentioning our prior... encounter."

"I thought when Lord Alderidge gave me the card, the banker must be one and the same."

"Yes. I thought it best for our previous meeting that we meet outside the bank. The walls have ears, you see."

"Of course." It was not lost upon me that the door remained open, and there was a window between us and the main lobby. "Then I shall get straight to the point. Lord Alderidge has informed me that I am nearly destitute."

He took a deep breath. "I am afraid your husband overextended himself."

"What of Matherscourt?"

"I don't quite follow you, Lady Mather."

"What is owed on it?"

"Why, nothing at all. The estate has been in your husband's family for generations."

"So, nothing is owed on it?"

"Nothing. I am pleased to report that if you rid yourself of your husband's other land holdings and investments, you can remain at Matherscourt. There are sufficient resources for its upkeep, at least, for the foreseeable future."

"And if I sell Matherscourt instead, Mister Watkins?"

"If you—what? Surely, you are not suggesting—"

"What is it worth, sir?"

His eyes flickered with a myriad of emotions. "I am afraid it is not that simple to sell an estate such as Matherscourt."

"And why not?"

He stared at me for a moment as if stunned. "You must realize, Lady Mather, that an estate such as yours would sell for an astronomical amount. It would be difficult to find a buyer with that kind of money, and the house could sit on the market for a decade or more."

"I see." I arched one brow. "And what if the contents were sold? What would they fetch?"

"The contents? I—" He stopped himself and looked down at his desk for a moment. "Are you quite serious, m'lady?"

"I am here," I responded. "And I am quite serious. You see, Mister Watkins, I am establishing an art gallery at Saint

Stephen's Green in my husband's office building. In addition, I am renovating the latest set of homes—"

"Tenements."

I hesitated. "Under my husband, yes, you are correct. They are slums. However, I have a very different vision for them."

Two hours later, I rose. Cups of tea had grown cold as we spoke, and his desk was covered in stacks of paper arranged by property. Two members of his staff had been sent scrambling for records and documents, and any initial gossip about my presence had no doubt been replaced with an understanding of my professional intent.

"Then I shall see you tomorrow morning at Matherscourt," I said.

"I look forward to it, Lady Mather. I shall bring an assistant or two with me to catalog things."

"I imagine it will take more than a morning. The artwork, of course, I plan to sell through my gallery."

"And—begging your pardon, m'lady, but what of your husband?"

I carefully slipped my gloves on and arranged each finger. "There will be no trouble with obtaining Lord Mather's signature. Prepare the papers, and I shall visit him myself at Reading Gaol."

He escorted me from his office and through the great doors, exiting onto the broad walk in front. His eyes searched the street. "Your carriage, ma'am?"

"I prefer to walk."

"I see."

"One more thing, Mister Watkins." I lowered my voice and extended my hand to him. As he reached for it, I said, "Was my donation the reason for our financial downfall?"

He held onto my hand as he looked into my eyes. "Not at all, Lady Mather. Your husband has been living beyond his means for years. It was inevitable."

I nodded as he gently dropped my hand. "And are you still involved?"

He frowned in a moment of puzzlement.

"Because I wish to be," I added.

"Then we have much to talk about, Lady Mather."

"Yes, Mister Watkins. Indeed we do."

A week had passed, a week of endless walking up and down the stairs and halls of Matherscourt. Everywhere I looked, people were buzzing with activity. The banker had supplied the personnel to catalog every item to be sold at auction before they were carted off in waiting trucks lining the drive. It turned out that while I could not sell Matherscourt itself without Stratford's signature and approval, there was nothing to stop me from selling everything inside its walls.

With Philip's and Nora's help, I had also assembled another workforce. A group of men was busy in the orangery removing all the materials that had been left before the Easter Rising. The supplies would go to a warehouse near the tenements, where they would be used in the renovations of those I planned to keep. I had carefully chosen several adjacent blocks which would be converted to apartments and filled with renters, providing ongoing revenue. What I didn't know, I inquired of Mister Watkins or Philip, who were both keen to assist me.

Meanwhile, at my office, renovations were underway in the top floor apartment. I was eager to clear the space of Stratford's presence. All the furniture had been removed and placed with the other auction items while Matherscourt's artwork was on display in my gallery. There were too many pieces to fit into the small area, so I kept the rest stacked against the walls in an empty first-floor office. It would ensure a steady stream of art for some time to come.

The wallpaper in the apartment was busy being removed, the floors refinished, the Oriental carpets taken away. I wanted air and space. I decided upon my bedroom furniture at Matherscourt, which would be moved to my apartment once the walls were painted a tranquil pastel. I had also selected several items from Matherscourt's many sitting rooms that would be moved to my apartment, including a settee, two chairs, and an assortment of tables. The kitchen was stocked with both dinnerware and food, and I had begun to feel contentment sweeping over me.

Even the land at Matherscourt was being subdivided. The house would remain on ten acres, which Mister Watkins had determined would be easier to sell than the thousand surrounding it. The parcels ranged from an acre to ten, and there was already interest from tenant farmers. The banker was working with them as well, having far more experience than I in negotiating such things. It was actually beginning to appear as though the accounts might be flush after all the transactions.

The only fly in the ointment was Nicky's absence. Heavy rains had moved in, settling over Ireland like a petulant child. I quietly made my way to the gatehouse each evening after all the workers had left for the day, traipsing down the muddy lane past the meadow, the horses tucked into the stable for the night. I would miss the horses. There would be no room for them in town and little need, as most of my business would be conducted in the office or within a short stroll. The dogs had begun to accompany me back and forth between Matherscourt and Dublin, and they would remain with me, the only family I had left.

This evening I ventured into the gatehouse as I had every night this past week, searching for clues that Nicky had been there. Perhaps there would be a bicycle propped against the wall or a few things left inside, or—my heart fluttering—he would be there himself waiting for me. But night after night, there had been nothing but the cold walls of the gatehouse. I'd sat for a while each night listening to the rain upon the slate and the brook rising and tumbling with the heavy downpour until eventually, I'd made my way out again, returning down the muddy lane as I dodged deepening puddles.

This evening was no different. I might have sat longer this time; it was difficult to tell, as the skies were ever darker with the storm clouds overhead. I lit a few candles and made my way from one window to the next, but as the night settled in, I could not see beyond the glass. I wondered when the surveyors would discover this gatehouse and when it would be sold, and my haven of the past would be gone.

I was so engrossed in my thoughts as I stared out the back window that I hadn't heard the door opening behind me. It wasn't until I turned that I spotted the hulking figure that filled the open doorway. He wore a black cape that had caught the rain like so many cups within its folds, the water now finding its way to the floor, where it puddled around his muddy boots. His face was in shadows beneath a dark cap, the water spilling over its long brim to splash into the puddles below.

I instinctively gasped when I saw him while my heart pounded in my chest. It wasn't until he lifted the cap from his head, shaking it out beside him, that I knew it was Nicky.

We crossed the open floor between us, his stride long and purposeful until he swept me into his arms. I didn't care if his rain-saturated cloak soaked through my gown as I flung my arms around him. I held him tighter than I ever had before, even as his arms squeezed me so firmly that I fought for my breath. Now that I was in his arms and he was in mine, I never wanted to let go, not even for the briefest of moments.

We might have remained in our embrace for seconds or minutes, for time became immaterial. The past was swept away, the future had not yet arrived, and there was only this one moment, a moment that would become seared into my consciousness.

Eventually, I felt his head turning toward me. His arms fell away from my sides to find my face as he held it. He stared at me for a long moment, his eyes wandering from my hair to my eyes, tracing my jawline and my lips and back up again, as though he intended to memorize every detail. Then his lips were on mine, wet with the rain and his passions, insistent, compelling, increasingly forceful.

I abandoned myself to him until I felt as if we were no longer separate but one, his soul reaching beyond his physical body to swirl around me, catching me in his desire, creating a whirlwind around me that I prayed would never cease. I don't remember when he pulled away just long enough to shed his cloak. I don't recall how we moved from the center of the room to the bed tucked against the wall. And I don't remember how I ended up in his arms upon the bedding while his trembling fingers sought to unbutton my gown.

I only knew that I was home when I was in his arms.

53

The grandfather clock heralded the four o'clock hour, but it awakened neither Nicky nor myself. We had already been awake all night, caught between our lovemaking and chatting. It was our third night together, and we had moved from the gatehouse, which was getting entirely too close to the surveyors' work, to the main house. It had been a risky move, I admit, but perhaps with my newfound freedom, I had also gained a sense of confidence I had not previously experienced.

We settled ourselves into the guest wing; it having been previously inventoried, there would be no need for the workers to reenter until the furniture was moved in another week to the auction house. The fire was low, and the room was becoming quite chilly, but neither of us wanted to leave the warmth of the eiderdown covers to stoke it. We made love as if each time would be our last, savoring every second, my mind memorizing every movement. I did not wish to think of the inevitable moment that inched ever closer, the moment he would announce his departure, and he would disappear once more. But I knew when that time would come and go, I would be left with the memories of these passionate nights.

Between lovemaking, as we lay recovering for the next round, Nicky had wanted to know all about my plans. He had heard about Stratford's arrest and was only shocked that he'd actually managed to get himself caught in such a compromised position. He knew, he said, that something was different about a man that could not recognize the gift he had in me. They were words I hadn't realized I needed to hear until he spoke them, and now my soul committed them to memory as well.

I told him of Stratford burning the barn and my art studio but my good fortune in finding the money intact, and we discussed my renovation of the tenements and my office across from Saint Stephen's Green. He was deeply interested in the business capabilities that had arisen within me and how both the banker and Philip had assisted me in transitioning from a neglected wife to a semi-successful art dealer and landlord.

I, on the other hand, was far more interested in Nicky's pursuits since we last met. To my chagrin, he could not tell me much about his missions. He spoke of the volunteers that had arisen as a direct result of Britain's heavy hand, particularly after the executions of the Easter Rising leaders. It was, as he had predicted, a guerrilla war. There were no more marches through the streets of Dublin carrying mops and brooms as units practiced the art of organized warfare. Instead, they had divided into smaller units, compartmentalizing orders and missions, so if one man was captured, he could not disclose much. It did not prevent the British from torturing the captives, and as it turned out, some were more loose-lipped under the circumstances than others. Every day was touch and go, moving forward, pulling back, sabotaging the Brits, and then running for their lives. Other times, they were in hiding, the boredom nearly unbearable but under orders not to move until given the command.

He did not know how many had been killed on either side nor did he know how many of his comrades had been captured and imprisoned. He saw a newspaper every now and again, but it was usually days or weeks old, and the world had moved on.

Nicky was a wanted man, his name having risen up the list as spies identified him time and again. It seemed that all of Ireland was filled with spies, some for the British, and others for Ireland's sovereignty. There appeared to be no one that could be fully trusted.

"Come with me to Dublin," I urged, my voice husky.

"Oh, but if I could," he said. He wrapped his arm around me and held me close to his chest.

"You were right about Michael Collins," I said. "I see him ride past my office on his bicycle."

"Do you now?"

"I do." I chuckled. "Right under the Brits' noses. He is known as 'Mister Brown.'"

Nicky laughed. "Ah, he's a cheeky one, he is. I heard tell that he was captured during the Rising, and they called out his name in the prison yard. But instead of coming forward, he moved further from the guards. They never knew they had him."

"If he'd have come forward, he would have been executed with the rest of the leaders," I sighed.

"So now he rides his bicycle right under their noses, does he?" he chuckled.

"I don't know how he gets away with it, frankly. His picture is everywhere; he must be the most wanted man in all of Ireland. But," I said, raising up to look him in the eye, "if he can do it, surely you can, too."

His eyes met mine. He had aged since last we met; there were lines beneath his eyes that had not been there before. His forehead was lined as well, the creases appearing deeper in the dusky room. His eyes were dark, shaded by his black lashes. He'd also lost a considerable amount of weight. "Oh, but if only I could," he said after a long moment. "But it is not my role, my darling."

"And your role takes you away from Dublin? Far from Matherscourt?"

He stroked my hair. "It could be far worse, you know. Great Britain has introduced universal conscription. If they could find me, they might cart me off to the front lines." He hesitated. "I admit it, I do, I feel more than a little guilty at not fighting at the front."

"Why?"

He shook his head, his hand moving to my neck, where it stopped to caress it. "I've heard the Germans have become more brutal, barbaric even."

"How so?"

"You don't know?"

I shook my head.

"They've introduced phosgene gas."

"What is that?"

"They released the gas at Verdun. From what I've been told, it can be nearly colorless, and it has the rather pleasant odor of mowed grass. Our troops never suspected it until they became violently ill."

It didn't escape my attention that he'd referred to the Allies as 'our troops,' despite Ireland's current circumstances. "Did they recover?"

"Some did. Some did not."

"What did it do to them?"

He hesitated. "Are you certain you want to know?"

"I do."

"Well, from what I hear, it gets into a man's lungs, especially if he thinks he is taking a deep breath of something as innocuous as grass. Fluid then develops within a few hours, and I gather it is an incredibly painful, slow death."

"And those that recover?"

"It is too soon to tell if the damage is long-lasting. It also creates skin lesions as if the person has been scalded, and nausea, vomiting…" He stopped. "I don't wish to say more."

"And the Allies? Will they use it, too?"

He shrugged. "I imagine so, eventually. It is a war, Penny. Wars are designed to create maximum suffering. It is in the breaking of one man's soul that allows another to rise."

"I wish that was not so." He didn't respond, and after a moment, I asked, "Will we win?"

He pulled me closer to him as he stroked my back. "I can't tell you what will happen, darling. Romania has entered the war now, and Italy has as well."

"On which side?"

"The Allies. Romania declared war on Austria-Hungary and Italy declared war on Germany."

"That is good, yes? More men to fight?"

"Is it good?" he mused. "Is anything in war ever 'good'? It is fortunate, yes, that they are on our side. It is a war of attrition, as all wars are. We have millions to throw into the fray; they have millions as well."

"And what of Ireland?"

"I do not know. We wish to rid our country of the English oppressors. Would Germany be any better? Would they even come to our shores? Perhaps we could make peace with them so we can rule ourselves as we once did."

"And if—" my question was interrupted by the sound of an engine, and we both scrambled out of bed.

"Are you expecting anyone?" Nicky said as he pulled on his trousers.

"Not until mid-morning. Certainly not in the middle of the night."

"Could anyone know I'm here?"

I slipped into my nightgown and then my robe. "I don't know. I thought we'd been careful enough." My voice revealed my doubt and rising trepidation.

"Penny, you can't—" His eyes swept over me.

"I wouldn't be dressed if I was alone in the middle of the night, now would I?" I asked. I slipped on my house shoes and made my way to the window, where I gently parted the draperies.

The window peered toward the northeast, providing me with a decent view of the long and winding drive. It was a single military vehicle, but it was too dark and a bit far for me to see how many were inside. It began to slow as it neared the front entrance.

I turned around to catch Nicky buttoning his shirt. "Stay here," I said.

"I won't leave you alone to them. They're vicious, Penny—"

"They wouldn't dare search Matherscourt. It's Lord Davies' headquarters now."

"I wouldn't be too sure of that if I were you," he answered as he bent to tug on his boots.

"No," I said. "You can't make an appearance. They'll arrest you for certain." I tamped down the anxiety that threatened to cut off my throat.

He joined me at the window. "Did you see that?"

"What?"

"By the stables."

"They're searching the stables? There must be more than one vehicle, then," I added as my eyes swept over the distance between the stables and the house.

"I think they were led here." He hurriedly strapped on his pistol.

"By who?"

"A volunteer."

"Stay here, Nicky. Please." I rushed to the door but hesitated with my hand on the knob. "If it is a volunteer, we can search the stables after they leave. But if you go out now—" My words choked as my eyes met his. God, no, please, please, don't, I found myself pleading silently.

We were interrupted by the sound of heavy banging on the front door.

"Go, Penny," he whispered, his voice hoarse. "Know that I am near. I will not allow them to hurt you."

I could only nod my head before another round of pounding, more raucous than the first, floated upward. I found myself darting out the door and down the hall, my feet moving of their own accord. With every step I took, I wanted to run in the opposite direction.

"Just a moment!" I called out as I descended the stairs. The banging persisted as I continued to call out. I felt for sure they were going to knock down the heavy wood door before I could reach it. I stopped momentarily at the foot of the stairs to peer upward. Nicky was not behind me. My mind raced to the second set of stairs the servants used. My heart was pounding, and my hands were growing clammy and cold.

"I'm coming! I'm coming!" I called as I reached the door and threw back the bolt with hands that trembled uncontrollably. I opened the door to find two men on my doorstep dressed in tan shirts and black trousers, their weapons visible. Their eyes were wild, like untamed creatures of the night. I wrapped my arms across my breasts, instinctively wishing to protect myself from their insolent prying eyes while my mind repeated the refrain, The Black and Tans, The Black and Tans. They were notorious throughout all of Ireland. Some said England freed violent prisoners to don the uniforms, and they did not abide by the same military protocol that dictated the regular troops' behavior.

"Are y'here by yourself, missy?" One said as his bloodshot eyes rolled past me into the foyer. He grabbed the doorjamb with one beefy fist as he teetered.

"This is Lord Davies' headquarters, you oaf," I answered, forcing my voice to sound deeper and with any luck, more authoritative, as I hoped they did not hear the tremor in it. "How dare you show up here like this."

"He's a bit green," the other said. I turned to him. They both reeked of alcohol, but this one seemed a tad bit soberer.

"What is it that you want?" I clipped. "Don't you realize it's the middle of the night?" I forced my spine straight and tall and hoped I'd assumed an air of righteous indignation as I sought to tamp down my fear.

"We're looking for a dangerous fugitive," he answered, slurring his words. "And we've an eyewitness that saw him come here."

"Well, he is certainly not inside the house." As I spoke the words, I saw Nicky's dark form rush from the house toward the stables.

"And we're just to take your word for it?" the man grinned insolently.

"On account o' she's a lady," the cruder one added, his eyes raking over my body.

I forced myself to turn in the opposite direction, so Nicky was at their backs. I dared not move my eyes from the two men even as I picked up Nicky in my periphery, hesitating at the entrance to the stables. The metal of his pistol gleamed in the waning moonlight as he watched us. "If anyone is running from the law," I said, pointing in the opposite direction, "and they cross this estate, they'd have to take that path there."

"I think we'll just have a look around, little lady," the first man said. He placed his hand on my shoulder as if to move me from blocking the doorway. I tried to stand firm though I knew if he insisted I could not physically restrain him. Out of the corner of my eye, I realized Nicky had disappeared, and I wondered if he'd slipped into the gloom of the stables. I was caught between disappointment that he might abandon me and relief that he had a chance to escape.

"Is your husband about?" the second man said.

"Of course he is," I said.

"And is he in the habit of allowing his wife to answer the door alone in the middle of the night?"

I felt the blood drain from my face as goosebumps formed along my arm. The drunker of the two men attempted to grab my arms as I wrenched away. I cried out, my voice carrying on the wind, as I stumbled backward. He plunged toward me, jerking my arm behind my back, as the second man joined him. I felt their hands pulling at my robe and gown, the chill of the night air riding my calves and thighs as the material was heaved ever higher.

A deafening shot rang out, and I found myself staring into the bloodshot eyes of the drunkest man. I felt frozen in time, every line on the man's face etching into my memory as he teetered. He looked surprised as he fell, hitting the marble floor with both knees before toppling forward until his face was planted against the floor. Bright red blood poured from his back, causing me to stumble backward and away from it.

Then my eyes found the second man mere inches away from me. He looked at his comrade lying in a heap at our feet before peering back at me. Then his hand moved toward the pistol on his hip. It came out as easily as a greased pig, and in mere seconds it was pointed at my head.

As the second shot rang out, I stumbled backward once more as the world spun around me. I felt weight against me, pulling me to the floor to land atop the first man as the second plummeted atop of me. The breath was knocked from my body, the cries that sought to escape, frozen on my lips.

54

I was covered in blood. My gown and robe were soaked in the crimson liquid even as the wet folds clung to my body. I sat in a chair in the grand foyer, shaking uncontrollably as the center table was moved, and the Oriental rug unceremoniously hauled in front of the two men.

I watched as though in a daze while Nicky rolled one man onto the rug.

"I need you, Penny."

His words didn't quite register.

"Snap out of it, Penny," he said. His voice sounded slower, deeper. "Come here. I need you."

Then I awakened as if from a dream, the adrenaline suddenly coursing through my body as I came to my feet, only to nearly fall from my unsteadiness.

"Get over there," he said, pointing to the opposite end of the rug nearest the man's feet. "Roll with me."

I found myself rolling the man into the rug until he disappeared into its folds and became a tidy bundle at the edge of the room.

Nicky was already at the door to the butler's old room. I heard knocking and the sound of furniture moving before he reappeared, hauling a second rug. We repeated our efforts with the second man until we had two bundles.

I don't know how I managed to help lift each bundle. Each man alone must have weighed a hundred and fifty pounds or more, plus the weighty rug around him. Yet I did. I helped to carry each to the army vehicle, hauling them inside the open bed.

"Listen to me, Penny," Nicky said. He was in front of me, obscuring everything except the vision of his face as he peered into my eyes. "Are you hearing me?"

I nodded. "I am."

"Clean up the blood," he said. "Not even a servant can see it come the morn, do you understand?"

I nodded again.

"Get rid of any bloody scraps you use to clean it, 'ey? And I'll be back. I promise you, I'll be back."

At the thought of Nicky leaving, I was hauled out of my stupor. "What about you, Nicky?" My voice was cracking, and I realized my throat and lips were dry and parched. "Where are you going?"

"I've got to dispose of the bodies. I'm taking them far from here, Penny, are you listening? Far from Matherscourt. Far from you."

"But you were defending me—surely—"

He grabbed him and pulled me to him. "It doesn't matter, darling. It doesn't matter."

"But—"

"We're Irish, Penny." He pulled my chin up to face him. "And I've just killed two British soldiers—"

"—black and tans—"

"It doesn't matter," he repeated.

His words sank into my consciousness. Of course, it did not matter. If the British could kill his brother and his nephew in cold blood without evidence of any crime, what would they do to him, having committed two murders? All the people I'd encountered during and after the Rising that told me being a Lady no longer mattered seemed to come at me all at once. The world had changed, and even the wife of Lord Stratford Mather could not save him.

55

Dawn arrived as a wide swath of red on the distant horizon, calling to mind the old mariner's adage, *Red sky at night, sailor's delight. Red sky at morning, sailors take warning…* It was an omen, I thought, as I carried a bundle of rags wrapped in my gown and robe across the front lawn and past the stables to the old dry well at the edge of the woods.

The front foyer was as clean as I was going to get it, having mopped it numerous times and scrubbed even into the grooves between the marble pieces until my weary eyes could not detect even the slightest pink. The rugs were gone forever, but should I be asked about their absence, I would assume the position that they'd been taken to auction. There had been dozens of workers on the estate in recent weeks, and by the time the auditors had discovered the discrepancy in the inventory, we would all assume they'd found their way elsewhere between Matherscourt and Dublin, perhaps gracing the dirt floor of a peasant's home. There were far too many concerns these days throughout Ireland, and my paltry rugs would not rate an investigation.

I lifted the heavy stone off the well, tipping it to the side just far enough to allow me to drop in the bloody rags. I'd expected to hear a thud when they reached the bottom, but I heard nothing. Panicked, I tried to peer into the well, concerned a rough-cut stone had snagged them on the way down, and with the light of day, they would be clearly visible to anyone searching for evidence. But the well was as dark as pitch in the waning hours of darkness, and I dared not remain there until daylight had shown its face.

I pushed the stone back into place, worrying over its exact location before realizing there was pine straw strewn about it from the copse of trees nearby. I picked up several boughs and scattered them across the well, hoping to give the appearance that it had been untended for years.

I had turned to make my way back to the house when I spotted blood upon the ground. I halted and wiped my eyes, thinking it was an illusion from the rising red sun. But as I stared at the ground in horror, I realized it was a solid trail. I kicked dirt over it and picked up more boughs, but as I followed the trail, I realized it did not lead to the house but to the stables.

Had Nicky mentioned something about the stables as the soldiers had driven up the drive? I couldn't remember now. He had been at the stable doors when the black and tans had begun to assault me; he hadn't had the time, I realized, to thoroughly check it. Once the men were killed, the focus had been on hiding the bodies and removing the vehicle.

Or had Nicky returned, perhaps attacked along the way, and he'd found his way back to me? Was he bleeding out in the stable even as I stood there staring at it?

I used the pine boughs as a broom to sweep dirt and debris over the bloody trail as I neared the stable doors. There was a bloody print on the frame and as I held my hand over it, I realized whoever was inside had placed their hand against the edge to pull the doors open before slipping inside.

In the time it had taken me to cover the tracks and reach the doors, the dawn had grown brighter. It now shone through the trees in fingers of red, orange, and an occasional yellow. The dark, hulking shadow of Matherscourt was becoming transformed in front of my eyes to easily recognizable structures. It was, perhaps, this light that emboldened me.

I opened the double doors and stood in the entryway. "Who's there?" I called out. I stopped to listen but heard nothing but my heavy, jagged breathing, and my heart pounding. After a few moments, I stepped inside.

I moved from one stall to the next, stroking each horse along the way. The ones closest to the door were calm and nuzzled my hand, looking for their customary carrots. By the time I reached the furthest stalls, they were nervous, jittery.

Horses were perfect barometers for their surroundings. A stranger not yet spotted by their human caretakers was instantly detected by the horses' strong sense of smell. They thrived on routine, and when it was broken, they became skittish.

I knew which stall he was in. I had a strong urge to rush in, to call Nicky's name, to do whatever was in my power to help him. I had made my way to him through the dawn of an Irish rebellion, helping to bring him back to me, and I could do it again now. I had to.

Another part of myself was trying vainly to reign in the adrenaline. That tiny voice in the back of my head cautioned me against hurrying forward.

In the end, I reasoned I had come this far.

"Who is there?" I called out again. When I received no answer, I said, "I can help you. I know you're injured."

The horse whinnied, and I moved closer to find a dark mound in the hay, curled into a ball. His head moved as I neared. "Are you alone, m'lady?" he whispered hoarsely.

"I am," I answered. It was not Nicky, I realized with a sinking heart, but in my next breath, I realized Nicky was out there still and may not have been wounded. "Who are you?"

"It's Éamonn, ma'am," he answered weakly.

"Éamonn?" I hurriedly unlatched the stall door.

There was a pause. "Aye, ma'am. And I've an urgent message I must deliver to Mister Collins."

The morning was fickle. The rains grew heavy, and the winds kicked up, pummeling the windows in earnest. I should have seen the vestiges of light on the distant horizon as the hours dragged past, but the skies remained a heavy gray-blue. I told myself it was better this way, that Nicky could remain in the shadows for longer, that the rain would help him along his way and keep him in its shadowy palm.

But as I tended to Éamonn's wound, the rains worried me. The roads and paths would be muddy and slow, sucking the tires into the soft earth with every step. Nicky could be out there now, burying the bodies in a swampy bog, soaked to the bone, and even in the summer, there wasn't enough warmth to ward off Ireland's perpetually chill air.

"I must deliver the message," Éamonn urged weakly, his fever rising with the passing minutes.

"There are many soldiers about," I answered, pressing into his flesh in a futile attempt to stop the bleeding. He'd been shot in the bicep of his right arm. It was the third time I had changed the bandages, the prior two attempts soaking the cloths until they were crimson. There was no exit wound, which could only mean the bullet lay lodged within, but my inexperience stopped me from digging it out.

"Were you shot at Matherscourt?" I asked as I worked.

"Ten miles away, more or less."

"And you managed to walk all that way, bleeding out as you are?"

"I had a bicycle."

"Oh?"

His face was pale as he leaned back into the pillow. He'd managed to walk from the stables to the big house, climbing the stairs with Herculean effort, before finally reaching the guest room in which only hours before, I had lain in Nicky's arms. It was the safest place I knew to hide him from the workers that would soon be arriving.

"I ditched it," he was saying, "in some brush a half-mile or so from the stables."

I gathered the bloody bandages and set them aside. "You need a doctor."

"I can't risk one."

"I can't dig out the bullet. I would cause more harm than help."

"I was on my way to Dublin," he said, his tongue lazy with exhaustion. "But I was ambushed."

A hundred questions were on my lips, but I remained silent.

"I am sorry to have involved you and Nick in this."

"How did you know he was here?"

The slightest of smiles tugged at his lips, but his eyes were closed now. "We know."

I watched the newly wrapped bandage grow red, my mind trying to wrap itself around the amount of blood that might have been lost in his journey to Matherscourt, the time he'd remained in the stables and up to the present time. The man would bleed out if he didn't receive the attention of a proper physician. "I thought you were incarcerated."

"They were transferring us a few weeks back," he said, his words growing weaker. "I escaped, and I've been on the run ever since."

"Do you trust Lord Davies?" I asked.

His eyes flickered as though he'd wanted to open them, but they fluttered shut again as if it was simply too much effort. "I do. I would trust him with my life. Lady Davies, also… I knew Brian well…"

I watched as he nodded off, unsure whether it was exhaustion overtaking him or a faint. I remained at his side, alternating between moistening his lips, wiping the perspiration from his face, and changing the bandages as I listened to the grandfather clock chime the hours all too slowly.

56

Philip arrived precisely at half-past eight, and I was waiting for him at the grand front doors. He appeared surprised to see me.

"Lord Davies," I said loud enough for his staff to hear me, "I have been up since the wee hours of the morning, thanks to soldiers pounding on my doors."

He strode across the drive to me, taking my arm gently and walking me into the foyer. "My apologies, Lady Mather, but it was necessary."

"Was it necessary for one to lay his hands upon me?" My voice rose to near hysteria. "To attempt to force himself into my home when I was alone here?"

We started up the steps together. "Now, now, Lady Mather," he said. In a lower tone, he whispered, "What the devil, Penny?"

"It's Éamonn," I answered. "He's wounded, and he needs a doctor."

It was noon before the doctor arrived, having been fetched by one of Philip's aids to tend to an overly wrought woman. It had exhausted me to play the role, but fortunately, he confined me to a bedroom just down the hall from Éamonn's where I could close the door and pace the floors without the staff's eyes upon me. There were dozens of tasks I should have been attending, between supervising the removal of furniture and household items to inventorying additional rooms, but I found myself stuck like a caged animal with nothing but my worries.

On top of everything else, Éamonn's cryptic reference to a message for Michael Collins wore heavily on me. I had searched his clothing thoroughly and extracted a single piece of paper. It was sealed, with the name "M. Brown" on the front. I didn't dare open it, but I knew I must get to Dublin and somehow encounter the mysterious Mister Brown long enough to press this note into his palm.

A tap came at the door, interrupting my thoughts, and I flew across the room to open it.

Philip slipped inside though he left the door ajar. "The doctor is gone now," he said.

"And Éamonn—?"

"The bullet has been removed. It was deep in a muscle; it had hit the brachial artery."

"Has the bleeding stopped?"

"Slowed significantly. With any luck, it will stop completely before the day is out."

I breathed a sigh of relief. "I must take my leave."

Philip took a step back. "Now, of all times, Penny?"

"I know it's inconvenient. It's just that—I have something to attend to at my office, it's very important that I weigh in on the budget and work will be stopped until I am there."

"I see."

"Can you send a man after Johanna?"

"I can." He rubbed his chin thoughtfully.

"Tell her she is needed in my stead here at Matherscourt, and then sneak her up to Éamonn. Is that possible?"

"I'll make it happen, Penny."

"Thank you."

"Do you need a ride into town?"

"Yes. I do." For the briefest of moments, I pictured sitting in the back of a military transport carrying a note for none other than Michael Collins himself, crossing through one roadblock to another. Then in the next instant, I was flying down the stairs with my scarf and coat in hand, heading to the vehicle that would take me to Dublin.

57

I snatched a small painting from the window display as soon as I entered my art gallery. It was one of the serene scenes Eliza liked so much. This one consisted of autumn trees at sunset. The grass was still a vibrant green, as it tends to be until it is covered in light snow or frost later in the season, giving way to brown bark and then vibrant yellow and red leaves before melting into rich red and orange layers of a perfect sunset.

I snagged one of Nora's daughters as I made my way toward the back. "Do you know Mister Brown?" I asked her, describing Michael Collins' clothing, which always consisted of a neat hat and heavy topcoat, along with the bicycle he rode. "Stand out front and wave him in when you see him. Tell him I have the painting he purchased for his wife."

As Nora, Jamie, and the others left for a day's work on the rental properties, I hurried into the room in the far back where I kept my supplies. I had a tidy pile of bark in all shapes and sizes, and now I selected one that would match the others I had added to the painting, which caused the entire work to pop out as if it were real.

I worked quickly. I retrieved the tiny note from my pocket and rolled it neatly into a shape resembling a cigarette before placing the bark atop it. A little bit of resin held it in place; experience told me it would dry hard in only a short amount of time. I left the bark natural, hoping no one would notice the slight difference in coloring between that one and those I'd painstakingly painted over.

Then I rushed back to the art studio, placed it back into the window on its petite stand, and placed a "Sold" sign in front of it. In all, it might have been only six by eight inches, the perfect size for a curiosity cabinet or table.

Then I cooled my heels over the next hour, fretting that he would not appear today or I'd already missed him. I busied myself with dusting and rearranging the displays, all while keeping an eye on the front windows. Nora's daughter Brigit took her assignment very seriously, walking back and forth in front of my shop while she looked this way and that.

I had stepped into the hall to retrieve another painting for display when the door burst open, the bell jangling wildly from the movement.

"He's here, m'lady!" Brigit called. "Mister Brown is coming down the road now!"

No sooner had I rushed into the front gallery than she dashed back outside, her tiny voice calling for him. "Mister Brown! Mister Brown! Lady Mather has your wife's painting done!"

I hurried onto the sidewalk as he neared. My God, he was a handsome man. It was no wonder half the women in Ireland swooned over the mention of him. He was young with a pleasant, round face and piercing eyes that peered at us under his dark brown hair, half-hidden by his cap. When he smiled, his entire face lit up, revealing deep dimples.

"Mister Brown," I called out as he drew closer, "I have the painting your wife is expecting. Thank goodness we spotted you."

I saw a flash of indecision cross his face. Out of the corner of my eye, I knew a group of soldiers was standing just across the street from us, and with Brigit and myself calling out to the man, all eyes were on us. Of course, he had to have been thinking it could be an ambush; I'd heard he often said it was only a matter of time before his number was up. Well, not today, it wasn't.

"It will only take a moment," I said. I hoped that he could see the urging in my eyes. "I know you're very busy."

A bit reluctantly, he stopped his bicycle in front of the shop, gently placing it beneath the front window. I hurried inside, grabbing the painting out of the front window. As I bent down to retrieve it, I looked through the glass at the soldiers watching me. It was a boring duty, sentinel duty was, and I imagine they looked for happenings out of the ordinary to keep themselves entertained.

I met Michael in the doorway, making quite a show of the painting. With his back to the soldiers, it was easy for me to display it so they could see it as well.

Michael had a slight frown on his face, and he hesitated before reaching for it.

"Remove the tree bark," I whispered hoarsely. "There's a message inside." I pulled my lace handkerchief from my pocket and wrapped it quickly. He made a move toward his pocket, and I waved it away. "Your wife already paid for it, Mister Brown." I hurried back inside. "Tell her I hope she enjoys it!"

When I turned back around, he was mounting his bicycle. For the briefest of moments, our eyes met. His were intelligent, perceptive, friendly. I had no doubt that he understood both my rapid instructions and my role in the war for independence. He placed the painting inside his coat and made a slight tip of his hat before he was off down the street. When I ventured back to the front window to rearrange the paintings there, he had already disappeared into the crowd at the end of the street.

58

Two days later, the front page of the *Irish Times* carried a story about an ambush planned by the rebels that did not take place. It was cryptic, and only those with knowledge of the actual events would have understood it's importance. There had been a spy in the rebel outfit planning the ambush on the road from Dublin toward Donnybrook as British troops moved further south to impose martial law across the island. The British had developed their own plan to ambush the ambushers. As it turned out, the rebels never showed, and the volunteer units identified by the spy were apparently disbanded.

The article was written as a triumph for the British and a major setback for the Irish. But as my mind wandered to the note I'd passed to Michael, I had a different opinion.

Three days later, I found myself standing outside of HM Reading Gaol, having traveled with Simeon Watkins to London. It was, without a doubt, the most imposing building I had ever encountered. It towered over Berkshire, England, a good days' ride from London, so by the time we arrived, I was hungry and tired. We'd been ushered through the entrance at the castle walls, our arrival expected, and our name on a formal list through a solicitor known by Mister Watkins. I stood now in full view of the forecourt, an area built especially for public executions. Though none had taken place since 1913, some three years prior, I could easily envision the prisoner marched to his death in full view of a thousand spectators or more.

Mister Watkins had filled me in on its history on the long drive out. Constructed in 1844 and modeled after America's Eastern State Penitentiary in Philadelphia, it was designed to punish. Prisoners were kept separated the majority of the time, and when they found themselves encountering others, complete silence was strictly enforced. Food was scarce, while rats, mites, and fleas were plentiful. Prisoners were required to work long hours without pay to repay their debt to society and their debt to the prison itself for housing them.

The entrance looked like something more suited to the castle of a wicked king, the steps designed to take the wind out of a visitor before they'd reached the top. On either side of the inset entrance were towers with guards peering at us curiously as we approached. The towers, including additional ones at the corners of the monstrous structure, contained windows, as did the front of the building. But wings jutted out from either side were completely bricked in, and I suspected those windowless cells were where most prisoners were incarcerated, including Stratford Mather.

The guards in the foyer wore the type of expressions that would have had me hurrying to the opposite side of the road had I encountered them in Dublin. Their eyes raked over me as though undressing me, their expressions were insolent, their manner of speech disrespectful and condescending. If they greeted visitors in this manner, I could only imagine how prisoners fared under their autocratic rule. I even felt sympathy for Stratford as we were escorted to the Irish wing, past wings marked for German, Hungarian, Belgian, and even Latin American prisoners captured during the Great War.

By the time we reached a tiny, windowless room where I was directed to sit and wait for my husband, the energy of the place hung about me like a heavy, dark cloak. I had difficulty breathing in the foul, stale air that smelled of unwashed bodies and something else I did not wish to identify.

"Only one visitor at a time," the guard said curtly, throwing his arm across the door to block Mister Watkins from following me inside.

I nodded to him and tried to smile reassuringly, but the smile never reached my face. It froze somewhere in my belly as the heavy door was slammed shut, and I found myself inside alone.

I surveyed the metal chair carefully before sitting down and fought the urge to rise quickly, lest mites or fleas find their way onto my clothing. An immersive bath would have to be my first priority once I was rid of this place.

A door separate from the one I'd entered was opened, and I gasped as Stratford walked in. "Five minutes," the guard said as he tethered Stratford's chains to the table leg. "No more."

I nodded that I understood. The guard stood behind the chair as though my husband was a dangerously violent criminal. It took me a moment to move past Stratford's appearance. He had lost quite a bit of weight and appeared as though he'd aged thirty years. The bald spot on his head was sunburnt, and the skin was peeling. His skin was an odd color, somewhat green and somewhat orange, and I wondered what sort of diet he must be on. He also stank as if he'd not been afforded a bath since his incarceration. Care of any sort was obviously lacking.

"Well, are you just going to sit there and gloat?" he snarled.

He had yet to look up from the table between us, and it occurred to me from the moment he appeared in the doorway, he had looked only at his feet as if trained to do so.

"I came," I said, trying to rid my voice of the tremor that threatened to surface, "to let you know that I have hired one of the best solicitors in England for your defense."

He made a derisive choking sound.

"He will be calling on you. I had to give his card to the guards," I added hastily, "I wasn't able to carry anything inside the prison."

"So you've told me. Now go."

I swallowed. "There is more. Our business is in financial tatters."

"*Our* business," he growled. "Keep your dirty little fingers off *my* business."

I pushed back from the table but stopped short of rising. "As a matter of necessity, parts have been sold off to protect some of the assets. Matherscourt will be placed at auction."

"You won't touch Matherscourt."

"As I said, a solicitor will be here to see you—"

"Two minutes," the guard announced curtly.

"—and he will have paperwork for you to sign. Once Matherscourt is sold, his bill will be paid as well as anything you owe for your incarceration. Then you shall go to France."

"You'd love that, wouldn't you?" He made a move toward me, but the chain prevented him from moving more than a few inches. "You little bitch. I'm in here because of you!"

"Me!"

"Look at your chubby, short body. Look at you! You're so pathetic, I had no choice but to find comfort elsewhere!"

"Oh!" I rose. "You'll go to France, and you'll stay there. If you do, you shall receive an allowance from the business. If you return to Ireland, you shall be destitute."

"Destitute like you, you fecking little—"

"Time's up." The guard made to unlock the chain from the table.

As he rose, he tried to lunge again toward me, but the guard's iron fist around the chain prevented him from reaching me. "Why don't you kill yourself?" he snarled, spittle whipping out of his mouth, so I found myself retreating from it. "No one wants you to remain alive. Do us all a favor," he yelled as the guard led him to the door, "and kill yourself!"

As the door closed behind them and I was left alone once more, I could hear him screaming down the corridor, "Do it! Do it!" Then the sound of something crashing replaced his voice, and a moment later, I heard whimpering.

The opposite door opened, and I shakily joined the guard and Mister Watkins. The banker peered at me curiously, but I could not meet his gaze. Instead, I focused on the back of the guard's shirt as he led us back through the maze to the front doors. I didn't know if I'd told Stratford everything I'd intended. I'd counted three things on the drive to Berkshire, and I recited them in my head over and over: solicitor, France, allowance.

Yet when the massive doors were opened, and we were allowed out of the dank, dark prison walls, and into the sunlight, I could no longer remember what I'd said to my husband.

"The solicitor will have all the necessary paperwork," Mister Watkins was saying as we made our way across the forecourt to the outer wall where more guards were waiting to escort us out. "Then I shall oversee the auction personally, rest assured."

I nodded as the final gates were opened, and we found ourselves outside the wall. I was quiet on the ride back to London. My appetite was gone, and when Mister Watkins insisted on a late dinner at my hotel, I found myself simply pushing the food from one side of the plate to the other. It had been a long and draining day with hours in a vehicle that bumped and jostled along uneven roads, all for five minutes in which my husband urged me to commit suicide.

Later, after I'd returned to my room and sat at the open window overlooking downtown London, I felt as though I had been physically kicked in the gut. I was to leave for Dublin first thing in the morning, and it couldn't arrive soon enough.

59

The best revenge, as it turns out, is not in dying but in living a full and useful life. I returned to Dublin as the Great War was turning in England's favor. On the surface, the Irish supported Britain's success, but an undercurrent existed now that was determined to seek sovereignty, regardless of the war's victor.

A note from Nicky was waiting for me upon my return, delivered through Eliza at my apartment above my offices and studio. He said little about that night, and I knew why: any note could be intercepted, and spies abounded in every direction. He said only that he'd discarded his cargo and had been recruited for additional assignments. And he professed his love for me so eloquently that I felt my heart surge with emotion. I longed for him in my arms, and yet I knew I must be content to know he was alive. He had not been caught on that fateful night, and as of this moment, he was not facing the firing squad or gallows.

Still, I yearned for him each and every night. While my days were filled with art and real estate, constant renovations and rentals, the dismantling of Matherscourt, and the ensuing auctions, my nights were something else entirely. They consisted of my dogs and me, a customary stroll with them through Saint Stephen's Green and dinner in my apartment, usually overlooking the Green through the open windows. Time became slow then, the nights tedious and often sleepless, the dawn arriving just as I was nodding off in exhaustion. And yet, I realized I was not as lonely now as I had been during dinners with Stratford at Matherscourt. I came to the conclusion that loneliness had nothing to do with being alone.

I had another, quite unexpected, assignment on my return to Dublin. I found a note awaiting me at my office and another one inside the first. The outer one informed me of the purchase of a painting, while the secondary note I left unopened. I carefully rolled that one underneath a piece of bark as I had with Mister Brown's painting, sealed it with resin, and placed it in the front window with a 'Sold' sign. Within a day, someone visited my studio with the same name as the outer note, and I bundled up the painting, and off they went. When they inquired about the price, I told them it had already been paid. I needed nothing for my part in the revolution.

A few days later, another note appeared, and then another. I could not paint fast enough. As more visitors were spotted at my gallery, more legitimate buyers emerged to purchase other, more valuable paintings that I had removed from Matherscourt. Mister Watkins regularly visited, often taking me to tea and discussing investments that would keep me in good stead throughout my life, should I be prudent about my earnings.

The London solicitor had been true to his word, arriving at Reading Gaol with several documents in hand. My divorce was finalized, Stratford's allowance set up in escrow, and within a matter of months, he was released with time served. Despite his treatment of me, I felt for the man, for I knew what it was like to love in the shadows. I would have wished him well, living in the more progressive south of France with his trusted Aindriú, but fate would have other ideas.

Aindriú did not have the means for a proper defense, and he was sentenced to twenty years at hard labor. It was a death sentence; I knew it the moment I read of it in the local papers. And, indeed, within a year, he had developed pneumonia and had perished in the unheated prison.

I was rearranging the window display for the umpteenth time when a vehicle pulled in front and out stepped Joanna and Éamonn. They were both dressed in their finest; Johanna's figure was more petite than my own, but she'd done an expert job of taking in several of the fancy dresses that no longer suited me. And as it turned out, Éamonn's physique was not significantly different than Aindriú's, and there had been several suits left when Aindriú and Stratford were detained.

Éamonn tipped his hat in greeting to the solders that milled about in front of the Green. He carried himself well, his head high, and the air about him significantly arrogant. There was a price on his head, but like Michael Collins' façade as Mister Brown, he'd learned he could go about his business under the noses of the British as long as he dressed and acted the part of a high society gentleman.

I welcomed them into my gallery, and we found our way to my office in the back, where we could speak more freely.

"You look exquisite, Johanna," I said, hugging her.

"Elizabeth," she corrected with a smile.

"And have you the documents?"

"She does, indeed," Éamonn said with a wide grin. He produced the paperwork for Elizabeth and George Centerton.

"Ah," I said, chuckling as I looked it over. "This will take some getting used to. And are you two—?"

"Married?" Johanna finished for me. "We are. By a priest in Newbridge."

"Congratulations!" I hugged both of them and handed back the valuable papers to Éamonn.

"We had to," Johanna laughed. "We'll be in one cabin together for the duration."

"I couldn't bear," Éamonn said, leaning in and whispering, "to be near her for that long without touching her. I am not a monk."

"Would you care for some tea?" I asked, finally discovering my manners. "We can go upstairs to my apartment—"

"We can't," Johanna said sadly. "We only have a moment."

I glanced out my office door and through the front windows, where their vehicle waited. The driver stood with his back to me as he leaned against the hood, and yet, he seemed familiar somehow. "The driver?"

"Brian," Éamonn said. "I believe you know him?"

"And I do. Has he paid a visit to Davies Castle yet?"

They shook their heads. "Too risky," Johanna said.

"Is he staying in Dublin?"

"No," Éamonn said. "He's going to America, same as us."

"Ah. And the ship awaits you then?"

"We have only a couple of hours, I'm afraid."

"Where is the ship docked?"

"Alexandra Quay," Éamonn offered. "We wanted to pop in and say goodbye, and to thank you for paying our fare."

"You can pay me back," I said as we made our way through the gallery to the front door, "by becoming as successful and happy as you've a right to be."

"We're already happy," Johanna said, "so success can't be far behind."

"Will you write?"

Éamonn opened the door. "Of course. We will never forget you, ma'am."

"Penny," I corrected. "And as soon as I have your address, I shall write you as well. Be well."

As they stepped through the door, I followed them onto the sidewalk. At the sound of our voices, Brian quickly came around to their door and opened it. His driver's cap hid part of his face in shadows, but I caught the gleam in his eye. I wanted to reach out and hug him, but I knew it was improper for a lady to touch a man of his class. "Someday," I said wistfully, "perhaps you will return to Dublin to find the soldiers gone and Irishmen in charge."

"Irishmen," Brian said, a smile spreading across his face. "And Irishwomen."

I watched as he closed the door and took his position at the wheel. Then the vehicle roared to life and noisily took off in the direction of the water. Just before they turned the corner, Johanna looked through the small back window, and I waved. It wasn't until they disappeared that I realized a tear had found its way to the corner of my eye. I dabbed at it as I hurried back inside my little shop, the ache in my heart growing a little bit larger.

60

November 1918

There was a strange mood in Dublin this evening, like a multi-headed cloak of dark and light clouds spreading across the island, bringing neither sun nor gloom. The Great War, the war so devastating, so brutal and so inhumanely horrific that it was touted as the war to end all future wars, had itself finally concluded.

While the rest of the victors celebrated, Ireland faced an uncertain future. Almost a quarter of a million Irish men had enlisted in the armed forces and had fought alongside Great Britain, France, and Russia. Around a hundred thousand were expected to return, but the country they'd known when they left in 1914 was not the same country they would find upon their return. It had changed completely, irrevocably.

Many of the men arriving on Ireland's shores were wounded in glaringly visible ways and others, deeply hidden. There were men without legs or arms, men whose faces had been permanently disfigured, men that suffered untold horrors with chemical attacks. They were returning to a painful, precarious future, a burden upon their families with little to no ability to provide for their loved ones, or even themselves.

But it was scores of others with hidden injuries that spoke the loudest even while they remained mute about their experiences. Those were the soldiers with vacant stares, the ones that seemed to sleepwalk through their days as if they had left their souls on the battlefields of Arras, Somme, Lys, and others. The number of Irish soldiers killed or wounded in the Great War was but a pittance compared to Russian or German casualties, but for a tiny island such as ours, there was not a family left unspared in one way or the other.

Unlike the other members of the Entente Powers, the Irish returned home without the hero's welcome, without the parades, and without the gratification of its citizens. Since the Easter Rising of 1916, those men that served alongside Britain were more often considered traitors to Ireland, and some even lamented the fact that Germany had lost. The Irish poet Francis Ledwidge was one of the men that had volunteered to perform their patriotic duty in 1914, only to witness from afar the executions of the Easter Rising's leaders. His words echoed throughout Ireland from 1916 to the present day: "If someone were to tell me now that the Germans were coming in over our back wall, I wouldn't lift a finger to stop them. They could come!"

Had Ledwidge lived, he might have been a pariah like the rest of the soldiers returning home, but he passed on the battlefield of Ypres in 1917.

Unlike the wounded soldiers, however, Ireland was not bent to its knees. It was rising.

The army of the Irish Republic, more commonly referred to as the Irish Republican Army or IRA, had risen earlier this year with a vengeance. In January, the Dáil had been formed, a break-away government consisting of Irish men and women determined to oust the British from our isle. America supported our quest for independence, largely through Éamon de Valera's tireless efforts in the States. Closer to home, Michael Collins had risen as had Countess Markievicz, leading a growing army of anti-British sentiment.

The Great War might have ended, but the Irish War for Independence had just begun.

For myself, I walked a tightrope that often seemed to waver. On the surface, I had risen like the Phoenix from the ashes of Stratford's arrest and conviction and his ill-fated business decisions. I employed more than two dozen now, from those that worked in the offices to those laboring to renovate or repair buildings or collect rents. I often worked six days a week from dawn to well past dusk. It was I that arose now and headed off to my desk, and I that returned. But instead of the massive estate that was forever under construction to impress others, I saw no need to alter perceptions. I lived quite happily in my apartment overlooking Saint Stephen's Green and was more than content to while away the hours in between managing the properties by painting and selling art.

In fact, the artwork I'd removed from Matherscourt fetched enough money to provide a comfortable existence if I was careful with my spending. I occasionally purchased other pieces, but the new pieces displayed in my window were those of my own making. I had gained a reputation for the odd three-dimensional pieces that protruded from my paintings, and my work had now been shown in London, Paris, and New York.

And underneath this façade lay my other life, my true purpose. I supported the effort for Ireland's independence directly under the noses of the British and often while they perused my gallery. I kept a supply of bark and natural substances ready at any moment to add to a painting, a note securely fashioned underneath, and a sold sign bearing a purchaser's name set firmly in front. The messages that made their way through my gallery often carried film that was developed in mainland Europe, eventually appearing in newspapers around the world, intensifying the pressure on Britain to grant Ireland her independence. Other times, there were simple messages on single pieces of paper, their content known only to a few. I checked the newspapers each morning for news of ambushes, arrests, and deaths as Ireland's war dragged on.

The sun grew ever more distant along the horizon. I was tidying up when my devoted assistant manager, Brad Beckwith, bid me goodnight. I watched as he strolled down the street, his cane, a recent purchase, twirling as he went as though he carried a marionette. The young man I'd met two years prior was now a landowner himself and engaged to be married.

I made my way to the front door and locked it. Nora's husband had arrived home from the Great War, and he, too, was employed by my company. Nora was expecting yet another child, and yet she continued to manage the workers as they moved from block to block. No sooner were the townhouses renovated than tenants were moving in, and even Mister Beckwith had an assistant to help collect the weekly rents.

I turned off the lights in the gallery just as the oil lamps along the street began to cast a buttery glow upon the walk outside my door. I made my way to the stairs, stopping to glance upward to briefly recall that fateful day when I stood upon the landing and stared into the faces of British soldiers. Once I had reached the second floor, I heard the rapid steps of my dogs, their claw marks against the hardwood floors above me. They would be ready for their evening walk, and tonight I was famished. Already I was thinking of the order of things—eating or walking—as I climbed the narrow stairs to the top.

But as I opened the door, I realized the decision had been made for me. The delicious aroma of lamb stew beckoned me in, and as I closed the door behind me, I noticed the candles on the small table, place settings for two, and the sound of dishes clinking in the kitchen. My heart soared, my mind springing forward to the kitchen even before my feet had made it there.

I petted the dogs as their attentions were turned from the stove to me. They'd been underfoot, apparently, hoping for morsels to fall onto the floor. My eyes took in Nicky's broad shoulders, his straight, purposeful back, his dark hair appearing newly cut, so he appeared more like a businessman than an Irish rebel. He'd gained a bit of weight since last I saw him. "You look rather fetching in your apron," I said.

Nicky grinned sheepishly. "Correction, m'lady. It is *your* apron I wear. And the scent of your perfume is still upon it, teasing my senses." As he spoke, he unfurled the tie at his back and tossed it onto the back of a chair. "Are you hungry?"

"I am," I said as he wrapped his arms around me. "And you?"

"Famished," he answered as he bent to kiss me. The months slipped away until I felt as though there had never been a gap between his lips and mine. His breath was hot and heady as I melted into him, his arms like steel encompassing my body and pulling me ever closer to him. If his objective was to soften the space between us until we became one, it was met almost instantly.

When he began to pull away, I moaned in protest, but when I opened my eyes, I found him merely an inch away. "How much time do you have this time around?"

"A week. Maybe longer. Plenty of time to give us both the memories we need to carry on a while longer, yeah?"

"Yes," I murmured. "I need more memories." I stared into his eyes as if I could memorize every minute variation in his irises, every black lash, every peek into the deepest, most sensuous place in his soul. It had been a few months since his last visit, but the days peeled away as though the absence had never existed. I snuggled against him, reluctantly breaking our eye contact while I closed my eyes. I inhaled the fresh scent of the outdoors on him and drank in all the places he had been, the meadows he'd crossed, the copses in which he'd hidden, and the sunshine and rain under which he'd traveled.

"I didn't hear you come in," I whispered.

"I used the key you gave me to come in from the alley," he said. His voice was low and husky. "I heard Brad speaking to someone in his office, but no one else."

"You must have arrived this morning," I said, peeking past his shoulder to the food cooking on the stove.

"Shortly after dawn. Honestly, I was hoping to find you still in bed, and I was prepared to awaken you."

A soft moan escaped my lips. "That would have been so nice."

"Would it now?" he grinned.

"I can't believe you were here all day, and I didn't know it. We've wasted hours—"

"Ah. So, in the future, perhaps you'll check your chambers more frequently, 'ey?"

"Most definitely."

"Then what are we waiting for?" he teased. "We're wasting time."

"I am never wasting time when I am in your arms," I protested. "Clothed or otherwise."

"Well, and it's 'otherwise' I'd like to see."

I laughed as he grasped my hand and pulled me momentarily toward the stove, where he quickly removed the stewpot from the flame, before escorting me into the next room. I surrendered to him there, trusting him completely as the months disappeared, and in its place, I was left only with the timeless warmth of his body and mine.

APPENDIX A

Casement, Sir Roger (1864-1916) – was born in Dublin and raised in Ulster, becoming a diplomat with the British Foreign Office and knighted by King George V. In 1913, he joined the underground movement for a free Ireland and in 1916, helped to facilitate United States support as well as German military aid on behalf of an independent Ireland. He was arrested at an ancient ring fort in Ireland and sent to the Tower of London. Charged with espionage, high treason, and sabotage, he was sentenced to death by hanging. Sir Arthur Conan Doyle, George Bernard Shaw, and W.B. Yeats pleaded in vain to have the sentence commuted. At the age of 51, he was hanged at Pentonville Prison in London. Throughout Ireland, there are parks, schools, statues, and landmarks named after him. He is recognized as a hero of the Republic of Ireland.

Collins, Michael (1890-1922) – was born in County Cork. He was imprisoned during the Easter Rising but released in December 1916. He was present in 1919 when the independence of the Irish Republic was declared and was given the task by Éamon de Valera of negotiating peace terms with London. While some Irish wanted complete independence and nothing less, Collins saw steps in that direction as progress upon which total independence could be built upon. When he negotiated the Anglo-Irish Treaty that included an Oath of Allegiance to the British Crown, he was seen as a traitor to some Irish, and he remarked at the time that he had signed his own death warrant. As the Irish Civil War ensued, he was placed in charge of the National Army as Commander-in-Chief and was shot and killed in August 1922 by an anti-Treaty unit of the IRA in County Cork. The passages in this book regarding Collins riding a bicycle under the noses of the British, who were looking for a ruffian and not a businessman, is true.

Connolly, James (1868-1916) – was born in Edinburgh, Scotland to Irish parents. He enlisted in the British Army at the age of 14 after falsifying his birthdate. He later deserted the Army rather than transfer to India, and he held a deep hatred of the British Army throughout his life. He lived in America for a short time, establishing the Irish Socialist Federation in New York and later, the Labour Party in Ireland. He returned to Ireland in 1910 and moved up the ranks of the Socialist Party and Irish Citizen Army (ICA). The ICA was originally separate from the IRB (Irish Republican Brotherhood), but they joined forces in early 1916. He was shot during the Easter Rising, and despite being given only days to live due to his injury, the British sentenced him to a firing squad. He was tied to a chair because he was unable to walk or stand, and executed at Kilmainham Gaol. Today, he is recognized as a hero, and many streets and organizations are named after him.

Connolly, Sean (1882-1916) – During the Easter Rising, he was charged with capturing Dublin Castle. When an unarmed guard, James O'Brien, attempted to stop them, Connolly shot and killed him. When they were fired upon through castle windows, they retreated to City Hall and took that instead. During a fight with the British in which the Irish rebels took position on the roof of City Hall, Connolly was shot dead by a British sniper. For the purposes of this storyline, I had Connolly shot on the first day of fighting, but it might have been during the first night or early morning. He was the first rebel to be killed in the Easter Rising. By the morning of the second day as British reinforcements arrived, they retook City Hall, and all remaining rebels there were arrested.

Éamon de Valera (1882-1975) – was born in New York to a Spanish father and Irish mother, and raised by a grandmother and other relatives from the age of two in County Limerick. His dual American citizenship allowed him to escape execution after the Easter Rising. Originally sentenced to life imprisonment, he was granted amnesty in 1917. One month later, he was elected a Member of Parliament (MP) in Britain, representing East Clare, Ireland. He was also elected President of Sinn Fein, President of Dail Eireann in 1919, and the first President of the Republic of Ireland in 1921.

Irish Civil War (officially 1922-1923) – Pressure mounted on Britain to grant Ireland complete independence after the Easter Rising and again at the end of the Great War. Due to the Plantation Era in the 17th century, six counties in Ulster remained largely Protestant and British loyalists. An agreement was reached to grant 26 of Ireland's counties the status of a Free State while declaring the remaining six counties of Ulster as Northern Ireland to remain part of Britain. To some, this was a necessary stepping stone toward complete independence. To others, Ireland would never be free of Britain's rule until all 32 counties were united under a free and independent Ireland. Things became further complicated under subsequent treaties, plunging the country into civil war. Though the time of violence began before 1922 and continues in Ulster as of this writing (2020), the official dates for the Irish Civil War remain from June 1922 to May 1923.

Mallin, Michael (1874-1916) – Second-in-command of the Irish Citizen Army under James Connolly, he had been a soldier in the British Army, serving in Ireland, Britain, and India. He witnessed atrocities perpetrated by the British upon Indian natives and, upon returning from India, realized the Irish were treated the same. While he worked as a silk weaver's apprentice, he became involved in the Irish Citizen Army, attaining the position of chief training officer due to his experience in the British Army. He was arrested by the end of Easter Rising Week, court-martialed on May 5, and executed on May 8 at Kilmainham Gaol.

Markievicz, Countess Constance Georgine (1868-1927) – founding member of the Irish Citizen Army, was sentenced to death for her participation in the Easter Rising, but her sentence was reduced because she was a woman. In a remarkable comeback, she was elected to the British House of Commons and was one of the first women in the world to hold the title of Minister of Labor (1919-1922). Her father was Sir Henry Gore-Booth, a famed Arctic explorer who fed all his tenants during the famine of 1879-1880. A childhood friend was W.B. Yeats. She trained as a painter and actor and met many of her other compatriots through those endeavors.

Pearse, Patrick (also Pearse, Pádraic) (1879-1916) – one of the most well-known of the Easter Rising, he was a teacher dedicated to the Irish Gaelic language as well as a writer and poet. It was Pearse who issued the orders for three days of 'maneuvers,' which was a code for the start of the rebellion. His orders were countermanded by Eoin MacNeill, which led to confusion throughout Ireland, resulting in a far lesser turnout than expected. Pearse read the Proclamation of the Irish Republic in front of the General Post Office (GPO). His unit was one of the last to surrender. The story told of Pearse observing an elderly man being gunned down in the street simply because he wanted to get his vehicle and go home was true, and purportedly led to his surrender in order to prevent further civilian casualties.

Sackville Street – Dublin's main thoroughfare, it was named Sackville Street in the 18th century after the 1st Duke of Dorset, Lionel Sackville. It was renamed O'Connell Street in 1924 when a free and independent Ireland named it after Daniel O'Connell, a nationalist leader. Today it is a popular thoroughfare for visitors to Dublin.

Shelbourne Hotel – Located at Saint Stephen's Green in Dublin, the hotel is now owned by Marriott International.

In 2007, it underwent a complete refurbishment and currently has 265 rooms.

Spindler, Karl (1887-1951) – was a German Naval Officer in World War I. He was tasked with delivering German weapons to the Irish rebels aboard the ship Libau, renamed Aud in an attempt to be mistaken for the Norwegian merchant ship. After detonating a charge that sunk the ship rather than risk the weapons falling into the hands of the British, he and his crew were taken prisoner and transferred to Donington Hall, an English castle and estate requisitioned as a prisoner of war camp during WW1. Before the end of World War I, he was part of a prisoner exchange with The Netherlands, and after the war, he migrated to the United States. He wrote a book about the mission in 1921 titled "The Mystery Ship." In World War II, he was held in an internment camp as an enemy alien because he was of German heritage but was released after the war. He died in 1951 in Bismark, North Dakota.

Wilde, Oscar (1854-1900) – born in Dublin, Wilde rose to become one of the most popular Irish poets and authors, extending beyond his death at the age of 46 in France. Among his most popular works are *The Picture of Dorian Gray*, *Lady Windermere's Fan* and *The Importance of Being Earnest*. At the height of his fame, he was brought to trial on charges of homosexuality, sodomy, and gross indecency. He was sentenced to two years of hard labor at Reading Gaol, where hunger, hard work, and poor medical care contributed to illnesses thought to later shorten his life. Upon his release, he moved immediately to France, where he died three years later of cerebral meningitis. In 2017, Wilde was among more than 50,000 men in the United Kingdom that were pardoned for homosexual acts, under the Alan Turing Law, named after the renowned World War II codebreaker credited with helping to win the war for the allies but who was imprisoned for homosexuality/gross indecency in 1952. Turing died in 1954 at the age of 42.

About the Author

p.m.terrell is the pen name for Patricia McClelland Terrell, the award-winning, internationally acclaimed author of more than 24 books in multiple genres, including contemporary suspense, historical suspense, computer instructional, non-fiction and children's books.

Prior to writing full-time, she founded two computer companies in the Washington, DC Metropolitan Area: McClelland Enterprises, Inc. and Continental Software Development Corporation. Among her clients were the Central Intelligence Agency, United States Secret Service, U.S. Information Agency, and Department of Defense. Her specialties were in the detection of white collar computer crimes and computer intelligence.

A full-time author since 2002, *Black Swamp Mysteries* was her first series, inspired by the success of *Exit 22*, released in 2008. *Vicki's Key* was a top five finalist in the 2012 International Book Awards and 2012 USA Book Awards nominee, and *The Pendulum Files* was a national finalist for the Best Cover of the Year in 2014.

Her second series, *Ryan O'Clery Suspense*, is also award-winning. *The Tempest Murders* (Book 1) was one of four finalists in the 2013 International Book Awards, cross-genre category. *The White Devil of Dublin* (Book 2) was released one year later.

Her historical suspense, *River Passage,* was a 2010 Best Fiction and Drama Award Winner. It was determined to be so historically accurate that a copy of the book resides at the Nashville Government Metropolitan Archives in Nashville, Tennessee.

Songbirds are Free remains her bestselling book to date; it is inspired by the true story of Mary Neely, who was captured in 1780 by Shawnee warriors near Fort Nashborough (now Nashville, Tennessee).

Inspired by the vast number of Neely descendants that contacted her after the publication of *River Passage* and *Songbirds are Free,* she researched her genealogy back to 1608 Scotland, resulting in a book of her ancestor William Neely entitled *Checkmate: Clans and Castles.*

She was the co-founder of The Book 'Em Foundation, an organization committed to raising public awareness of the correlation between high crime rates and high illiteracy rates. She was the founder of Book 'Em North Carolina, an annual event held in Lumberton, North Carolina, to raise funds to increase literacy and reduce crime, serving as its chairperson and organizaer for its first four years. Robeson Community College now chairs and hosts it.

She also served on the boards of the Friends of the Robeson County (NC) Public Library, the Robeson County (NC) Arts Council, Virginia Crime Stoppers and became the first female president of the Chesterfield County-Colonial Heights (VA) Crime Solvers.

For more information, visit the author's website at www.pmterrell.com.

Other Books by p.m.terrell

Black Swamp Mysteries:

Exit 22 (2008)
Vicki's Key (2012)
Secrets of a Dangerous Woman (2012)
Dylan's Song (2013)
The Pendulum Files (2014)
Cloak and Mirrors (2017)

Ryan O'Clery Mysteries:

The Tempest Murders (2013)
The White Devil of Dublin (2014)

Historical:

River Passage (2009)
Songbirds are Free (2007)
Checkmate: Clans and Castles (2018)

Other Mysteries:

Kickback (2002)
The China Conspiracy (2003)
Ricochet (2006)
The Banker's Greed (2011)
A Thin Slice of Heaven (2015)
April in the Back of Beyond (2019)

www.ingramcontent.com/pod-product-compliance
Lightning Source LLC
LaVergne TN
LVHW020040110826
845155LV00029B/566